23
9,
29/
11/ ∩

Pleas
show

www

Ren

Text

sp

L3.

WARTIME FOR THE DISTRICT NURSES

Alice Lake and her friend Edith have had everything thrown at them in their first year as district nurses in London's East End. From babies born out of wedlock to battered wives, they've had plenty to keep them occupied. As rationing takes hold and Hitler's bombers train their sights on London, Edith tries to battle on bravely while bearing her own heartache, but there's no escaping the reality of being at war, or the new terror of the bombing raids. The girls find themselves caught up in the terrible aftermath, their nursing skills desperately needed by the shaken locals on their rounds. With the men away fighting for king and country, it's up to the nurses to keep up the spirit of the Blitz, and everyone is counting on them . . .

ANNIE GROVES

WARTIME FOR THE DISTRICT NURSES

Complete and Unabridged

MAGNA
Leicester

First published in Great Britain in 2019 by
HarperCollins*Publishers* Ltd
London

First Ulverscroft Edition
published 2020
by arrangement with
HarperCollins*Publishers* Ltd
London

A catalogue record for this book is available
from the British Library.

ISBN 978–0–7505–4815–1

Published by
Ulverscroft Limited
Anstey, Leicestershire

Set by Words & Graphics Ltd.
Anstey, Leicestershire
Printed and bound in Great Britain by
T. J. International Ltd., Padstow, Cornwall

This book is printed on acid-free paper

Many, many thanks to Teresa Chris, Kate Bradley and Pen Issac — the dream team.

1

Summer 1940

Edith Gillespie woke up and for a moment could not work out where she was. Her brain was too befuddled with sleep to remember and there was no light to give her a clue. She struggled to work it out.

Not in the house where she'd grown up in south London, that was for sure, because there would have been the sound of at least one of her many siblings breathing, or snoring, or sneezing. She'd never had the luxury of a room to herself for all those years, not until she'd left home to train as a nurse. She didn't think she was in her nurses' dormitory, though. That had been near a station and you could always hear the trains, or porters and drivers shouting. After that she'd chosen to take extra training as a district nurse, but this didn't feel like the home in Richmond. It must be wherever she'd gone after that.

Now it all came back to her. She was at the North Hackney Queen's Nurses home on Victory Walk, in Dalston. This was her little attic room, and the reason it was so dark was that the blackout blind was firmly in place. The country was at war, and had been for nearly a year. It was warm as it was summer, and from the birdsong outside it was already dawn. Slowly she sat up and shook her head, trying to wake up.

1

Her dream lingered on the fringes of her mind. The details had gone but the sensation of happiness — of being cared for — remained, and she smiled in the darkness, savouring that comforting and thrilling feeling. Somebody loved her and she loved them back.

Then she remembered and cried out despite herself. Harry was gone. Harry Banham, the most handsome and wonderful man in the world, had not made it back from Dunkirk, and she was alone. Her dream had lied. There was nobody to hug her, to hold her and tell her how beautiful she was. There was no golden future for the couple who'd attracted envious glances wherever they'd gone. The life they'd so recently begun to plan was never going to happen. Sobs came from her throat and dimly she realised that she started most of her days like this, waking in the hope of seeing Harry and then coming back to reality with a sickening bump.

Her alarm clock began to ring and she reached automatically to silence it, then crept across the rag rug to the window and pulled back a corner of the blind. Sunshine edged its way into the little room, revealing that it was far from luxurious but had all the essentials. The room of a woman who had a job to do.

Edith turned to her wardrobe. The full-length mirror on its door reflected her slight figure, with her short, dark hair sticking up from where she'd slept on it. Her dark eyes took it in and she automatically smoothed it back down. Then she took out her uniform, shaking out the creases. Time to start the day. No matter that her heart was still raw from recent bereavement. Plenty of others were in the same boat. She had to carry on as normal and do what was required of her. After all, she was a nurse.

★　★　★

'Gladys, whatever are you doing?'

Edith arrived downstairs for breakfast to be greeted by her colleague, Mary Perkins, complaining loudly. Mary had never been one for waking up in the best of tempers and now her voice rose over the clattering of saucepans and pots being stacked on the lino floor of the storeroom, which was squeezed between the stairs and the large area they all used as a canteen and common room.

Gladys, who helped out their cook and with general domestic duties, stood up and pushed her lank brown hair from her eyes. Even though the morning was still young she looked as if she'd already been up for hours.

'We got to hand over all our scrap metal,' she said. 'The government says so. There's going to be a collection or we can take it to the council. So I'm sorting out all our old pots what aren't no real use any more.'

'Yes, but can't you do so quietly?' Mary wailed. 'Surely they can't need it right now? The council depots won't even be open, and I'll bet all their staff are still safely asleep, like anybody sensible would be.'

Gladys shook her head. 'I got other things to do later. So I thought I'd get on and do this now,

3

then it will be one job done and ticked off me list.'

Edith nodded to herself. This time last year, Gladys wouldn't have said boo to a goose, but she'd changed in the months in between, gaining in confidence and learning to read. Now she was standing up to Mary, who had a heart of gold, but was used to a lifetime of speaking sharply to servants.

'Come on,' Edith said, not wanting to start the day with a row. 'I'm starving. Let's have some toast.' She steered Mary away and over to a vacant dining table, as Gladys resumed her sorting and stacking.

Mary plonked herself down on the hard wooden chair, which made her rich brown curls bounce around her cross face, and allowed Edith to fetch her some toast and a cup of tea. 'It's too bad,' she grumbled.

'What? That Gladys has to get up even earlier than usual to clear out the broken saucepans?' Edith thought that was a bit much, even for Mary.

Mary shook her head. 'No, of course not. I know I'm being silly.' She sighed as she smeared a small amount of butter across the toast. 'It's nothing to do with Gladys really. It's Charles.'

Edith raised her eyebrows in sympathy, even though she sometimes envied Mary for the fact that her boyfriend was still alive and so she really didn't have much to complain about. However, she liked to hear about what her friend's beau was doing, partly because he was a captain in the army and generally knew what was going on in

4

the wider world, even if he wasn't permitted to tell them the half of it. 'What's wrong, then? Spill the beans.'

Mary crunched into her toast and took a second slice. It would take more than a minor argument to make her lose her appetite. She finished her mouthful and looked up, her expression changing from annoyed to sad. 'Well, of course I hardly see him, he's so busy. Then, when we do manage to find an evening when he's not on duty, he's so preoccupied that I sometimes wonder if he hears a word I say.' She patted one of her curls into place. 'Yesterday I spent ages doing my hair, wearing my nicest silk blouse and making sure I looked my very best to cheer him up. Boost his morale and all that. But he didn't even notice. Didn't say a thing.'

Edith set down her own piece of toast. 'I expect he did and just didn't want to mention it,' she suggested.

'But I want him to mention it!' Mary cried, her usually bright blue eyes now filled with irritation. 'It took me ages, and you know how hard it's becoming to buy nice makeup and find a way to make your favourite perfume last. I don't want to let him down when he takes me to lovely restaurants.'

'Of course,' said Edith, although her experience of lovely restaurants was nonexistent. Harry used to take her to a local pub, the Duke's Arms, or one of the nearby cinemas, and that was all they had needed.

'He keeps going on about the threat of Hitler invading,' Mary confided. 'I tell him, he won't.

5

He wouldn't dare. Mr Churchill will defend us. That's what he's promised to do and I believe him. There's no need to worry on that score. Charles won't tell me any details but he looks so tired and drawn, poor lamb. Yesterday he couldn't even spare the time for a proper meal. We just went to the hotel bar nearest to his office and had a quick supper there. Not that it wasn't lovely,' she added loyally.

'I bet it was,' said Edith. Mary had been adamant up until the actual outbreak of hostilities that there wasn't going to be a war, that Mr Chamberlain would stop it. So Edith didn't have any great faith in her friend's abilities to predict the future. Yet she could not fault her for steadfastness and optimism, qualities which might be very important in the days to come, if her own worst fears of invasion came true.

'I'm beginning to think he's a bit of a fusspot,' Mary admitted. 'He was so carefree and fun when we first met, and now his mind is always on something else, I can just tell.' She reached for the marmalade and carefully helped herself to a small amount, to leave enough for whoever sat at the table next. Nobody could slather it on their toast any more, the ingredients were too scarce. Sugar had been rationed since the start of the year and oranges had all but disappeared.

'Well, he's got an important job to do,' Edith pointed out. She checked her watch. 'As have we.'

Hastily Mary finished off the last of her breakfast. 'I'd better go and restock my Gladstone bag. I didn't get around to it last night, what with preparing to go out with Charles. I don't want to run short of anything.'

Edith made a face of mock horror. 'I should think not. And don't so much as breathe such a thing in front of Gwen.'

Mary glanced hastily around, as if mentioning the name of their fearsome deputy superintendent was enough to conjure up her presence. 'Heaven forfend. Right, I'm off. See you later.'

Edith grinned, although she knew that Gwen's bark was worse than her bite. The older woman had been kindness itself when they'd first learnt the news about Harry. But that was a side of Gwen that few people saw. She would have been perfectly right to berate Mary if the young nurse had been mistaken enough to set off on her rounds without a properly stocked bag. Every district nurse relied upon this most vital piece of equipment, which contained everything she might need when visiting a patient's house. It was no exaggeration to say that lives depended on it.

'You're up early.'

Edith turned around at the sound of a chair scraping beside her, and looked up into the steady blue eyes of her best friend, Alice Lake, who lowered her tall frame to sit at the vacant place at the table.

'Couldn't sleep for ages and then I woke up before the alarm,' Edith admitted.

Alice nodded in sympathy as she set down her bowl of porridge. 'Again,' she said.

Edith shrugged. Alice was the only nurse who knew about her dreaded moments when she

7

awoke thinking Harry was still alive and then remembered that he wasn't. Yet she was getting better. At first the realisation would make her feel so sick that she couldn't face breakfast, and would end up shaking with exhaustion by the end of her morning rounds. Now she could manage some toast and set off with something like her old energy, because she knew that neither Harry nor the rest of his family, who lived nearby, would have wanted her to fail in her chosen profession.

'Who's your first patient?' Alice asked, knowing that the best way to help Edith was to concentrate on work.

'Dennis,' Edith replied. He was one of their favourites, a teenager with a tubercular hip who required regular visits, and whose life was one of discomfort at best, but who never complained. 'He's been pretty bright recently, and Dr Patcham thinks we might even be able to try him walking for short periods with crutches. I don't want to rush him though. His leg muscles are wasted from lying in bed for so long.'

Alice beamed at the idea. 'Imagine how happy his mother would be. I know she thought her son would never walk again.'

Edith agreed. 'It would be a small miracle — but don't tell anyone or it might jinx it. Anyway, I'd better go.'

'Give them my best and tell them I'll see them soon,' Alice called, raising her teacup as Edith departed.

The sunlight flooded the corridor of the big old Victorian house as Edith strode along it, to pick up her own bag before setting off on her bicycle for the day. It was true that there was finally a ray of hope for young Dennis, and it was moments like that which had led her to do this job in the first place. There was a long way to go for him, and he might always have a limp; everything would be easier if he could leave his crowded street and move to somewhere with fresh air, but she might as well recommend him to fly to the moon. Besides, even the countryside was open to attack; areas around airfields had started to see enemy planes overhead and nowhere was guaranteed to be safe.

'So you aren't missing much, Harry Banham,' she murmured to herself, carefully wedging the bulging leather bag into the bicycle basket. She knew she didn't mean it, though. She would have given anything for him to be back with her, laughing with his friends, joking with his family, throwing his beloved little niece into the air and catching her before his mother could tell him off. She shook her head, and automatically checked that her dark wavy hair was secure under her cap. It was no use; he was gone, and she had work to do.

★ ★ ★

'Gillian! No, put it down.' Mattie Askew, nee Banham, pushed herself to her feet and padded on swollen ankles across the family kitchen to try to stop her daughter from pulling a china bowl off the low shelf where it shouldn't have been in the first place. 'Ma, stop her, I'm too slow.'

Flo Banham swung around from where she was peeling potatoes at the kitchen sink and in one swift movement rescued the bowl with one hand and caught her granddaughter with the other, lifting her up and holding her so their eyes were level. 'No you don't, my girl,' she said lovingly but firmly. 'You know that's not a toy. Heaven knows you've got enough of those, so when I put you down, you're to play with them and not with my china.'

Gillian roared with laughter and tapped her grandmother's nose.

'Don't you try and get around me like that.' Flo put the little girl back on the mat and wiped her hands on her faded and threadbare apron. 'Oh, she's got a surprise coming. Just wait until her baby brother or sister arrives.'

Mattie groaned and rubbed her growing bump. 'Can't come soon enough for me. Whatever was I thinking of, carrying a baby through the heat of summer. We'll both melt before it's due. Nearly three more months! I don't think I can do it.'

Flo tutted. 'Of course you will. That's Lennie's child you've got there, and you owe it to him to bring it safely into the world.'

Mattie rolled her eyes. 'You don't have to remind me. As if I'd forget.' Her husband Lennie had been taken prisoner at Dunkirk, only weeks after she'd written to him to say he was going to be a father for the second time. He'd been beside himself with joy at the news, and it was knowing that which kept her going. That and caring for their firstborn: Gillian, now nearly eighteen months old, and growing better at walking and talking every day. The toddler assumed, quite rightly, that she was the centre of everyone's attention, and wasn't old enough to miss the people who should have been there: her father and her doting Uncle Harry.

The third missing face belonged to Mattie's older brother, Joe, who was in the navy. Nobody knew exactly where he was or what he was doing, as letters arrived home in no regular pattern, depending on if and when he was in port. He was a master at writing long, funny, affectionate letters without actually telling them anything. She looked forward to them, as they were as entertaining as reading a real book. Lennie, even Mattie would be first to admit, wasn't a great one for letters, but he had managed to send one from his prison camp to assure everyone back home that he was alive and as well as possible. Mattie had already sent off one parcel via the Red Cross to make his stay more bearable.

Mattie sank back down onto the comfy chair, keeping a close eye on Gillian, who had found her teddy bear which had rolled under the kitchen table. Then came a gentle waft of welcome cool air as the door to the back kitchen opened and Stan Banham strode in. He was an imposing figure, tall and straight-backed, although his face had grown etched with new lines ever since the news had come through about Harry. He was the local trusted Air Raid Precautions warden, as well as working full time, and Mattie knew that whatever happened, her father would be there to make everything better. He was the rock on whom they all depended. She struggled to her feet. 'Fancy some tea?' she asked as brightly as she could, despite the heavy weight of the growing baby.

Stan smiled at his only daughter and then at his granddaughter, who ducked out from beneath the table and held her arms up, demanding a cuddle. Stan obliged. 'No, you sit yourself down, I'll just have a glass of water to cool off,' he said, tousling Gillian's fine brown hair before gently putting her down again. 'It's warm out there. The heat will have died down before I go out on my rounds; that's something to be thankful for.'

Flo looked at him. 'Well, that's good,' she said slowly. 'Have you heard anything more today? About what's going on? Down the market there are all sorts of rumours. Some say Hitler's just waiting to pounce, that he's got all his tanks lined up on the French coast.'

Stan shook his head. 'You know better than to listen to rumour. People will repeat any old rubbish.' He took a deep breath, easing off his light jacket. While he didn't want to give anyone false hope, one of his foremost duties as an ARP warden was to prevent panic and keep everyone calm. If necessary that applied to his own family too. 'We'll take whatever comes and do our best. That's all we can do. We won't be frightened by silly tales or scaremongers. Worrying never solved anything, you know that as well as I do.'

Flo nodded, reassured as ever by her

12

husband's presence. 'Then that's what we'll do,' she said with determination. 'And we'll start with my potato pie.'

2

Billy Reilly wiped his itching eyes. They were red from tiredness, not helped by his underlying anxiety that this was the calm before the storm. He gazed up at the darkening sky, searching for any enemy planes. They'd been spotted in small numbers in Kent and along the south coast, sneaking over the Channel, as was common knowledge down at the docks where he worked. You couldn't stop sailors and dockers talking to each other. How much everyone else knew was anyone's guess, but he had a pretty good idea of what was going on.

He forced himself to concentrate on the job in hand. As well as working his full shift of hard manual graft, he now had an evening of ARP duty, walking the streets of Dalston, checking that everyone had put up their blackout blinds correctly and generally helping out whenever he was called upon. He'd learnt most of what he needed to know from his colleague Stan, who everyone looked up to. Billy had known Stan since he was at school, as Stan's sons were two of his best friends. Or, rather, they had been; now there was just Joe left.

He was used to his duties now and found it easier to confront householders who refused to obey the regulations. In some ways it was easier in summer, as the longer hours of daylight meant nobody needed to use their gas — or, in rare

14

cases, electric — lamps until late in the evening. During the winter months, when he'd been new to the work, there had been plenty of rows, as people pointed out that the expected air raids and gas attacks hadn't happened and so what was the point of putting up ugly black blinds? Some wardens were lenient, insisting on the blinds only when there was a warning siren, but Billy thought that was the start of a slippery slope and aimed to be equally strict with everybody. Lives might depend on it.

He wondered whether he could find an excuse to call in on Kathleen. He wanted to more than anything else in the world but didn't like to push his luck. He could tell himself it was out of simple concern for her welfare, as she had nobody else to look out for her and her little son. She struggled to make ends meet and he loved helping her out in small ways. Yet, if he was honest, he knew the real reason was that he'd been in love with her for years but had missed his opportunity to tell her.

She'd been another person Billy had known from school, and he'd always thought she was the prettiest girl there. Gradually they had drifted into the same circle of friends and they had all stayed in touch after leaving, when Billy had gone to work down at the docks. Just as he was gathering his courage to tell her how he felt, she'd met that handsome wastrel Ray Berry, and before you could say knife she'd gone and married him.

Billy drew a sharp breath at the thought of the man who had treated Kath so badly. She'd

15

hidden his true nature from them all for ages, but it had got to the point where anyone could see the bruising. And it wasn't only Kath who'd suffered. Ray had resented their baby son, which was unforgivable. When the news had come that Ray had not survived Dunkirk, most people had felt relief.

Yet Kathleen had been more distant since that day. It was as if she felt guilty at sharing the relief, the knowledge that Ray could never hurt her or little Brian ever again. So Billy was biding his time, not wanting to rush things, to ask for too much too soon. One thing was certain though; he didn't intend to be pipped to the post again. Kathleen was the only woman for him, and if he had to wait until she realised that they were destined to be together, then so be it.

★   ★   ★

Peggy sighed as she dutifully fastened the blackout blinds in her mother-in-law's kitchen. This was not how she had imagined her life turning out. She had moved in after she and Pete had got married in the autumn, with the plan that they would have their own house as soon as the war was over. Pete had been happy at the thought of his wife and his mother keeping one another company while he fought for his country. He hadn't hesitated to enlist in the army when war broke out, even though their long-awaited wedding had been only weeks away. Everything had been going so well; they still managed to marry, and he'd had a wonderful period of leave at Christmas. She'd realised she was pregnant and they'd been thrilled. But then she had miscarried, and before that really sank in, Pete had been killed at Dunkirk.

'Are you finished in there, Peggy love?'

'Nearly,' Peggy called back, from between gritted teeth. She hadn't minded Mrs Cannon at first. They'd always got along well, and the older woman had welcomed her into her home, pleased that Pete was so happy in his choice of bride. Everyone could see how well suited they were; they'd been together since meeting at school, although they'd only become serious once Peggy had started working at the gasmask factory.

Now, though, every tiny request or comment drove Peggy to the point of screaming. Nothing she did was ever quite right. The forks weren't the right way round in the cutlery drawer. She hadn't used enough Reckitt's Blue in the washing. She didn't know the best way to darn the frayed elbow of a jumper. None of these complaints on its own was enough to spark a row, but added together they were stifling.

It wasn't that Peggy had to do all the housework. She knew she was lucky; plenty of young women her age were expected to do the lion's share of the cleaning and cooking as well as working full time. Mrs Cannon was not like that and had been heard to boast that Peggy was a good girl, putting in all those hours at the factory and then helping out around the house. Peggy groaned inwardly. It was just that when she did help, it always provoked gentle criticism.

'Come and listen to the wireless,' called Mrs Cannon from the front room. 'That Wilfrid Hyde-White is going to be on — he's ever so good.'

'Thank you, I will,' Peggy replied, wanting to hit her head against the wall. Another evening beckoned of sitting either side of the fireplace with the wireless in pride of place in the middle of the mantelpiece, knitting or sewing on buttons while the Home Service played at full volume. Peggy preferred the music programmes, especially if Ella Fitzgerald came on, but her mother-in-law didn't like those kinds of singers. Peggy had often wondered if she could get away with simply turning the sound down a few notches. Mrs Cannon was a little deaf but would not admit it.

Running out of excuses to stay in the kitchen, she painted on a smile as she went through to where her mother-in-law was already sitting in her armchair, knitting at the ready.

'Thank you, dear,' said Mrs Cannon, her eyes twinkling in appreciation. 'I don't know how I'd manage without you around, I really don't. I find it so hard to reach the tops of the windows now, what with my lumbago, and arthritis in my fingers. You're so nimble, you're lucky.'

'It's nothing,' said Peggy, keeping the smile in place though her cheeks ached. She took the other armchair, the slightly less comfy one, and reached for her sewing bag. She brought out a skirt on which she had optimistically let out the waist when she'd been pregnant; she might as well take it in again. Her fingers trembled slightly

18

at the memory as she threaded her needle.

'Oh, what good eyesight you have,' Mrs Cannon said warmly. 'I remember when I used to be able to do that without my glasses. Not any more. Those days are long gone.'

Peggy nodded. 'What are you knitting?' she asked, for something to say, although she already knew the answer. It was the same cardigan her mother-in-law had been working on all week.

'Just a little something to keep me warm when autumn comes,' she answered, the same as she always did. 'I can do one for you if you like.'

Peggy tried not to shudder. The colour, a dull brown, was not at all to her taste. 'No, you save the wool for yourself,' she said hastily, knowing that if she were to wear such a shade it would drain every ounce of colour from her face.

So Mrs Cannon thought she was lucky, did she? Peggy could not imagine feeling much worse. Stuck in here, with the sound of those blasted needles clacking away, knowing that any minute now there would be a well-meant but undermining comment about her sewing technique. How was that lucky? No baby, no Pete. How she had loved him, with his athletic frame and dark eyes that sent her weak at the knees every time he looked at her. How she missed holding him, being held by him. She'd never feel like that again. No man could ever come close to Pete, and that heady rush of first love that grew stronger by the year until they'd realised that they were meant for each other. All that had gone, vanished in the waters off Dunkirk.

The only way in which she counted herself

19

lucky was that she was certain how he had died. One of his comrades had seen it happen: one quick, fatal bullet. He wouldn't have suffered. He had been serving his country, which was what he had wanted to do. He was no coward, had never flinched from physical confrontation. If there was a wrong to be righted, Pete had been the man. For a minute Peggy thought of Edith; nobody was able to reassure her of Harry's fate. His body hadn't been found. He had failed to return to his unit, and wasn't on any of the wounded lists, and so they had to assume he'd drowned and not resurfaced. How unbearable for them all.

Peggy had liked Edith on the occasions when they'd all gone out together. She always seemed keen to enjoy herself, to have a bit of fun, to let her hair down after a hard day's work, and had fitted in easily to their group of old school friends. A thought occurred to her and she accidentally jabbed the needle into her finger.

'Are you all right, dear?' Mrs Cannon asked at once. 'Haven't made yourself bleed, have you?'

'No, no,' Peggy said, swiftly hiding the telltale dot of blood. She pretended to search for her scissors while the idea grew. She really could not stand the thought of every evening turning out like this, cooped up in the little front room full of trinkets, every one bearing some kind of memory of Pete, with just his old mother for company. Perhaps Edith would like an evening out. They could go to the Duke's Arms and nobody would mind two women out on their own as they were well known there. Harry and Pete had been regulars, and were well liked. They could sit in the beer garden at the back and watch the world go by. Anything was better than this. Peggy gave a genuine smile and Mrs Cannon smiled back.

Peggy decided she would send a message to the nurses' home the very next morning.

3

Edith sped along Dalston Lane on her bike, the breeze catching at her dark hair escaping from her starched cap. She was heading for one of the smaller side streets but had been there often enough not to have to check her bearings. That was often the way with a patient who required nursing twice a day. What with Dennis and this patient, she had a busy round even without any new cases.

She was on her way to see a three-year-old boy who not only had measles but had developed the complication of pneumonia as well. He was a very sick child, and Edith's heart ached for him and his mother. She had not yet met the father, who was out working all hours at one of the local factories which had changed from producing pencils to munitions. He must have been earning a decent wage as the house was in a reasonable condition compared to many she visited, and yet it was barely big enough for the family, which numbered five children altogether.

Edith knocked smartly at the door, which must have been painted fairly recently, as it was nowhere near as chipped as its neighbours. Mrs Bell opened up at once, and ushered Edith inside. 'I'm terribly glad to see you, nurse. Vinny's been all hot and he can't sleep, poor little mite.' She turned to another child right behind her. 'Out you go, Freda, you know you're to keep out of nurse's way and not go near any of her things. We don't want you down with it as well. One's enough, one's more than enough.' The woman sounded at the end of her tether.

Freda, who looked about six, regarded Edith with big, curious eyes. 'Is me brother goin' ter die, miss?' she asked.

Edith crouched down to the girl's level and met her gaze. 'Not if I have anything to do with it,' she said cheerfully. 'We're going to look after him and see that he has the best possible chance of getting better. So you can do your bit by making sure you're quiet when you go past his door and letting him rest.'

'All right, miss.' The little girl seemed reassured. 'He's got my bedroom, though. I want it back.'

'Freda!' cried the mother. 'You know it's because it's the smallest room, and Vinny can't share with the boys if he's so sick. You'll just have to put up with it. He needs it more than you do.'

Edith smiled, feeling sorry for the little girl. It wasn't her fault that she had been turfed out of her room. 'When he's properly better you can go back to how it was before,' she assured her. The girl nodded solemnly and ran into the kitchen.

'Nurse, I'm so sorry,' gasped the mother, stricken. 'You'll think we brung them up with no manners.'

Edith began to climb the stairs towards the back bedroom on the topmost floor. 'Not a bit, Mrs Bell. Sometimes we forget how the other children are affected if one of the family is sick. They can be frightened and don't know what to

23

do to make it better. Sometimes they think it's their fault.' She paused. 'All you can do is keep telling them everyone's doing their best and they aren't to blame one way or the other.'

'You're very kind, nurse,' Mrs Bell replied, sounding unconvinced. She and Edith paused on the top landing outside the bedroom door. As quietly as she could, Edith took off her coat, nurse's cap and apron and hung them over the banister. From her bag she took out an overall and handkerchief to wear over her hair, along with everything she would need to treat the little boy. They had to minimise all risk of contamination, even though it meant carrying around extra items and added to the length of the visit.

Mrs Bell had queried why this was necessary to start with, but Edith promised her it was set down in the strict guidelines for such a case. She also required a bowl of disinfectant and a nailbrush to be left outside the bedroom door so that she, Mrs Bell or the doctor when he came could ensure their hands were clean going in and going out. Mrs Bell had protested. 'Where can I put that without the other kids knocking it over? This ain't a hospital where you can see what's going on. The older boys sleep in that room opposite, and they'll stick their noses into everything.'

Edith had looked around and noticed a small bookshelf at her head height; she was on the short side. 'That might do,' she said.

Mrs Bell had tutted. 'We ain't got many books and, those we have, the little darlings scribble all

24

over, so we put our good ones up there. I'll have to put them in me and Terry's room, otherwise they'll draw animals all over the pages.' She removed the precious copies of *Pears' Cyclopaedia*, the Bible and the *Children's Everything Within*.

Now Edith carefully reached for the bowl, standing on tiptoe, making sure not to dislodge the envelope she had to leave for the doctor containing the patient's report and chart. Grimly she thought that the people who devised the guidelines might have meant well but they hadn't reckoned on big families living in confined spaces. And this was one of the luckier households.

Finally they were ready to go into the little bedroom. It was warm inside, but Mrs Bell had left the window open as instructed, so that what passed for fresh air around Dalston could freely circulate. On the narrow bed under a threadbare candlewick bedspread lay a little boy, propped on pillows and scarcely making a sound. Edith gently crouched beside him. 'How are you feeling, Vinny?' she asked.

'Hot,' he whispered.

Edith turned to Mrs Bell, lingering in the doorway. 'Could you fetch him a glass of cold water?' she asked, reaching for the tray set on the battered dressing table. All the crockery and cutlery that Vinny used had to be kept separate, so as not to infect the rest of the family, although that presented another hurdle for his mother.

Glad to be of use, Mrs Bell set off back downstairs, and Edith could properly assess her patient without causing his anxious parent even more worry. As she would with every case, she took his temperature, pulse and respiration, and noted them for comparison later. 'Oh, you are a spotty boy,' she said softly. 'How am I going to recognise you when you're better, eh? You'll look so different.' The little boy tried to smile but he was clearly too exhausted.

Edith shut the window and then set about sponging him down, noting that his spots were actually fading slightly. Perhaps he was turning the corner. 'Are you hungry?' she asked encouragingly. 'Maybe Mummy can bring you some beef tea.' But he shook his head.

She went on to check his eyes and ears in case of any extra complications. 'And have you had a pain in your tummy?' she wondered, knowing that any disturbances of that kind could indicate still further problems. Wearily he shook his head once more, and turned his face into the pillow.

Edith swiftly finished her work and was just opening the window again when Mrs Bell returned, glass in hand. She had put on the flannel overall that Edith had lent her so that her own housecoat wouldn't spread infection throughout the rest of the home. 'See if you can get him to drink it,' Edith urged. 'He might still be off his food but he's got to keep up his fluid intake. That's more important than getting him to eat anything. Maybe some thin soup, when his appetite returns.'

Mrs Bell sat on the bed and looked at her boy with exhausted, concerned affection. 'He's a good little chap usually. Loves his pie and mash.'

Edith smiled. 'It might be a while before he manages any pie. Mash would be good though, with beef gravy if there's any going. But whatever you do, don't let anyone else eat his leftovers or they might still catch this and we don't want that.'

Mrs Bell's shoulders slumped. 'That's easier said than done. We can't afford to waste food. There's too many mouths to feed and that's a fact.'

Edith nodded in acknowledgement. The guidelines insisted that a patient's leftover meals should be burnt or flushed down the lavatory, which was fine if you had a bathroom upstairs, but far from easy if not. Again the rules were hard to apply in circumstances such as these. 'Just do your best,' she said encouragingly. 'You've managed very well so far. Having a mother who is prepared to go to all these lengths makes a great difference — you'd be surprised. I know all these rules seem silly, but they work. I do believe he might be on the mend.'

Mrs Bell's expression changed to one of hope. 'Really? Do you think so?'

Edith bit her lip, wondering if she had said too much too soon. After all, it was only an impression she'd formed and she wasn't the doctor. However, she had seen such cases before and knew what to look for. 'It's early days,' she cautioned, 'but I'd say his spots have gone past the worst. Also his temperature is down a notch even though he feels hot. So keep on doing what you're doing, and we'll see how he goes on.'

Mrs Bell hurriedly wiped one eye. 'Thank you,

27

nurse,' she said softly. 'I don't know what we'd do without you.'

★ ★ ★

'There's a message for you,' Mary greeted her on her return.

For a moment Edith's heart flew to her mouth and her pulse quickened, but then she damped down the feeling. The one person she most wanted to hear from would never write to her again.

'Looks as if it's from Peggy,' Mary went on, oblivious to what Edith was thinking. 'I haven't seen her for ages, have you?'

'No,' Edith replied, taking the envelope and sticking it in her skirt pocket while she set down her bag. 'Blimey, my arm's aching from carrying all that extra stuff. So many infectious cases at the moment — or is it just me?'

Mary shrugged. 'I had two confirmed of measles today, and one suspected case. I shall have to notify the school. What a palaver. Fancy some tea?' she added, heading for the stairs to the common room.

'I'll see you down there,' said Edith, knowing she would have to sort out her bag first.

When she eventually joined her friend, several other nurses had gathered on the same table, comparing measles cases.

'It's so hard on the mothers,' said Belinda, a tall, dark-haired nurse who had joined the home in the New Year, fresh from her QNI training, but who was now thoroughly used to working on the district. 'They all say the same thing — they wish they'd never come back after being evacuated. They think that if they'd stayed away in their billets, the children would still be all right.'

Edith sat down. 'That's daft, though. You can catch measles as easily out in the countryside as in the city. It doesn't care who it infects.'

Alice agreed. 'Yes, of course, but it's true that the parents feel awful and blame themselves. Anyway, it will be the end of term soon and perhaps some families will go back to where they were evacuated because of the threat of invasion.'

Mary immediately turned on her. 'Don't talk rot. There won't be one.'

Alice looked at her levelly. 'We don't know that, Mary. There might well be. We just can't say. The fact is that some parents have told the schools they're taking their children away again, and it's making the teachers' lives very difficult as they don't know what to plan for the new September term, invasion or no invasion.' One of Alice's friends was a teacher at a nearby primary school, and so she was up to date on their day-to-day problems.

Mary wasn't prepared to argue with Alice, who — it was generally acknowledged — was better informed than anyone else when it came to current affairs, as she spent much of her spare time reading the newspapers or glued to the news on the wireless. She decided to change the subject instead.

'What did Peggy have to say?' she asked, turning to Edith.

29

Edith had quite forgotten about the envelope in the hurry to sort out her potentially infected clothing, find a fresh set for tomorrow's visit, and to restock her Gladstone bag for the morning. 'I don't know. I haven't had a moment to look.'

'Well, how about now?' demanded Mary impatiently. In the absence of any letters for herself, Edith receiving one was the next best thing.

Edith obligingly reached into her pocket and drew it out, jagging it open with her index finger. 'All right . . . she says it's a shame we haven't seen each other for a while, and she knows what it feels like . . . ' Edith took a quick gulp and went on, 'so why don't I come and meet her in the Duke's Arms on Friday evening after work and we can pretend it's like old times. Well, without Harry and Pete, of course.' There, she'd done it, she'd said his name in front of a group of people and not broken down. She silently patted herself on the back.

'Would you want to?' asked Alice doubtfully.

Edith sighed. 'If you'd asked me even last week, I'd have said no. But she might have a point. I don't want to spend the summer moping around. Harry wouldn't have wanted it and neither would Pete. After all, what harm could it do? It's only down the road and we'll know lots of people there. Clarrie might come.' Peggy's friend Clarrie worked in the gas-mask factory as well. She too was part of the old school gang. 'Why don't you come along, Al? Or Mary? Belinda?'

Alice shook her head. 'I don't think so. You go, but I'll stay in.' Everyone knew her idea of a good time was an evening spent reading a book in her room.

Belinda raised her eyebrows. 'I might. There's a chance my brother will be in town, and if he is I'll want to try to meet him, but who knows with the trains these days. So I'll see, if that's all right with you.'

Mary beamed. 'Count me in. Charles will be working late again, and so just you try to stop me.'

★ ★ ★

Gwen let her good friend Miriam take the window seat as they stepped onto the bus. Miriam had been adamant that Gwen should not waste her day off but accompany her to the West End for a shopping trip. Gwen had gone along, but more for the pleasure of spending the afternoon with her friend than with the intention of buying anything. She wasn't particularly interested in what she wore; clothes served a purpose and that was that. Most of the time she wore her nurse's uniform anyway. Miriam, however, had other ideas.

'You can't let what's going on in the world stop you doing what you enjoy,' she had said. 'For me, that's buying nice clothes. No, don't wrinkle your nose like that. If you don't want to buy anything yourself, I shan't make you, but do me the favour of coming along and telling me what suits me best.'

31

Gwen had recognised this was simply a ruse, as nobody knew what suited Miriam better than Miriam herself. Now she glanced at her friend, beautifully turned out in a lilac skirt with matching light cotton jacket over a cream blouse with a delicate lace collar. She had kept her figure and it was hard to believe she had an adult son. Other women might have been jealous, but Gwen was happy for her, as she knew it mattered to Miriam that she looked smart. She had her role to play as the wife of a successful businessman. Also, she simply loved clothes.

'I'm sure this little summer coat will come in useful,' she said happily, patting the bag on her lap. 'And how lucky that they had a scarf to go with it. You could have got one as well, Gwen.'

Gwen laughed. 'Where would I wear it? Teaching first aid? I don't think so.'

'You'd wear it for the pure pleasure of it,' Miriam laughed. 'I always feel better when I have a nice scarf. It can make or break an outfit, you know.'

Gwen raised her eyebrows. 'I'm sure it can. Just not one of mine.' She glanced down at her plain grey skirt and serviceable beige blouse, which she'd run up from material she'd found at Ridley Road market.

'Yes, even yours.' Miriam tapped her on the arm. 'Something in dark green would lift it. I have something I could lend you if you like.'

Gwen shook her head. 'Thank you, but it would be wasted on me. You keep it. You'll enjoy it more.'

They fell silent as they passed the shop fronts

of Tottenham Court Road. There were still goods to buy but not as many as this time last year. There was an unspoken air of people going shopping while they still could. It was partly why Gwen had come. Even if she didn't want anything, it was still a spectacle, and she didn't know if or when she would be able to do so again. Like so many Londoners she was filled with a sense of deep foreboding.

A young couple got on and sat a few seats in front of them. The young man wore the uniform of the RAF, and the girl looked as if she had been crying as her eyes were red and puffy. She clung to his arm and looked imploringly up into his face. They were too far away for Gwen to hear what they were saying, but it wasn't hard to guess.

She caught Miriam's gaze.

Miriam shifted in her seat. 'Did I tell you what I have decided to do?'

'I don't think so.'

Miriam nodded in determination. 'I'm joining the WVS.'

'The Women's Voluntary Services?'

'Yes, exactly.' Miriam's face was serious. 'I am tired of hearing the news and feeling I'm doing nothing.'

'But you're always so busy,' Gwen pointed out. 'You've opened your house to families escaping Hitler.'

Miriam shrugged. 'The families are no trouble — this new couple don't have children, and they see to themselves most of the time. I have plenty of spare hours and I want to do something worthwhile with them. They need people who are organised and prepared to turn their hand to anything, so I thought I might fit in.'

'Well, I should think they'd welcome you with open arms,' Gwen said decisively. 'You must let me know how you get on. If I can help, I will, but I won't be able to join full time or anything like that. We're going to be even busier from now on.'

'Really?' Miriam asked. 'Do you know something I don't about what's happening over in France or Germany?'

Gwen realised her friend had misunderstood. 'No, I meant at the home. We're taking on two more newly qualified district nurses. These ones are Irish. They start as soon as we can sort out their accommodation.'

Miriam looked surprised. 'I thought your home was full?'

'It is,' said Gwen, 'but the woman who owns one of the flats next door has told us she's going to live with her sister, and she's given us first refusal on renting it from her. Fiona says we'd be silly to turn down the chance. It's only small but it has two rooms. They don't need a living room, as they can share our common room and canteen. It's ideal, even if highly irregular. I don't say I approve of bending the rules like that but, as long as Fiona's happy, who am I to say no? She's in charge.'

Miriam nodded in assent. 'These aren't normal times, are they? I could be wrong and I hope I am, but you might need every pair of hands available soon.'

Gwen stared out of the window, as the bus went past Sadler's Wells. 'I'd love you to be wrong, I really would,' she said, 'but I have a horrible feeling you aren't.'

4

'Look, there's Billy,' said Peggy, tugging on Edith's arm as they rounded the corner to the Duke's Arms. 'Doesn't he walk well now? You'd never think he'd been in that awful accident before Christmas, would you?'

Edith waved as Billy glanced along the street and saw the group of young women. 'That's nice, we can go in with him,' she said. Once she wouldn't have thought twice about going into a pub on her own, but that was when she had been young and carefree. Meeting Harry had steadied her — that and a year of district nursing. 'He was lucky, though,' she went on. 'His leg has healed properly and he doesn't have a trace of a limp. If he'd got an infection it would have been a different story.'

Belinda, walking just behind them with Mary, joined in. 'Why? What happened?'

'Oh, of course, it was before you came,' said Edith. 'Billy saw a car careering out of control down the high road and heading straight for a woman and her baby in a pram, so he threw them all into a doorway and saved their lives. The car hit him and broke his leg. Alice was the first nurse on the scene and she said it could all have been so much worse if he hadn't been there.'

'Goodness.' Belinda looked with respect at the young man now walking towards them. 'He must be very brave.'

Peggy nodded. 'He wanted to join up but he's got flat feet. Just as well, though, or he wouldn't have been walking along at just the right time, and Kath and little Brian would be dead.'

'Oh, so you know the woman?' Belinda asked.

'Yes, she's our friend. She was all shook up about it but wasn't really hurt. A few cuts and bruises, that was that. Now we all think Billy's a hero. And he went over on one of them little boats to Dunkirk.'

'Did he?' said Belinda, her eyes glinting with interest.

Billy tugged at the lapels of his jacket as he strode towards the women. 'Evening, ladies.' He grinned broadly. 'What a lovely evening it is an' all. How you doing, Peggy?' he asked his old friend with concern.

'Not so bad, Billy.' Peggy smiled gamely, pushing her hand through her light brown hair. 'Me and Edie thought it was time we showed our faces in public again, and we brought along Mary — you know each other, don't you? — and this is Belinda.'

'Pleased to meet you,' said Billy, offering his hand, which Belinda shook. 'Are you a nurse too?'

'I am,' said Belinda. 'I've been at the same home as Edith and Mary since January, but I've never been to the Duke's Arms before.'

'Well, you're in for a treat,' Billy promised. 'I arranged to meet a couple of mates from the docks and they're bringing some others, so we'll make a proper night of it.' He waved his arm to usher them forward, then dropped back to speak to Edith in a quiet voice. 'You all right, Edie? Not too soon to come out after . . . well, you know?'

Edith took a deep breath. In all honesty she was feeling rather shaky, but she was determined not to show it. She didn't want to ruin her friends' evening out. 'No, I'm doing well, thanks, Billy,' she said as steadily as she could. 'I'll take it easy, and if I feel like going home before the others then I will. But thank you for asking.'

Billy nodded solemnly. 'I'll walk you back if you like.'

Edith smiled at him in gratitude. 'We'll see how we go.'

★ ★ ★

Billy's colleagues were gathered around a wooden table and bench in the beer garden, taking advantage of the warmth of the evening sun. He hurried to make the introductions. 'This is Ronald, and this is Kenny,' he said. 'We were all down the same warehouse this morning and they fancied seeing my neck of the woods.'

'Didn't tell us that you had such lovely lady friends, though,' said Ronald, the taller one, with a kindly face. 'Kept that under your hat, you did, Billy.'

Peggy stepped forward a little. 'We didn't tell him we was coming,' she said. 'We kept it as a surprise, though we thought he would be here.'

Edith watched her friend with a hint of amazement. She herself was in no mood for talking pertly to a group of strange men, even if

38

they were Billy's mates. She couldn't imagine flirting with anyone ever again. But perhaps this was Peggy's way of coping.

'Then we're lucky twice over,' smiled Ronald. 'And this here's my brother, Alfie. He's not one of us from the warehouse, as you can see.' He indicated a man with tightly cropped sandy hair, in Royal Air Force uniform, who turned to acknowledge the newcomers.

'Hello,' he said, and his voice was pure East End, just like his brother's. 'Yes, got a spot of leave so came to see my kid brother. Brought along my mate Laurence, as he's so far from home.'

Another man turned to the group, his uniform jacket over his arm. 'Hello, ladies,' he said, his accent immediately marking him out. 'Thanks for brightening our evening.'

Mary perked up. 'I say, are you Canadian?'

Laurence's eyes crinkled in appreciation. 'Got it in one. Must say I'm impressed. Most folks think I'm from the States.'

'Oh, it was a lucky guess,' said Mary.

Edith smiled to herself. Before her colleague had met Charles, she had been extremely keen on going dancing to meet Canadians. She could see that this particular Canadian liked Mary's attention — but then, plenty of men took notice of her friend's curves.

'Where are you stationed?' asked Belinda.

Billy and Edith looked sharply at her. Everyone knew that it was best to say as little in public as possible when it came to such matters, as you never knew who might be listening.

There was even a new poster out from the government, warning that 'Careless Talk Costs Lives'. Belinda registered their disapproval and hastily explained. 'I mean, my brother is in the RAF and I know it's a long shot but maybe you know him. He was meant to be in London this weekend and I was looking forward to seeing him, but he wasn't able to make it in the end.'

Edith noted with relief that she hadn't said why. A call had come through to say his leave had been cancelled. Gwen had been cross that the home's single telephone had been used for a personal message, but their superintendent, Fiona, ruled that it was allowable in such circumstances as long as the message was kept brief.

'Suppose we might. What's his name?' asked Laurence.

'David. David Adams,' Belinda replied, but both men shook their heads.

'But if we bump into him in the future we'll say we met you,' offered Alfie, picking up on her disappointment.

She shrugged, and her tight black curls caught the evening sun. 'I know it was a bit unlikely,' she said. Rallying again, she turned to Laurence. 'So, where have you visited so far?'

He smiled easily and even Edith admitted to herself he was very good-looking. 'Well, my mother's from Scotland and so when I first got here I went to see my long-lost relatives up near Edinburgh. But for the rest of the time I've been down south. Alfie here took me to Brighton yesterday but it wasn't how we imagined it.'

'No,' said Alfie. 'For a start you aren't allowed on the beach now. Even the streets near the sea have a curfew, so you can't go down the seaside pubs after nine thirty. Put a bit of a kybosh on our plans.'

Peggy patted her hair. 'All the more reason to enjoy tonight then,' she suggested.

Billy met Edith's gaze behind their friend's back, and gave her a quizzical look. Edith gave him a little shrug. She didn't know what Peggy's game was either, but this wasn't turning out to be the quiet night out she'd foreseen.

Laurence and Alfie offered to get in a round of drinks. Edith didn't mind that; she only wanted half a shandy, and it was well known that the RAF men generally weren't short of a bob or two. Peggy ordered a port and lemon, while Mary and Belinda chose lemonade.

'They seem nice,' Peggy said, coming over to her. 'Makes a change, seeing new faces in here. Usually it's full of people I've been to school with, or at least their brothers and sisters.'

'Yes, but that's why I like it,' said Edith. 'Not that I was at school with them all but . . . well, you know, Harry was, and so I felt like I had this new group of friends to count on. It was never like that where I came from.'

Peggy bit her lip. 'I know. I'm only having a bit of fun. You don't mind, do you? It feels as if I've been sitting in Pete's mum's front room for ever. It was driving me nuts. It's a real breath of fresh air coming here again.'

Edith recognised that Peggy was dealing with her grief in a very different way, but didn't want

41

to blame her. 'Of course not. I'm just not feeling very chatty yet. It's nice to be out, so don't mind me if I'm a bit quiet.'

Peggy's face broke into a big smile. Then the RAF men returned and she hurried over to help hand round the glasses. She took her own and raised it. 'Cheers!' she said, beaming at Alfie and Laurence, then knocked back half of the gleaming purple drink in one go. 'To having fun.'

'Blimey,' said Billy under his breath, yet loud enough that Edith heard, while Laurence raised his own pint and said, 'To a fine evening, in the best city in England!'

'To the best bit of the best city in England!' said Peggy, and knocked back the rest of the port and lemon.

★   ★   ★

After a couple of hours, Edith was more than ready to go home. She'd tried her best, keeping up her end of the conversation when one of the others spoke to her, but it was an effort and her heart wasn't in it. After a while she drifted to the edge of the group and watched them rather than joining in. Billy's friends seemed nice enough, but she wasn't remotely interested in getting to know them any better. What would be the point? She'd probably never see them again anyway.

Peggy, however, continued to accept the port and lemons, which the RAF men obligingly bought her, and to drink them down as if there was no tomorrow. Her voice grew louder and she laughed at everything they said, playing with her hair or shaking it loose around her shoulders. Edith was slightly shocked. She was no prude, but it was no time at all since Pete had died, and here was Peggy behaving as if she hadn't a care in the world.

Mary detached herself from the conversation she'd been having with Ronald and Kenny and came over. 'You all right, Edie? You've gone quiet.'

Edith grinned awkwardly. 'Just tired.'

Mary nodded. 'Me too. Shall we go?'

Edith nodded, grateful that Mary had made the suggestion. As a point of pride she hadn't wanted to say anything, but the light was beginning to fade and she wasn't keen to stumble back in the blackout. Besides, she simply didn't have any energy left to socialise. She longed for her bed in her little attic room, where she wouldn't have to speak to anyone.

'Would you mind?' she said.

'Not a bit. I'll see what Belinda wants to do.'

After a brief chat with Belinda, and a word or two with Billy, Mary came back and told Edith: 'Belinda wants to stay longer, but Billy said he'd make sure she gets back all right. I've said goodbye on your behalf, so we can leave whenever you like.'

Edith sighed with relief. 'Let's go right now. No point in hanging around. Thanks, Mary.' She shrugged into her bolero and drew it around her. 'Come on, we can go out the back way.' She linked her arm through her friend's and they quietly made their way through the gate into the little lane behind the beer garden — where once

Harry had led her, the night she'd realised he was the only man for her.

★ ★ ★

At breakfast the next morning, Belinda was last down, almost missing the porridge. Edith, who had been chatting to Alice, waved her over. 'How was the rest of last night?' she asked. 'Did Billy walk you home like he said he would?'

Belinda looked guilty. 'Yes, but I lost track of time and I missed the curfew. I didn't realise it was after ten o'clock until he looked at his watch. I had to sneak past the front door and hope nobody was watching. I remembered what you used to do, though, and found the loose fence panel. I almost ripped my skirt getting through the gap — I'd hate to think what would have happened if I'd been any bigger. Mary said she'd leave a window open just in case and so I climbed in that way.'

Edith grinned. 'Good job you're so tall. I always needed help to reach the windowsill. I'd have been completely stuck on my own.'

'I scraped my knee as it was,' Belinda said ruefully. 'Still, it was worth it. I really enjoyed myself and it took my mind off David. I'm trying not to think about what he's doing, you see.'

Edith and Alice nodded in sympathy, although Alice had no brothers and sisters, and Edith wasn't close to any of her brothers in the way Belinda evidently was.

'Billy's ever so nice, isn't he?' Belinda went on. 'He had to come out of his way to bring me

44

back. I assumed he must live near here when he offered but, no, his house is in the opposite direction, yet he swore he didn't mind.'

Edith agreed. 'He's one of the kindest people I know. That's typical of him.' She watched Belinda with curiosity. Was there something more than friendly appreciation behind what she'd said? Had Billy taken her fancy? Belinda had never talked about a boyfriend so perhaps it was possible. Edith decided not to mention the complication of Kathleen.

'Anyway, Peggy certainly seemed to enjoy herself,' Belinda continued. 'She and that Canadian airman got on like a house on fire. I think she's going to see him again.'

Alice raised her eyebrows in surprise. 'Really? Isn't that a bit soon?'

Edith pulled a face. 'Well, I'd have thought so, but if that's her way of getting over Pete then I don't suppose we can blame her. Perhaps it's just a bit of fun.'

'What's he like?' Alice asked.

'Very good-looking,' Belinda said at once. 'Dark hair, dark eyes, easy to talk to. Generous as well — he bought everyone drinks all night.'

'Yes, you couldn't fault him for that,' Edith agreed, remembering all the port and lemons Peggy had had.

Alice picked up on the tone of her friend's voice. 'But what? Didn't you like him, Edie?'

'No, it's not that.' Edith stopped to think about her impressions of Laurence. Everything Belinda said was true, and yet there was something about him she hadn't warmed to. Was

45

it the way he had eyed up Mary when they'd arrived? Then again, she was hardly in the mood to start taking an interest in men. 'I'm just being silly, pay me no notice. I didn't really speak to him enough to say either way.'

Alice glanced at her sceptically but Belinda didn't see. 'Well, I thought he was a bit of a catch. I don't suppose he'll be around for long, though. They're based down on the south coast somewhere, so they're bound to go back there soon and that'll be that.'

Edith got up, clearing her plate and cup. 'I expect you're right.' But she couldn't shake that faint feeling of unease.

5

'You're getting too big for this!' Kathleen exclaimed, lifting her son into his pram, which had seemed so huge when she'd first got it. Brian beamed up at her, his face now almost chubby. He still fitted in but gone were the days when she could easily sit him at one end and a bag of shopping at the other. It was finally being able to give him proper food that had made the difference.

Kathleen had struggled when he had been a small baby, with scarcely any money to feed the pair of them and make ends meet. If it hadn't been for her best friend Mattie insisting that she came round to the Banhams' house so often, they would have been in deep trouble. Then Ray had joined the merchant navy and some of his wages found their way back home, which had helped. Kathleen automatically rubbed her wrist and arm at the mere thought of him. She was never going to forget the way he'd hurt her, throwing her to the floor and all because she'd needed to feed Brian before paying attention to him. She had loved Ray with all her heart, even more so because her family had been so against the match. It had taken that day when he'd come home and she'd feared he would attack his own son to make her fully realise the sort of man he was.

Now he was dead, lost at Dunkirk along with

47

so many others. Plenty would say he was a hero, and she supposed he was. At least she could tell Brian that his father had died for a noble cause. She would try to hold on to that, rather than the cold truth of Ray the wife-beater, jealous of his own son. While one part of her still longed for the passion they had shared, a greater part felt nothing but relief. He could never hurt either of them again.

Yet she blamed herself for not mourning him more deeply. He had been her husband, after all. Shouldn't she feel terrible, as if life had no meaning, that she'd never be the same again? Like poor Edith did. The guilt was eating away inside her. She knew she was avoiding her friends, those who wanted to help her, like the Banhams and Billy. Especially Billy.

He'd always been so kind to her and come to her rescue more than once, very discreetly lending her money when he correctly suspected she had no other way of paying the rent. She'd been too proud to tell anyone just how bad her financial problems were, but somehow he had known. That was before he had saved her from the speeding car with its drunk driver. She and Brian would have been badly hurt, even killed, and he hadn't thought twice. So really she should show him just how grateful she was.

However, the more she acknowledged how she felt, the worse the guilt became. She'd failed to see what a good man Billy was and had been taken in by Ray's shallow charm. More fool her. Now she was too confused to know what to do.

'Off we go,' she said, forcing herself to sound

bright and encouraging, not wanting Brian to glimpse the darkness inside her. She manoeuvred the heavy pram down the narrow pavement of Jeeves Place, waving to her old neighbour Mrs Bishop who sometimes babysat, dodging the broken slabs on the corner, and headed for Ridley Road market.

No matter how miserable she was, Kathleen usually enjoyed the bustle of the market, where many of the stallholders knew her, and some even saved little treats for Brian. He would sit up straighter in his pram when they drew near to the best fruit and vegetable stall and start to wave his arms when he caught sight of the man who ran it. Sure enough, today the man came around to the front of his stall, still piled high with colourful produce despite all the difficulties of the war. At least fruit and veg weren't rationed. 'How's my favourite customer today?' he asked, bending down to Brian's level, and Brian squealed in delight.

'He's giving me no end of trouble, growing so fast,' Kathleen laughed, pleased to see that Brian didn't mind relative strangers. He was becoming a sociable little boy. That was exactly what she wanted. He hadn't been around his aggressive father enough to taste real fear.

The stallholder reached into his pocket and drew out a shiny apple. 'This will put colour in your cheeks,' he said solemnly to the child. Brian immediately reached for it and beamed as he held it, fascinated by the bright colour and delicious smell.

'Good boy,' said Kathleen, reaching around.

'Now you give it to Mummy to keep safe and you can have it when we get home.' She didn't want him taking big bites out of it when she couldn't see him or he might choke.

Brian didn't object and she turned her attention to the business in hand, buying ingredients for the next couple of days. It was a sad truth that receiving a pension as Ray's widow meant she had money coming in more regularly than ever before. It wasn't a fortune, but it was so much better than hoping for handouts from him, never knowing when they would come — or if at all. She and Brian had never eaten so well. Kathleen was clever at making something out of nearly nothing, having had to do so out of sheer necessity for so long, and now she found they could eat like kings if she budgeted carefully. Thanking the stallholder for his help, she loaded her bulging bag on to the wire basket beneath the pram, and made her way down the crowded thoroughfare to the stall which sold grains.

'Shall we get some oats for your porridge?' she asked Brian. 'And pearl barley too,' she said to the new stallholder. Barley stew was something she made a lot of; it was filling, and nourishing, and safe for Brian with his new teeth. She propped the big paper bag of it at the bottom of the pram. 'Now you keep your feet away from it,' she instructed her son, mock sternly.

The stallholder laughed. 'He'll be big enough to kick that soon,' he observed.

'It's all your good food,' Kathleen replied, thankful as she'd seen he had added a little extra to the bag before fastening it. That left only the fish stall. As meat was rationed, she had taken to buying fish when she could, but that meant coming more often as she had nowhere to keep it fresh.

Turning back into the fray of busy shoppers, some with small children tugging on their mothers' coats, she became aware of a strange sensation, almost like a prickling at the back of her neck. She rubbed her scarf, hastily flung on earlier that morning. She must be imagining things. Frowning, she drew up at the fish stall and joined the small queue. Clarrie's sister, who she knew slightly, was just ahead of her, and they passed the time while they waited.

'And how are you getting on?' asked the young woman, who had hair the exact same shade of red as Clarrie. 'I heard about your husband. I know Peggy's proper cut up about Pete, and I'm sorry you are on your own now.'

'Oh, not too bad, thank you for asking,' Kathleen said hurriedly. 'This little one keeps me going. You have to carry on, don't you?'

The woman nodded. 'Well, I think you're very brave,' she said. 'Oh, two fillets please.' She turned to pay the fishmonger and Kathleen sighed with relief. She could not say what she really meant: she was glad Ray was dead.

She waved goodbye to Clarrie's sister as she reached the head of the queue. The fishmonger recognised her and chatted easily as he took her order, making sure she got a good fillet and wrapping it carefully. Kathleen was pleased. That would be enough for her to eat simply grilled, with a little left over to break up and mash into potato for Brian. He wasn't keen on fish on its own yet. She began to daydream about when he might be old enough to enjoy fish and chips as she pushed the pram back down between the stalls towards the main road.

There it was again, that strange prickling at the back of her neck. Kathleen turned round in puzzlement. A movement several stalls away caught her eye and she squinted in the bright sunshine to make out what it was. A figure had gone behind a striped awning but now appeared to be standing still. From what she could see of the person's clothes, it was a man. He moved a little but did not step into the pathway between the stalls. It was almost as if he was teasing her.

He swayed towards the edge of the stall and then back again. This was silly, she told herself. What grown man would play games like this? She was seeing trouble where there was none. She moved to the next stall and examined the bolts of fabric, more for the pleasure of enjoying their contrasting patterns than with the intention of buying anything.

Just as she was about to turn around and resume her journey home, the man reappeared, but backlit by the sunshine she could not make out any definite details. He seemed to take a step towards her and then moved back into the shadow of the awning. It was very peculiar, to say the least.

Kathleen stood still as the crowds milled around her. What was all that about? Was he having a stupid bit of fun, or was he following her for some more sinister reason? Shaking her head, she told herself not to be fanciful. She had to get back to her dingy rooms on Jeeves Place and cook the fish before the heat of the day spoiled it. She didn't have time to worry about men behaving oddly. She would put his strange behaviour straight out of her mind.

Yet as she pushed the pram along the main road, heavier now with all its shopping, the kernel of worry would not be dislodged.

★   ★   ★

Gladys flapped her duster out of the common-room window, careful to avoid two of the nurses who were propping their bikes in the cycle rack at the side of the yard. The dust rose in a puff, the air almost still and very warm. She glanced up at the sky, wondering if she might catch sight of any of the brave aircraft heading to the coast or Channel to defend the country from the Luftwaffe, in what was being described as the Battle of Britain. She wondered if she would have had the courage to be a pilot if she'd been a man. Sometimes she wished she could do more, something directly useful.

'Penny for them.' Alice stood right behind her.

Gladys wheeled around and almost banged her head on the window frame. 'Oooh, you startled me.' She still had to bite her lip not to call Alice 'Miss'. Old habits died hard. 'I was just looking for any planes. They must be up there somewhere. Going off to — what do they call them? — the dogfights.'

53

Alice came to stand beside her at the window and gazed into the cloudless blue. 'Perhaps they're further south. Or over Kent. It's hard to say. But that's where the dogfights are happening, apparently.'

Gladys nodded and then cleared her throat. 'I been meaning to ask. How's Edith? She's so quiet around the place, I don't like to speak to her direct.'

Alice took a moment. 'She's going to be all right,' she said slowly. 'She wouldn't mind if you spoke to her, you know. She's keeping going. The work helps.'

'I can understand that.' Gladys twisted her duster in her hands. 'It's so important, the work you all do.'

'Well, so is yours,' Alice pointed out. 'We couldn't manage if we didn't have board and lodging all sorted out for us. It's teamwork.' She smiled but Gladys did not smile back.

'I want to do more, Alice. I love going to the first-aid classes. I remember everything we're taught. I wish I could read better and take exams and that.'

'You're improving so fast,' Alice assured her, knowing that the young woman had hidden her shameful secret for years. Now she was finally learning she was making progress — but not enough yet to cope with nurses' exams.

'Anyway I can't stop work to study. We need the cash, simple as that.' Gladys grimaced. 'Me ma can't do without me wages, and I can always get home round the corner if something goes wrong with the little ones.' It had been the burden of caring for her many younger siblings that had brought a halt to Gladys's schooling in the first place.

'If you keep up the reading and the first-aid course then something might come up,' Alice ventured. 'We don't know what's around the corner, but nurses will be needed even more than at the moment.'

'Perhaps things will get easier when me sister is a bit older,' Gladys replied, looking down at her feet as if she didn't really believe it. 'I was younger than she is now when I stopped everything to look after them. She helps a bit but not like what I had to. She's a good girl though, doesn't try to get out of her chores like some.' She shook her head. It all seemed impossibly far in the future and gave her a headache to think about it. She tried to change the subject. 'Oooh, what's that you got there, a letter?'

Alice's hand went to her skirt pocket, where Gladys had noticed the corner of an envelope sticking out. 'Yes, it came earlier.' She broke into a grin. 'It's from Dermot. Do you remember him? The locum doctor who helped Dr Patcham out last autumn.'

Gladys took a moment to think who she was talking about. 'The one everyone got in a tizz about? I didn't meet him but I know all you nurses went into a flap every time he was mentioned. Didn't some swap shifts so they could stand more chance of seeing him? There was a right to-do.'

Alice laughed. 'Not me. I've known him for years. He was a trainee doctor when I began nursing, back home in Liverpool. But you're right — the first thing anyone notices is his looks. Not that they'll be much use to him at the moment.' She drew out the letter and reread it. 'He's back from France, thank goodness, and survived more or less in one piece. Now he's somewhere near Southampton at a guess, as he can't say exactly, but hints that it's not too far from where he was before. He's got his hands full with casualties from the fighting overhead. Those dogfights that you were talking about, I expect.'

'See, he's doing something useful,' Gladys said.

'So are you,' Alice reminded her. 'Who knows, we might make a nurse of you yet.'

6

Peggy was sure her mother-in-law suspected something. The older woman hadn't been waiting up for her when she'd come in late from the pub that time, hardly able to remember what she'd been saying or doing after all the port and lemons, but ever since then she'd been on the alert, even more keen to point out the smallest mistake. She always claimed it was for Peggy's own good, so that she wouldn't make the same error in the future, but Peggy was permanently on the verge of screaming.

She knew she'd given her address to Laurence before eventually leaving the pub, but vaguely recalled he was on leave and so might not be around for long. She hadn't worried too much. It had been a fun evening and she would have loved to repeat it but, if it wasn't to be, then that was that. She wasn't going to pine away if he didn't get in touch. That wasn't what she'd been looking for.

Perhaps she should have made more of an effort to talk to Edith, Peggy thought with a flash of guilt. That was what the evening was meant to have been about. But Edith had brought two other nurses along and then they'd bumped into Billy with all his friends — it had grown into something else entirely. She vowed she would see Edith again on her own and then they could have the heart-to-heart she dearly wanted. The pain of missing Pete never left her, and whatever she now did or said didn't begin to touch it. That sense of overwhelming loss was at her very core; everything else was on the surface, far away from what really mattered. Perhaps Edith would understand.

She'd been on the point of scribbling a message to leave at the home on Victory Walk when the letterbox opened and an envelope landed on the doormat. Swiftly she moved to pick it up. It was for her, in handwriting she didn't recognise, loopy and forward-slanting. Peggy hurriedly jammed it into the handbag she'd left on the stairs, ready to take to work. She would read it when she got to the factory. Despite the scores of people there, it was easier to find a private moment than here in Mrs Cannon's house.

Right on cue Pete's mother called out from upstairs. 'Was that the post, Peggy love?'

Peggy gritted her teeth but made her voice as neutral as she could. 'I can't see anything. It must have been the wind.'

There was a brief pause. 'I could have sworn I heard something,' said Mrs Cannon, appearing at the top of the stairs, a fresh print overall on to greet the new day.

'There's nothing there,' Peggy assured her truthfully. 'Were you expecting anything?'

Mrs Cannon's face fell. 'No, dear. Not any more.'

Peggy immediately felt a rush of new guilt. She knew Mrs Cannon missed her son dreadfully and yet she couldn't bear to think about it or it would open the floodgates of her own grief. Pete's letters had been something they had been able to share, but there would be no more of them.

The older woman visibly pulled herself together, straightening her shoulders and smoothing down the cotton of her overall. 'Well, I'll see you later then,' she said, in a voice that must have been intended to sound bright but which was so full of sadness that Peggy couldn't bear it.

'Yes, I'm just going to write a quick note then I'll be off to work,' she said, grabbing her bag and ducking around the corner of the corridor so that she wouldn't have to witness Mrs Cannon's brave attempt at normality, because it was all too painfully close to her own.

★   ★   ★

'We gave Jerry's planes a pasting last night,' said one of the sailors as he made his way up the gang-plank to board his vessel. 'Sent 'em back where they came from good and proper.' He waved to the dock workers who were lined up ready to deal with the cargo.

Billy rolled back his sleeves and prepared to move the first lot of crates. Sometimes his leg gave him trouble when he had to deal with heavy weights, but he wasn't going to admit that. He was dog tired after having been on shift half the night but he wasn't going to admit that either.

'That's good news, then,' said Ronald, coming up beside him. 'Help me with this one, will you?'

Billy grunted in assent and took one side of

the big crate, while Ronald manoeuvred his corner onto the trolley to drag it towards the warehouse. 'Suppose so,' he managed, as they set the big wooden box down.

'Warm one today,' Ronald went on, wiping his forehead with his dusty hanky. 'What I wouldn't give to be sitting around on me arse doing nothing. Like that lot.' He tipped his head towards a small group of men who weren't even bothering to watch all the activity, let alone come across to help. Ronald spat onto the sawdust floor. 'Makes me sick. They might as well join up; they're a fat lot of use round here.'

Billy looked up at his taller friend. 'It's true, you got a point there.'

Ronald shrugged. 'That one — what's his name, Bertie — seems to have it in for you.'

Billy laughed grimly. 'It's cos he got drunk and drove into me leg, and almost killed me friend and her little boy. Then he blames her for him being slammed in the nick for a bit. Not for long enough, if you ask me.'

'Longer the better,' agreed Ronald, pushing his hanky back into his trouser pocket, frayed where it had caught on the rough wood of the crates. 'All the same, he don't half bear a grudge. He was going on about her the other day, nasty piece of work that he is.'

'He's just trying to make himself sound more important than he is — and that's not hard,' Billy said.

Ronald thought about it for a moment. 'Could be — he likes to strut about like he's cock of the walk, and for no good reason,' he conceded. 'All the same, he's up to something. Wish I could say what but I can't.'

'Should I warn Kath?' Billy asked. 'I can't very well go worrying her if we don't know what it's all about, can I? That would be no help at all.'

Ronald spread his hands. 'Wouldn't hurt to go round and check on her, would it? You seen her recently?'

'No,' Billy admitted. He'd kept to his resolution to give her some space, to let her grieve for that bastard Ray Berry, and not to pester her, even though the effort of staying away had cut him to the quick.

'Why not pop round, just friendly like, and don't say anything in particular, just see if she's doing all right,' Ronald suggested. 'Look, there's the boss. We'd better get to that next crate.'

Billy nodded. 'Fair enough.' His mind was racing. He could not let Bertie attempt to hurt Kath again. He'd be doing her a favour if he dropped round, just like old times. It was a happy coincidence that it matched what he wanted to do more than anything.

★   ★   ★

Peggy hummed to herself as she put away her overall in her locker and shook out her hair from its protective scarf. When Pete had been alive she used to lighten it with lemon juice in the summer, but lately she hadn't bothered. Now maybe she might start again, if there were any lemons to be had. She brought out the little mirror she kept tucked in the side zip of her handbag and pouted at herself in the reflection. Not looking too bad, she decided, given what she'd been through recently.

'You're cheerful today,' Clarrie observed, arching a carefully shaped eyebrow at her. Peggy noticed her friend had managed to use a brown pencil to taper the brows, as she hated her naturally red tone; it was all right on her head of hair, but not her brows, she always moaned.

Peggy shrugged noncommittally. It was true, she was fizzing inside after reading her surprise letter, but she wasn't going to tell anyone why, not even her oldest friend. She had a feeling Clarrie wouldn't understand. 'Sun's out, sky is blue,' she said vaguely. 'I can't be miserable all the time, can I?'

Clarrie nodded approvingly. 'That's the spirit. That sounds like the old Peggy is on her way back.' She grinned mischievously. 'Don't suppose it was anything to do with that piece of paper I caught you looking at before dinnertime?'

Peggy almost blurted out a shocked reply but gathered her wits quickly. 'Oh, I wrote a note to Edie to ask her out on Friday to the Duke's Arms, so we can have a bit of a chat,' she said easily. That was true, insofar as it went, but it had been a different piece of paper. She'd delivered the note that morning before arriving at the factory. She'd been reading her letter just before their dinner break.

'What a good idea. Shall I come?' Clarrie asked. 'I've been wondering how she's been getting on.'

'Let's wait to see what she says,' Peggy said quickly. 'She might just want a heart-to-heart. I'll let you know.'

Clarrie nodded. 'Got to dash. I promised Ma I'd try to get some tripe on the way home and the place will shut in fifteen minutes.' She sped off.

Peggy gave her friend a little wave and then her thoughts returned to the contents of the letter. It had been from Laurence and was very flattering. Best night he'd had for ages. Didn't realise London had such pretty girls. Would she do him the honour of meeting up again, just the two of them this time? He'd suggested a pub closer to the centre of town, but Peggy knew she could get there with just one change of bus.

It wasn't as if she was being unfaithful to the memory of Pete. This was just a bit of fun, a way of getting out of the house and having a respite from sitting eye-to-eye with Mrs Cannon. It didn't mean she missed Pete any the less. It was just so tempting to hear someone, especially someone as good-looking as Laurence, tell her she was pretty when she felt so withered and empty inside. It was a little plaster over the top of a deep wound, nothing more.

She debated saying no, claiming she had to be up early for work, which was true, or that she shouldn't because of her recent bereavement. Yet she knew she could do her work without thinking — she'd done so often enough when out courting with Pete. And why would she even tell Laurence about her husband? This was just a bit of fun.

Pushing her conscience to one side, she decided to accept.

7

Billy rounded the corner to Jeeves Place, turning over in his mind what he would say. He'd had a couple of days to think about it, as he hadn't been able to come round immediately after the conversation with Ronald. He'd been exhausted after working at night and then going straight to a day's graft at the docks for a start. He also wanted to say the right thing, to somehow encourage Kathleen to be vigilant without scaring her unduly. But now, as he approached her door, he still hadn't decided exactly what to say.

All he knew was, he was desperate to see her. It felt like years, even though it had been more like weeks. Every moment away from her was too long. When he was with her, time sped by. Even though he yearned to hold her and protect her, just being in her company would be enough, or at least for now.

Yet he hesitated, his hand raised above the letterbox which Kathleen had clearly polished recently. His heart ached at all the attempts she made to make her home look nice for little Brian, even though it was only two small ground-floor rooms with poor daylight and a noisy family upstairs. She couldn't have shown more love and pride if it had been a palace.

Taking a deep breath, he rapped on the door.

It swung open immediately. 'Oh, Billy, it's you.'

Kathleen looked relieved and yet her smile was reserved, not the wide welcoming grin he'd grown used to. 'I could see someone was out there and wondered who it was. You better come in.'

'Expecting someone else, was you?' Billy asked anxiously, not wanting to intrude and yet immediately on his guard as to who it might be.

'No, no.' She moved inside and he followed her, into the dimness of the small living room with its single bed pushed up against the far wall, everything immaculate as ever but still shabby. 'Time for a cuppa?'

Billy nodded at once. 'As long as I'm not interrupting — is the nipper asleep yet?' He cast his eyes towards Brian's cot, but the little boy was sitting up, and he waved his arms and called out when he saw who it was.

Billy went over and tousled his hair. 'Only me, Brian.'

Brian sat back down from where he'd pulled himself up on the bars and, satisfied, began to play with his teddy again. Billy nodded to himself, pleased the boy hadn't forgotten him. He sat at the wooden table near the window and watched as Kathleen busied herself. Her quick, neat movements never failed to make him catch his breath, as she took the milk from its cooler and set aside the small piece of muslin she used to cover it to keep out the flies. Then he remembered what he had in his pocket.

'Got some biscuits,' he said awkwardly, reaching inside his jacket and pulling out the packet.

Kathleen turned. 'Oh, you shouldn't have. They're like hen's teeth these days.'

Billy grinned and handed them to her, watching as she set them out on a plate. 'Well, what's the use of working down the docks if you can't get some treats?' Seeing her expression change he hurried to reassure her. 'No, no, they're legit. I got a tip-off from me mate who knew which shop down Limehouse they was going to.'

Kathleen let out a breath. 'I didn't mean . . . I know you wouldn't do nothing wrong, Billy. But you hear such stories these days. I don't want to get you in trouble.'

'Can the boy have one?' Billy asked.

'Maybe a half. I don't want to spoil his supper. Anyway, he can't go getting a taste for these things, they're too hard to come by,' Kathleen said ruefully, as Billy broke a biscuit in two and gave half to Brian.

'See, he likes it.' Billy watched him fondly. How could Ray have failed to love his son? He was the sunniest little boy, hardly ever complaining, despite the grim conditions he'd often had to endure. Billy sat back in his chair. 'So, Kath, how you been?'

Kathleen sat carefully down opposite him. 'Oh, you know. All right.' She smiled but cautiously.

'Been seeing much of Mattie?' he asked. 'She must be quite a way along now.'

Kathleen brightened up. 'She is, the baby's due around the end of September. I been round there helping out, what with her being so big and

Joe away and . . . ' She stopped.

Billy sighed and voiced the inevitable. 'And no Harry any more.'

Kathleen bit her lip. 'No Harry. No.'

A silence stretched between them. Billy was unsure how to broach the topic he knew he had to bring up, all the more so because he could sense Kathleen's tension. The last thing he wanted was to make her feel under threat. Then Kathleen gave him the perfect opening.

'Sorry I was a bit jumpy when you came, Billy,' she said, rubbing her hand across her forehead. 'It wasn't cos I didn't want to see you, you know that. It's just . . . it's the silliest thing. I was down the market and I thought a man was acting strange, sort of lurking in the background. Hanging around the stalls he was . . . '

'He didn't do nothing to hurt you, did he, Kath?' Billy burst out, his blood boiling at the very idea.

Kathleen shook her head. 'No, nothing like that. He didn't even say anything. He sort of came out from behind a stall and went back into the shadows a couple of times. Not normal but that was all.'

Billy frowned. 'You sure that was all?' He knew Kathleen would always seek to downplay anything bad that happened to her, rather than worry anybody. She'd put up with Ray's mistreatment for ages before it became too obvious to hide. He couldn't bear it if she was hiding something now.

'Really, Billy, that was all it was. I'm probably making something out of nothing, so don't mind

68

me.' She tried to smile to take the edge off her words.

Billy nodded slowly. 'All right. Fair enough. But Kath, if you see or hear something more, anything at all, you let me know, all right?' Suddenly his voice was full of intensity. 'It don't matter if it's day or night, you get word to me. If I'm on shift then Stan or Flo will know where I am. I'm not having any — ' He bit back the word he wanted to use as he realised Brian was taking an interest in what he was saying. 'Any strange man interfering with your safety. You been through enough.' Without thinking, he rubbed his injured leg.

Kath at once grew alarmed. 'Your leg still hurting you, Billy? After all this time?'

Billy swiftly folded his arms. 'No, just habit. It don't bother me at all now. Think nothing of it.' He finished his tea. 'Look, I better be going. I don't want to hold up the boy's supper, or yours either for that matter, and I got to be on duty later on.' He rose to go and Kathleen rose with him.

'Thank you for coming,' she said. 'Sorry again for being all jumpy.' She smiled but kept the table between them, before turning and opening the door. 'See you again, Billy.'

He took a step towards her then, recognising her reticence, went no further. 'Yes, hope so, Kath. And you remember what I said. Day or night, you let me know if you need me.' He could hardly keep the pain out of his voice as his emotions threatened to overwhelm him. He was desperate to draw her close, to enfold her safely

— but he could tell that was not what she wanted at all.

She nodded. 'I won't forget,' she said softly.

★ ★ ★

Kathleen shut the door and leant against it, shutting her eyes for a brief moment. She had seen the longing in Billy's eyes but could do nothing about it. She was torn between the urge to accept all he was so clearly ready to offer and the suffocating guilt that it was too soon after Ray's death. It was so much worse because she wasn't sorry Ray had died. She should be grieving, as were so many others — for husbands, lovers, sons and brothers. Edith and the Banhams were mourning Harry with every waking breath, and yet she was secretly glad she was free of her violent husband.

Nobody must know how she felt. It had to remain her secret. Brian must never suspect the sort of man his father had truly been. The shame of it all flooded through her again, that she should have been reduced to that mangled heap on the floor, that she had misread the man's character so completely. It would kill her if anyone found out what she felt deep down.

So all she could do was keep Billy at a distance, because the love she saw in his eyes threatened to undo her and break her resolve. She couldn't let it happen. Better he thought she had stopped caring than he knew the truth — even if it cost her what she longed for most.

Peggy glanced around the interior of the pub. It wasn't quite what she had expected. Somehow she had imagined that Laurence would have a taste for the good things in life, after he had appeared to have money to spend so liberally on drinks for a group of people he hardly knew. This place could not be described as luxurious. It was even a bit rundown, if she was honest, but she made up her mind not to be disappointed. He had probably chosen it because of its convenient location, halfway between the station where his train would pull in and where she lived.

It wasn't as if she was out to snare a rich husband either. Nothing could have been further from her mind, although she knew some of the women she worked with were targeting airmen as they were most likely to have plenty of cash. This was solely to escape from everything that now weighed her down. She took in the sight of the other customers. There were plenty of young men in uniform, but mostly army rather than RAF. There were equal numbers of young women and older men, some who had perhaps come straight from work, as she herself had. She'd taken the precaution of telling Mrs Cannon that she might stay at Clarrie's so the older woman would not wait up for her. Not that she intended to stay out, but she didn't fancy a grilling about where she'd been and with whom.

There was no sign of Laurence yet. Peggy was not sure if he was staying in London or coming up from his airfield that day, and she'd heard that the trains were now often delayed and so it was nothing to worry about. She knew the sensible thing to do would be to find a table and sit there to wait for him, but she was in a reckless mood. She elbowed her way to the bar, its deep wood surface marked with scores of rings from where glasses had stood. The bar staff at the Duke's Arms would never have stood for that, but this place evidently had different standards.

There was a middle-aged man serving at one end, his thinning hair combed unconvincingly across his pink scalp. Peggy looked away before he could meet her eye. She didn't fancy getting stuck in conversation with him. Then, from around the other side of the bar, a youngish woman appeared, older than Peggy but with a far friendlier demeanour than the barman. 'Evening,' she said brightly, her big brass necklace flashing in the beams of the overhead lights. 'What can I get you?'

Again Peggy thought of the sensible choices, lemonade or ginger beer. 'Port and lemon please,' she said decisively.

'Port and lemon coming up.' The barmaid reached for a glass, held it up to the light and hurriedly wiped it with a tea towel. 'Your first time in here, is it?'

Peggy nodded. 'I'm meeting a friend.'

The barmaid raised an eyebrow. 'A male friend, might that be?'

'He's in the air force,' Peggy told her eagerly. 'He's a pilot.'

The woman pulled a face. 'Is he now? We get some of them in here all right. Well, don't go getting too fond of him if you take my meaning.'

Peggy was confused. 'Not sure I do. What do you mean?' Now the woman was standing more closely Peggy could tell that she was older than she'd first appeared, with worry lines across her forehead and the beginnings of crow's feet at the corner of her eyes.

The woman sighed. 'Because they're getting shot down like nobody's business,' she said brusquely. 'Day after day, all those fights with Hitler's planes. You can call it the Battle of Britain if you like, but all I see is customers who suddenly don't show their faces again.'

Peggy bristled. 'That's not what they say on the news,' she began, even though she often didn't listen properly. It hadn't saved Pete, after all.

'I'm only giving you a friendly tip,' said the barmaid. 'You can be friends with whoever you like, no skin off my nose. But those boys have a habit of not coming back, so have a care.'

'Enough of that, Marge, you'll frighten her off,' growled the man. 'Don't go saying such things in public.'

Marge tossed her head and the necklace flashed. 'Still true though,' she said. 'You mark my words.' She slammed the full glass on the counter, gave the barman a filthy look and disappeared around the corner of the bar to the snug.

Peggy took her drink and gave the money to the barman, who glared at her as if it was all her fault. She took a quick sip and turned, scanning the room for a table. There was one in the corner. Making her way across the saloon, she decided that the woman was jealous, probably because she was stuck with the miserable barman and couldn't flirt with the pilots any more. Well, that wasn't Peggy's problem. Marge must have gone straight to the wireless as the sounds of the Andrews Sisters rose over the hubbub of chatter from the punters.

Taking her seat, Peggy toyed with her glass, knowing she had better not finish this drink too quickly. She ignored all the interested glances from the young lads in army uniform, or those from the men old enough to be her father. Dirty so-and-sos, she thought.

Finally, when she was over halfway through the port and lemon, there was a flash of movement and he was there beside her. Laurence, even more handsome than she remembered.

'I'm so sorry I'm late,' he said, in that relaxed accent that made her knees go weak. 'Have you been waiting long? Here, let me get you another.'

Peggy beamed up at him and stood. 'I don't mind if I do,' she said.

★ ★ ★

'Got a moment?' Edith stuck her head around Alice's bedroom door. Her friend was sitting by the window to catch the last of the daylight, the sunset fading from bright gold to deep red over the rooftops. Her hair, swept up into a loose bun to keep it out of the way, picked up the golden highlights. In her hand was a letter. 'Sorry, are you busy?'

'No, no, come in.' Alice folded the sheets of paper and tucked them back in their envelope. 'It's from Joe. I was only rereading it.'

Edith gave a small smile. Joe, Harry's older brother, wrote frequently to Alice, and there had been plenty of their friends who took this to mean more than it actually did. Edith knew for a fact that most of their correspondence consisted of comments about books they had recently read and there was no romance to speak of. Alice was not looking for anything of that sort; she had had her heart broken once already and had no intention of repeating the devastating experience. Yet she and Joe had formed a close bond and Edith was glad for her friend, who otherwise would throw everything into her work.

'How is he?' she asked now, sitting on the neatly made bed, leaning back and stretching her feet. She groaned a little — they ached as she had cycled or walked for hours on end earlier that day, or that was what it felt like.

'Lots going on, by the sounds of it.' Alice raised her eyebrows. 'Of course he doesn't say where he is, but he does mention he's just finished a novel by Eric Linklater. So my bet is he's at Scapa Flow.'

Edith frowned. 'How do you know that?'

'Because that writer is from Orkney,' Alice explained, a little embarrassed to be caught out knowing such details. 'That's where our big naval base is, so it would make sense if he was there. That's my guess anyway. He sends his love.'

Edith nodded. 'Send mine back.' She was very fond of Joe, who was as reliable as Harry had been impetuous. From a distance they had looked very similar, but she had never had any doubt which brother she preferred. 'I've had a letter too.'

'Oh?' Alice put down her envelope. 'Not Peggy again?'

'No. Well, yes actually, she left a note to suggest meeting this Friday but not in a crowd like before. That's not why I wanted to talk to you, though.' Her face twisted and Alice leant forward in concern. 'It's from one of my brothers.'

'Your brothers?' Alice sat up in amazement. Edith's contacts with her family were few and far between, and in all the time she had known her, there had never been word from any of her brothers.

Edith nodded. 'Yes. It's from Mick — the one who's only a couple of years younger than me. He's had to join up, of course, and he's back on leave for a few days. He says we should meet. I think he's worried that our younger brother Frankie will try to join up too, even though he's not old enough.'

Alice grimaced. 'The way this war is going, Edie, he might well get his chance anyway. Sorry, that's not fair. Will you go? To see him, I mean?'

Edith's dark eyes grew bright. 'I don't know. It's a bit rich, coming to me now, when there hasn't been a dickybird from any of them for ages. My mother did send a Christmas card, but she forgot to put a stamp on it and it reached here after New Year. I wouldn't be surprised if he's out to cadge some money off me or something like that.'

Alice spread her hands. 'But you won't know unless you go.'

'Exactly.' Edith got up and walked to the window. 'That's the dilemma. If he really needs to see me then I should let bygones be bygones and go. If he's just after a handout I'll be back to square one.' She gazed sadly out at the ridge tiles and chimneys knowing that, far away over the houses, what remained of her family still lived on the other side of the Thames. She could not in all honesty say that she missed them very much. Yet, since meeting Harry's family, she had become aware of what she was lacking — a big, caring group of people who welcomed friends into their fold. It had broken through the hard shell she had placed around the idea of family. Perhaps her brother really had changed.

'Then you won't have lost anything by going, will you?' reasoned Alice. 'You might regret not giving him a chance.'

Edith sighed. 'I suppose so. Part of me doesn't want anything to do with him. We never got on as kids, and after Teresa died he hated me; well, he hated all of us, but me especially. It was as if I was meant to have kept her alive. But how could I have? I was only twelve.'

Alice got up from her seat and stood by her friend. 'It wasn't your fault, Edie. She would have died whatever you did. It was nobody's fault, just bad luck that your big sister got diphtheria.'

Edith kept her gaze steadily on the rooftops, not trusting herself to look into Alice's face. She never spoke of Teresa as a rule, the one person in her family who had loved her without question and whom she had adored. Just one year older than her, Teresa had been her best friend for all her childhood, but then she had taken sick and died in no time at all. The shock had never quite left her. She knew deep down it was why she had fought so hard to become a nurse; she might not have been able to save Teresa but she would do her best to save all those other children with that dreaded disease.

'I know,' she said eventually. 'Well, we know better than anyone, don't we? We saw cases of it while we were training. Not much of it in Hackney, touch wood.' She tapped the window frame. 'So it makes sense for me to meet Mick. If he's changed, then so much the better. If he hasn't then I'm no worse off.'

'I think you're right,' Alice agreed. 'Expect the worst but hope for the best. You never know. Do you want me to come with you?'

'No,' said Edith decisively. 'Thanks, but this is something I will do alone.' She knew that her brother would quite unreasonably think that Alice was snooty, as she didn't have a London accent. Edith was quietly protective of her friend, who had not grown up on the same tough streets.

'If you're sure?'

Edith nodded firmly. 'I've made up my mind.

I'll see him. As you say, he might be different now.' The old proverb about leopards not changing their spots sprang into her mind but she dismissed it. Perhaps joining up had made him see that there were other sorts of people in the world. War was proving to be a great leveller. Time would tell if that was how it had affected Mick Gillespie. 'You go back to Joe's letter and his funny old writers. I'll try to sort out my nuisance of a little brother.'

8

Peggy opened her eyes and squinted because the light of the ugly bedside table hurt her eyes. Where was she? Her throat was dry and she ached all over. There was an odd noise too, a rhythmic sort of rumbling. Then she remembered.

Some of the details were hazy but she knew Laurence had bought her many more port and lemons. At first it had been fun and she had enjoyed their conversation, relishing his wit and good looks and the way everyone was staring at him in his smart pilot's uniform. Then she'd begun to get rather wobbly but he'd still continued to buy her drinks. It turned out he was staying in a room above the pub, which had surprised her, but when he'd suggested she go upstairs for a lie-down as she seemed a bit tired, it had made a kind of sense at the time. That had been a big mistake.

He'd been on her in a flash, pushing her up against the door, kissing her roughly and not at all in the way she liked, pulling off her clothes as he undid his trousers. She'd tried to protest but she was too drunk, and her body wouldn't move as she wanted it to. She tried to call out but he stopped her mouth with his own. It was useless and in the end she'd gone along with it, just to get it over with. It hadn't lasted long. In a moment he got her on the cheap carpet, forced himself on her then rolled off. 'Payment for all the port and lemons,' he'd said, and suddenly his accent didn't seem as attractive any more. 'Don't pretend you haven't done this before. You aren't exactly an innocent, are you.' It wasn't a question.

Peggy tried to recall if she'd told him she was a widow, but decided it didn't matter. Pete's memory was too precious to her to share with this man who had turned out to be the very opposite of a gentleman. He'd taken advantage of her, but then she'd allowed him to get the drinks all evening. She'd offered herself up like a willing sacrifice. No wonder he'd thought she wouldn't mind, or rather hadn't bothered to check if she did or not.

Groaning, she rolled over. She was in an unfamiliar bed, and the strange noise was Laurence snoring. She had to get away from him as quickly as possible as she could no longer bear the sight of him. Those good looks covered a black heart and the sooner she was away the better. Wildly she scrabbled for her clothes and put them on, her hands shaking as the effects of the alcohol wore off. Her head pounded but the most important thing was to get out.

If he'd heard the noise she was making, Laurence didn't react. That told her all she needed to know. She was less than nothing to him. He didn't care if she was awake or not, let alone if he'd hurt her. She knew she'd have bruises tomorrow, and marks from the horrible carpet, which was slightly sticky under her feet as she crept to the door.

Pausing in the dimly lit corridor, she checked her watch. She would still have time to catch the last bus, just. Swiftly she made her way down the stairs and out of a side door that she hoped would lead her to a road she recognised, but not before Marge caught her eye as she wiped the bar. The older woman shook her head, but Peggy was too hungover to react. She didn't care what the barmaid thought; she'd never have to see her again. All she wanted now was her own bed and to forget the whole evening.

★   ★   ★

'What have you got there, Mary?' Belinda, who was a half-head taller than her colleague, leant over to see. Mary was standing at one of the common-room windows, overlooking the bike rack at the side of the yard, and admiring a small box in her hand. It was Friday lunch time and Belinda was ravenous after a tough morning, but not so hungry as to overcome her natural curiosity.

Mary looked up and smiled, patting her rich brown curls. 'A present from Charles,' she said, giving the box a little shake. It rattled, and Belinda raised her eyebrows. 'Hairgrips.'

'They'll be useful.' Belinda shook her own dark hair, which held its tight waves no matter how much she tried to straighten it under her nurse's cap. 'I'm running out and can't seem to find any in the shops or market.'

Mary nodded. 'Charles said that's because all the available metal will be going to munitions and to build new aircraft and that sort of thing,' she explained. 'Not that I can see how a few little hairgrips will make much difference. They're only small. But he says they will be tricky to come by and so he got me these.'

'You're lucky to have someone as thoughtful as that,' breathed Belinda with just a hint of envy.

Mary tried not to look smug. 'I know. Most chaps wouldn't think about it. But he knows how hard I try to keep my hair tidy for work, and how important that is.'

'Exactly,' said Belinda. 'We can't afford to spread infection if we let loose our beautiful tresses.' She sighed. 'I need some food after the morning I've had. Let's go and eat.'

After settling themselves in front of their bowls of oxtail soup in the dining area, Mary looked up. 'So what happened this morning?'

Belinda took a couple of spoonfuls. 'That's better. Now I feel human again.' She put down her spoon. 'It wasn't any one major problem, just the way lots of small things built up. There was one middle-aged woman who had broken her wrist. I mean, it was painful and awkward but no worse than that, no complications. She was so upset, though. In the end I realised she just wanted someone to talk to. She's missing her sons, her husband is hardly at home because he's started fire-watching, and now she's hurt her wrist she's no use for minding her daughter's baby. On top of all that she's terrified the Nazis will invade. There wasn't much I could say to that; only to reassure her that she'll be as good as new soon and that we're all trying our best.' She paused to draw breath.

'There won't be an invasion,' Mary declared, confident as ever.

'Mary, we don't know that,' Belinda pointed out.

'Our boys in the RAF are defending our skies. That's what the wireless tells us,' Mary replied, steadfast in her belief. 'Charles says the Luftwaffe aren't getting away with anything. Our boys are stopping them getting through and it's a marvellous triumph every day. So you can tell your patient to set one worry aside at any rate. But isn't it funny how cases go in batches?' she asked hurriedly, reading the scepticism in her colleague's eyes. 'A short while ago it was measles everywhere. I had two sprained ankles and a broken arm this morning. One was an accident in the blackout . . . '

' . . . though we're seeing fewer of those now the evenings are light,' Belinda pointed out.

'True. One was a young boy who'd decided to help out around the house with jobs his big brother used to do before joining up, but he didn't really know what he was doing and fell off a ladder while trying to put up a shelf. So now his poor parents have double the worry and no shelf.' She shrugged. 'It could be worse.'

Belinda nodded as she took another welcome mouthful of soup.

'My other one was an old man who tried to mow his lawn and wasn't strong enough to take his mower out of the shed,' Mary went on. 'He told me his neighbour used to do it but now he's in the army. So many things we used to take for granted are much more difficult now that there aren't as many young men around.'

Belinda rolled her eyes. 'Tell me about it.'

'Belinda!' Mary pretended to be shocked. 'And over lunch, too!'

'Well, it's all right for you, you've got Charles,' Belinda pointed out. 'Not only does he take you to the snazziest restaurants, but he remembers you need hairgrips too. He's a man in a million. Does he have any friends?'

'They're all in the army, most of them away. You can share my hairgrips if you like,' she added generously. 'I'm sure I shan't need them all.'

'No, no. I couldn't let you do that. They were a present,' Belinda said. 'I was only teasing. Sometimes the least expensive presents are the best, aren't they, because they are what you really need, and Charles knew you well enough to find them. You're a lucky woman, Mary Perkins.'

Mary had the grace to blush. 'Well, I think so. Most of the time.' She grinned and stood up, taking her soup bowl to the serving hatch. 'Must be off, more patients to see.'

Belinda waved to her friend and tipped her bowl to spoon up the last of the soup. She'd been half joking, but it was true that there seemed to be far fewer eligible young men around, or at least those who weren't simply passing through en route to active service somewhere. Her mind turned to that nice young ARP warden who had been at the pub and who knew Edith well. He'd had such kind, lively eyes and a lovely head of dark hair, gently wavy — not tight like hers. Admittedly he was not quite as tall as her, but many men weren't. He'd been a real gent, walking her home even though it was out of his way. What was his name again? She frowned in concentration until it came to her. It was Billy — Billy Reilly.

★   ★   ★

Edith pushed open the door of Lyons Corner House with trepidation. Perhaps she should have chosen a smaller café but it was too late to change her mind now. She'd wanted to go somewhere she wouldn't bump into anyone she knew, so that ruled out all the Dalston ones, and to be somewhere central so her brother would have no cause for complaint about being dragged north of the river and so far east. Lyons near Charing Cross seemed the easiest bet. But gazing round at the waitresses in their smart uniforms, and the women customers sipping their tea with bags of shopping stacked around their chairs, Edith could hear her brother's snide comments in her head even before he turned up.

In for a penny, in for a pound, she told herself, smiling at the nearest waitress and ordering a toasted teacake. She could pretend sugar and butter wasn't rationed for once. Might as well enjoy the place before her brother arrived to ruin it. Then she berated herself. Everything might be all right. He might just surprise her.

Edith's thoughts turned to the night before,

when she'd met Peggy in the Duke's Arms. She'd tried not to look shocked when Peggy had confessed to getting blind drunk with Laurence, but any disapproval had melted away when Peggy described what had happened next.

'I don't know how we went from having a lovely time to him behaving like a pig,' she'd said, quietly so nobody else in the busy beer garden could hear. 'It was like he was a different person altogether, more like a filthy animal than the bloke we all met in here. I couldn't do a thing to get away. Truth was, I was afraid to try after a bit, I thought he'd really hurt me.'

'Oh, Peggy.' Edith had put her hand on her friend's arm and squeezed it gently, but even that made her wince.

'Sorry, it's the bruises,' Peggy said. 'They're coming out all over me, I'm blue and purple from head to toe. It's a proper palaver hiding them from Pete's mum.' Her lip trembled.

'Peggy, you should report it,' Edith said. 'Who knows, he might try to do it again.'

Peggy had laughed off the suggestion. 'And say what? That I had too much to drink and agreed to go into his room? They'll say I was asking for it, you know they will. It's not as if I'm completely wet behind the ears. I thought we were going to have a bit of fun. I just didn't realise what his idea of fun was.'

Edith shook her head. 'All the same . . . '

Peggy was resolute. 'No, there's nothing to be gained by complaining. All that will happen is I'll get a reputation for being fast. Who knows, perhaps I deserve it.'

Edith tutted. 'Don't say such daft things. Of course you don't.'

Peggy glanced away, suddenly unable to meet her friend's eyes. 'Perhaps it's my punishment. You know, for going out when Pete's not long dead. That's what everyone will say, and maybe it's right. You aren't going out gallivanting; you're staying in and mourning Harry like he deserves, aren't you?'

Edith shrugged. 'I don't feel like going out, that's true. It's different coming here and seeing you. But, as for the thought of meeting another man . . . no, I couldn't. It wouldn't feel right to me. But I'm not saying you shouldn't. We're not all the same, are we?'

Peggy sighed. 'That's right. Thanks for not blaming me, Edith. I feel terrible, like I've disrespected Pete's memory in some way, and yet whatever I do won't change the fact that he's gone. I don't want another husband, there ain't ever going to be anyone like him, but I just can't sit in and do nothing cos that makes everything a thousand times worse. I've got to cope in my own way, just like you have.'

Edith had raised her glass. 'That's all we can do, isn't it? You can talk to me any time, Peggy, you know that.'

Peggy had let slip a tear and dashed it swiftly away before anyone else could notice. 'Thanks, Edith. You're a mate. I might take you up on that. I really hope he hasn't got me up the duff — that would be more than I could stand.'

Edith had looked her steadily in the face. 'Well, tell me if that happens.'

Peggy's lip trembled. 'I know you'd help. Well, I only ever got pregnant once with Pete and I admit we took lots of risks before we got married, so it probably won't happen. But I'll be sure to tell you either way.'

Now she spread the butter on her teacake, watching the golden liquid melt onto the plate, almost like before the war had started. She shut her eyes as she took the first bite. Pure heaven.

'Very fancy.' She was woken from her moment of bliss by a familiar voice. 'You must be doing all right for yerself, hanging round places like this.'

Edith forced herself to smile, though her heart sank at the tone of the greeting. 'Mick. You look well.'

Before her stood a young man in uniform, smarter than she remembered, who bore a striking resemblance to her and, she remembered with a pang, their dead sister Teresa. They shared the family characteristics of wavy hair, almost black, dark eyes and small stature.

He bristled. 'No thanks to you.' He pulled back the chair opposite her and took a seat.

Edith didn't rise to the bait. 'Do you want a cup of tea?'

Mick looked at the neat menu. 'You got to be joking. Not at these prices.'

Edith sighed. 'It's on me.' It wasn't as if she'd taken him to the Ritz, or one of Mary's favoured haunts, but her brother was trying — as always — to make out that he was the injured party. So much for the notion of the army making a man of him.

'Suppose I will, then,' he accepted grudgingly. He sat back, taking a good look at her. 'Nursing suits you, then.'

Edith nodded. 'I still like it. No, it's more than that, I really love it.' She bit her lip, cross with herself for saying so much. Childhood had taught her to give away as little as possible, or Mick would take anything that was dear to her and try to ruin it in one way or another. Still, she thought, she wasn't a child any more. She was a woman, in a profession, who had briefly been the unofficial fiancée of a wonderful man — a champion boxer, what was more. She had status. It would not be so easy for her brother to knock her down.

'Love it, do yer?' Mick sneered. 'Got yer eye on all the doctors, have yer? Better not let them get their highfalutin hands on you.'

He paused only because the waitress brought the tea.

'Oh, leave it, Mick,' said Edith, pouring from the neat little pot. 'If that's all you've come to tell me, we can say goodbye now.' She glared at him, refusing to back down. She was heartily glad she had never mentioned Harry to any of her family. At least Mick couldn't use that to taunt her.

'Suit yerself,' he muttered, slurping noisily, at which several of the customers nearby turned round to look. He smiled at them, pleased to have been a source of annoyance. 'Well now, seeing as you can stand me a cuppa in a swanky place like this, seems like my humble little request will be no bother at all.'

Edith raised her eyebrows. Of course, there

was going to be a request. She could make a very good guess what it was going to be.

'Yes, see, we got to look after our Frankie,' Mick went on. 'He's been in all sorts of trouble and he thinks the best way out of it will be to follow his big brother,' at this he puffed out his chest a little, 'into the army. He's got some vicious types on his heels saying he owes them money, so he reckons his best way of staying safe is to scarper down to enlist.'

'Mick, he's sixteen,' Edith pointed out. 'They won't have him.'

Mick snorted. 'Since when did you grow so keen on playing by the rules? You was the one who said they was there to be broken.' He pointed his finger at her. 'They're signing up all sorts and no questions asked.'

Edith shook her head. 'I can understand it if a lad looks eighteen. Come off it, Mick. None of us Gillespies looks older than we are; we're too short, we stand absolutely no chance of passing. You barely look old enough to wear that uniform now. There's no way on God's earth a recruitment officer will accept Frankie.'

Mick pulled a face. 'Prepared to risk it, are you?'

'What's the alternative?' Edith thought they might as well get to the crux of the matter.

'Glad you asked me,' he said smoothly. 'It's all about this inconvenient amount that our Frankie owes. He pays that off, there'll be no further questions asked, and he won't have to go into the Forces. Or at least till he's officially old enough. So, knowing how much you love your little

91

brother, I'm sure you'll want to see him right.'

'No.' Edith folded her arms.

'Aren't you even going to ask how much?'

'Doesn't matter.' Edith kept her face impassive. 'If he's old enough to get into that sort of trouble, then he's old enough to sort himself out. Or at least come to speak to me directly.'

Mick pushed his chair further back with a loud scraping noise, receiving even more glares. 'What, don't you trust me? D'you think I'd take a cut of a lump of cash that's going to save our brother?'

Edith decided to call his bluff. 'Yep. That's exactly what I think.' She pressed home her advantage. 'You think I earn a fortune, do you? Since when did nurses ever get huge pay packets? And what about you — you're serving in the army for nothing, are you? I can't see that happening somehow.'

Mick glared at her in fury. 'I deserve my pay. A man needs his earnings. Whereas you, look at you, what do you need cash for? Bet they feed you and you get to live in one of those fancy nurses' homes. I been inside one or two of those,' he leered, 'and they was like little palaces. You're living the life of Riley.'

Edith stared heavenwards, thinking of all the sad cases she had had to deal with in the past week. Yes, she loved her little attic room, and if the canteen food wasn't as delicious as a Lyons teacake, at least there was plenty of it. It was a world away from what she had grown up with and she'd worked hard to get there. She wasn't going to give Mick the satisfaction of upsetting her. She didn't even know if he was telling the truth about Frankie, but she was sure that if she gave him any money, then their younger brother would see very little of it.

'Think what you like,' she said evenly, 'but you'll get nothing from me. If Frankie's genuinely in trouble, ask him to get in touch directly. That's if you can't sub him yourself, after having all your bed and board paid for, that is.'

Mick slammed down his cup so hard she thought it would break. 'I might have known it. You've only ever been out for yourself. Ma told me that's what you'd say but I thought, oh no, now she's a nurse she'll have changed. She'll be kind; everyone knows nurses are kind.' He brought his face close to hers. 'But not you, eh, Edith? Hard as nails, that's what you are.' He threw the chair to one side, causing a nearby woman to squeal, as Edith swiftly reached out and caught it before it could fall or knock into anyone. 'Wish I could say it was nice seeing you again, but that would be a lie.' With that he flung himself towards the door and out onto the Strand.

Edith sighed but made herself finish the tea and the last bite of the teacake. She would not let his familiar viciousness get under her skin. In truth, she had expected little else from him, and in one way it was good to have her suspicions confirmed. He was trying to con her out of her hard-earned money, just like the old days, but now he thought she'd be a softer touch. Well, he'd picked on the wrong person. She knew his ways and had no intention of falling for them.

Taking some coins from her purse and leaving them for the waitress, she rose with dignity and steadily made her way to the door. It was only when she had reached the outside and the cooler air hit her that she felt a pang. Why did her family have to be so difficult? Did they really still blame her for Teresa's death, or would they have been like this anyway? There was no way of telling.

Edith exhaled sharply. All right, so her family weren't much of a comfort, but she knew one that was — and one that had made her welcome. Suddenly she knew she had to be back in that room she thought of as the source of all comfort and safety. She would go to visit the Banhams — at least she knew she would always have the warmest of welcomes there.

9

Mattie had been hanging out the washing when she'd first sensed something wasn't right. It was never her favourite chore, but she knew her mother found it increasingly difficult to carry the heavy tub into the back yard, hoick up the line and prop it up with the weathered old pole, and then lift the dripping clothes and bedding into place and nip the pegs into position before the items could slip off again. Flo's hands were beginning to swell with arthritis, much as she tried to hide it. Mattie had seen her wince as she twisted the sheets to squeeze out the water.

She wanted to save her mother the bother, and also to save her face; now she was a mother herself she recognised how Flo had to maintain the front of being the one in charge, capable of anything. In most respects that was exactly what she still was — but age was starting to creep up, and stiffen her poor hands.

Mattie gritted her teeth as she balanced the laundry tub to one side of her sizeable bump. The sun was out and it had seemed a good idea to wash the sheets, a brisk breeze promising to dry them quickly. Now she was faced with manoeuvring the unwieldy armfuls of cotton onto the frayed old line. Usually it was easy, but now her bump kept getting in the way; she couldn't bend properly, she had to twist, and that pulled on her back muscles which were already sore from lifting Gillian out of harm's way scores of times a day. Gritting her teeth harder still, she flung the sheets over the line, tugging at them until they hung properly, by which time she was covered in water. Suddenly it all seemed too much. A wave of sadness came over her from nowhere, and she wanted nothing more than to sit down and put her head in her hands. At the same time, she recognised that this was not like her at all. Anyway, there was no helping it — the washing was not going to peg itself out. She simply had to get on with it.

When she heard someone knocking on the front door she wondered if this would be her excuse to take a break, but then came the sound of her mother's voice greeting the visitor. She sighed as she hung up the last few items, Gillian's small smocked dresses and her own well-worn pale blue blouse. The sight of it threatened to bring tears to her eyes. Lennie had loved her in that. She took a deep breath. No point in thinking about that now. Wincing as she bent to pick up the basket and peg bag to stack them by the side fence, she realised she had to run to the outside privy, and never mind who had come to visit.

★ ★ ★

'Come through, come through to the kitchen.' Flo beamed in delight as Edith stepped inside the hallway. 'I was just going to put on the kettle. You'll have a cup of tea, won't you? Or is it too hot?'

Edith was wilting from the warmth of the crowded bus back from the city centre. Everyone on it had been chattering about what was going on over the south coast, the brave RAF lads tackling the Luftwaffe, but it had only served to underline her sadness that her own brave hero was no longer there to comfort her. 'I'd love some water. I'll get it, you sit down.'

Flo pretended to be affronted. 'I've not got to the stage where a guest in my house has to fetch their own drink,' she admonished. 'I can see you're in need of something cool. Sit yourself there by the window and catch the breeze. Now, that's better.' She set a heavy glass tumbler down at Edith's elbow.

Edith took a long draught and almost groaned in relief. 'That's just what I needed. Those buses are busy today. Whatever was I thinking of?'

'Never mind, you're here now,' said Flo, 'and very welcome you are too. I'm pleased you dropped by. It seems like ages since we last saw you. You aren't staying away, are you? Not afraid we'll make you think of Harry?'

Edith felt a pang that Flo might even have imagined such a thing. 'No, no. Not a bit. I've been run off my feet with work, I've hardly had a moment to call my own.' Except for two trips to the pub, the voice of her conscience whispered.

Flo nodded. 'That's only to be expected. In a job like yours, you'll always have to put the patients first. We understand.'

Edith smiled gratefully. 'It's only what everyone else is doing too.'

Flo grinned conspiratorially. 'Well, I'll tell you

something. Stan has been so flat out — what with working all day and then going on his ARP rounds — that he's in bed at this very minute! Catching up on his sleep, he is, and in all our years of married life I've never known him to do such a thing. But take the chance while you can, I told him. You can't burn the candle at both ends any more, not at your age.'

Edith's eyebrows rose in surprise. To her, Stan was indefatigable. Then she found she was quite envious. 'It sounds like a good idea.' Sleeping late was unheard of at the nurses' home. Even if she'd wanted to skip breakfast, the noise of her colleagues starting their days would have roused her. She knew that was not the real reason she felt tired, though; it had been the emotion of the day so far, foolishly allowing herself to hope her brother had changed and that familiar sinking feeling when she realised he hadn't.

Yet now she had the chance to unburden herself to Flo, a rare moment of quiet in the usually busy kitchen. She took a deep breath and explained how she had set off that morning and how adrift she had felt.

Flo's open, kind face betrayed its sadness at the very idea a brother could treat a sister so badly. 'You poor thing,' she said with heartfelt sorrow. 'And him your own flesh and blood. I'd be ashamed if Joe said anything like that to Mattie. Or vice versa. I know they tease each other — well, they all did.' Edith nodded in acknowledgment as she knew full well that Mattie and Harry had bickered non-stop and then would immediately make up again. 'But that's not the same. You need to know you can count on your family. That's what they're for.'

Edith gave a short laugh. 'Well, I can count on mine — to be unreliable. Works every time.' She finished her water. 'It isn't as if I really expected anything different. It's what they're like.'

Flo reached across and gave her a quick hug. 'I wish it was different,' she said. 'You've got us, though. Even without Harry, you're still family to us now. You can come to us with anything, we won't turn you away.'

Edith smiled in gratitude. 'I know. I'm very lucky.' Suddenly she felt better again, more like her old self. She had found somewhere to belong. All right, it wasn't how she'd imagined it when Harry was with them, but here was proof that they accepted her for herself, not simply as his girlfriend.

'Harry was lucky,' Flo told her, 'and therefore we all were. Now, come and see what I bought down the market the other . . . good heavens, Mattie, whatever is wrong?'

Mattie stood in the doorway to the back kitchen, all colour drained from her face. 'Ma . . . Edith, thank God it's you. Something's not right.' Her normally wild hair was plastered to her head and she was sweating. 'I came over all strange and . . . and . . . I went to the privy and there was blood. From . . . You know.' A sob escaped her.

Edith instantly sprang into action. 'You come over to the couch, Mattie, and raise your feet, that's it. Now lie still and try to keep calm. I'll take your pulse and see if you have a temperature, but I must wait until you're steadier. What were you doing before?'

'Putting out the washing,' Mattie gulped, trying to keep a lid on her fear of what this might mean. She could not lose Lennie's baby. It would break her heart, and she could not even begin to imagine what she would write to him. It was the hope of seeing this new life that was keeping him going in his prison camp.

'No wonder you're hot,' Edith said.

Flo grimaced. She regretted allowing Mattie to take on the heavy task at such a late stage in her pregnancy, but her daughter had insisted. She would never forgive herself if anything were to happen now. Yet good sense told her not to panic, that this might be nothing.

Edith rose and fetched another glass of water. 'Here, drink this.' She knew that her friend's mind would be racing with the most horrible thoughts and that her first job was to cool her down. 'Take little sips, not all at once. There, that's better. Now give me your arm.' Swiftly she brought her fingers to the pulse in the wrist. She had none of her usual equipment with her and would have to improvise, but this was better than nothing. Shutting her eyes she willed herself not to panic but just to observe, as she would do for any patient.

Nodding, she set Mattie's arm back onto the cushion. 'Absolutely normal.' She rested her own hand on Mattie's forehead. 'And there's no worrying temperature that I can see, nothing that wouldn't be caused by working in the garden on a hot day.' All the while she had been watching her friend's breathing, noting that it too was normal, allowing for her panic. 'Right, so how much blood, Mattie? And was it all just now or has there been anything before?'

Mattie screwed up her eyes. 'No, it was only right now. And there wasn't a lot . . . it's just that I wasn't expecting anything . . . I must be all right, Edie, the baby has to be all right.' She turned pleading eyes to her friend. 'You know why.'

Edith nodded. 'Of course.' She took a breath. 'Mattie, this will sound easy for me to say, but try not to worry. Honestly. This sort of thing happens all the time.'

Mattie sniffed. 'It didn't with Gillian.'

Edith acknowledged the problem. 'No, maybe not. But in plenty of pregnancies, all the same.'

Flo stirred from her kitchen chair. 'It's true, love. I had a bit of it when I was carrying — now, which one of you was it? It didn't come to anything.'

Mattie looked a little more reassured.

Edith took a decision. 'I think it's best if you take it easy for the rest of the day, and don't do anything like heavy work. I can pop over to Dr Patcham to see if he can call in, as he's so close by. I'd put money on him advising the same thing, though. You have no other symptoms — you have no pain anywhere, do you?'

Mattie shook her head.

'Well, then. As long as there's nothing else I reckon you'll be fine. It's just a little scare.'

Mattie raised her eyebrows. 'I'll say. A big scare, if you ask me.' But she smiled. The calm reassurance was working its wonders.

Edith got up. 'I'll go to see him now. Then I'll come back again, if you like.'

Mattie nodded. 'You'd better. We haven't even had a moment to chat.'

Flo walked Edith to the front door. 'Will she really be all right?' she asked in a low voice.

Edith pursed her lips. 'I'm not a doctor, but I've seen this many times. Well, you know yourself. One moment it can feel like a disaster about to happen, the next you're right as rain again. The odds are that this will pass and both Mattie and the baby will pull through with no problems at all.'

Flo exhaled slowly. 'I hope so, for all our sakes. Somehow this baby is all the more special what with Lennie being held prisoner.' She stood up straight and put back her shoulders. 'Right, you tell Dr Patcham I'll have some of my cheese scones ready for him if he would care to drop round. And there'll be some for you too, of course.'

Edith beamed at the mouth-watering thought. 'Then I'll hurry back. And don't either of you dare try to take in the washing. I'm staying until it's dry and then that will be my job.'

★   ★   ★

Belinda twisted her dark, tightly curled hair into a rough plait and shoved it under her nurse's cap as best she could. This was not a good moment for it to come undone — she needed to keep both hands free. She just hoped it would stay put

102

long enough before help arrived.

The day shift had been busier than the usual Monday for some reason. In addition to the regular patients, there were always some casualties left over from the weekend. Sometimes it was adults who had been overdoing it on the day of rest and who wanted an excuse not to turn up for work at the start of the week. None of the local doctors or nurses had much sympathy for those cases, and they generally got short shrift. Then there were the older patients who didn't want to be a nuisance over the weekend. 'I was sure I'd be all right by Monday,' they would say, when they could have done with a proper medical visit on Saturday morning. It was hard to be stern with such people, but it did mean a lot of extra work when it happened.

Then there were the children. Plenty of parents suspected — often rightly — that their offspring developed mysterious illnesses overnight on Sundays in order to avoid school the next morning during term time. These were normally easy to diagnose. Belinda had begun to carry an impressive-looking medicine bottle filled with coloured water, and would administer a dose of two spoonfuls that was guaranteed to get any malingerers on their feet. The children felt they had been taken seriously and the mothers were grateful for somebody else sorting out the situation in a way that caused no harm to anybody — except for using up precious time.

Today, though, there had been a late call for a nurse to come to an accident, just when most of them had thought their day's work was over. A child had fallen from a height onto something sharp — that was all the information they had been given. Often Edith would be the first to volunteer, but Belinda knew she'd had a busy weekend of it, unofficially nursing her friend through what luckily turned out not to be a miscarriage after all. Still, it hardly seemed fair that she should have to turn around immediately after tea and go out again. So Belinda had said she'd go.

Now she sat in a cramped back yard, careful to avoid the pieces of broken glass all around. She shook her head at her young patient. 'Don't try to move, Percy,' she instructed, trying to be authoritative but sympathetic. 'It will hurt more if you do.'

'It hurts now!' wailed the little boy. He could not have been more than ten, and his earlier bravado had all gone. Now he was frightened, as well he might be.

'I know, but it could have been so much worse,' Belinda said, giving him a steady smile. 'It won't seem like it, but you're actually very lucky. You've hurt your leg but it will mend.' She hoped she was right. The boy had leapt off a pile of boxes in the yard, landed badly and crashed back into the pile — which turned out to have contained glass jars of some corrosive substance. It was very obviously a black-market operation. Percy had told her this wasn't where he lived, but he'd seen the pile of boxes from his bedroom window and thought they looked like a good thing to climb on. He wouldn't say whose yard it was. 'I don't know nothing,' he'd repeated, before the pain in his leg had rendered him silent.

At least he'd avoided falling in the worst of the evil-smelling liquid, merely splashing himself a little, but that was bad enough. Belinda had made him as comfortable as she could, cleaning the injuries with plenty of cold water — she hadn't wanted to use anything else in case it reacted to the acid, or whatever it was. It was strong enough to burn holes in the boy's jacket, so she'd made him take it off and it lay ruined in one corner. Now they were waiting for an ambulance, as she couldn't move him on her own. His leg had to be kept straight so that any broken bones would set properly, and she had strapped it to his other leg as a makeshift split. She dared not try to reach for anything else; she wasn't sure what had been splashed by the acid. She could see a puddle of the stuff advancing across the concrete towards them. Where was that ambulance? She didn't want to end up sitting in a pool of acid but she didn't want to move the boy either. She dug her nails into her palms as the shiny liquid moved closer, careful to position her body to shield it from Percy's gaze.

Was acid flammable? Belinda couldn't remember. What if somebody walked by and lit a cigarette, throwing the match over the wall, unaware of what was happening? Would they both go up in flames? The other jars might catch fire and explode, and she wouldn't be able to get Percy to safety in time . . .

Firmly she told herself to get a grip and stop thinking the worst. The ambulance was on its way; there were all sorts of reasons it might have been held up, but it would come. She just had to sit it out. 'Not long now,' she said brightly to Percy, who was hanging on her every word. 'You'll look back at this and laugh one day. You can tell your children how you escaped getting cut to ribbons by the skin of your teeth.'

'I ain't having any, miss,' said Percy. 'My little brothers and sisters are proper little bleeders, I don't want none like that.'

'You might change your mind when you grow up,' Belinda suggested, wondering how he'd made his mind up so definitely at such a young age. But before she could ask him about it any further, there was a welcome cry of 'Anyone in there? Nurse, can you hear us?'

Through the rusty back gate came two figures, one in the ambulance service uniform and the other in ARP colours, which she could just make out in the now-fading light.

'In here!' She waved so they could see her in the shadow of the tall wall. 'Mind that liquid! We don't know what it is but it doesn't smell very nice.'

'Proper stinks, miss,' added Percy, who had perked up considerably now that help was at hand. The men unrolled the canvas stretcher they had brought and gently, between them, the three adults helped Percy onto it with as little disturbance as possible, anxious not to cause him more pain. Only then did Belinda recognise the ARP man. 'Wait — it's Billy, isn't it?' She knew that broad smile even in the dimness of the twilight.

Billy nodded. 'Bet you wasn't expecting to see me,' he chuckled. 'It should have been the other ambulance man come in here, but he couldn't find nowhere to park that wouldn't block the back lane, so I said I'd do it while he waited on the main road. Quick, let's get ourselves away from whatever that stuff is. You ain't got any on you, have you?' His gaze grew anxious.

Belinda shook her head as they all made their way down the narrow back lane and out to the waiting ambulance. 'No, thank goodness. But I'm glad you turned up when you did. I might have been in a bit of a pickle if we'd been there much longer.' She shivered at the thought of it.

The ambulance driver got out and helped lift Percy into the back of the vehicle. 'All right, son,' he said, his voice kindly and reassuring. He was old enough to be her father, Belinda saw, and was just the sort of figure she would have wanted to rescue her if she'd been unlucky enough to break her leg like that. Percy would be in good hands now, and she could breathe easily again.

'I better go back and make sure that gate is closed, then I'll have to wait for my colleague,' Billy said, shoving his hands in his pockets. 'They'll send someone what knows about chemicals.'

'Good,' said Belinda, who had been worrying about this for much of the time she'd sat with Percy in the fading light. 'I think it will take more than a quick mop-around. Heaven knows what they've been doing in there, but we weren't far away from a very nasty ending indeed.'

Billy tutted as he carefully shut the old gate.

107

'Some people got no morals at all. To think they was storing that right where all these people live. Anything could have happened.'

'It nearly did,' said Belinda, trying to stop her teeth from chattering. Now that she was out of danger, she realised how scared she'd been.

'We'll get them,' said Billy soberly. 'We told the police and they'll go round asking everyone who might have seen whoever was in here. Big stack of boxes like this, stands to reason somebody will have seen something. They won't get away with it. Look, there's Mr Dawson. He's our expert for things like this. Used to work in a chemical factory, knows what he's about.'

Belinda sighed with relief as Billy quickly updated the man, who'd appeared out of the shadows from the other end of the service lane. He was tall and thin, again almost her father's age, and seemed totally unsurprised by the evening's events. 'Well, no need for you two to stick around any longer,' he said. 'Well done, Reilly, you kept your head and secured the place. I'll take over now. You're due off shift, aren't you? Best get along and give my regards to your mother.'

Billy nodded and needed no further encouragement. 'I will. Good night then. I'll be getting along, like you say. You going this way, nurse?'

Belinda grinned to herself as she fell into step beside him, noting how he hadn't revealed he knew her first name in front of his more senior colleague. 'My bike is by the railings right next to where the ambulance parked,' she said, swinging her Gladstone bag. 'I'm glad the police are taking this seriously, Billy. I hate those black marketeers; they're the lowest of the low. Taking advantage of there being a war on. I hope they catch them, lock them up and throw away the key.'

Billy nodded, and if he was surprised by her vehemence he didn't show it. 'They're scum all right,' he agreed. 'Leaving all that poison where a kiddie could hurt himself on it like that, it beggars belief. Course he should never have been in there in the first place, but even so.'

'He thought he was on an adventure,' said Belinda sadly. 'He told me he'd seen the stack of boxes and thought he could be like a mountain climber. He didn't stop to think beyond that.' She came to a halt. 'Ah, well. This is me. That's my bike.' She pointed to the sturdy frame of one of the old boneshakers all the nurses were now so used to.

Billy grinned at her and she thought again that he really did have the friendliest face. 'I dunno how you lot get around on those old things. I seen Edith on one that made so much noise it was like a tram coming round a corner.'

'They're not so bad.' She tucked another stray curl behind her ear.

'Why don't you push it and then I can walk back your way, make sure you get to the home in one piece,' he suggested.

'But you live in the opposite direction,' Belinda pointed out, knowing Victory Walk was out of his way, but pleased at the offer nonetheless.

Billy shrugged. 'It's not that far. I can easily

cut through the Downs and get back to Ma that way. Can't have one of our precious nurses coming to harm after saving someone with a broken leg. It's a nasty injury — I should know.'

'I'm used to cycling back even when it's dark, you know,' she said lightly, but not in such a way as to make him change his mind. She remembered the accident he'd been in and how brave he was. He hadn't hesitated tonight, either, even when — for all he knew — it could have got very nasty indeed. He obviously had plenty of courage. She liked that in a man.

'Nope, I'm seeing you home and that's all there is to it,' he said cheerfully, falling in beside her as she slung her bag into the basket on the front of the old bike and began to wheel it along the pavement. There was just enough daylight left to see where they were going.

They passed a few people heading back to their houses after a late shift, or going to the factories which carried on producing essential materials through the night, but the streets were relatively peaceful. The stars were beginning to come out in the twilight and, for a moment, Belinda thought she could almost convince herself that there was no war, that the RAF weren't preparing to go into battle over the south coast and the Channel even as she walked along the familiar road. Her brother would be one of them. He was another one who didn't lack courage.

'Penny for them,' Billy said, and it seemed the most natural thing in the world for Belinda to tell him how much she missed David; how she tried not to worry but knew from all the reports about the Battle of Britain what sort of danger he might be in.

Billy listened and didn't try to interrupt or to tell her that her brother was bound to be all right. She respected that. There was no point in pretending all the airmen came home unscathed. She had to hope for the best but be prepared for the worst, just as everybody else who had a loved one in the air force did.

'You must be very proud of him,' Billy said when she had finished.

She paused for a moment. 'Yes. I am. He didn't wait to be called up; he was off to the recruitment office as soon as he could,' she replied.

'Well, I expect he's proud of you too,' Billy told her. 'It's no joke what you all do; it's proper opened my eyes getting to know your mates Edith and Alice and hearing the sorts of things you have to cope with. I know it ain't no picnic.'

Belinda shrugged as they turned the corner into Victory Walk. 'It's not usually as exciting as this evening. It's often just changing dressings on people who've fallen over. Then again, sometimes it makes you long for a stiff drink.'

She stopped herself from saying more, conscious that he might misunderstand and think she was asking him out for a drink, when no lady would do such a thing — or admit to a liking for stiff drinks in the first place.

'Know what you mean,' he said, and for one moment Belinda thought he might ask her to join him at the pub one evening. But instead he came to a halt outside the nurses' home, and the moment — if there had even been one — passed.

'Thank you, Billy, for everything you did this evening,' she said, a little shy suddenly, which wasn't like her at all.

'Think nothing of it,' he said easily. 'See you around then.'

'Bye, Billy.' Belinda stood at the gate as he waved and walked away. She wondered what she would have said if he had asked her out. Then she pushed the thought away and wheeled her heavy bike across to its stand, to join the others.

10

'You'll never guess what I just heard.' Mary rushed across to where her friends were sitting for their evening meal. 'It's rather sad.'

Edith and Alice looked up, while Belinda made space for one more person. They moved their bowls out of the way as Mary set hers down.

'What's it like?' she asked, nodding at the nondescript liquid.

'Healthy tasting,' said Edith with a scowl.

'Filling,' said Alice, trying to find something cheerful to say about it. 'What's your sad news, Mary?'

Mary sat down, picked up her spoon and then put it down again. 'Oh, it's something I heard from one of my patients this afternoon. Old Mrs Massey. The one with the failing eyesight — do you remember, I've told you about her before.'

Edith nodded. 'The one with all the cats?'

'That's right,' Mary said. 'Her place is full of them, I've no idea how she manages to feed them all. Anyway, it's such a small world, it turns out she's the auntie of those friends of Billy's — you know, those brothers? Ronald who works with him down at the docks, and Alfie the airman.'

'Oh, right,' said Edith, vaguely recalling them from the evening at the Duke's Arms when she couldn't wait to go home. She hadn't spoken to either of them, so they had made very little impression.

'Well, she got quite upset because one of the men Alfie had trained alongside and then fought with has just been killed in action.'

Belinda looked up, her face set. 'Was he shot down?'

Mary realised why Belinda was looking at her so intently. 'I'm afraid so. In fact it's an even bigger coincidence because we met him. It was that Canadian pilot, Laurence. You know, the really handsome chap with the dark hair. Isn't that a shame? What a waste.'

Edith put down her spoon with a clatter but nobody noticed, as Belinda gasped and even Alice frowned. 'I remember you talking about him, although I didn't meet him. That is sad.'

'And he didn't even have to fight. He wouldn't have been called up or anything; he only did it because his mother was Scottish,' Belinda added. 'He told me all about it that night, and he bought us all drinks. He was so generous. It doesn't seem fair.'

Mary sighed. 'No, it doesn't, does it? He was a real hero, dying in the defence of somewhere that wasn't even his home country.'

'You have to admire someone like that,' Alice said. 'He must have known what the odds were, and yet he still went ahead and did what he thought was right.'

'Oh, they know the odds all right,' Belinda said grimly. Then she brightened a little. 'And yet, as you say, they go on and do it anyway. Yes, heroes, the lot of them.' She choked a little.

Edith remained silent. She was the only one there who knew that Laurence might well have been a hero in everyone else's eyes, but he had a dark side too. He was no hero to her after what he had done to Peggy. Yet she would say nothing. It was not her secret to tell. Besides, it didn't do to speak ill of the dead — even when they were capable of such evil acts. She pushed away the remainder of her soup, suddenly revolted at the thought of eating any more.

Mary looked across at her. 'Oh, don't you want that? Shame to waste it, even though it's a bit like potato water.'

'Because that's exactly what it is,' Belinda suggested.

Edith gave a weak smile. 'You go ahead and have it. As you said, no point in wasting it.' Already her mind was turning over when she could go to see Peggy and what she would say. Her friend ought to know, and as soon as possible, before she heard it from someone else. What if she was in the pub after a few port and lemons and one of the lads mentioned it in passing? She might blurt something out that she'd later regret. Edith had to protect her from that.

'You all right, Edith? You've gone very quiet,' Alice asked under her breath.

Edith flashed her a glance. Trust Alice to pick up on her abrupt change of mood. But this wasn't something she could tell her closest friend, it wouldn't have been fair to Peggy. 'It's nothing,' she said softly. 'Just reminded me of something, that's all.'

Alice nodded in sympathy, and Edith bit her lip, feeling guilty because she knew that Alice would assume she was thinking about Harry. In one way, she could see why; anyone killed in battle meant a sad loss. But when it came to Laurence, Edith realised that what she really felt was relief.

★ ★ ★

Kathleen drew her front door key out of her pocket, sighing with exhaustion but feeling pleased with herself nonetheless. She swung the pram around so that she could more easily push it into the front room, a move she was now expert at. 'Ready for your tea, Brian?' she asked, even though she suspected Flo had given him more cheese scones than she'd let on about.

Kathleen was always looking for ways that she could make it up to the Banham family after they had shown her such kindness when she'd been down on her luck. More than that — she felt she wouldn't have survived without them. Now she had the perfect opportunity. Flo was having trouble coping with the washing, and Mattie was too heavily pregnant now to manage it — she reckoned she had about six weeks to go if she'd got her dates right. So Kathleen had volunteered to do it and combine it with her own, as it was no trouble to her, and in fact it was a benefit because their line in the back yard was so much larger than the cramped one in her own small yard, which she had to share with the Coyne family upstairs. It was also easier to share the soap powder, making it go further. She loved the smell of Oxydol, Flo's preferred type.

She bent to the shelf underneath the body of the pram to retrieve her bag of freshly clean laundry, tugging it free and propping it by Brian's feet. She was about to push open her door when a window opened just above.

'Ere, what you been doin' to piss people off?' Mrs Coyne stuck her head out of the gap and gave a malicious grin. 'You must have done somethin' really bad. Swearin' and shoutin' blue murder, she was.'

Kathleen looked up. 'What do you mean? Who was swearing and shouting?'

Mrs Coyne glared. 'Well, you should know. She seemed to know all about you. Really got it in for you, she has.'

'There must be a mistake,' Kathleen said, baffled.

'I said to her, I can't be of any help to you, I can't,' Mrs Coyne went on. 'I told her, just cos I live above her don't mean I'm privy to all her business. I sent her over to Mrs Bishop. I said: if anyone round here knows what Kathleen is up to, then it'll be her. Was I right?'

Kathleen set the heavy parcel of laundry down on the pavement. 'I don't know what you're talking about,' she said. 'I don't have a clue who it is or what she could want. She must have got the wrong door.'

'No, she definitely asked for you,' said Mrs Coyne, obviously enjoying Kathleen's discomfort. 'Knew you had a little boy and everything. You better watch out for yourself.'

Kathleen sighed, picked up the laundry once more and tucked it by Brian's feet. 'You be good and don't kick all the lovely clean clothes,' she warned. 'We're just going to drop in on Mrs Bishop before tea after all.' Perhaps it was a good thing that Flo had fed him those extra scones. As she turned the big pram around, the upstairs window slammed shut. Mrs Coyne had clearly decided there was no more fun to be had in taunting Kathleen.

Mrs Bishop was in, as the front-room curtains twitched, which was no surprise as she hardly ever left her house. She had often complained to Kathleen that none of her family ever bothered to come and take her out, and Kathleen prepared herself for the usual litany of grievances as she knocked on the woman's door. At least she had been willing to mind Brian, and Brian was happy enough to go there, probably because he couldn't yet understand what she was moaning about, Kathleen thought uncharitably.

Mrs Bishop was only too happy to talk about the visit from the strange woman. 'She looked about your age, maybe a bit younger, dear, and pardon me for being rude, but she wasn't what you'd call a lady. Downright sluttish in fact — sorry, but you know what I mean. No better than she should be, if I'm any judge. I thought she was going to sit on your doorstep and wait till you got back at one point.'

'She'd have had a long wait then,' said Kathleen. 'I've been doing laundry since first thing this morning. You'd think she'd have better things to do.'

'Well she must have, dear, because she went away again after a while.' Mrs Bishop raised her eyebrows. 'I hate to think what sort of profession she's in, if you get my drift. No doubt had to start getting herself ready for her evening shift, if you see what I mean. Not that I want to cast aspersions, but really . . . I thought to myself, this is a respectable street, and if she comes round here again I've a good mind to tell her so. Are you sure you don't know her?'

'Completely sure.' But Kathleen was no further forward in finding out who it was. 'Sorry you got caught like that, Mrs Bishop. I haven't the foggiest what it could be about, but I suppose if she's that desperate she'll be back. Not much I can do about it till then.'

'No, dear. But if she comes around and causes trouble, you can always bring the boy to me.' A smile cracked the sour old woman's face, as she had a genuinely soft spot for Brian.

'Thank you, Mrs Bishop. I'm sure it won't come to that.' Kathleen trundled the pram back down Jeeves Place and finally made it to her own house. But the question kept nagging away at her as she put away the laundry and fed Brian his tea. Who on earth could it be and what did she want?

* * *

The little café off Ridley Road was busy but not full to bursting, which was exactly what Edith had hoped for when she'd arranged to meet Peggy when she came off shift. Too many people and they wouldn't have been able to hear themselves think; too few and everybody else might have overheard their conversation. That was the last thing Edith wanted.

She arrived first, scanning the small room for a vacant table where they could be fairly private. The one in the far corner was free and she walked swiftly to take it, smiling at the middle-aged waitress who looked familiar, but not so much so that she would enquire too closely why Edith was there.

'Table for one?' the waitress asked, straightening her clean but well-worn apron with its threadbare seams.

'There'll be two of us; my friend will be here in a minute,' Edith explained, sitting down. 'I bet she'll want a cup of tea, so can I order it for both of us now?'

'Course you can, ducks,' said the woman, and turned back to the counter.

Edith draped her light jacket over the back of her chair and tried to marshal her thoughts. It wasn't easy, as she'd had yet another busy day. Now that the children were on summer holidays, they seemed to get up to all sorts of mischief, and therefore there had been a flurry of minor accidents — nothing as dramatic as Belinda's episode with the broken acid jars, but time-consuming nonetheless. The current craze was for playing Battle of Britain, in which the children sped around the Downs and other parks on their bikes, dodging the trenches that had been dug for people to shelter from the air raids that the council believed were coming, chasing one another and pretending to fire guns at their friends. This meant trying complicated moves with one or no hands on the handlebars, with the predictable consequences of plenty of falls, and injuries consisting mostly of bruises and scrapes but sometimes broken arms or legs. There was at least one suspected concussion and plenty of the parents were at their wits' end. Edith had spent at least as much time reassuring them as treating their sons and sometimes daughters.

'Sorry I'm a bit late. I came as soon as I could.' Peggy pulled out the chair opposite, shaking her hair from its factory scarf. 'Ugh, these things make my scalp itch when it's so warm. I don't know how you manage when you have to wear your cap all the time.'

Edith grinned. 'It's better than having hair in your face when you're working. I don't think my patients would thank me if I couldn't see what I was doing when giving them an injection or taking out their stitches.'

'Suppose not.' Peggy paused while the waitress brought across their pot of tea. 'Oh, that's lovely. I'm parched. I never get time at work to have enough to drink and it can get really hot in there.'

Edith waited until her friend had finished and the waitress had gone away again.

'Anyway, I heard something yesterday that I thought you should know.'

Peggy looked up, alarmed. 'That sounds serious. What do you mean?'

Edith's face twisted as she tried to think of an easy way of saying what she had to say, but there

121

simply wasn't one, so she jumped straight in.

'It's about Laurence. He's been killed in action.'

Peggy put down her cup abruptly. 'Oh.' A confusion of emotions played across her face.

Edith stared at her anxiously. 'Sorry to come out with it like that, but I thought you should know.'

Peggy dropped her gaze but it was several moments before she spoke. 'Yes. Yes, you're right, I wouldn't have wanted to hear it as gossip. That bastard. Now everyone will say he's a hero. How did you know about it, anyhow?'

Edith explained, knowing full well that Peggy's prediction had already come true. That was how he would be thought of from now on. There was nothing they could do about it, though; that would be the rest of the world's opinion. Only they knew otherwise.

Peggy nodded. 'I don't suppose Alfie and Ronald know what he was really like. Oh God, Edie, I don't know what to think. I suppose he was brave and all that, it's just he was also a monster. I'm glad I'll never have to see him again. Does that sound awful? I shan't say it again but, really, when I think about what he did . . .'

'I know.' Edith didn't rush to fill the silence. It was all too difficult. 'He's paid the ultimate price, hasn't he,' she managed eventually.

Peggy shrugged. 'So he has. And at least now I know he can't do what he did to me to anybody else. That was playing on my mind. I didn't want to tell anyone, but I worried that it would mean he'd just attack some other poor girl. Now I can rest easy on that score.' She sighed. 'That's just between us.'

Edith nodded. 'Of course.' Neither of them had touched their tea. She raised her cup to her lips to prevent the waitress coming over to see if anything was wrong.

'At least the bastard didn't leave a bun in the oven.' Peggy grimaced. 'That's the only good thing. I was worried for a while, but that's one anxiety out of the way.'

Edith met her gaze. 'Just as well. You didn't need that on top of everything else. I was concerned before, I've been wondering.'

'I know. I'm glad you knew, it made it a bit easier.' Peggy drummed her fingers on the table top. 'I think I'd better go, Edie. My mind's going round and round, I won't be good company.'

'You do what you think is best,' Edith told her. 'It's bound to take a while to sink in.'

Peggy nodded briefly as she stood. 'Do you know what gets me really angry? That people will say he's the same as Pete and Harry. When we know they were proper good men, while underneath it all Laurence was an evil bastard. He couldn't hold a candle to my Pete.' For a moment she looked as if she would cry, but then she won control of her feelings again. 'So I'd best be off. Thanks, Edie. I know that can't have been easy.' She swung around and headed for the door.

Edith slowly drank her tea, staring at the posters, some advertising Bovril and others reminding the customers that 'Careless Talk

Costs Lives', then left some loose change on the table so that she wouldn't have to engage in conversation with the waitress. She could always make up an excuse as to why Peggy had had to rush off, but would far rather avoid having to do so. She picked up her jacket and slung it over her shoulder as it was really too warm to wear it. She could sympathise with Peggy, Clarrie and the rest of them in the overheated factory.

Pushing open the café door, she thought she could see Billy in the distance down by one of the market stalls, but she couldn't be sure. She hoped he hadn't noticed her as, while she didn't want to be rude, the last thing she felt like doing was having a friendly conversation about how their day had gone. Peggy's face, with its stark look of pain, guilt and anger, had stayed with her, and she didn't feel like having a light-hearted chat. Feeling a little guilty herself, she took a slight diversion so she could avoid Billy, if it really was him.

★　★　★

Billy caught a glimpse of Peggy rushing along the central aisle of the market, but paid little attention to her as he was too busy with the task in hand. Stan had taken him aside yesterday to ask if he knew of anyone who would be suitable to join them as an ARP warden. He was concerned that they simply didn't have enough manpower to provide the necessary service. All the wardens they knew were working flat out, and few were getting enough sleep. That meant

124

mistakes might be made, and that would not do at all.

Billy had had a think overnight and had come up with the owner of the hardware stall. He'd hurried up after his shift at the docks to catch the man before he closed down for the evening, and fortunately he had made it in time. The man had been reluctant at first, but Billy thought he'd managed to persuade him, or at least to come along to see what was involved. 'You never know, the government might decide everybody has to be conscripted into something at home, even if they aren't eligible for the armed services,' he had said. 'So it stands to reason that it's better if you choose yourself. The wardens are a good bunch; we all pull together when there's a crisis. Makes you feel you're doing your bit.'

Mr Richards had nodded, even as he was securing his awnings and putting away his boxes. 'You could have a point there, Billy,' he conceded. 'I know I'm too old and past it to go off to France or wherever, but I don't want folk to think I'm dodging my duty. I'll have a word with me better half and, if she agrees, then I'll come along like you say.'

Billy had beamed with delight and shaken the man's hand. 'You would be a natural, Brendan, cos you already know everybody.' As he looked over the man's shoulder, he could have sworn he saw Edith some distance away, but he might have been mistaken because she didn't show any sign of recognising him and then turned away from her usual route home.

As he began to make his own way back to the

125

house he shared with his mother, he reflected that she had every right to be out and about and he'd have a chat with her another time. He was very fond of Edith, and felt extremely protective of her after what she'd been through, losing Harry like that. He had known very well that Harry had been a proper ladies' man but, once he'd met Edith, he had seemed to change overnight. Edith had been just what he needed: good fun, bright as paint, a real looker, but not one to take any of Harry's nonsense. All that, and she did such a responsible job too. Truly, Harry couldn't have done better for himself, and all their gang had been delighted when the pair became an established couple. For the thousandth time, Billy cursed the beaches of Dunkirk. He'd never forget the scenes of horror he had witnessed there.

As he strode along the pavement, his mind turned to Edith's colleague. He'd enjoyed their conversation when he'd walked her home for the second time. There was another one who took a difficult job in her stride. He was sure that Belinda's patients loved her, knowing they were safe in her hands. He was also aware that she had beautiful dark eyes, which brightened with laughter, and a warm voice that was very easy to listen to. She was about the same height as him, and he knew that must put many men off, but he had been conscious that he was at a level with her lips, her wide smile.

To tell the truth, he had almost asked her to come with him to the pub one evening. It would have been so natural, and he sensed that she might have said yes. He was tempted to seek her out and see if he was right. If things had been otherwise, he would probably have done so.

However, he knew he was still in love with Kathleen, even if he could do nothing about it at present. He had hoped that — with Ray out of the picture — she would have turned to him and they could start their life together as he so dearly wanted. Yet, if anything, she had been even more distant since the news of her husband's death. He sensed that she needed more time and he told himself that he had to respect that and give her as long as she wanted. She was worth waiting for.

He should be glad that she was showing proper respect to her late husband, however badly he had treated her, since he was Brian's father and the little boy would want to know that his mother had done the right thing. In his head, Billy recognised this was good and correct, but in his heart he longed for nothing more than to take her in his arms as soon as possible and show her just how much he loved her. He had an overpowering urge to make her feel safe, to show her that not all men were bad lots like Ray Berry. She would never have to fear the sound of the front door opening or to hide the bruises from her friends. He would never dream of hurting her. She just needed more time.

So, however attractive Belinda was, and however strong his suspicion that she had feelings for him, Billy would do nothing about it. His heart belonged elsewhere, and he wasn't the sort of fellow to mess around with a girl, however pretty and admirable. Other men might, but not him. She would make someone a fine girlfriend — but not him.

11

Alice was making a quick visit to the service room to check how much cocoa she had left in her own personal supply when she almost collided with Gladys, who was coming out.

'Sorry, miss. I mean Alice.' Gladys smiled brightly.

'You're in a good mood this morning,' Alice observed. 'What's happened? Have I missed some news?'

Gladys laughed, as Alice was the person least likely to be behind with any sort of news. 'No, nothing like that. I just helped our Walter, that's my youngest brother, when he burnt himself. He should have known better; then again, my sister was meant to be minding him but she's got her head in the clouds sometimes.' Her face lost her bright smile for a moment.

'So what did you do?' asked Alice hurriedly. She knew Gladys was pinning her hopes on her sister taking on responsibility for the younger ones at home, to free her up for her long-abandoned education.

'Silly boy was playing too near the kettle,' Gladys said with a mixture of affection and annoyance. 'Burnt his hand cos he weren't looking what he was doing. Got carried away with his wooden planes, he did. So I remembered you should put the affected part under running water, only of course we ain't got any at home. So I did that other thing, when you bathe a burn in tea.'

Alice nodded approvingly. 'That's right, it's because of the tannin in it. It's meant to help burns.'

'I know,' said Gladys proudly. 'I read it in the magazine.'

Alice's eyebrows shot up. 'Which magazine?'

'Well, your magazine, Alice. The special one for nurses. The *Queen's Nurses' Magazine*. It's ever so useful.'

Alice beamed. 'Gladys, that's marvellous news. I know you can read the newspaper, although sometimes that's easier as we all go round talking about what's in it every day. But some of the articles in the magazine are quite difficult, with all the technical terms. You've really come on.'

Gladys nodded in delight. 'I found it ever so hard at first, but I kept going cos I know that's where you find out what new things have been decided or learn how to treat different cases. I read about the tannin only last week. Just as well for Walter that I did. I got our Evelyn to take him down the doctor's after just in case.'

'That's probably for the best,' agreed Alice.

'And he's never to play with his plane in the kitchen,' said Gladys firmly. 'I can't be worrying about him doing the same thing all over again. Him and his friends, they pretend they're Spitfires fighting the Luftwaffe from morning to night. But not in our kitchen, they won't. Not any more.'

★　★　★

Kathleen's first instinct was not to let the woman in. She had been out in the back yard, annoyed by the mess of broken boxes the Coynes had left to blow around in the breeze, when she'd heard the banging on the front door. Perhaps if she ignored it, the woman would go away, she thought as she peered through the window. Then again, better to confront her on her own territory than let her shout her quarrel to the whole street, whatever it might be about. She carefully shut Brian in the small back kitchen, swiftly checking any sharp implements were safely out of his reach, and that he had his teddy. Then she squared her shoulders and opened the door.

There was no doubt that this was the same person Mrs Bishop had spoken about; she had got the description to a T. Definitely not a lady: bottle-blonde hair, over-bright lipstick, even though it was only mid-morning, a low-cut blouse which left little to the imagination, and a tight skirt that barely reached the knee, with high-heeled shoes that Kathleen wouldn't have known how to get into, let alone walk in. This was a woman to remember all right.

The woman looked her up and down. 'So . . . ' she drawled, 'this is what you look like.'

Kathleen folded her arms. 'And who might you be?' she forced herself to say, calmly, not screaming as she felt like doing.

'You don't know?' The woman cocked her head. 'No, I don't suppose he ever mentioned me, did he? That wouldn't have been like him.' Her eyes narrowed. 'But I know all about you.

You and your saintly ways, but not knowing how to give a man what he really wanted. He had to come to me for that.'

Kathleen took a slow, deep breath. 'I haven't got a clue what you're talking about.'

'No, I bet you haven't.' The woman gave her a condescending look. 'I'll spell it out then. I'm what's called a common-law wife. Or rather, now a common-law widow. And d'you know who my husband was? Ray Berry.'

Kathleen reached for the doorframe for support in her shock. 'What?' she gasped.

'Yes, that's right. Half the time you thought he was away at sea, he was no such thing. He was with me, in his other house, leading his other life, which was a damn sight more fun than the one he led down here. Oh, I'm sorry, surprised you, have I? Aren't you going to ask me in? Or do you want all your neighbours to hear what I've got to say?'

Kathleen almost fell back through the door and the woman followed her like a shot.

'How did you find me?' Kathleen gasped.

The woman gave a bitter laugh. 'That was easy. He talked non-stop about all his contacts down the London docks, how they could get hold of everything, you name it. He was going to be part of something big. Then he went and got himself killed.' She sighed theatrically. 'So don't I get a cup of tea? It's hot out there.' The woman was taunting her now.

'No, you don't.' Kathleen's eyes flew to the kitchen door, willing it to stay shut. She didn't want Brian anywhere near this imposter, who she was sure would mean him no good. Unthinkingly she rubbed her wedding ring, which she still wore, more for her son's sake than anything else.

'Charming, I'm sure.' The woman looked around, sizing up the small room and its meagre contents. 'I can see why he couldn't wait to get away from here. Not exactly cheerful, is it?'

'Is that what you've come to say?' Kathleen burst out, stung at the insult to her home, into which she had poured such care. As for the devastating news the woman had just delivered, it was too much to take in.

The woman turned to face her squarely. 'No. It isn't.' She paused to draw out the moment, enjoying Kathleen's discomfort. 'All right, I'll tell you straight. You've got something that I want. That I need.' She stepped forward and Kathleen instinctively drew back.

'Wh-what?' She couldn't imagine what this woman could be talking about.

The woman fixed her with a steely glare. 'His pension, stupid. Stands to reason, we're both his women — '

'But I was legally married to him,' protested Kathleen.

'And I gave him full marital rights, make no mistake about it. What's a piece of paper anyway? He promised me he'd leave you and marry me. So I deserve it every bit as much as you do.' Her voice was growing ever more vicious. 'I'm not greedy, I'll split it down the middle with you. But I want half and I'm going to get it.'

Kathleen felt faint at the idea. Just when she'd finally got something like enough to live on, here was someone threatening to take it away from her again. She couldn't let it happen. She had to fight for Brian's rights as well as her own. The thought of her son gave her strength.

'No you're not,' she breathed. 'I'm the legal widow and I am entitled to the money. I need it for my son.'

'Hah! Where is he then? I've heard all about him too,' the woman spat. 'Suffocating little brat that wouldn't stop crying, that's what I heard he is. Not like my boy. Yes, you heard me.' She took in Kathleen's horrified face. 'That's right, you aren't the only one with a boy to bring up, a boy who won't ever have the loving support of his daddy. That's why I need the pension just as much as you do. Ray wouldn't have wanted our boy to go without. So it's just a matter of us coming to an arrangement.' The woman stepped even closer and Kathleen realised she was all but backed up against the fireplace. For a moment, neither of them moved.

Then, just as Kathleen thought the woman would actually hit her, there was another knock on the front door. This time it opened immediately, and Mattie stepped inside.

'Hello, Kath, just wondered if you had any . . . ' Mattie came to an abrupt halt, taking in the scene before her.

Kathleen pushed herself upright and pushed back her hair. 'This is . . . I didn't catch your name.'

'Elsie,' said the woman. 'Elsie Keegan. Or

should I say, Elsie Berry.'

'Elsie was just leaving,' said Kathleen, getting her confidence back now that Mattie had turned up. She moved to the door and held it open. 'Weren't you, Elsie?'

Elsie regarded her steadily, her grey eyes cold behind their heavily mascara'd lashes. 'I'm just off, yeah. I don't want to stick around here any longer than I have to. But I'll be back. You'll be hearing from me.' With that she swept out, slamming the door behind her.

Mattie turned to her friend in utter bafflement. 'Blimey,' she said, 'who was that?'

12

'Nurse! Nurse! Over here!'

Edith slammed on her brakes and expertly swung herself off the bike, assuming it was an emergency. Then she saw the waving arms of the small figure and realised it wasn't. At other times she might have been cross to have been called to stop for anything non-medical in the midst of her shift, but now she gave a wide smile of delight.

'Freda! And Vinny, is that really you? Look at you, aren't you doing well?' She crouched to the little boy, who was clutching the hand of his not-much-bigger sister, twisting shyly.

Mrs Bell, their mother, came hurrying up. 'Oh, Nurse Gillespie, how nice to see you. You don't mind stopping, do you? Freda was so excited when she spotted you cycling by.'

Edith shook her head. 'It's always a pleasure to see a former patient,' she assured the anxious woman. 'He's much better, isn't he? Vinny, how do you feel now?'

The little boy gave a grin. 'Very well, thank you,' he said quietly, shuffling his feet in their scuffed plimsolls.

Freda took charge. 'He got better, just like you said he would, Nurse. His spots have nearly all gone. He don't scratch nearly so much neither.'

Vinny nodded. 'The spots all went away.'

Edith made a show of checking his face.

'You're right. I would hardly know it was the same boy, except your hair hasn't changed.' She knew he'd made a good recovery as he seemed so lively, and his eyes were bright with interest rather than fever. She turned to his mother.

'You did a grand job there,' she said. 'I know it was a right royal palaver to keep everything disinfected and preventing contamination to the rest of the house, but look at him now. Are all your other children all right?'

The woman gave a heartfelt sigh. 'Yes, thank the Lord. I can't praise you enough, Nurse. You showed us what to do — we wouldn't have known without you.'

Edith shrugged. 'That's what they train us for, you know.'

'I suppose so.' The woman nodded decisively. 'Freda, do you want to tell Nurse our good news?'

For a moment, Edith thought that she meant there was yet another child on the way, and wondered if that could really be good news, given the number of little Bells already in that house. But Freda soon put her right.

'We're goin to the countryside. Me and Vinny and Ma,' she said. 'We ain't stopping round here no more. Some of me big brothers might come, but Da and the eldest don't want to go.'

'That's right,' said Mrs Bell. 'We're ever so excited, aren't we? Me brother found somewhere out near Northampton where we can all go together, only my Terry says someone has to stay behind and look after the house. Besides, he don't want to lose his job, and he's started fire-watching. But I don't want the young ones in the filthy air no more. That was what did for Vinny before.'

Edith opened her mouth to start explaining that wasn't quite the whole story, but the woman went on, dropping her voice. 'Anyway, if what everyone says is true and Hitler's got his sights set on London, I'm not letting them stay here. We'll be safer out of the way. So we're off next week.'

Edith nodded in acknowledgement. Even though the news was full of the RAF holding the Luftwaffe at bay, everyone still expected an invasion. 'That's probably for the best. Who knows what's just around the corner. Sorry,' she pulled her bike upright once more, 'I'll have to be off, but I'm so glad to see you. Vinny, you've made my day.'

The little boy came over all shy again as she waved to him, but Freda waved back enthusiastically. 'We'll send you a postcard!' she called out as Edith cycled off.

★ ★ ★

'So that's what she said.' Kathleen fell back into her one comfortable chair, exhausted by the effort of explaining to Mattie the outrageous but terrifying claims that Elsie Keegan had made. 'You saw her, Mattie. She means business. She wants money for her son and sees me as the quickest way to get it.'

Mattie rested against the table top, her hands across her swollen stomach. Brian, now released

138

from the kitchen, pulled at her dress for a cuddle but Mattie shook her head. 'Sorry, Brian, not now. I can't reach you properly any more. Go to your ma.' She frowned. 'Look, Kath, we don't even know that she's got a son, let alone that it's Ray's. This could all be nothing but a load of lies.'

'I know.' Kathleen tipped her head back and shut her eyes. 'But there must be something to it or why would she bother? She'd pick on someone with more cash for a start, if she was just after getting rich quick. She must be able to see there's nothing going spare round here. That's why I can't give her any.'

Mattie sat up. 'No, you won't give her any because she doesn't deserve any. That pension is all yours, Kath, and you've paid for it already by putting up with Ray for so long. God knows you deserve a fortune for doing that. Anyway, she didn't claim to be his first wife, did she? She knows she hasn't got a leg to stand on. She's just trying her luck.'

Kathleen could feel the tears pricking at the back of her eyes as the depths of her late husband's possible betrayal began to sink in. 'How could he? He told me he was on a ship nearly all the time, that's why he couldn't send money home regular . . . when really he was shacked up with her. God knows where, not round here.'

'She sounds like she's from Liverpool,' said Mattie. 'Didn't you pick it up? It's the same accent as Alice's but much stronger. That was where he used to dock a lot of the time, wasn't it? That'll be it, then.' She got up. 'I'll make us some tea, that always helps.'

Kathleen flapped her hand ineffectually at her friend. She didn't think she could ever touch food or drink again. She was totally drained. She realised she was shaking, the shock now beginning to hit her properly. Ray had been cheating on her with that awful woman, leaving her high and dry with hardly any money, but with her believing at least that he was off doing his best for his family. To top it all, he had another son. That meant . . . Brian had a brother somewhere out there. Or at least a half-brother. The thought made her feel sick, and she dashed from the room through the kitchen to the privy in the back yard.

When she came back in, white-faced and weak, Mattie had the tea ready. 'Come on, drink some, it'll do you good,' she cajoled, stirring a precious teaspoon of sugar into one cup. 'We'll make a plan. We'll all help, you know we will.'

Kathleen shook her head. It was hard to speak without sobbing. 'Is this some kind of punishment for not taking the kids to be evacuated?' she wondered. 'We could have done it, you and me, gone somewhere with Brian and Gillian. Should we have? Should we think about it now?'

Mattie spread her hands. 'Not with me like this. Anyway, I don't want to be far from Ma. We ain't had any of those raids they talked about, and the news on the wireless says our planes are keeping the Jerry ones back. We should stay put, Kath. It's not some kind of punishment, it's just Ray still causing trouble from beyond the grave.

140

Typical, if I may say so.'

Kathleen almost smiled at that. 'And I don't want to go away on me own. I can't manage without you lot. Besides, Brian would miss Gillian something awful.'

Mattie shifted to try to get more comfortable. 'So let me help you now with this Elsie creature.'

'But I can't ask you to, Mattie. You're due in a few weeks now. You can hardly walk through the door, let alone see off the likes of Elsie.'

'Well, I wasn't thinking of fighting her,' Mattie pointed out. 'We need information, that's what. Forewarned is forearmed. We have to find out just how much of her hokum is complete lies, or if any of it is based on the truth.'

Kathleen nodded slowly. That made sense. Mattie was thinking more clearly than she was.

'We need someone who's out and about, who knows everyone round here. So we ask Billy,' she said simply. 'He'd do anything to help, Kath, you know that.'

Kathleen shut her eyes briefly. That was true — he'd said so often enough. She'd spent too long avoiding him recently. She had to put aside her guilt and mixture of feelings to find some way out of this trouble. She sensed the threat was real — and not only to her but to Brian. For that, she would overlook any feelings of her own discomfort.

'Yes. We'll ask him.' She set down her teacup decisively.

Mattie paused for a moment. 'I know he'll help. I'm sure of it. Only . . . ' It looked as if she was debating whether to say something or not.

Kathleen frowned. 'What is it, Mattie?'

Mattie twisted her hands together. 'It's probably nothing. But I bumped into Clarrie queuing for tripe a couple of days ago, and she said someone at the factory had seen him out one night, walking along with a young woman. A nurse, he thought she looked like. A tall one.'

Kathleen blinked in surprise. 'A tall nurse? What, Alice, you mean?'

'I don't know. She didn't have many details. But I'm sure I'd have heard if it was Alice.' Mattie shrugged. 'There's most likely nothing in it.'

'Were they . . . you know? Holding hands or something?' A cold sense of dread started to creep through her bones.

'Oh, I don't think so. I'm sure Clarrie would have asked and said if that was what they were up to. On no, I don't think it was like that. Sorry, I shouldn't have said anything.' Mattie's face fell as she realised the impact of her words on Kathleen.

Kathleen tried to put a brave face on it. 'Don't be silly. Anyway, I'd rather know, rather than put my foot in it. That would be far worse.' She found she was gripping her hands together.

'Right.' Mattie put down her own teacup. 'You and Brian had better come home with me. I don't want you here worrying about that horrible woman coming back, I know what you're like. Pack an overnight bag and put everything you need in the pram. Then you can help us cook tea. You'll be doing us a service. After that, we can ask my father to speak to Billy. They're on duty together this evening. That's what we'll do.' She nodded firmly at her friend. 'What are you waiting for? Get your things.'

Relieved at the idea of being protected by the Banhams, Kathleen did as Mattie asked. But the thought went round and round in her head: what if she had left it too late? What if Billy had found someone else, just when she was in her greatest hour of need?

★　★　★

Fiona pursed her lips as she reread the costs of the lease for the flat next to the nurses' home. What had seemed a simple transfer had gone on far longer than she had wanted, but now it looked as if the place was finally theirs to let out to the two Irish nurses who had been waiting to join the North Hackney team. The two rooms had been redecorated. What had once been a living room was now an airy bedroom, and they had the luxury of a small kitchen and bathroom to share between just the two of them. If all was well with the trains, they would be arriving that very evening.

'And not a moment too soon.' Fiona realised she was speaking out loud. The threat of Nazi attack was growing ever stronger, as the RAF airfields were now becoming targets. What would be next? Logically it would be the cities. She needed all her staff ready and fully prepared for what was to come. On paper the two new recruits looked excellent, but Fiona had no idea how they would settle in, or

143

whether they had ever left Dublin before. Then there was the question of how they would fit with the other nurses. Some had no problems, while others were homesick, found the rigours of working on the district too tough or simply went wild when set free from the limitations of living in a big hospital. Experience had taught her that it was impossible to predict which way it would go.

Still, the obvious thing to do was to enlist the services of one of the experienced nurses who had fitted in most quickly. Rising from her desk, she set off for the top floor of attic bedrooms, and knocked on Alice's door.

★   ★   ★

Alice had been taking advantage of finishing her shift early for once, and for the best of reasons — a regular patient no longer needed her, having made a full recovery. She'd gone to the house, finished off the report for the doctor and waved the old man goodbye. She sighed with satisfaction at a job well done. If only they all had such happy endings.

Now she'd had a drink of lemonade with Gladys in the common room and come up to read the letter that had arrived with the morning's post, but which she hadn't yet had time to open. She was just reaching for the slim paper knife she kept on her bedside table when she heard the knock on her door. Before she could finish saying 'come in', the superintendent had already done so.

'Alice! Glad I caught you.' Fiona sat down on the bed.

Alice had long since given up being surprised at Fiona's lack of formality, in such marked contrast to every other matron she had ever worked for. Fiona simply had no time for any of that. She was far too busy getting things done. True to form she launched straight in.

'We have two new nurses arriving from Ireland today, travel arrangements permitting, and I would appreciate it if you could give them a hand settling in,' the superintendent began, her grey eyes bright with enthusiasm.

'They're the ones who'll be living next door?' Alice asked.

'Yes indeed. And a very nice little flat it is too,' said Fiona proudly. 'So, now, their names are Bridget and Ellen, and they've come from a big hospital in Dublin. They will be new to working on the district. Therefore they might well need help making that transition.'

Alice nodded. 'I've been to Dublin. My father took me to see Trinity College once as a friend of his had studied there.'

Fiona smiled. 'Excellent. You'll have something to talk about then. Of course, you're from Liverpool. I expect you could get across easily before the war broke out, couldn't you? Yet another thing that will have changed for the worse. Ah well, can't be helped. You can explain to them how we go about things and iron out any little problems, can't you?'

'Of course.' Alice smiled. 'The biggest problem that I remember is trying to ride those bikes. I had a shocker when I started.'

'Ah, yes.' Fiona came as close as she ever would to looking guilty, and patted her copper hair. 'Still, cope with that and you can cope with anything. We have two new bikes ready and waiting in the rack. I say new. New to us.'

Alice raised her eyebrows. With all the money needed for the upkeep of the house and staff, she knew that expenditure on bikes was well down the list of priorities. She just hoped the brakes worked.

'Will you be in this evening? I shall let you know when they're here if so. Good.' Fiona rose. 'And sorry to have interrupted — I see you have a letter.'

Alice picked it up from where she had dropped it. 'Yes, it's from Joe Banham.'

'Such a lovely family.' Fiona sat on a committee on which Stan Banham represented the ARP, and greatly admired his steadiness and refusal to become involved in the petty infighting that frequently threatened to break out. 'So sad about Harry. But Joe is well, I hope?'

Alice blinked in acknowledgement of Harry's loss, but said, 'Yes, so far at any rate.'

'Quite so. Well, I shall leave you to his news.' With that Fiona swiftly left Alice in peace once more.

She once again picked up the paper knife and carefully slid it along the envelope, drawing out the pages of the letter. She loved this moment, the delicious anticipation of news, the way Joe's writing sounded just like his voice. It was as if he was in the room talking to her. The letters were unlike anything else in her life, and she valued their arrival more than she cared to admit. She spread out the pages to flatten them and then gasped in delight as one phrase leapt out at her.

He was coming home on leave in about ten days' time. She would see him again, hear his voice in person, not only in her imagination. Only now could she acknowledge how much she had missed him. The last time they had spoken had been that heartbreaking phone call he had managed to make after the news had come about Harry, to check if she had heard, and to see how Edith was. Even at such a time of sorrow, it had been a deep comfort to hear him.

Now he would be home and they could see each other properly, resuming their friendship in person. Alice was aware her heart was beating a little faster. If she was honest, Joe always had that effect on her. She had started off by being angry with him when they first met, and it had taken a while for that to change to friendship, but he had always provoked some kind of strong reaction from the first day she'd seen him.

It was nothing more than friendship, though. She could not take that extra step. Mark, the doctor she had fallen in love with back home in Liverpool, had well and truly broken her heart. She wasn't going to risk that again. Neither was she prepared to entertain the idea of ever giving up nursing. Besides, who knew where Joe would end up on his next posting. She skimmed the letter and caught another reference to Eric Linklater, and reckoned he must still be at Scapa Flow, but there was no telling where his ship would go after that.

She mustn't get too excited, Alice told herself. Leave could be cancelled at short notice. Trains could run late or not at all. Even so, she could not resist imagining how he might look and what they would say to each other. Truth be told, she couldn't wait.

13

'Two down,' Edith thought dully, shutting Mrs Massey's front door. It was hard to believe. It was only last month that she had gone to the Duke's Arms that sunny evening and they had met the airmen. Since then, Laurence had been killed in action. Now Alfie had been shot down, his tearful aunt had just told her. He was still alive, but injured and in hospital. Nobody in the family yet knew how badly he had been hurt.

'They can't say, he's all bandaged up,' she had sobbed. 'He was such a lovely little boy, I do hope his precious face is all right, I couldn't bear it if he was all ruined. My sister doesn't know what to do with herself. She wants to go to see him and yet she doesn't know if the sight of him would be too much for her. She's not well herself, you know, she's got a dicky heart. I told her, don't you go, you won't be able to do nothing for him, and if he hears you crying it could make him worse. You send Ronald, I said.'

Edith had agreed. Her brief impression of Ronald had been of someone sensible, as she might have expected of a friend of Billy's. Not one of the wide boys who were known to work down at the docks. If his mother had a bad heart then she would be ill advised to make the journey to Portsmouth, where Mrs Massey said the hospital was.

She hadn't really taken much notice of Alfie that evening, beyond noting his uniform and that he seemed like a friendly enough chap, but Belinda had spent a long time chatting to him, Edith recalled. Mary had seemed quite taken with him too. With a heavy heart she began to pedal back to Victory Walk, knowing she had to be the bearer of bad tidings to her friends. As always, it would be better if they knew as soon as possible, before the rumour mill swung into action and blew the story out of all proportion.

★ ★ ★

Bridget and Ellen looked at each other aghast as Edith broke the news to Mary and Belinda. They had just sat down for their evening meal.

'So you knew this man?' Ellen asked. 'And he's in the hospital now? The poor creature.'

Belinda gave a small shrug. 'We didn't know him well, but his brother is a friend of someone we do know pretty well.' For a moment she wondered how Billy was taking the news. 'It's just the way it goes. All we can do is hope for his recovery.'

'And we'll pray for him,' said Bridget at once. 'Isn't it terrible? I don't think I've ever known anyone who was hurt in the war before.'

Mary pulled a rueful face. 'I wish we could say the same. We've all known someone who was killed.' She said no more, not wanting to cause Edith any further pain. 'But even though it's terrible, we have to carry on. Sorry you had to hear this in your first week here. But how are you getting along? Do you know your way around a bit more yet?'

Ellen laughed. 'I don't think I'd go so far as to say that. I've got lost a fair few times. Then when I ask the way, some people don't seem to understand the way I talk.'

'Or I don't always understand what they're saying if they speak quickly,' added Bridget, who was the smaller of the two, with startling blue-green eyes and plenty of freckles peppered over her snub nose. 'It takes some getting used to, your London accent.'

'I'll say,' Ellen agreed, while pouring herself a glass of water.

'Alice has been grand though,' Bridget said.

'What's that, what have I done?' asked Alice, coming over with her tray, overhearing her name but nothing else.

'I was just after saying you were grand, helping us find our feet,' said Bridget, giving a wide smile.

Alice picked up her fork and took a bite of the corn-beef fritters. 'Oooh, not bad.' She raised her eyebrows. 'That's another thing you'll have to get used to, the ever more limited food now some things are rationed.'

Ellen twirled a curl of her black hair. 'We'd been warned. I'll get Mammy to send us some of her cakes. Or even just the ingredients. We've been lucky, my parents live in the countryside and they can always get hold of eggs and fresh things and use them to bargain for whatever they need. Since we've got our very own kitchen here, we could do a spot of baking.'

Mary instantly brightened up. 'Now there's an idea. How very civilised. We can make ourselves hot drinks, of course, or even a sandwich or two if we're lucky, but anything more than that gets tricky. It's not that the cook begrudges us the use of the big kitchen, it's just that she has so much to do that she can't really fit us in.'

'And Gladys would probably be left to clear up,' added Edith, who was always on the defensive when it came to the general help.

Alice had an idea. 'If she can send us the ingredients soon, we could do a 'welcome home' cake for Joe.'

'Now there's a thought. That would be a big help to Flo,' Edith said, eyes shining. 'Do you think we have time?'

'Sure, who's this Joe?' asked Ellen, sensing a change of tone. 'Would there be any romance going on there?'

Alice looked a little abashed. 'No, he's just a friend. A very good friend. Some of us know the whole family, and they've often fed us, so this would be the perfect chance to return the favour.'

'Then I'll send word right away,' Ellen assured them. 'Meanwhile, we will make proper acquaintance with our oven. It would be dreadful to ruin our very first attempt at baking.'

'Perish the thought,' said Mary, visions of cake already before her. 'There you go, Alice. Even more reason to look forward to Joe coming home.'

★ ★ ★

Billy spent most of his afternoon shift working mechanically, there was so much else on his mind. Ronald had already gone home early, having won permission to take time off to travel to Portsmouth to visit his injured brother. He had no idea of what the travel conditions would be like, and so had decided to pack enough to last him for a few days, as well as all the presents his mother and aunt had gathered together, things they hoped would help Alfie get better and let him know his entire family was thinking of him.

'I'm dreading it, Billy, I really am,' he'd confessed. 'I don't like to tell me ma or auntie or they'll think I'm a coward, but the idea of seeing me big brother just lying there all bandaged up — well, I can't tell you what it does to me. He was always the one I looked up to, you know, when we was kids. He's always been the brave one. But now, well . . . ' He stopped before he broke down.

Billy had given him a pat on the back. 'You're doing the right thing, Ron. He's been fighting for all of us, up there in the air above Blighty. He'll be glad to hear your voice, he will. Specially as your ma is in no fit state to go.'

'I hope so, Billy, I hope so. I just don't want to let them down.'

'You won't, Ron. And don't even think about work. Me and Kenny will keep the show on the road, so you take as long as you like,' he assured his friend, although part of him wondered how the two of them could possibly do the work of three. Billy was managing on little sleep as it was, thanks to his ARP duties, and Kenny had just begun fire-watching two nights a week. Yet they would find a way, somehow. While he didn't know Alfie well, he had liked him on the few occasions they had met, and he was very fond of Ron, who had always been a steady and reliable colleague as well as good company after the day's shift had finished.

He was desperate to see Kathleen, even more so now that Stan had passed on the news about Elsie's appearance, to reassure himself that she had not been harmed, but had resisted doing so until he had something to offer her. She didn't need his sympathy — she was getting plenty from the Banhams, who had agreed to let her and Brian stay in Harry and Joe's old room for the time being. She was relying on him for something more concrete. He had to come up with the goods. The thought of her being threatened was driving him crazy, and so heaven knew what it must be like for her.

Billy had kept a close eye on Bertie from the day Ron had talked about his muttering about the grudge he clearly still held, and particularly since he had heard about the woman who was making a claim on Kathleen's lifeline of a pension. Billy sighed. Bertie had had the temerity to come up to him directly, to taunt him. The odious man had hinted that things were going to change, that fate was for once going in his favour. Billy had challenged him to say what he meant, but Bertie had sneered and then laughed, before strolling off, whistling.

Billy was left with a sick feeling in the pit of his

stomach that somehow his crooked colleague and the awful woman were connected. Why would Bertie have started hinting of trouble now, when he'd been out of prison for so long? What was he playing at? He would have to follow the man home to see if anything happened this evening. While Billy was in dire need of extra sleep on his night off, keeping Kathleen safe was more important. It wasn't much to go on but he had to start somewhere.

Kenny called across to him to count a new load of crates, shaking him out of his reverie. He checked his watch. Another hour to go and he could put his plan into action.

* * *

For once Bertie appeared to be in no hurry to leave work, but finally the man sauntered towards the main gates and Billy could drop his time-wasting and follow behind from a distance. He checked his ready change in his pocket in case Bertie hopped on a bus.

Bertie headed east, away from the route he would usually have taken towards his mother Pearl's house. Billy tried not to make assumptions. He might be going anywhere: to a pub, to meet friends, for a game of darts, or — more likely — to drum up more black-market business. Billy had no wish to get drawn in to any of that activity. He drew the line very firmly between what was legal and what was not, refusing to operate in the murky area in between, where so many of his colleagues lined their pockets with a little extra. Bertie didn't look as if he was trying to avoid detection; his flashy clothes made him stand out. Billy knew he himself would fade into the background in his dull work clothes and dusty boots.

Just as he was beginning to believe that he was wasting his time, Bertie came to a halt on a street corner near a small shop. He pulled out his tobacco and, as if he had all the time in the world, started to roll a cigarette, then lit it and took a relaxed drag. Was this the action of a man enjoying his leisure time, or was he hanging around until a particular person turned up?

Billy tucked himself behind a garage wall that stuck out into the pavement slightly, providing a good cover position. He drew out a copy of the *Daily Express* from his inner pocket and pretended to read it, all the while keeping an eye on Bertie over the top of the page. Two could play at this game. Billy was sure that he looked for all the world like someone just catching up with the news after a hard day at work.

He'd almost reached the sports pages when a new figure came into view, emerging from the shabby shop. Billy squinted to get a proper look.

It was a woman, with bright blonde hair, tottering in high heels, and wearing very tight clothes with a skirt far shorter than anyone he knew would dream of going out in. She appeared to be friendly with Bertie, putting her hand on his arm, looking up at him coquettishly. She spoke too quietly for Billy to catch what she was saying.

There was a lull in the background noise that

was usually a constant around the dock roads, the buses and other vehicles, the bike brakes, the conversations and shouts of everyone going about their business. There was hardly anyone around and Billy could make out Bertie's words loud and clear.

'What the bleedin' 'ell are you playing at, keeping me waiting like that? Have you got anything for me or what?'

'Don't be like that!' the woman squealed, and then dropped her voice, her body language suggesting she was wheedling, but then the roar of dockside life resumed and Billy could pick up no more. He watched, glued to the spot, as Bertie shook off the woman's arm, shouted something else and then whirled away, his whole posture indicating fury.

The woman gave up attempting to look seductive and made a rude gesture at his retreating back, shouting something while doing so. She dashed into the shop and immediately reappeared, this time with a rusty-looking pram.

Billy did a quick calculation. This must be the infamous Elsie, as she fitted the description so perfectly. Folding away his paper he began to walk towards her, keeping his eyes to the ground, not wanting to draw attention to himself.

As he drew closer he could hear her talking. 'Mummy's not going to take that sort of treatment lying down, is she. Who does he think he is, filthy bleeder? Happy enough to take advantage when it suited him,' she fumed, coming towards him at speed. She barely noticed as he edged out of her way. 'He's got another think coming, he has.'

Billy stepped back into the centre of the pavement once more as she passed him by and turned to look, trying to catch a glimpse into the pram. He was in luck. He had an unimpeded view of the child inside.

The boy was wearing a pale blue knitted top, rather grubby and far too heavy for the warm weather. His face was bright red, looking as if he was about to cry.

His hair was bright red too. It was as red as Clarrie's.

He looked absolutely nothing like Ray Berry.

14

Ronald could have taken a bus but he wanted to walk along the unfamiliar streets. He had to clear his head of what he'd just seen. There was a part of him that wanted to break down and howl like a small child, but he knew that would never do. And what did he have to complain about? He was still fit and able, with full use of all his limbs and faculties — not like the patients in his brother's ward, or all the wards he'd passed on the way in and out of the hospital in Portsmouth.

The only good thing was that their mother had not come with him. It would have been the end of her, witnessing the wreck that was once her eldest son. Ronald had been girding himself to expect the worst but, even so, he had recoiled as the kind young nurse led him towards Alfie's bed. 'Now he won't be able to see you but make sure you speak nice and clearly,' she said. 'His hearing's been affected by the impact of the crash but it's coming back slowly. Take it easy and you'll be fine.'

Ronald wasn't sure how what happened after that could ever be thought of as fine, but he'd done his best, after stifling a gasp at the prone figure, bandaged as far as he could see from head to foot. 'Alf,' he'd gulped, 'Alf, it's me, Ron. Can you hear me? I come down on the train. Ma and Auntie Ida send their love.'

The body in the bandages had waved a hand and a low noise came from the small gap where the mouth must be. 'Ron? That you? Thought I could hear me brother.'

'You can, Alf. I'm here.' Ronald had drawn up the functional wooden chair provided by each bed, and gingerly sat down, lowering his bag of goodies from home onto the floor. 'I got something from Ma and Auntie Ida. I'll tell the nurse it's there, I'll put it on your side table.'

There was a pause then the body took a sharp breath. 'Thanks. Good of them. Good of you.' Another pause. 'Tell me about what you been doing.'

Ron understood that it cost Alfie to talk, and so he'd prattled on about life on the docks, down the pub, how Kenny had joined the local fire-watch team, the coincidence of Auntie Ida getting treated by one of the nurses who had gone to the Duke's Arms with them.

Alfie almost seemed to smile. 'The pretty nurses? Which one?'

Ronald tried to remember. 'The little one with black hair. You know, I said her fella got killed at Dunkirk.' Then he stopped, not sure if he should even mention that disaster when so many sick and injured servicemen lay all around him, in various levels of distress. 'Auntie Ida likes her. What are the nurses like in here?'

Alfie gasped for breath again. 'Very kind. Haven't seen them yet. Are they pretty?'

Ronald shifted on his chair to look around. He hadn't even noticed, he'd been so preoccupied, although usually he would have been as keen as the next man to spot any attractive women. 'Yes,' he said, even though he couldn't see any of them at that particular moment, but sensing it was what his brother wanted to hear.

Two beds along, a man was groaning softly, his eyes screwed shut. There was some kind of contraption under the blankets to raise them off his legs — or rather, as Ron looked more closely, his leg, as there seemed to be a space where the other one should have been. Next to him, a young man was propped up on pillows, his face grey, his breathing laboured and rasping. Still further along, in the corner bed, was another man no older than his early twenties, with half his head covered in luxuriant rich brown hair, the other half completely shaved, angry red welts along the cheek beneath. The arm on the injured side was raised in another complicated contraption.

The nurse who had led Ronald in came past Alfie's bed and caught the direction of his gaze. 'So sad,' she breathed. 'That poor soul doesn't even know who he is. He came here with no papers or anything and he doesn't really speak. We only know he's British because he sometimes shouts out in the night. Terrible damage to his arm and face there. He's taken a head injury and he's hurt all down that side. Ah well, he's slowly on the mend.' She raised her voice a little. 'As is your brother. Feeling a little better, aren't you, Alfie?'

'Better and better every day, Nurse,' Alfie managed to say. She walked away to the other end of the ward, her heels tapping lightly on the linoleum floor. 'Is she one of the pretty ones?' he asked after the footsteps had faded.

Ronald nodded and then realised Alfie couldn't see him doing so. 'She is,' he said honestly. 'Too good for the likes of us, Alf. A bit like that Vivien Leigh.'

'Classy, then.' Alfie started to laugh but it made him cough.

'God, Alf, I'm sorry, didn't mean to set you off.' Ronald was mortified.

'No, no, done me good, this has.' Alfie paused again. 'I'm a bit tired now, Ron, but will you come again tomorrow? Did you get a spot of leave?'

'Yes, I'll be here tomorrow,' Ronald said, though for two pins he would never have set foot inside the ward again. However, he had to do it — Alfie had asked. If Alfie could endure fighting in a Spitfire, being shot at, crashing and winding up in here, unable to move or see, then it was the least he could do to visit and seem cheerful. 'I'll be off now, then.'

'Bye, Ron.' Alfie's voice was fading.

Ron all but staggered towards the door, but the nurse who resembled Vivien Leigh saw him and came over. She drew him into the corridor.

'Look, I realise it looks bad and it's a bit of a shock, but he's doing really well,' she told him.

Ronald stared at his feet. 'God, is it that obvious?'

'You went white as a sheet,' she said crisply, 'but then many of the relatives do. I can assure you I've been caring for your brother every day since he arrived and there has been marked improvement, and every reason to hope he will continue to recover. We just have to give his body time to heal. You see all those bandages and you imagine the worst, but they're there to protect his open wounds from infection. He won't be covered in them for life, you know.'

'Oh.' Ronald was embarrassed that she had read his mind so accurately. 'But what about his eyes, nurse? Will he be able to see?'

The nurse faced him squarely and he met her gaze. 'I don't know,' she said. 'I'm not the one to be able to tell you. If you're here for visiting hours in the morning, you may be able to speak to the doctor. He can give you a better idea.'

Ron swallowed hard. 'Right you are then. I'll do that.' He turned to go. 'Thank you, Nurse.'

She nodded. 'It's nothing.'

Now Ronald dragged himself along the terraced street, counting the houses and wondering if he would recognise the place where he was staying. A friend of a friend who'd once worked at Limehouse Docks and now was at Portsmouth had agreed to put him up, and so Ronald had left his bags there. At least he wouldn't have to pay for lodging. He could stop here a couple of nights if it would do Alfie good to see him every day, but his stomach heaved at the thought of the smells, sounds and sights of the ward. His admiration for Edith and the other Victory Walk nurses grew with every step he took. Up until now, he'd gone along with the generally held view where he worked, that women were the weaker sex and it was men's duty to protect them. He now realised you needed nerves of steel and a stronger stomach than he himself had to deal with the everyday realities of life on the wards. Those nurses were tougher than they looked.

★　★　★

'Won't you need the room back when Joe gets home?' Kathleen asked Flo, anxiety pulsing through every nerve. She really didn't want to return to Jeeves Place yet. The threat from the woman who claimed she was as good as Ray's wife hung over her. Sometimes she would be helping around the house and would forget, and then it would hit her twice as hard as the memory came back.

Flo put her hands on her hips. 'Now you listen to me, Kathleen Berry. You and young Brian are welcome here for as long as you want to stay. Haven't you been like my own daughter these past few weeks, doing all the chores that Mattie's too far gone to manage? I won't hear of such a thing. Joe can have the front-room settee. I dare say that will be like luxury compared to where he's been lately. I will not have you going back to your house on your own when you don't feel safe. So there's an end of it.'

Kathleen swallowed hard with relief, even as she moved to stack the clean plates ready to carry over to the dresser in Flo's generously sized kitchen. 'All right. If you're sure.'

Flo gave a mock-exasperated smile. 'And why wouldn't I be sure? Enough of such talk. Pass me

164

those plates and then you can sort out the cutlery.'

Kathleen did as she was asked, wiping the slightly mismatched knives and forks before lining them up in their drawer. Everything in Flo's kitchen had its place, the result of her bringing up three children and a grandchild there, not to mention catering for their various friends who were never turned away. She felt she could breathe easy again. While she hadn't really thought Stan and Flo would throw her out, she had feared they might resent her taking up the room now Joe was due home in just over a week.

Gillian raced into the room from the yard, followed by Mattie huffing and puffing. 'I tell you what, I can't wait for this baby to arrive,' she said. 'I know Edie said I should take it easy but I hate doing nothing.'

'Will you listen to yourself,' her mother admonished her. 'Plenty of people would love to have nothing to do.'

'You wouldn't,' Mattie pointed out waspishly. 'No, Gillian, put that down. See, Granny will sort you out. Thank you. No, you'd hate being told to lie around and not lift a finger. It's downright tedious, that's what.'

Kathleen laughed. 'Make the most of it. You'll be busy soon enough. Once the baby gets here, you won't know which way to turn, what with Gillian able to walk around and reach everything.'

Mattie subsided onto the sofa. 'Have you heard from Billy?'

Kathleen's face clouded over. 'Not yet. I don't

know what to make of it.' In fact she was longing to see him, just for the comfort of knowing he was there, but she knew she'd been distant with him and couldn't blame him from staying away.

Flo caught her expression. 'He'll be doing his best to find out what's going on,' she assured her guest. 'He probably doesn't want to come round until he knows something definite. He'll be pulling strings behind the scenes, just you wait and see. Why don't you do something to take your mind off it a bit? I saw some patterns in my *Woman & Home* the other day for little siren suits. You could make Brian one of those, and I have some big buttons that would be just right. Wouldn't that be lovely for him? I'm not saying those Jerries will manage to invade or nothing, and Stan says the RAF are doing a sterling job, but it could keep the boy warm in the winter anyway. How about that?'

Kathleen sighed. 'Yes, I'm sure you're right.' Yet her heart sank at the idea that Billy might be interested in somebody else, and that it was her fault for failing to encourage him at the right moment. Maybe he was spending his free evenings with this other woman rather than helping to find out who Elsie Keegan really was. The thought sickened her — because in that case she would have nobody to blame but herself.

★   ★   ★

Ron's kind host assured him his wife would cook him a good breakfast before setting off the next morning, but Ron couldn't face the thought of food, let alone anything fried. He nibbled on a piece of toast to show willing but that was his limit. He slung his bag on his back, knowing he should return directly to the station after the morning's visiting hours were over. He was actually looking forward to being back at work. It would be a doddle compared to this.

As he approached the hospital his stomach was churning, but he knew it meant a lot to Alfie to have his brother there beside him. He knew where to go now, and threaded his way along the corridors, which smelled strongly of disinfectant, making his nose itch. For a moment he was irritated, but then he reminded himself how unimportant that was when set alongside what the patients here were enduring. Shoving his hanky back in his pocket, he opened the big double doors to Alfie's ward.

There was the pretty nurse on the other side of the room, who recognised him and smiled. He thought he detected an expression of approval. Had she really thought he had been so distressed at the sight of his wounded brother that he would not return? Ron straightened his shoulders. He might not like it but he would never let Alfie down.

'Morning, Alf,' he forced himself to say, just as if he was joining him for breakfast.

Alfie stirred. 'Ron, is that you? When I woke up this morning I thought I'd dreamt it, that you'd come all the way down here to see me. And now you're back. Sucker for punishment, you are.'

'Course I came back. Ma and Auntie Ida would have my guts for garters otherwise.' Ron settled himself on the uncomfortable chair.

'Thank them for their parcel. One of the nurses gave me some of Auntie Ida's gingerbread last night. Lovely, it was. Do you want some?'

Ron was briefly tempted, as their aunt was known for her baking skills and nowadays found it hard to get the ingredients. He couldn't remember the last time she'd made gingerbread. But he couldn't deprive his brother of the treat. 'No, you save it for yourself. Or share it with the nurses,' he suggested.

'I might an' all. Doesn't hurt to be friendly to them.' Alfie sounded more like his old self, and was catching everything Ron said. Perhaps he really was on the mend.

'Has the doctor done his rounds this morning?' Ron asked casually.

Alfie's body might be a wreck, but his mind was still sharp. 'Checking up on me, are you?' he replied at once. 'Want to know what he really thinks my chances are?'

Ron thought about denying it and then realised that would just be to insult his brother.

'Well, yes.'

Alfie shifted a little in his bed. 'Don't blame you. I'd do the same. You're in luck, he hasn't been yet. Dry old stick, he is, but seems to know what he's doing.'

Ron noted how Alfie was able to speak for longer this morning without running out of breath, but he didn't know if he was always better at this time of day. He didn't want to get his hopes up for nothing. He cast his eyes around the ward and noted the empty bed where the young man who had gasped for breath had been. His heart went out to the poor soul and his family, but he didn't want to mention it to Alfie.

'Tell me more about what's been happening back home,' Alfie said. 'I think about you all, wondering how you're getting by.'

Ron recounted more everyday stories about life in the East End, trying to play down the ever-present fear of invasion and increasing restrictions of rationing. Instead he told his brother which children had been evacuated, which ones had come back, who'd been in trouble with the ARP, how their neighbours had finally finished their Anderson shelter. 'Done it up like a palace, they have,' he said. 'I told them, there's no point in doing that, you don't want to be spending more time in there than you have to. But they insisted. Said they didn't see why they should be uncomfortable just because Jerry decided to turf them out of bed. She's gone and put up curtains, made matching cushions, the lot.'

'You can't teach common sense,' Alfie observed.

Ron nodded and then turned round at the sound of a discreet cough. A man well into his sixties stood there, with hair almost as white as his coat. 'Good morning,' he said in an accent that bore traces of Scottish. 'Nurse tells me you are my patient's brother. If you would be good enough to step aside so that I can see how he is this morning, I'll be happy to spare you a few moments afterwards.'

Ron did as he was asked, moving away to give Alfie some privacy as the doctor assessed him. He gazed at the man with the missing leg, then looked away as he didn't want to be caught staring. Instead he turned to the man in the corner, who wouldn't be likely to realise if he was being stared at or not. Ron thought what a shame it was that he was so marked along his face. He must have been handsome before his injuries. Well, Laurence had been handsome too — and it hadn't helped him.

The doctor gave another of his discreet coughs and tipped his head towards the double doors. Ron acknowledged him and retook his seat beside Alfie's bed. 'I'd better be making a move,' he said. 'I'll try to come again now I know how to get here. You take care of yourself. Don't go chasing the nurses or anything like that.'

Alfie gave a short laugh. 'We'll have to see. If I keep on getting better it might be good exercise. Thanks for coming, Ron, but don't worry, don't go missing work to visit. I know it's a fair old hike to get here. You look after yourself as well, and look after Ma and Auntie Ida. Your job is protected still, isn't it? They can't make you join up? Well, don't go doing anything daft like enlisting. One of us has to make sure Ma is all right.'

Ron cleared his throat. It had crossed his mind, of course it had. Yet he knew that it was vital to keep the docks working and, although he tried not to think about it, that he might be in almost as much danger there as in the armed forces if the threatened invasion or bombing campaign took place. 'I'll look after them, don't you fret,' he said, trying to keep his voice steady. 'You just concentrate on getting better. I'll come back if I can. If not I'll write. You can get that pretty nurse to read my letters.'

He got up. 'Bye, Alfie.' He did not look back at his brother as he walked away, afraid his eyes would mist up. He dreaded what the doctor might have to say.

The older man was waiting for him on the other side of the double doors. 'You'll not mind if we walk back to my office while we speak? It's a busy day, like every day.' He set off at surprising speed and Ron had to hurry to keep up. 'Well, I'll not keep you in suspense. I'll not deny that your brother has been very, very sick, and we were concerned that we would lose him when he first arrived. Now, though, I'm pleased to say he's making an excellent recovery. He's young, he's fit — this stands him in good stead. With the careful nursing that we can provide, I am confident he will pull through.'

Ron let out a breath he hadn't realised he had been holding. 'And his sight, Doctor? What about that?'

The doctor pursed his lips. 'It is too soon to say. We won't even risk removing the bandage for a wee while yet. But I have high hopes he will have some sight, even if not full twenty-twenty vision. Look how well his hearing is recovering — you might well have noticed that yourself, even over the course of two days. So try to hang on to that.'

Ron gulped. 'But he's a pilot . . . if he can't see properly . . . '

The doctor grew solemn. 'Let's not race to any conclusions yet. He may well have to face the future without flying any more planes. We'll tackle that problem if it arises. Meanwhile, chin up. He's doing far better than we ever could have expected. You may tell that to your mother.' His eyes crinkled in good humour. 'Now I must be about my business. Goodbye.'

Ron could only try to smile back. 'Goodbye. And thank you, Doctor.' He watched as the man strode away down the corridor with an energy that belied his years. Alfie was in good hands — and the rest was in the lap of the gods.

15

Billy had tried his best to find out more about the blonde woman who'd turned Kathleen's life upside down but had got nowhere. He'd asked around on the quiet at work to see if anyone knew if Bertie had a new girlfriend, or if he'd been seen with a woman they didn't recognise, but to no avail. The general consensus was that Bertie had it too cushy living with his mother — who spoilt him rotten — to court any girl, and any sensible woman would run at full speed in the opposite direction rather than have Pearl as a mother-in-law. Billy wholeheartedly agreed but it didn't help his cause.

He owed it to Kathleen to tell her what he had seen, which at least should help to put her mind at rest. If the baby had been a little replica of Ray, it would have been a different matter but, as things stood, he was more and more certain the woman had been trying it on. He had to let her know.

He got the bus from work up to Dalston and passed the spot where Belinda had chained up her bike on the evening of the acid accident. That felt like ages ago. He'd scarcely thought of her since he'd learnt of Elsie's arrival on the scene. He almost laughed to himself that he had even entertained the idea that he might ask her out. There was only one woman who was important to him in that way.

Billy got off the crowded bus on the main road, turning left into Jeeves Street. He still half-expected to see Harry coming out of the front door, strolling down the pavement as if he didn't have a care in the world. Billy had been walking down this street since his schooldays, coming round to call for his friends. Now here he was still in his dusty docker's work clothes, carrying his ARP uniform in a bag under his arm so that he could get changed for his shift without going home first. Those carefree years were a long time ago.

He knocked on the door and it was Kathleen who answered. His heart sped up at the sight of her as it always did. Yet he hesitated, not knowing if she would be welcoming or if that new distance between them would still be there.

For a moment she paused, and then the old familiar smile was back. 'Billy. Come in,' she said, and he followed her into the kitchen with its delicious smell of something cooking for the evening meal.

'Sit down. I'll make you some tea,' she offered, clearing away her sewing from the armchair. Brian's little siren suit was beginning to take shape, in bright emerald green with big buttons down the front. 'Have you come to see Stan? He's not back yet.'

Billy shook his head. 'Only if you're having one. It's a bit warm for tea, I've just been on a bus full of factory workers and it was roasting in there,' he said. 'And no, I mean yes, I have come to see Stan as we're on shift together later on, and I thought we could go together, but it's you

I've come to see.' He realised he was all flustered.

Kathleen blushed a little. 'Have you got any news, Billy? Have you found out anything?'

Billy clasped his hands together. 'I saw them, Kath. I saw Elsie trying to talk to Bertie and then I saw her kid.' He took a breath, and swiftly recounted what he had witnessed. 'Kath, he's nothing like Ray. Even from a quick look it's obvious. He looks completely different. He's got red hair.'

Kathleen gasped in relief and then frowned. 'But that doesn't mean he's not Ray's kid, does it? He could just look like his mother. Not all kids look like their dads.'

'But proper red hair, Kath. It's more unusual, ain't it? Who do we know with red hair? Clarrie, her sister, and their dad. Well, when he had any hair. I'm sure I read it somewhere, you don't often get red hair without it running in your family. It's science.'

'You could still be wrong, though. You said yourself you only saw him quickly.' It was as if Kathleen couldn't believe it was good news.

Billy wasn't giving up. 'Yes, but you couldn't miss it. Bright red, it was. Not brown or blonde with a bit of red in it. I don't suppose Elsie's really a redhead and dyed it blonde?' he suddenly wondered.

'No, she's really a brunette,' Kathleen said decisively. 'Did you see her eyebrows? They're natural, not painted, and they're dark.'

Billy shook his head. 'I can't say as I noticed. I wouldn't know how to tell the difference.'

'Well, I can.' Kathleen was growing in confidence. 'Perhaps you are right, Billy, but why would she say such a thing if it wasn't true?'

'Maybe she lied to Ray as well,' Billy suggested. 'Then she might have thought she'd got away with that, so why not go for the jackpot? He might have laid it on thick, said you were all alone in the world with nobody to advise you. Made out you were weaker than you are.'

'But I have got somebody, haven't I? You've come to my rescue again, Billy.' Kathleen's eyes shone. 'I can't thank you enough.'

Billy smiled but then looked away. He didn't want to press home his advantage, or she might think he was taking liberties. 'I know, I could go back to the shop where she left the pram and ask in there if they know more about her,' he said. 'Don't know why I didn't think of that before.'

Kathleen nodded. 'Is it far?'

'Sort of between Limehouse and Poplar. Not that far,' he replied. 'But where's everyone else? I just realised, it's quiet round here for once.'

'Flo and Mattie have taken the children to the park,' Kathleen explained. 'Mattie was getting fed up with not doing anything, so Flo reckoned she'd be all right if they took it slowly. She put the stew on before she left and I'm minding it. They'll be back soon.'

Billy looked at her steadily, sure that his feelings for her were clear for her to see. 'Kath . . . ' he began, but then there was a noise at the door and Stan strode in, taking off his jacket as he did so.

'Billy! You're early.' He sat down at the table.

'Oh, it's good to get the weight off me feet before we go out again this evening. Have you come round to get changed?'

Billy recovered himself. 'Y-yes, that's it,' he said. 'I'll go out to the privy and do that now, and let Kathleen tell you what I discovered. All right, Kathleen?'

If she had been wondering what he was about to say, she didn't show it. 'Of course. So, the thing is, it might be good news . . . '

★ ★ ★

'Don't you miss the greenery?' asked Mary as several of the nurses were refilling their Gladstone bags at the end of the day's shift.

Bridget stopped what she was doing, wrinkled her freckled nose and looked at her new colleague. 'What greenery would that be?'

Mary shrugged. 'Well, everyone says Ireland is very green. London must seem very built up, very crowded. I know we've got the Downs and Victoria Park nearby, but I dare say it doesn't compare. Lots of the parks are ruined with those trenches anyway.'

Bridget expertly rerolled a bandage as she laughed at the idea. 'Mary, we trained and worked in Dublin. It's a city too. We didn't learn our nursing in a field.'

Mary looked confused. 'No, not a field, obviously. But doesn't everything seem different here?'

Bridget packed away her bandage. 'Sure, it's different, but it's more that food is rationed and

177

the blackout and all that. We do have buses and trams, believe it or not.'

'Oh, I didn't mean . . . ' Mary trailed off, glancing up as Alice walked in, imploring her friend for help with her expression. 'Hello, Alice, you've been to Dublin, haven't you? I was just saying, it must seem very crowded and grey over here.'

Alice nodded, setting down her own leather bag. 'It was pretty busy there as well, to tell the truth. But I've only been to the city centre. I remember there being lots of people on the streets. It was quite like Liverpool in some ways — everyone talking quickly and passing the time of day — but I hadn't been to London then so didn't know what it was like here.'

Bridget decided not to tease Mary any longer. 'The countryside is very green, it's true, and that's because it rains all the time. Isn't that the case, Ellen? That's why we came over here, to get out of the non-stop rain.'

'Really?' Mary's eyes were wide. 'Oh, I see, no, you don't mean that.'

Ellen shook her head. 'We came for several reasons,' she said honestly. 'There's more work to be had, and at better pay. Also for a bit of adventure. You can't get up to anything without your mammy knowing back home.'

Bridget nodded. 'That's right. And of course we wanted to stand up to Hitler and his Nazi forces. It didn't seem right for that to be happening just across the water and for us to do nothing.'

Alice reached for some more bandages. 'Even

though it's not strictly your fight? I think that's very brave.'

Bridget sighed. 'My father says it's foolhardy. He thinks we've run mad. Mind you, he never wanted me to leave home in the first place. Besides, it's everyone's fight, isn't it? This is for human decency, or at least that's how I see it.'

Mary blinked soberly. 'Yes, when you put it like that, I see what you mean.'

'Anyway we're very glad you're here,' Alice said warmly.

Ellen shrugged but smiled back. 'Now you're just saying that to have use of our little kitchen. Oh yes, I forgot to say. We've had a letter to say the ingredients are on their way, but will take longer as they're in a parcel. So we should be able to make your friend's 'welcome home' cake we spoke about.'

Edith joined them, stuffing a piece of paper into her pocket as she came in to the district room. 'Budge up, Al. Ta. That's good news to come back to. We love a bit of cake, don't we?'

'Certainly do,' said Mary, who was worried that their necessarily more restricted diet was causing her to lose her curves, of which she was very proud. 'I must go, I'm going to be late. Fiona asked me to help out at one of the first-aid classes. Said I hadn't taught at many and it would be good practice, so I had to say yes. See you later.' She took her now-full bag and left, followed by Ellen and Bridget.

Alice glanced sideways at Edith, now they were left on their own. 'What's that you were putting away as you came in?'

Edith sighed. 'More trouble from my family. You know I sent Mick away with a flea in his ear? Well, now Frankie is asking me directly for help.'

'He's the next eldest one, isn't he?' Alice had a job to remember all Edith's siblings.

'Yes, Mick's twenty and Frankie's sixteen. He wanted to join up, but mostly because he thought he could get away from these thugs he owes money to. The army won't take him; he looks even younger than he is.' She took out the letter, on cheap yellowing paper, covered with an unruly scrawl. 'I think he's realised he's on a hiding to nothing and so he's trying to bring me into it. At least he's writing to me direct and not via Mick. I wouldn't trust that one as far as I could throw him.'

Alice could only nod. She knew Edith rarely mentioned her family simply because she could not bear to.

'So, of course he wants money. I don't know if I should give him any.'

'How much? Is it a lot?' Alice asked.

Edith made a face. 'It's enough. It would be a huge amount to a kid like Frankie. Well, I shan't give him all of it. If Mick gets wind of it he'll want a cut for asking me in the first place. That's what he's like. I could send Frankie a bit to tide him over. Enough to get the thugs off his back for a bit. He can work to pay the rest of it off. I don't want him to get hurt though.' For a moment her face creased with worry. 'Why do I bother? They wouldn't do this for me. They wouldn't lift a finger if I was in trouble.'

Alice gave her friend a straight look. 'You

never tell them if you're in trouble. They don't have the chance to help.'

Edith turned her gaze to the floor. 'I'm not giving them the satisfaction. I don't need them. I've got you, I've got the Banhams. I've made my own life. God knows it was hard enough getting here. They aren't going to drag me back there. All the same . . . ' She kicked her feet. 'I don't want him to get in any deeper. He's daft enough not to realise the hold these sorts of people have over you. I'll send him some money. Not all of it, but a little. I can't have him saying I abandoned him completely.'

⋆ ⋆ ⋆

Kathleen held her breath as she opened her own front door for the first time since leaving in such a hurry, half wondering if the vile Elsie would appear, but there was nothing but the silence and slightly stale air of a place that had not been lived in for a while. She let out a sigh of relief as she set down her bags. She would make the place ready and then go back for Brian.

Despite Flo's protests, she had decided to move back into the little ground-floor flat, as Joe would be home any day now. She didn't want to outstay her welcome. Besides, if she'd been Joe, away on his ship for months, and up in the north of Scotland if Alice was to be believed, she would value her home comforts.

Although she was full of trepidation, Billy's latest information had helped to put her mind at ease. He had gone back to the shop and got talking to the owner, who had got to know Elsie a little. She was apparently living in a one-room flat above a bookmaker's near Poplar, with a dark-haired man who hardly ever came out. He never came into the shop but the owner had occasionally seen him waiting outside while Elsie popped in to buy essentials. He remarked that when she'd first arrived she had been lively and excited, almost as if she was full of anticipation, but lately had been more deflated, her early confidence gone. Billy had taken this to mean she'd started off thinking she could con the share of the pension out of Kathleen, but had then realised it would not be possible.

Kathleen had let him talk her into believing this was the explanation. She hung on to his conviction, wanting it to be true, even if a secret dread still lurked. She told herself not to be so fearful. The woman had done her best to extract the money, but had backed off when she'd stood up to her. That would be the end of it.

She wished she could be certain that the baby wasn't Ray's. Somehow that felt like a deeper betrayal than his unfaithfulness; not only had he got himself another woman, but he'd given her a child too. It made Brian less special, and anything that hurt Brian cut Kathleen to her very core. It was defending Brian that had provoked Ray's worst attack, when he'd left her broken on the living-room floor, without a care if she was alive or dead. He hadn't deserved to be Brian's father. He hadn't deserved to be anybody's father, full stop. He had been feckless, unreliable, untrustworthy and completely selfish.

She knew that this was the polar opposite of Billy.

Even though she had tried to shut Billy out after the news of Ray's death, he had persisted and not let her down after all. She had been silly to believe he was seeing another woman. Everything he had done proved to her that his feelings were unchanged. Perhaps it was time for her to let down her guard a little. She knew now how terrible it was to imagine he might care for somebody else. She couldn't have blamed him; he was only human. 'Kathleen, my girl,' she murmured to herself as she began to unpack her bags, 'you need to decide what you want to do. You can't ask him to wait for ever. And you'd be lost without him.'

She went to her kitchen cupboard and hunted for something to drink. She fancied a treat. That was strange; she could have sworn she had some Ovaltine left in a tin. There didn't seem to be any there now. She shook her head. 'Losing your marbles, you are,' she admonished herself. 'It's all that moving from one place to another. Making you forgetful.' Reaching for her packet of tea leaves, she decided that she had better get on with the job of making this a fit home for Brian to return to, and not to get any more fanciful ideas.

16

Alice studied herself in the mirror that hung on the back wall of her small attic room. She was not in the habit of spending much time looking in it. Usually it was simply a case of making sure her hair was tucked properly under her cap and that she was neat enough for her working day. Tonight, though, she had wanted to look her best.

She had brushed her hair out so that it lay lush and golden over her shoulders rather than curled up in a bun. Somewhat self-consciously she straightened her collar. By good fortune, her mother had sent her a new blouse as a surprise gift and it had arrived that very morning. Alice gave a wistful smile. Her mother had loved to go shopping with her when she'd lived at home and would have gone into the centre of Liverpool specially, making her way down the familiar street to John Lewis. She had chosen well, though; she knew her daughter's taste, and also that her daughter would be unlikely to find the time or have the inclination to search out such a thing for herself. It was a delicate cream muslin with matching lace around the neck and sleeves, and tiny mother-of-pearl buttons down the front. Alice had to admit that it was a lovely choice.

'Oooh, what have you got there?'

Alice's quiet moment was shattered as Edith came in and stared admiringly at the blouse.

'My mother sent it.' She tugged at the lapels one last time and turned to smile at her friend.

'Well, it's bloomin' gorgeous,' Edith declared, sitting herself down on the bed. 'If I didn't know better, I'd say you were dressing up for a special occasion.'

Alice pulled a face. 'But you do know better. Don't you start. There's nothing more than friendship between Joe and me, and well you know it.'

Edith relented. 'Don't take on. I know, I know. But it's gorgeous all the same. I shall feel shabby in comparison.'

'Nonsense. That dress is really smart.' Alice recognised the navy frock in artificial silk from two summers ago, but Edith had refreshed it by sewing big white buttons in a double row down the front and adding a shiny white belt. Alice pointed at it. 'Is that new?'

Edith grinned. 'No, Bridget lent it to me. I had to add an extra hole to it, but she didn't mind. In fact I got Stan to do it with the bradawl from his toolkit when we took the cake over earlier. Thought I'd better not go using anything from my medical bag to puncture the leather; Gwen might hear about it, then there'd be hell to pay.'

Alice sat carefully down beside her friend, smoothing her skirt as she did so. That was the trouble with light cotton — it creased so easily. 'So did they like the cake? What did Flo say?' She paused. 'Was Joe there?'

Edith shook her head, registering that Joe's presence was far more important to Alice than the reaction to the cake. 'His train was due in a bit later. Not to worry,' she added hastily, 'Flo was sure he'd be back in time to be at the pub tonight. But yes, they all loved the cake, well, of course they did. What a stroke of luck the new nurses are such dab hands in the kitchen. Bridget did the actual baking and then Ellen did the decorating. She's very clever, she wrote 'Welcome Home' in icing and then dotted on those pieces of lemon peel. It was as good as anything you'd find in a shop. Flo was impressed.'

Alice raised her eyebrows. 'Must have been good, then. I think it's terribly kind of them to help — they don't even know the Banhams. They're really friendly, aren't they? I'm so glad they joined our home.'

'Yes, when you think of some of the misery guts we trained with, we've been lucky.' She stood up. 'Can I borrow your navy handbag, Al? That's if you weren't planning on using it?'

Alice got up and went to her wardrobe. She had intended to use the bag herself, but recognised Edith had dressed up extra carefully for the first time since Harry's death. That was far more important, and she could equally well take the classic leather shoulder bag her parents had given her when she'd first qualified back in Liverpool. If she gave the clasp a quick polish, it would be good as new. She lifted out both bags and passed the navy one to her friend.

'Thanks, Al, you're a life-saver.' Edith grinned broadly as she realised the literal truth of what she'd just said. 'And you were going to use it, weren't you? I can tell. But to tell you the truth, that other bag goes better with your new blouse. Trust me.'

'If you say so.' Alice knew that Edith had a better eye for these things than she did. 'Anyway, it doesn't matter. A bag is a bag. It's just somewhere to put your money and your keys when all's said and done.'

Edith gave her a look of mock horror and pretended to block her ears. 'Don't even say such a thing. A bag is just a bag! Have I taught you *nothing* these past couple of years? Honestly, Alice Lake, you might know who wrote what and who's in the war cabinet but, when it comes to the really important things in life, you have no idea, none at all.'

'Good job I've got you, then.' Alice hastily stuffed her purse, keys and a clean hanky into the second bag.

Edith rose to her feet. 'Come on. You don't usually take so long — do you realise how late it's getting? Belinda's lost patience and gone on ahead. We can't keep the hero waiting.'

★   ★   ★

The Duke's Arms was already busy by the time they arrived, pushing their way through the highly polished doors into the noisy bar and into the welcome coolness of the beer garden beyond.

There was Billy, and for once, standing beside him, they could see Stan, his shirtsleeves rolled up and his collar undone, chatting affably to a couple of men with their backs to them. Belinda was already there, her tall frame easily noticeable

187

in the group. 'Goodness,' breathed Edith, 'who's running the ARP post tonight then?'

Stan spotted them and waved them over. 'Good evening! Here, we've saved you some room at the table.' He stepped to one side and Billy did likewise, revealing two empty chairs by the wooden table they had claimed. The familiar figure in the third chair rose to greet them, a smile slowly spreading over his face until it reached from ear to ear.

'Edith. Alice.'

Edith ran forward into the very informal hug of the man who would have been her brother-in-law. 'Joe! Look at you. Whatever they're feeding you in the navy must suit you.'

Joe set her free again. 'That's not what Ma says. She reckons they've been starving me and it's my bounden duty to eat every hour on the hour for as long as I'm home.' He looked up at Alice, who had hung back to allow her friend to greet him first. 'Hello, Alice.' His eyes brightened at the sight of her, and his face broke into a slow smile.

'Hello, Joe.' For a moment she almost didn't know what to say. She had forgotten the reaction he always provoked in her; something intense which nobody else brought out. Why was it so hard to speak when she'd been writing him long letters for these last months? Their eyes rested on each other for a moment, seeming to drink each other in before she came to her senses and found her tongue. 'How good to see you. Was your journey all right?'

'Not too bad. Only two hours late.' She felt

the warmth flood through her as she realised how much she had missed seeing that humorous grin.

'A luxury, then.'

'Yep. Even had a seat for some of it. What will you have to drink?'

'Lemonade, please.' Alice was far too hot for anything else.

'Shandy for me,' said Edith. This was a night out to savour, not to dwell on the past.

'One lemonade, one shandy. Coming right up. Pa, Bill, anything for you?'

The other men shook their heads and Joe set off towards the noisy bar, leaving Alice and Edith to take their seats.

Edith exhaled loudly. 'Bit of a scrum, isn't it?' She craned her neck to look around. 'I thought Peggy and Clarrie might be here but I can't see them.'

'We can't see much from here,' Alice pointed out.

'You can usually spot Clarrie's red hair, though. And you can often hear them if they're anywhere near.'

Stan leant down. 'Thank you for the cake,' he said. 'I know you had something to do with it, Alice.'

'Oh, not really.' Alice shrugged, feeling she couldn't take credit for anything other than suggesting the idea.

'Well, it helped mark the occasion and we appreciate it.' Stan's kindly face was solemn. 'It does us all good to see Joe home again, and his mother's thrilled to bits.'

'I bet she is,' said Alice, knowing how proud both parents were of their clever son. She couldn't imagine what it must feel like to have raised a family, only to have one son killed and the other put in equal danger, with no way of knowing when it would end. Yet Stan and Flo were among thousands of others facing the same agony.

She turned at the sound of Joe coming back, bearing their drinks. Behind him she could see still more people arriving. 'Thank you, Joe,' she said.

'Yes, thanks,' Edith echoed. 'Who's that just come in?' She squinted over at them and answered her own question. 'Oh, it's some of Billy's friends from the docks. I don't think you know them, Alice.'

Alice shook her head, and Joe frowned and then did the same. 'Can't say as I've seen them before,' he said. 'So, how's the world of nursing? What have you been up to?'

'Coping with a measles outbreak for a lot of the time,' Edith said, and launched into a vivid description of the trials and tribulations of the summer. Alice sat slightly back and enjoyed her friend's tale, knowing she had written about this to Joe on several occasions, but that Edith could talk about it far more entertainingly in real life. It gave her pleasure to see her friend coming back to something like her old lively self, chatty and outgoing, a side of Edith that had been sadly lacking since Dunkirk. Perhaps she was finally emerging from her shell. Not that she would ever forget Harry; but life had to go on, even if it was fundamentally changed.

'. . . and we still don't know how many of our young patients will be here when school starts again in September, do we, Alice? Oh look, there's Clarrie after all. And Peggy. Maybe their factory shift went on longer than usual. I might wave at them to come over. You don't mind, do you, Joe?'

'Not at all, the more the merrier,' said Joe, grinning again, clearly taken with the idea of being surrounded by a group of young women. He shifted a little to allow the newcomers to come through and welcome him home. Then, once they'd found free chairs and dragged them over, Joe manoeuvred himself into a seat next to Alice and turned his full attention to her. 'You're as busy as you said in your letters, then? You weren't making it up to make me feel better?' His eyes crinkled in amusement and focused on her alone.

She pulled a face. 'It's been busy all right. We've managed so far.' She glanced quickly around. 'All we can do is hope we continue to do so if and when it gets worse. We're as ready as we can be. Two new nurses have just joined us — they're the reason we could make you a cake — and everyone's up to date with their training; plus we're teaching more and more first-aid classes, so we won't be the only ones who know what to do in an emergency.' She sighed. 'Then we just have to wait and see what happens. But anyway, what about you? You've been in Scapa Flow, haven't you?'

'Of course.' He gave that grin again. 'I knew

you'd work that out. I honestly can't say what comes next, though.'

'Not that you would.'

'Well, no, not in as many words. But I don't think anyone really knows. It all depends on whether our boys in the air can continue to hold off the Luftwaffe, doesn't it. Makes the invasion that bit less likely.'

'Although Hitler's bound to deploy another tactic. He won't be content with bombing airfields, will he?'

Joe shook his head. 'I don't want to depress you, but it's not likely, no.' They fell silent for a moment, neither wanting to voice the idea that the next step would be air raids on the big cities.

'How long are you home for?' Alice changed the subject, realising nobody had said.

Joe shifted a little. 'Four days. That's unless I hear otherwise. I thought it might coincide with the arrival of Mattie's baby, but she's still got a few weeks to go, hasn't she?'

Alice smiled, aware that as he'd shifted in his seat their legs had briefly touched. 'Yes. Poor Mattie in all this heat. She's due in September.'

'Not far off now.'

'Yes, she'll be glad to be heading down the home straight, all right.' For a moment Alice imagined they could be anywhere, away from the perpetual pressure of war, chatting about his sister and the anticipation of the baby's birth. It hadn't taken long to get back to this easy way they had with each other, and she felt, as she often had, that she could tell him anything. She had missed that as well. She made herself forget about it when he wasn't here, but how she relished it now he was back.

Joe, for his part, felt himself relaxing in a way he found impossible when he was away. Even when he was off duty he could never fully let go; there was always a chance he would be needed for something, and the atmosphere had an undercurrent of perpetual uncertainty. Plus, it was often so cold. He'd taken to sleeping wearing his heavy jumper and the thick socks Flo had knitted for him many months ago. Taking in the scene before him: the evening sun; the plants, now a little faded by the heat of the summer; the pints of beer, golden in the shafts of light, he felt he was in a different world.

And next to him sat Alice, her hair golden too in this light, smiling back and gamely insisting all was as well as could be, as if they weren't all under threat from the Germans escalating their terror from the air. For a brief moment he wondered what had happened to that good-looking doctor they'd all talked about last autumn who, Alice insisted, was just an old colleague from her training hospital. Then he pushed the thought away and told himself it was none of his business; and besides, if the man was a doctor in the active services, he would have his work cut out, as much if not more than any of them.

Irritated at his own idiocy to be thinking of such a thing when Alice was nothing but a friend in the first place, he briefly turned his gaze from her and onto the crowd of people by the back gate. Billy was there, talking nineteen to the dozen to several of the others, the tall nurse with tight black curls laughing at what she'd heard. For a moment he thought one of the young men was staring at him, but he must be imagining it. Joe didn't know him and the bloke didn't know Joe. 'Sorry, what was that last thing you said?' he asked Alice, caught out when she came to a halt and seemed to be waiting for a response.

'Good job you're not on duty now,' she teased. 'I only asked if they let you see any films up in the frozen north.'

'Not many. What's on around here at the moment?'

'I think *Laugh It Off* is back again.'

'That Tommy Trinder one? I missed it the first time around. Shall we go?'

Alice nodded. 'We could. It'll take our minds off everything else that's going on.'

From the other side of the wooden table, Clarrie perked up. 'Did somebody say Tommy Trinder?'

Peggy and Edith looked up as well.

'Yes, I was just saying that musical he was in a few months back is showing again,' Alice explained. 'Joe and I were thinking of going.'

'Oh, when? Shall we all go?' Clarrie looked delighted. 'It'll be just like old times. We could make a night of it. Go for fish and chips as well.'

Alice nodded. 'We could.' She couldn't tell from Joe's expression if he was pleased it would be a whole crowd of them or not. After all, it wasn't to have been what anyone would have called a date. And if Edith was thinking of all the times she'd been to the cinema and then on for fish and chips with the younger Banham brother, her face wasn't giving anything away either.

'Lovely,' said Joe. 'What could be better?' But he didn't meet Alice's eye as he spoke.

★ ★ ★

'Billy, who's that?' Ron asked, pointing to the group of young people sitting around the wooden table.

'Oy, mind my pint,' Kenny said mildly, swinging his glass out of the way.

Billy looked across the beer garden. 'Him near Edie? He's the reason we've all turned out tonight. That's Joe Banham, that is. Local boy made good, he's some hotshot engineer doing telecommunications in the navy now. I forgot you don't know him, do you? Can't think why your paths never crossed before.'

'I don't think I met him either,' said Kenny, adjusting his glasses on his nose. He hated wearing them but he'd recently come to accept he couldn't manage without. 'Heard you talk about them all, of course, but I've never actually come across him in the flesh until this evening.'

'Just one of those things then,' said Billy. 'Why, is there any particular reason you asked, Ron? Introduce you, shall I?'

Ron scratched his head. 'No, no, he's there with the girls. Don't let me get my ugly mug in the way.' Something was bothering him but he couldn't put his finger on it. That's what happened if you drank two pints on an empty stomach, he told himself. 'I'm going to the bar to get a pickled egg. Anybody else want one?'

Kenny pulled a disgusted face. 'You can keep it, Ron. I don't care for them meself.'

'Me neither. And Ma cooked a lovely fry-up before I came out,' Billy added.

'See you in a moment, then.' Ron carefully placed the remains of his second pint on the makeshift shelf by the gatepost and headed inside.

'Don't suppose his ma is up to much cooking at the moment,' said Kenny. 'Not well, is she? And his auntie's only just on the mend. Poor old Ron. We'd better keep an eye on him, see he doesn't waste away.'

'Fat chance! Did you see that pie he put away at dinner time?' Billy didn't lack sympathy for his colleague, but felt he had enough people to look after at the moment. There was a limit, and Ron was big enough to take care of himself. 'Come over and meet Joe. You'll like him, everyone does.' He led his friend over to the group at the wooden table and made the introductions.

Edith nodded to him in recognition, but then turned back to Peggy, who had claimed the seat next to her.

'Good to see you out again,' she said quietly.

Peggy nodded resolutely. 'I'm not going to lock myself away just because . . . well, you know.' She dropped her voice. 'Because one evening went so wrong. I don't deserve to feel like I'm in prison, I went through enough at the time. So he's not going to win.' She sat back and spoke normally again. 'Good to see you out, too. That's a nice dress, that is. Is it new?'

'I wish it was.' Edith laughed but enjoyed the compliment nonetheless. Peggy liked clothes — she wouldn't have praised anything that she didn't approve of. 'New buttons though, and a borrowed belt, and Alice's handbag.'

Peggy nodded approvingly. 'You're looking proper smart. That's more like it.'

'Why, was I so terrible before?' Edith teased. 'You mean you let me go around looking like a drab? Some friend you are.'

'Silly.' Peggy tapped her on the arm. 'No, but you've paid attention to putting your outfit together, haven't you. That's more like the Edie we know.' She took a swig of something Edith noticed wasn't port and lemon.

'What's that you're drinking?'

'Ginger beer.' Peggy lifted an eyebrow. 'Thought I'd keep me wits about me for once. I've gone off the other stuff.'

Edith gave a short laugh. 'And here's me on the shandy. I won't have more than one, though. Got to have a clear head tomorrow.'

Peggy nodded in acknowledgement. 'Still, Edie, do you fancy coming out one night? I mean, proper out, not just down the pub? We could go dancing in the West End.' Her eyes sparkled.

'Really?' Edith took a moment to absorb that her friend was ready to pick herself up. 'You'd want to do that? I'm not sure, Peggy. It feels a bit too soon for me, to be honest. I don't think I'd be much fun.'

Peggy's face fell. 'Really? Bet you'd love it once you got there. We wouldn't have to stay for long or nothing.' She tried to water down the prospects but it wasn't working.

'Look, thanks for asking, but I know deep down I'm not ready to go out enjoying myself,' said Edith seriously. 'Tonight is all right — it's for Joe, and I'm here with all of you, and if I want to go back then it's not very far. But the West End . . . no, that doesn't seem right to me. I'm not saying you shouldn't,' she added hastily, not wanting to sound judgemental, 'I think it's good you're ready to hit the dance floor again. But go with Clarrie, or her sister, or Belinda even.' She nodded across to her animated colleague, enjoying herself a few yards away. 'I couldn't. Not yet, anyway.'

Peggy tipped her head to one side. 'All right. I'll let you off the hook. But I won't stop asking, you know. One day you might feel like it, and then we'll have the best time ever.' She sipped her ginger beer. 'This stuff's not bad once you get used to it. I must drink it more often. Will you at least come to the pictures with everyone when we see Tommy Trinder?'

Edith smiled. 'I think I can manage that.'

★　★　★

Ron fished into the packet for the tiny blue paper sack of salt and untwisted the top. Two pickled eggs, followed by some Smith's crisps — that would set him right. He wandered back to the beer garden and located his almost-empty glass, thought about getting himself a half and then decided to wait for his food to go down. Where were Billy and Kenny? It had grown darker, but after a few moments he could see they were over by the big table and, he might have guessed it, surrounded by the girls, including two pretty nurses with the dark hair, one tall and one short. Two of the others were school friends of Billy's, although he wasn't sure who the blonde one was. She looked a bit on the serious side compared to the rest of them. She was deep in conversation with the man Billy had said was the reason they were here, the chap who had taken his attention earlier.

Could he have met Joe Banham before? Maybe through someone other than Billy? It wasn't impossible if they had grown up in neighbouring areas of the East End. That had to be it, because there was something about him that felt familiar. But what? For the life of him Ron could not remember. That was what two pints did to your brain cells. Perhaps if he delayed getting that next drink in, it would come back to him. He made his way over but stood on the edge of the group, smiling and nodding in the right places in the general conversation but not adding anything, waiting to see if his memory would wake up.

The hum of their talk filled the air and for a second he was back at that gathering earlier in the summer when Alfie had been with them, smart in that uniform he'd been so proud of, his open face unmarked, his eyes sparkling with humour and taking in everything around him, his hearing perfect. He'd never be like that again. Ron felt a prickling at the back of his eyes and squeezed them shut, desperate for his sorrow not to show. He'd have to cut back on his pints if he started giving in to his emotions in public. He'd never live down the shame. And didn't everyone here know someone who'd died or been injured? It wasn't as if he was the only one mourning the loss or ruin of a young person's life. All the same, it was his big brother, his hero, Alfie, who could do anything . . .

The cogs started whirring. Alfie. The hospital. The young man in the corner bed. Almost the same profile as Joe Banham's, and similar hair — or what the poor patient had of it. Surely a coincidence. Lots of people had thick brown hair. But with a face so alike? It had to be the beer, affecting his brain. And yet . . .

17

'I'm here to help and that's all there is to it,' said Kathleen the next morning, turning up at the Banhams' doorstep as usual even though she was no longer staying there. 'Don't talk daft, Mattie. You can pass me the pegs if you like, but you aren't going to lift anything heavier.' She ushered Brian through to the kitchen, carrying her own bundle of washing to add to the family basket.

Mattie didn't bother to argue. She was grateful that Kathleen had come round, as she didn't want Joe to see how much she struggled to do everyday tasks. He didn't need to be worrying about her when he went away — he would have enough on his plate as it was.

Now he leapt up from the remains of his breakfast on the big wooden table and greeted their friend. 'And who's this? Brian, how you've grown,' he said to the toddler, who gave him a nod before making a beeline for Gillian.

'He has, hasn't he?' Kathleen gazed proudly at the back of her little boy as he climbed up beside Gillian on her heap of cushions in the corner. 'They play by themselves for hours on end, good as gold.'

'And how are you keeping, Kath? You're looking well,' Joe said. 'Ma told me you'd been helping out. I'm very grateful to you.'

'Well, it's only right,' Kath said, shaking out her hair. 'It's good to see you, Joe. Can I just squeeze by to the back kitchen? I'll get the copper on for hot water to get this lot started.'

'Here, let me help.' Joe got up. 'No, honestly, let me. I've got to keep in shape, after all. A bit of exercise — after all that cake, followed by more pints than I'm used to — wouldn't hurt me.' He swung the big laundry tub off its hook.

'Oh, what did you do last night?' asked Kathleen, taking out the Reckitt's Blue and Oxydol. She quickly sorted the whites from the rest of the laundry.

'He's got a sore head,' said Mattie. 'Let himself be dragged down the Duke's Arms, of course. Even Pa went, though he's made of stronger stuff and was up bright and early this morning, which is more than can be said for some of us around here.' Her eyes gleamed at the now-rare opportunity to tease her big brother.

'I might have known it.' Kathleen pretended to be stern. 'And who else was there?'

'The usual gang. Clarrie, Peggy, Billy, and some of his mates I didn't know. Alice and Edith, and their friend Belinda.'

Kathleen took this in. 'Which one is she?' she asked lightly. Mattie caught her eye but Joe didn't pick up on it.

'I think Alice said she'd joined them since I was last down — I didn't recognise her anyway. Very tall. She spent most of her time chatting to Billy and so I hardly spoke to her. I was glad to see Edith out and about, as I understand she's been keeping herself to herself since . . . since Harry died.'

'She came round here a few times though,'

Mattie said, leaving Kathleen to think about what the tall nurse might have been talking to Billy about all evening. Surely, if this Belinda and Billy were anything other than occasional acquaintances, Joe would have noticed and said something? Or didn't men spot these things unless it was so blindingly obvious that it was impossible to miss? Perhaps her fears were groundless and there was nothing in it. She hoped that was true. She had to hang on to that.

'Alice said there's a Tommy Trinder film on,' Joe continued. 'It looks as if we're all going to go. Almost like old times.'

'You like Tommy Trinder, don't you, Kath?' asked Mattie.

Kathleen looked up from her assortment of whites. 'Of course. Everyone does.'

'Well, why don't you go?'

Kathleen's busy hands came to an abrupt halt. 'What, me? Go to the pictures? How would I do that? Now you're having me on, Mattie.' She racked her brains for the last time she had gone to the cinema. It must have been before Ray left to join his ship, which would have meant before he had met Elsie, when he still loved her. She wrestled her thoughts away from that painful image.

Mattie sat up in the chair where she had collapsed, suddenly animated at the idea. 'Yes, why not? We can have Brian to stay; he can fit in with Gillian or something. You haven't had a night out since he was born, have you? Don't bother thinking about it, I know you haven't. You of all people deserve it, don't she, Joe?'

Joe nodded, wondering why he hadn't thought of the idea himself. 'It'll be on me, Kath,' he said hastily, concerned she would back out because she had no spare money for the treat. 'By way of a thank you for the help you've given Ma and Mattie.'

'I can't let you do that. If anyone's grateful then it should be me . . . ' Kathleen began, but Joe stopped her.

'I won't listen to any arguments, you're coming with us,' he insisted. 'Just think how glad everybody will be to see you.'

'Yes, you won't have seen most of them for ages.' Mattie pressed home her advantage, pleased that Joe had seen the merits of her idea so readily.

'Well . . . ' Kathleen was tempted. An evening out — and with Billy there. It was too good to turn down. She hoped the tall nurse wasn't included in the party, but it wouldn't stop her going. Besides, she didn't have to worry about Brian; he was as at home here as in their own little flat. 'If you're sure . . . '

'Then it's settled.' Joe beamed, happy to be able to do something to help. 'You pop back to your place, pick up a change of clothes for the boy, and come round here in time for tea.'

'There's a bit of that cake left,' added Mattie, in case Kathleen needed more persuading. 'Brian will come to no harm, you know I'll see to that.'

Kathleen's cheeks grew rosy with anticipation at the unexpected treat. 'I . . . I don't know what to say. Thank you. I'd love to.' Then she turned to the business in hand. 'So I'd better get

204

cracking with these.' She poured the Reckitt's Blue into the tin bucket.

* * *

Gwen pursed her lips as she waited patiently for Fiona to finish adding up the column of figures. Somehow they had to work out how to provide more nursing with less money, and yet even with the two new Irish nurses, they were uncomfortably stretched as it was.

It felt like ages since her shopping trip with Miriam, which was the last time she had left Dalston. With Gwen's commitments to her work and all the extra classes she was teaching, there simply had not been time. Miriam, meanwhile, had thrown herself into WVS activities, alongside welcoming into her home more Jewish families fleeing the Nazi clampdowns, before finding them more permanent places to stay. The latest ones were a couple in their seventies, who had had to drop everything to leave at a moment's notice, and now faced settling in a country where they could not speak the language. Yet at least they were alive.

The shafts of late summer sunlight from the office window caught Fiona's copper head as it bent over the columns. She pencilled in some totals, stared at them and then struck them through.

'Still no good?' Gwen asked.

Fiona looked up, her face showing pure frustration. 'Not yet. I'll find a way. We can't let anyone down.'

Gwen drew up a chair on the other side of the

superintendent's desk. 'Absolutely. And you always come up with something.'

'Just as well.' Fiona glanced at her friend wryly. 'So, distract me from these blessed sums and tell me what else has been going on. It feels as if the only conversations we've had recently are about shortages, extra demands and requests for even more first-aid classes. I've lost track of what our nurses are up to when they aren't actually working.'

Gwen folded her hands over her knees. Even though it was strictly her day off, she was still in uniform. 'Well, young Edith seems to be perking up at last. She's taking a pride in her appearance when off duty and has been out several times, which is a big improvement.'

Fiona beamed. 'That is certainly good news. The loss of her young man was such a blow. She has been faultless in her work, but still, you can't help but worry.'

'True. And the Irish girls are settling in. Alice has been a great help. Mary is as silly as ever but I admit it was a good idea to make her teach more classes. She may be daft as a brush but she is an excellent communicator, I have to hand it to her.' Gwen pursed her mouth, as if admitting that Mary was useful gave her actual pain.

Fiona nodded. 'I hate to say I told you so, but I did tell you so. You always underestimate that young lady. She has calmed down since she met her army captain. Not broken curfew for ages, has she?'

Gwen stared at the stubborn columns on the paper in front of them. 'No, that is true. The one who's causing problems on that front is Belinda Adams. I caught her earlier this week. I dread to think how many times she's done it; you know they get in through the downstairs window. She's one of the few tall enough to do so without a problem or accomplice, and she might have evaded my notice on other occasions. It's not good enough.'

Fiona frowned. 'Has she a young man, do you know?'

Gwen shrugged. 'Not as far as I'm aware. No, she told me she had lost track of time when meeting her brother. He had some unexpected leave from his squadron.'

'Ah, her brother. A pilot, I understand?' Fiona's face relaxed.

Gwen nodded. 'I believe so. He flies Spitfires.'

Fiona looked at her friend. 'The poor girl must be worried sick, then. We know full well that the losses are being played down in the newspapers and on the wireless reports, but the chances for those brave young men . . . well, let's just say that I'd be inclined to cut her some slack in this case. She must be trying to spend every extra minute with him, as who knows when and if she will have another opportunity?'

Gwen sighed and turned her head a little so that she could stare out of the first-floor window. The rooftops beyond were silhouetted against pale clouds. 'I know, I know. It's desperately sad, and I know exactly how it feels to lose a beloved brother.'

'Of course you do.' Fiona was acutely aware of the personal tragedies Gwen had endured in the previous war. 'So, then . . . '

Gwen raised her hands and let them drop again to her lap. 'But it's standards, Fiona! Let one get away with it, they'll all want to do it. And most of them won't be doing anything as worthy as meeting up with a brother in the services. They'll be out fraternising with unsuitable men given half a chance. Discipline must be maintained.'

Fiona cocked her head to one side. 'Normally I would be the first to agree with you. But in this case I have some sympathy with the young woman. In fact, a lot.' She paused. 'Did you issue her a warning?'

Gwen looked at her feet. 'As a matter of fact, no. I spoke to her sharply, of course, but . . . '

'But actually you let her off. You did feel sympathy, Gwen, I can tell, although it would kill you to admit it.' Fiona's eyes danced with merriment. It was so rare to catch out her punctilious friend.

Gwen refused to concede for a moment, but then she relented. 'Oh well. Yes, if you put it like that.'

'I knew it!' Fiona crowed. 'You're softer than you would have us believe, aren't you?

'Not a bit — ' Gwen began, but then Fiona leapt up.

'I have it! Thinking about something else for a few minutes has worked. I can see where we can save something. Look here, if we just reallocate these payments . . . ' She was bent over the figures again, scribbling as fast as she could, and Gwen could only sit back and marvel at the superintendent's ability to magic something out of nothing.

★ ★ ★

Ron was paying for his rash decision to have another pint at the end of the evening in the pub. What had come over him, he asked himself, as he dragged his hungover body around the warehouse. It hadn't even been a Friday. He'd really let himself go. All right, he was upset about Alfie and worried about his mother, but it was no excuse. He'd go easy in the future, he vowed under his breath. He couldn't face the idea of conversation, and somehow managed to avoid Billy and Kenny until the mid-morning tea break.

'Something wrong, Ron?' Kenny teased, knowing full well what the trouble was. 'Been burning the candle at both ends, have yer?' He grabbed a large mug. 'So you won't be going to the flicks tonight then?'

Ron groaned.

'Look at him, he needs his bed,' Kenny said to Billy.

'Reckon he does.'

'Can't take the pace, not like some of us.'

'Shut up, stop it,' Ron begged. His head was ringing and the noisy docks weren't helping. 'So I had a couple of beers, what of it?'

Kenny was about to start up again when he was summoned by the boss for an urgent task. Billy looked at his woebegone friend with wry amusement.

'Oh dear, Ron. We ought to leave you at home next time.'

Ron wiped his face with his hand. 'Might be for the best an' all.' He dimly recalled that he'd wanted to ask Billy about something. He could feel the cogs in his brain creaking around, rusty as anything. 'Bill . . . that bloke last night.'

Billy frowned. 'Which bloke? There were a lot of them.'

Ron shook his head. 'Don't take the mick. I know I'm in a bit of a state but I remember now. Whatshisname — Joe. The one everyone came to see.'

'What about him?'

Ron wondered if his friend would think he was crazy, or put it down to the hangover. 'Well, he looked familiar. But you said I didn't know him.'

Billy shrugged. 'Well, as far as I'm aware. Suppose you might have bumped into him around the place. He's a bit older than us.'

Ron was gradually piecing together what he wanted to say. 'That pretty nurse with the dark hair, the little one, Edith. Did you say her bloke got killed? At Dunkirk?'

'That's right,' Billy answered shortly.

'And he was Joe Banham's brother.'

'Right again. Harry. He's more our age, we was at school together.'

Ron made the leap he'd been puzzling over. 'When I went to see Alfie, there was a fellow in a really bad way in the same ward. So badly hurt he didn't know his own name, could barely speak. Half his head was all cut up and that. But I spent ages looking at him and the rest of his

210

face and hair ... and don't go mad, Bill. He looked just like Joe Banham. Gave me a proper fright, last night, when I saw him.'

Billy looked sceptical. 'Yep, but you'd had a few, mate. You could have seen a unicorn for all I know.'

'No, I mean it.' Ron took a big gulp of tea. 'All right, answer me this. Did they look alike, the two brothers?'

Billy didn't have to think about that one. 'Yes, everyone said so. Joe was the quieter one, Harry was life and soul of the party, but you couldn't mistake the fact that they were brothers. It can't be right, Ron. Harry's dead. We got to accept it. He ain't coming back no more.'

'So you said. But I know what I saw. I was stone-cold sober when I visited our Alfie. I went twice, remember. There wasn't much to do but stare around the ward. There's someone there who's the spitting image of Joe Banham. Nobody knows his name. I can't say if it's Harry back from the dead. But don't you think it's odd?'

Billy didn't know what to think. Common sense told him Ron had been in no state last night to see anyone properly. Then again, his mate was usually reliable, not given to making things up. He didn't want to let his hopes grow. Harry was dead and nothing would change it. But what if ...

'What do you say, Billy?' Ron pressed. 'Wouldn't it be a miracle? Wouldn't Edith want to know?'

Billy shuddered. 'Don't you go saying nothing to Edie. She's been through enough. She's

211

hardly shown her face all summer; she's only just started coming out again, so don't go giving her ideas. We got to sort this out ourselves. If there's anything in it — and I mean *if*, it's a very big *if* — I'll find out. Don't even whisper it otherwise. Got it?' He was suddenly fierce, wanting to protect the young nurse, but also hoping against hope that there was something in this wild idea. 'Do you promise, Ron?'

'I promise,' said Ron, wondering what he'd set in motion. There was no going back now.

18

Alice could hardly believe that she was going out for two evenings in a row. The last time she'd done that was when she'd been with Mark, back in Liverpool, in those heady days when they'd told themselves that love would conquer all. That had been before he'd joined the International Brigade and set off to fight in the Spanish Civil War. It had turned out that love had come a poor second.

Of course going to the pictures with a group of friends was nothing at all like that, even if one of them was Joe. If she was honest, she wouldn't have gone if he hadn't been there. She'd seen the film already and would happily have opted for a night in. But she had no way of knowing when his next leave would be. If she was even more honest, she would far rather have spent the evening with him alone, talking like they used to. Yet she could hardly expect him to prefer that to a night out with his many friends.

'Come on, Al. Get your skates on.' Edith tapped on Alice's doorframe, where she was leaning, waiting impatiently. 'I've been on my feet all day as well, you know. There's no excuse.'

Edith's day had started badly when one of the patients who had been on the verge of recovery from a chest infection had taken a turn for the worse, and then it turned out Dr Patcham had taken a few days' holiday, and his locum was totally unprepared. 'Made me wish that Dr McGillicuddy was back,' she'd confessed to Mary over dinner. 'He took to Dalston like a duck to water. This one looks as if he's never seen a tram before.'

'Oh, that lovely Dr McGillicuddy used to brighten my day in so many ways,' Mary had said longingly, and Edith had felt so sorry for her that she'd asked her along to the cinema as well.

Now Mary bounded along from her room at the end of the attic corridor. 'Ready yet?' she demanded cheerfully. 'Oh, nice scarf, Edie. Goes with your eyes. When did you get that?'

'Saw it in the market in between patients and I thought I deserved it after the morning I'd had,' Edith confessed. 'Don't look at me like that, Al, I had a bit of time to spare and I wasn't late for my next call or anything. It was hanging at the end of a stall and it called out to me, I swear.' She patted the knot in it.

Alice picked up her old handbag and declared herself ready. She knew she didn't look as smart as yesterday, now she was back to her serviceable pale blue shift dress, but it didn't matter. It was just a night out with friends.

* * *

Kathleen could see the nurses approaching the cinema on busy Hackney Road, and breathed a sigh of relief that the tall dark-haired young woman wasn't one of them. If there was anything between Billy and her, she really didn't want to witness it on her first night out for so long. It would have ruined everything.

There he was now, speeding along the pavement towards her. He had tried to slick down his curly hair with Brylcreem, but nothing could subdue it for long. Still, she could tell he had made an effort, in his smartest light jacket and the shoes he kept for best, not his work boots or heavy-duty ARP ones. She was glad she'd made an effort too. When she'd gone home to fetch Brian's clothes she had taken the opportunity to change into her nicest skirt and the cardigan she had knitted herself from some fine cherry-red wool that Flo had had left over. She'd worried that it would be too bright, too attention-grabbing, but tonight it fitted the mood of celebration. Joe was back amongst them and they were all going to make the most of it.

She couldn't help smiling as Billy drew up beside her, even though she knew she should still be in mourning. He looked at her with such feeling that she almost reached out for him, even though she knew she must not. But there was no harm in basking in that feeling of safety that he always brought to her. Maybe everything would be all right. They'd heard no more from Elsie, and Kathleen was beginning to think the woman's threats had been empty — unpleasant, but nothing to them.

'You look lovely, Kath.' The words were out of Billy's mouth before he could stop them. He was very aware of how her silky cardigan brought out the natural colour of her lips. He mustn't think about that, whatever he did. 'Is everyone here? Where's Edie?'

'She's over there with Alice and Mary. They just got here too.' Kathleen approved of the way Billy had kept an eye on Edith since Harry's death. He was such a good, kind man. Why hadn't she seen it before? She prayed it was not too late for them.

'Here's your ticket, Kath.' Joe came over and handed her the piece of stiff paper. 'We'd better make our way in, there's quite a crowd.' He nodded to Billy and then turned back to the group of nurses. Kathleen wondered if he would make a point of sitting next to Alice.

Sure enough, as they filed through the lovely Art Deco entrance hall, Joe had made sure he was standing next to the tall blonde nurse, while Billy positioned himself between Kathleen and Edith. Clarrie and Peggy arrived in the nick of time and had to squeeze themselves at the end of the row next to Mary.

Billy wanted to savour the delights of sitting next to Kathleen: the way it felt natural for their arms to rest next to one another's; the way their legs couldn't help but touch in the crowded auditorium. As the lights dimmed he could allow himself to dream that they were on their own settee in their own living room in their own home. But he couldn't drift off into a reverie. He had to think. On his other side sat Edith, bravely determined to enjoy her night out, oblivious to the bombshell Ron had dropped. What was he going to do? He couldn't let her suspect a thing. It would break her heart to believe Harry was alive somewhere only to have those hopes dashed. Without knowing he was doing it, he drew away from her a little, moving ever closer to Kathleen.

Edith noticed his arm retract from the armrest they shared, but assumed that Billy was simply being gentlemanly in allowing her to use it. Billy had seemed a little distant but she made nothing of it. She knew he was working long hours and then spending half the night on duty with Stan, and so she reckoned he was entitled to behave how he liked on his time off.

Alice, meanwhile, was basking in the enjoyment of sitting next to Joe, a sensation she'd almost forgotten. She fancied that his arms had grown stronger since the last time they'd sat pressed together like this, and he held himself a little differently — more alert. She hoped he wasn't already thinking about his return to Orkney. She wanted him to make the most of being here, away from the pressures of his work, the demands of service. She'd treat him to something nice to eat at the interval. Somehow she wanted to make tonight special for him, so he'd have it to remember back on his cold ship. Then the fanfare for Pathé News began and she attempted to put aside all other thoughts to concentrate on the latest bulletin. It was only right at the end of the main feature that Joe spoke quietly in her ear. Her skin shivered a little at the touch of his breath.

'I know you'll have to go straight back after this or you'll get in trouble for breaking curfew, but shall we go somewhere tomorrow, just the two of us? I've missed our chats. Don't worry if you're too busy.' Alice flushed at the very idea she might turn him down. She swivelled in her seat so she could face him. 'Of course,' she said quickly, 'I've missed them too.' Her arm brushed against his more forcefully as she turned back, and she was sure his newly toned muscles reacted. She could sense his warmth and it made her secretly smile, even as she leant to pick up her bag as the credits rolled and the crowd began to move towards the exit.

'I'll see you back to your place, or are you staying at Joe's?' Billy asked Kathleen as they allowed themselves to be swept along through the foyer.

'I'll stay with the Banhams. So there's no need,' she said, glad he had suggested it all the same.

'No, but I want to. Anyway, I could do with a word with Stan,' Billy said, trying to make it sound like an excuse, when it was really why he had to come with her. Of course Joe could see her back, but not only was Billy glad of every extra moment with her, he had formulated a plan while watching the film. Half of his brain had followed Tommy Trinder and his antics, and he'd laughed along with the rest of them, but the other half had been working overtime.

He was due some time off from the docks. It had been ages since he'd taken so much as a day. Changing his ARP shift would be harder, but Brendan Richards, the stallholder from the market he'd recruited, was coming into his own, and they weren't quite as stretched as at the beginning of the summer. If he spoke to Stan tonight, without saying why he had to swap, he

218

could go to Portsmouth and see this mysterious patient for himself. The hospital would gladly let him in as a friend of Alfie's family, and he could do Ron a favour and bring along some extra food and clothes for his brother. He just had to plan it well, keep his nerve and not reveal to anyone else what was going on.

'You're quiet tonight, Billy,' Joe remarked as they rounded the corner to Jeeves Street. 'Something on your mind?'

Billy came to with a jolt. He'd almost fallen at the first fence. They mustn't suspect a thing. 'No, no, just a bit tired,' he said as convincingly as he could, with a pang of guilt as Kathleen looked admiringly at him.

'You shouldn't have gone out of your way, you should have gone straight home,' she admonished him gently.

'Not a bit, I'm glad of the walk,' he insisted. 'Anyway, I'll just have a quick word with Stan about some shift problems and then I'll be off.'

'If you say so,' she said dubiously, and Billy's heart beat faster at the secret he was keeping, but knowing he absolutely could not say one word about it.

* * *

Alice's mind was distracted with memories of Joe as she made her way along Dalston Lane the next morning, pushing her bike, so that she didn't see the child in front of her until they almost bumped into each other.

'Blimey! I thought you was going to run me

219

over then,' the little girl exclaimed crossly. 'You got to look where yer going, that's what me gran always tells me.'

With a start, Alice realised who it was. It was one of the pupils she'd met at the local school when she'd been co-opted into teaching them to clean their teeth properly. 'Pauline! I haven't seen you for ages. How are you?'

Pauline scuffed her feet against the dusty pavement. 'All right, I suppose. Me little brother's being a proper nuisance, so I'd rather be out here on me own.' Her eyes brightened. 'I've grown since you last saw me, Nurse, so can I have a go on your bike this time? Me legs are bound to be long enough by now.'

Alice shook her head. 'Sorry, Pauline, but I don't think so. You'll have to do a lot more growing yet. Besides, it's not for playing on. It's to get me from place to place for work.'

'Is that where you're going now?' the girl asked.

'Yes, I should be on my way.' But Alice couldn't go without asking the question she always felt obliged to put to the child. 'Has your gran changed her mind about taking you away from London to somewhere safer?'

Pauline gave her a look of derision. 'She ain't ever goin' to do that, Nurse. She's stayin' put, and she don't hardly go out no more cos her leg ulcers are givin' her gyp. Anyway, you heard her before. She says we'll stay exactly where we are and beat the Jerries and that's all there is to it.'

Alice nodded as it was the answer she had

expected. 'Well, you know if she does decide it would be best to leave, then you can always come to me. I could find someone to help you, you know.'

'Thanks, Nurse, but we won't be needing no help,' Pauline said matter-of-factly. 'This is where we belong, see. That's all there is to it.'

Alice knew that plenty of families had returned after agreeing to be evacuated last year, as the expected gas attacks had not taken place. But, with the battle raging in the skies overhead, and the threat of invasion looming, she was far from convinced they were right. Yet she could not force them to change their minds. All she could do was keep stressing that she was there to turn to if needed. 'I'd best be going. It was good to see you, Pauline,' she said, and smiled as the girl gave her a cheeky wave before running off. Trundling her bike along, she reflected she really had better watch where she was going and concentrate, rather than thinking ahead to her evening with Joe.

★   ★   ★

It took Bridget several minutes to realise that she was lost yet again in the warren of terraced streets that all looked the same to her. So many near-identical houses, their window panes taped against possible bombing, stared back at her. She'd been so sure she was headed in the right direction and that she would recognise the house when she saw it. She had been there before but had approached it from another route. 'You can't miss it,' Alice had told her that first time. 'It's just off Cricketfield Road, behind the pub on the corner.' That had been easy. So where on earth was she now?

Two dead ends and one very dingy alley later, she finally caught sight of the pub, and knew she was in the right area. Now she had made herself late, despite having eaten an early breakfast. That was exactly what she hadn't wanted. Everyone knew that you had to treat diabetic patients as early in the morning as possible as they could not have their own breakfasts until half an hour after the nurse's visit.

Bridget did not like to admit that she was nervous. She tried to tell herself that there was no reason to be; this was a procedure she had performed many times when she'd worked in the big hospital on the outskirts of Dublin, and also when undertaking her district nurse training. Of course in both those situations she had had somebody else alongside her, whom she could turn to for help if needed. Not that she ever had; it was just that knowing the help was at hand made it all so much easier.

She didn't know if it was dreading the visit that had made her lose her way, or if losing her way had made her more nervous about the visit. 'Chicken and egg, chicken and egg,' she muttered as she dismounted her bike and secured it to a lamppost. The fact remained, she did not enjoy giving insulin injections. They were the bane of her life.

Taking a deep breath, and willing her face to appear confident and friendly, she knocked on her patient's door. Millicent Gates opened it at once, ushering her inside with no fuss, as befitted a woman who had had to become used to welcoming nurses into her home on a regular basis. Bridget noted how Millicent had little embarrassment when she needed to check her urine for sugar levels, how the woman simply got on with what had become a normal part of her day. She then began to prepare her delayed breakfast while Bridget wrote up her results and readied the syringe. The wireless was on, with a cheerful woman's voice instructing housewives on how best to cook vegetables, scrubbing but not peeling them to ensure maximum nutrition. Bridget realised it must be 'The Kitchen Front', which some of the nurses had on during breakfast themselves.

She hoped that Millicent had not noticed her agitation and willed her hands not to shake as she entered today's figures on the report. She knew it was her duty to project an image of calm, but sometimes she felt anything but. No wonder: new city, new country, new colleagues, and a whole different way of working. Even if most of the elements were those she knew backwards, the fact that she was performing them on her own, on the district, in people's homes with nobody else watching, made her want to gasp aloud at the weight of responsibility. Didn't they know she was just Bridget O'Doyle, originally from Kilkenny, fourth of five children and often told by her teachers she'd never make anything of her life? How come she was now in charge of such serious matters as the health and well-being of so many inhabitants of northeast London? Sometimes the impossibility of it made her wake at night.

She hadn't told anyone, not even Ellen, whom she'd met in their first week of training at the Dublin hospital. As far as she could tell, her friend suffered from no such nerves. She had settled into working on the district as if she had been born to it: loving the visits to different houses; always coming back with an anecdote about the way a patient had arranged their furniture or planted their garden, eager to swap stories. Bridget had tried to oblige, but often the details escaped her, as she was focusing so intently on doing everything right.

Millicent appeared not to have spotted anything different about today's nurse, as she pottered about, sorting her cutlery in its painted drawer, wiping the countertop with a dishcloth, humming along to a tune now on the wireless. 'My nephew came the other day,' she began, and Bridget nodded, as if she was paying full attention to the small talk. 'He helped me with my Anderson shelter, I don't know how I'd have managed without him, he's very kind to his old auntie.'

'That's grand,' said Bridget, hoping that a short reply would be enough.

'Oh yes, he's always been like that,' said Millicent, and happily related a tale of what the boy had been like when at school. Bridget made the right noises in the right places, but really she was counting the seconds until she had to do the inevitable.

'Right,' she said brightly, 'shall we have your injection now?'

Millicent agreed readily, putting aside her dishcloth and rolling up the sleeve of her housecoat.

Bridget took a deep breath and prepared the syringe, carefully tapping it and then inserting the needle, smoothly and swiftly. 'There you are. All done until the next time.'

Millicent rolled her sleeve down again. 'I don't know how you nurses do it,' she said cheerfully. 'You're so calm and steady. I never even think about it nowadays, and it barely hurts at all. You do wonders, all of you.'

'Oh, it's nothing,' said Bridget, gathering her paraphernalia together. 'All part of the service.'

Millicent shook her head. 'It's far from nothing to me. I couldn't manage without you. It's thanks to you I can lead a normal life. Still,' she gave Bridget a smile, 'I bet you were nervous the first time you did one of those! I bet your hands were shaking!'

Bridget almost let out a high-pitched laugh. If only Millicent knew the truth. She was heartily relieved that the woman evidently hadn't guessed. She had to maintain her confident front. 'They probably were,' she said lightly. 'Now, have you got some sugar put by in case of an emergency? Excellent. Doesn't hurt to be prepared, does it?'

'Very true, Nurse, very true.' Millicent followed her the short distance down the rather worn but immaculately clean hall. 'Will I see you tomorrow, or will it be one of the other girls?'

'I expect it will be one of my colleagues,' Bridget replied, trying to keep the relief out of her voice. 'But I might see you next week.'

Millicent beamed as Bridget freed her bike and got on it. 'I shall look forward to that. I know I'm in safe hands with you, Nurse.'

Bridget set her foot on the pedal in readiness. 'You get in and enjoy your breakfast, and sorry again for keeping you waiting,' she said as she pushed off.

'Thank you for everything!' Millicent called, waving as Bridget started back down the small street.

Bridget exhaled deeply as she rounded the corner back on to Cricketfield Road. She'd done it, the sort of visit she dreaded the most. At least the next patient was a simple case of changing a dressing to a minor burn. Not too much to go wrong there. Then a case of suspected rickets. She could manage that.

Bridget hoped that after a while she would get used to the pattern of work, and laugh off the mistakes while learning from them in the way the others seemed to do. Mary would often recount how she got so lost in her first weeks that she ended up all the way up in Tottenham and had had to call on the nurses' home there to get advice about finding her way back. Bridget would have been mortified to admit such a thing. Surely that would make her seem incompetent and then they would doubt everything else that she did? Yet nobody thought that about Mary.

Bridget was not sure what she could do to help herself. She hated waking in the middle of the night in a panic. Often she would dream of running along a coastal path and then she would look down, only to find that the path had run out and she was running on thin air, the rocks far beneath her, and she knew she had to keep going faster and faster in order not to plummet down onto them. She dared not tell any of the doctors she worked with. They would think she was mad, and question her suitability for the job. She could not tell Gwen or Fiona, who had put their faith in her when choosing her for the post. She would have to face it alone and keep hoping nobody guessed.

Slowly she pedalled along, remembering where to turn for the next patient's house, shivering slightly despite the warm air. She had to make this a success. She could not afford to fail. Too much depended on it.

★   ★   ★

Alice had been uncertain where to go with Joe. She didn't want to return to the Duke's Arms or the café they used to frequent before he'd joined up. She knew deep down it was because she didn't want their precious time together to be interrupted. Two nights of sharing his company had been enough.

She hadn't been able to wash her new blouse and so she reluctantly put on a dress that she felt was old and staid. It wasn't as if he would notice, she was sure, but new clothing was a boost to her confidence. Not that she was trying to make him look at her in that way . . . and yet her sense of her own attractiveness had taken a beating when Mark had chosen the International Brigade rather than her. She had been able to park that uncomfortable knowledge quite successfully at the back of her mind for some time now, but having Joe around somehow awoke all those old insecurities, along with a wish for them not to matter.

'It counts for nothing,' she told herself sternly, tugging at the cap sleeves to straighten them, smoothing the well-worn cotton in now faded turquoise. 'You're meeting a friend, that's all.' All the same, she brushed her hair out over her shoulders, and picked out her sandals with a slightly raised heel rather than her sensible flat ones.

In the end they had decided simply to go for a walk around Victoria Park. Joe met her at the end of Victory Walk and they strolled to the bus stop together, getting off at the Regent's Canal and wandering along the towpath until they reached the park itself. The towpath was narrow, making it tricky to walk side by side, and it wasn't until they reached the park gates that Alice could really turn to talk to Joe.

She had planned to ask him so many questions about what he had done, what he really thought would happen if the cities were bombed, but she ended up breaking into laughter when she realised the significance of where they had come to.

'What is it?' he asked, his dark eyes fixed on hers, but puzzled.

She smiled up at him. 'I just remembered that

this is the place where I first saw you. You know, the day that Edie, Mary and I had brought a picnic here and you and your family were here as well. Edith and Harry set eyes upon one another and that was that.'

Joe laughed as well. 'You're right, that hadn't occurred to me when we agreed to come here. That feels like a lifetime ago.' He grinned ruefully. 'I thought you were one of those stuck-up nurses who think they are better than everyone else.'

'I know.' Alice cast her mind back to their first encounter. 'And I thought you were a proper stuck-up killjoy, making Mattie go home early.' She remembered how indignant she had been, and how furious at the idea he had disapproved of her.

'Yep, that's me,' he said easily, and they smiled more widely at each other, in silent acknowledgement that their friendship had got off on totally the wrong foot. Slowly they turned and began to stroll along, as the leaves on the trees rustled in the evening breeze, not yet ready to change colour and fall. All around the trenches bore witness to the fact of the war.

'Ah well, I know better now,' she said, falling comfortably into step with him, remembering how well their strides were suited. Edith had often complained that she had to run to keep up and it wasn't fair as she had much shorter legs.

Joe had rolled back the sleeves on his pale grey shirt, and Alice could not help but check to see if she had been right in the cinema about his arms becoming more muscly.

'What are you looking at?' he teased.

'They must make you do lots of PT,' she answered. 'Your arms have changed shape, you're like Popeye the Sailor now, I swear it.'

He rubbed them self-consciously. 'You're probably right. Even we engineers are meant to be halfway fit, you know. I'll end up with a physique that even Harry would be proud of. Or maybe not quite that extreme.'

'Perhaps.' Alice was pleased he could say his brother's name so naturally, but still felt a pang of sadness. As a boxer with his eyes on the big championships, Harry had taken his keep-fit regime very seriously, brooking no mockery about it. She couldn't imagine Joe taking it to such lengths.

'It's no bad thing,' Joe went on. 'I want to feel that I'm ready for anything, not just able to mend the telecommunications . . . I shouldn't say any more about what I do, not really.'

Alice looked around. 'There's no one listening. No, you're right, though, best not to get into the habit.' She had a surge of pride that his skills had been recognised, that he was doing something he believed in and that not many men would be qualified for.

As if he had read her thoughts, Joe said, 'Not bad for a bloke from Jeeves Street.'

She looked up at him and nodded. 'No, you're doing well, Joe. We're all proud of you. I for one feel safer for knowing that you do what you do.'

He smiled but almost in embarrassment. From the early days, once they had got over their misunderstanding, their friendship had been based on gentle mockery and shared humour, as well as a mutual love of books. Now she sensed a shift to something more serious.

Harry's cruel fate had underlined that anything could happen at any time. Plenty of young people were rushing into relationships after knowing one another for next to no time. Nobody could say how long anyone would have; what was awaiting any or all of them in the future.

Yet she knew she was not one to rush into anything. Nor, she sensed with every fibre of her being, was Joe. She realised she was keenly attuned to him, to his moods and feelings; whatever else, their friendship was vitally important to both of them. She didn't want to risk it, for so many reasons. For two pins she could have reached out to see how that golden muscled forearm really felt, but something more powerful held her back.

He halted and turned to face her, and to her surprise rested his hands on her shoulders, lightly, but the heat of his touch shot through her. 'And I'm proud of you,' he said, his voice quiet but ringing with sincerity. 'I can't imagine what horrors you've already seen, let alone what might be coming soon. I wish I could stop it, protect you from it — but I can't. And you wouldn't want that anyway, would you?'

She shook her head, certain of that without even having to consider it. 'No. A nurse can't run away and hide. Nursing is what I do, it's who I am.' Before she could explain that she was grateful for what he'd said, surprised that he'd revealed so much in that short statement, that if circumstances had been different, who knew what direction their friendship would take, a group of teenaged boys on bicycles came around the corner of the path and only swerved around them at the last moment.

Joe pulled her to one side, instinctively protective. The boys had long past them before they broke away. Joe smiled down at her, his face strong and handsome and Alice smiled back, comfortable in his gentle embrace.

The spell was broken, yet, as they returned the way they had come and finally said their farewells on the corner of Victory Walk, well in time for curfew, she sensed that their friendship was even stronger now, with an undercurrent of deep connection.

19

Billy didn't know what to think as he stood at the window of the crowded train to Portsmouth. Everywhere he looked there were men in uniform, mostly naval but from the other services too. A couple of soldiers must have been well under eighteen. How had they got through the selection process? Billy's face flushed red with shame as he remembered being turned down just because of his stupid feet.

The train lurched along, any pretence at sticking to the timetable long gone. Billy wondered if he'd even make visiting hours, or whether he would be forced to wait until morning. He had the address where Ron had stayed so he wouldn't be stuck kipping out in a park, but he wanted to get this over and done with. The further he got from London, the more unlikely it sounded. Ron was a good mate and not given to flights of fancy but, really, he had to have been mistaken.

This was one big case of wishful thinking, Billy told himself. If this poor man on Alfie's ward was injured so badly, how on earth could Ron have spotted the likeness? Impossible. Why was he wasting his own precious leave on such a wild-goose chase? And he'd had to lie to Stan — well, not lie exactly, but certainly by omission. He'd allowed Stan to assume it was his own family who had a spot of bother. There had been no trouble swapping shifts, but Billy liked to keep such measures for emergencies as it didn't do to use up all your favours too soon.

This wasn't an emergency, it was a futile waste of time, he thought, flexing his leg muscles and cursing his feet, sore from hours of standing in the same spot. He wished he'd brought more to eat on the journey, and wondered if he could break into the food parcel that Ron's auntie had made, delighted at the chance to send her sick nephew more of her famous gingerbread. No, that would be mean. He knew she'd begged and bartered for the extra sugar coupons for a start. His stomach rumbled at the thought and he cringed with embarrassment. Everyone was so tightly packed together that there was no hiding it.

The young man next to him, in a Fleet Air Arm jacket, turned and grinned at him. 'Sounds as if you could do with a sandwich,' he said cheerily. 'Here, have one of these.' He leant over and opened his duffel bag, drawing out a parcel wrapped in greaseproof paper. 'I've got far too many. My old dear must have thought I was headed for Australia, she's done enough to last a fortnight. It'd be doing me a favour.' He passed them across. 'Ham and mustard do you?'

Billy stared wide-eyed at the offer. He had heard that the war was breaking down barriers and pulling people together but, apart from his voyage to Dunkirk, he had hardly left the East End for the last year, and that had been on a small boat.

'Go on,' the man urged.

'Thanks, I will.' Billy took a sandwich, made of thick-cut crusty bread, and bit in with gusto. It was slathered in butter and the ham was generously sliced. It was like nectar. 'Tell your ma she's a wonder,' he said when he'd swallowed the first mouthful. 'That is the best sandwich I've ever had. That hits the spot, that does.'

The man shrugged. 'We're spoilt where I come from. It's farming country, we don't go short of butter or meat or anything like that. When I'm aboard ship, it's a different matter.'

'I bet,' said Billy, remembering some of the stories Joe had told down the pub about what they'd had to eat in Scapa Flow. A bigger contrast to Flo's home cooking couldn't be imagined.

'What about you?' the man asked, but then one of his companions nudged him in the ribs. 'Ah, sorry, shouldn't ask, should we? Never know who's listening.'

Billy nodded. It seemed strange to be able to accept a sandwich from a stranger but not to tell them where you were from, what you did or why you were going to the same place they were. 'Let's just say I could support Arsenal or Spurs,' he said with a grin.

'And do you?'

'Nah, my old dad was a West Ham man. But really I don't have time to support any of them,' Billy confessed. 'There's Ma to look after, and me job, and the ARP work.' He wondered if he'd said too much, but what harm could that do? He was proud of being an ARP warden. 'You get to see all sorts, doing that.'

The man nodded, and they passed the time in conversation, eating sandwiches now and then, while the countryside turned to suburbs and finally into the buildings of Portsmouth, which the Fleet Air Arm crew recognised. 'Here we go, good old Pompey,' said one. 'Back where all the fun begins.'

Everyone began to pack away their flasks, books, newspapers and remaining food, secure their duffel bags and prepare to leave the train as it finally creaked alongside the platform. Billy smiled and said goodbye, his heart full of trepidation at what he might be about to find. What would be worse: for it to be a complete stranger? Or a Harry too injured and maimed to recognise him, a shadow of his former extrovert self? Was it a mistake to have come? Too late to consider that now, Billy my boy, he told himself, and swung down from the train's high step onto the teeming platform.

★   ★   ★

Kathleen quickly rinsed out the few items of handwashing and looked around for her peg bag. It had been so long since she'd hung anything out in her shared courtyard that she'd forgotten where she'd left it, but there it was, next to her iron in the cramped kitchen. She grabbed it and took the bucket of Brian's clothes over to the line. The weather was taking a turn for the worse and she needed to get this out fast.

She would have to buy him some bigger shirts soon, she thought, straightening the collar of the little checked one he had nearly grown out of. She could put this one aside in case it was useful for Mattie's baby. She had collected a pile of such clothes, believing you could never have too many when children were small, as they had so many ways of making them dirty and needing to be changed. She tugged at a tiny cotton vest to remove most of the creases and pegged that to the line as well.

Mrs Coyne emerged into the yard with a few items of laundry in a basket. 'Haven't seen you doing this for a while,' she observed, making it sound like a criticism.

Kathleen would not let herself be riled by her upstairs neighbour. 'No, I've been helping out my friends with their washing and doing most of mine at their house while I'm about it,' she explained.

Mrs Coyne nodded. 'I thought you was away a lot. Haven't heard your baby for a while.'

Kathleen gave a short smile in acknowledgement.

'I could have sworn there was someone around yesterday,' the woman went on. 'Thought there was noise at your door. Early evening, it was. Expecting visitors, was you? Did you miss them?'

Kathleen pushed her hair out of her eyes. 'Not that I know of. It can't have been important. There was no note or anything like that.'

Mrs Coyne pulled a face as she took a much-patched apron from her basket and straightened up again. 'Oh, my back. It's really giving me gyp. I don't know what I done to it. I blame the rain, look, it's coming in before too long, I can feel it in me waters.' She slowly pinned up the apron, moving cautiously to avoid further twinges. 'Well, maybe I made a mistake, it could have been next door. I didn't look out or nothing.'

Kathleen adjusted her final items, some little socks that had once been white but were now pale grey, with a faded design of rabbits at the heel and toe. 'That must have been it, then. Right, I must get on, the flat needs a good clean and then I should go shopping.'

Mrs Coyne didn't reply, only groaned again as she lifted up her next piece of laundry. Kathleen hurried inside with her bucket and peg bag so that she didn't have to hear any more about the woman's bad back. Although she wasn't lacking in sympathy, she couldn't help but suspect Mrs Coyne was exaggerating, perhaps in the hope that Kathleen would offer to help her too. Doing the Banhams' laundry was one thing; adding the Coynes' to her chores was something else entirely. She didn't owe them any favours, and had no wish to know them any better than she had to. It was bad enough having to hear all their noise through the floorboards.

'Right, all done!' she sang out cheerfully to Brian, who was sitting on the rug under the front window, making a wall out of wooden bricks. He looked up at her, giggled and pushed the wall over.

Kathleen reflected that only a few days ago, she would have panicked at Mrs Coyne's gossip, assuming that it was Elsie chasing after her once more, ready with her threats. Today, though, she felt safer, sure that the woman would leave her alone in future. After all, she didn't have a leg to stand on. Kathleen needed every penny of that pension and she was going to hang on to it.

She wondered whether she should discuss it with Billy, to set her mind completely at rest. She was longing to see him again. That night out at the cinema had been wonderful, a real treat, and extra-special because she had managed to spend so much time feeling him sitting close beside her, bringing that sense of being protected that she loved so much.

Perhaps she could get a message to him to come round, just to be certain. He was so good at reassuring her, with his sensible advice and practical perspective on things. Yes, that's what she would do.

'Shall we build it up again?' she asked Brian, crouching to his level. 'Then we'll sweep the floor, and go to buy bread, and we'll see if Billy can pop by later on. Won't that be a lovely afternoon?' She picked up several of the bricks, and in doing so noticed something shiny under the chair. 'What's that, I wonder?' she asked cheerfully, reaching for it. It was a dark brown button. Brian reached for it out of curiosity, but Kathleen drew it away from him. 'No, let Mummy see, and she doesn't want you to swallow it.' She turned it over in her hand, struggling to recall where it could have come from. Nothing came to mind. Perhaps it came from a visitor's clothes; Mattie or Billy could have dropped it. 'Silly Mummy,' she said, and

Brian laughed, then gave his wide smile. Kathleen felt her heart fill with love. She would never, ever let Elsie do the tiniest thing to hurt her precious boy.

★   ★   ★

Billy glanced again at the pencil sketch Ron had drawn on the back of an envelope, giving directions to the hospital. Billy thought that it was a good job Ron wasn't in the armed services making maps. He'd done his best but he'd misremembered the street names and Billy had gone round in a circle before he realised what had happened. Now he was concerned that visiting hours would be over. It also felt like rain in the air. He walked as quickly as he could, slinging his canvas grip over one shoulder.

He arrived with just twenty minutes to spare. It was a big hospital and Ron's instructions about how to find the ward were about as accurate as his main map, but a helpful nurse pointed out where to go. Billy was by now completely convinced he was on a hiding to nothing, but at least he could see Alfie and report back to his family. He took a moment to take a breath and compose himself. If Alfie was as bad as Ron said, then he wouldn't want to hear frustration and disappointment in his visitor's voice.

As he pushed through the big double doors, he caught sight of the ward matron in her unmistakable uniform and went to let her know who he was.

'A visitor for young Alfred?' she said, her stern face breaking into a smile. 'That will be very welcome, I'm sure. His days must pass very slowly at present. I shall take you across to him.' Billy sensed dread spreading through him and recognised he hadn't really considered what kind of condition Alfie would be in and how he would react. He was about to find out, and felt very underprepared. 'Here you are. Alfred, you have a visitor, Mr . . . Reilly, was it?'

'That's r-right.' Billy stuttered as the shock hit him. Alfie was almost totally bandaged, with just a small gap for the end of his nose and another for his mouth. 'Er, Alfie, it's me, Billy. Billy Reilly, what works with Ron down the docks.' He cleared his throat as the matron walked purposefully off.

'Billy? From down the pub?' The words came out muffled, but otherwise it was recognisably Alfie's voice.

Billy blushed with embarrassment. He really hadn't thought this through. He and Alfie were barely more than acquaintances when all was said and done. The poor man must be wondering why a colleague of his little brother had bothered coming all the way to Portsmouth to visit someone he only met occasionally down the pub.

'Yep, that's it, Alfie.' Billy's mind was racing. 'I had some ARP business down this way and Ron had said you were here, so he's got me being his delivery boy. I got yer auntie's cake in my bag.'

Alfie shifted a little. 'Auntie Ida's gingerbread? I'm very grateful to you, coming out of your way

241

like that. It's very popular round here, I can tell you. The lot Ron gave me went in no time at all. I'm bribing the nurses with it.' The hole over his mouth changed shape a little and Billy realised he was smiling.

'How you feeling, Alf?' he asked, sinking cautiously onto the hard bedside chair. He was tired out from standing all the way and then the swift walk, but didn't want Alfie to know that.

'Not so bad,' said Alfie staunchly. 'Better than when Ron was here. I couldn't hear him very well, did he tell you that? Now my hearing's much improved. They haven't let me take the bandages off my eyes yet, but I reckon I can see the light changing behind my eyelids and I couldn't do that before either. My plan is to have the prettiest nurse standing in front of me when they do take off the bandage, so she'll be the first thing I see. That's why I need the extra gingerbread — to bribe the doctor to do it only when she's on duty.'

Billy relaxed a little against the back of the chair. Alfie couldn't be too bad if he was coming up with schemes like that. 'Good plan,' he said. 'Shall I put it in your bedside cupboard? Then you'll know it's safe for when it's needed.'

'That would be best,' agreed Alfie. 'Be sure to get Ron to thank Auntie Ida for me. She's always on to us to get ourselves proper girlfriends, so you can tell her I at least am working on it.'

Billy was impressed. 'You don't let the grass grow under your feet, do you?'

Alfie snorted. 'I figured that I had better make the most of this. I could either lie here and give up, or use the time wisely. I'm not daft, now that I can hear again I know what they've been saying about me. Well, you can tell our Ron that I'm not about to snuff it, far from it. I'm not even taking as many painkillers as before. I said to them, I can't think clearly on that stuff, so let's be having less of it. I don't need it. My burns are healing, I can sense it. I might not be taking up a career in film once I'm out of here, but I don't intend to be some invalid wheeled around in a bath chair.'

'Glad to hear it,' said Billy sincerely, but his eyes had begun to search the rest of the ward as Alfie spoke. He counted the number of beds, as Ron had told him to. That must be the man he had seen, in the corner. The sheet was pulled over most of him, just one arm slightly raised by a complicated contraption, and there was no way Billy could see who it might be underneath.

Alfie shifted again. 'Don't you worry about me, Billy, and tell Ron and Ma not to either,' he said firmly. 'Now you don't have to stay around here. I can imagine what it's like, rows of us all laid up just like me. Not a pretty sight. It's not that I don't appreciate you coming, God knows I do, but you'll be busy. ARP business was it, you said?' If he didn't believe the lame excuse, he had the good manners not to say so.

'That's right. It's about protecting the docks,' Billy improvised. 'We know you been taking a bit of a pounding down here and want to know how you defended yourselves.'

'Glad to hear it. It's good to know that my little brother will be looked after. When the trouble really starts he'll be right in the firing line, won't he? Well, you both will.' Alfie's voice grew serious. 'Brave men, you are. Sticking to your jobs even when you know the dangers.'

'Nah, we're just doing what we always do. You're the brave one. Flying Spitfires and that.' Billy was deeply moved and for a second he couldn't speak.

'Just doing what I was told,' said Alfie. 'Go on, you get back to your digs or whatever you're doing. Wish me luck with the nurse.'

Billy recovered himself and laughed as he stood. 'Hope the cake does the trick. See you down the Duke's Arms soon, I hope.'

'Bye, Billy. Mine'll be a pint of bitter.'

'I bet there'll be a queue waiting to shout you one,' Billy predicted, picking up his grip. 'Bye, Alfie.' He wondered when the brave young pilot would be well enough to return to the Duke's Arms. Not too soon, by the looks of it. But then, given how determined he sounded, who could tell?

He stepped away from Alfie's bed and then came to a standstill, wondering how to do what he had come for. Noticing him, the matron made her way across the ward. 'Mr Reilly. Is there anything further we can help you with? You will be aware that visiting hours finish very shortly.' She spoke in a friendly fashion but there was a firm warning in her voice.

Billy shuffled his feet. 'Well . . . yes. You might think I'm crazy but . . . '

'Out with it, young man,' said the matron, clearly having no time to waste.

Billy looked at his hands and then dived

straight in. 'That man in the corner. He seems familiar somehow. Do you know who he is?'

The matron eyed him keenly. 'No. I'm afraid we have no idea. We have to keep him heavily sedated as he's had a very bad head injury and he doesn't talk. He has no papers, he came here with nothing, not even his uniform. I believe he was wrapped in a blanket. Why, do you think he is familiar?'

'Ron — Alfie's brother — thought so. We've got a mate who was killed, or that's what we were told. But they never found his body. Dunkirk, it was. So there's an outside chance it could be him.' Billy gulped. It sounded so far-fetched.

The matron looked doubtful but did not dismiss him out of hand. 'The timing would fit. But we had so many young men back from Dunkirk. It is very unlikely; surely you must see that?'

Billy nodded. That was understating the matter. Yet he'd come this far. 'Could I just go a little closer?' he asked. 'Then I could tell, I'm sure I could.'

The matron weighed up her options while glancing at the fob watch attached to her neat uniform. 'Very well. It is my duty to caution you against false hope, however. You do realise the odds are stacked against you.'

Billy could tell his face was going crimson. 'I know. But I can't go home without checking. His family . . . his fiancée . . . they don't know I'm here, but it would mean everything to them.'

'I cannot deny it would be of the greatest help

if he were to be identified,' the matron admitted. 'Now you are not to disturb him. We cannot tell how much he is taking in of his surroundings, or which of his senses are damaged. If you stand on the far side of the bed I will move the sheet.'

Billy, by now almost sick with anxiety, moved to where she had indicated, so that he would be able to see the uninjured side of the man's head.

The matron stepped forward and gently, slowly, lifted back the sheet. It seemed to take forever.

Billy gasped. His hand flew to his mouth. 'Oh my God.' He almost stumbled as he took a stride forward. 'My God. I don't believe it. It can't be.' He turned to the matron, who was wary now, signalling to him to keep the noise down. 'It's him, Nurse. It's really him. It's Harry. Oh my God. Harry's alive. After all this time, Harry's alive.'

20

Kathleen hadn't expected Billy to come rushing round immediately, but when Stan told her he wasn't on duty that evening, she had at first assumed he would turn up at some point, even if only briefly. It wasn't as if it was an emergency; she just wanted his steady reassurance.

The evening crept on and the light began to fade as she sat at her table, attempting to concentrate on darning the rabbit socks. Soon she would have to put up the blackout blind and try to finish the task by candlelight or the gas lamp, which hissed and gave everything a greenish tinge. Brian had fallen asleep in his cot without a fuss, his hair flopping over his soft cheek, his hand outside the blanket grasping his teddy. He was a picture of contentment.

With doubts now threatening her earlier confidence that all would be well, Kathleen caught her breath and prayed that he would continue to be so placid and cheerful. He was making a snuffling sound, deep in his dreams. His hand loosened its grip on the teddy, which rolled back towards the pillow. Kathleen knew that she should count her blessings.

Yet those doubts would not disperse. What if Billy was out somewhere with the tall dark nurse? Mattie had mentioned that her name was Belinda. Kathleen had absolutely no cause to believe he was, and knew that there were a hundred reasons why he might be unable to come round. His mother might need him. He might not have picked up the message. Something could have happened at work. He might, and her heart turned over, have had an accident. What if he was lying hurt somewhere? She couldn't bear it.

But would that be worse than him going out somewhere with Belinda? They could be at the cinema, sitting as close if not closer than she and Billy had done at the Tommy Trinder film. She bit her lip. This was a stupid train of thought. She had to stop it. How could she be so cruel as to think it would be preferable for him to have had an accident rather than see the tall nurse?

If that was his choice, then somehow she would have to bear it. There was no point in being jealous. She had had her chance and had blown it. He deserved somebody special and could easily have grown tired of waiting for her. If that was the case she would have to cope. She had no idea how she would go about doing so, but she might simply have to. Billy didn't belong to her. She had no claim over him. She would have to find the courage to accept it.

★　★　★

Billy could scarcely contain himself, he was so agitated. He hopped from foot to foot, his nervousness causing other people to look at him askance. He was in Portsmouth station, waiting to see if there would be a train back to London that night. He hadn't wanted to go to Ron's friend's digs after the hospital visit. He was too wound up and knew he wouldn't be able to sleep. He had to get back as soon as possible to tell everyone in person. He had debated phoning with the unbelievable news, but had decided against it. The Banhams didn't have a telephone in their house; he'd have had to call the ARP post, which might mean that a vital message got delayed. He could have tried to ring Edith at the nurses' home but, again, that phone was only meant to be for important messages, and he knew how strict the senior nurses there could be.

Besides, he had a feeling that everyone would say he was making it up. It really was almost beyond credibility. He'd spent some time in the matron's office, giving her all the details: Harry's full name, date of birth, home address, names of parents. He'd struggled to recall who he was serving with but remembered the name of the superior officer who had recruited him, a former champion boxer himself. When he had exhausted his store of information, the matron had let him go. She had asked if he had somewhere to stay as it was getting late, and Billy hadn't lied when he assured her he had. He just had no intention of going there.

Rumour had it that there would be a train leaving around midnight or after, and so he'd hung on in the railway station, hopeful of cramming on it with all the other men in various uniforms who were milling around waiting as well. Some looked dog-tired, some were injured, others sat patiently on the platforms playing cards or chatting. Billy was too anxious to get home to talk to anyone. He fought against the frustration that was building inside him. He had to get back, he absolutely had to. This news was too great to keep to himself, but there was nobody here he could share it with.

Eventually there was a flutter of activity on one of the platforms and a train came in, a mixture of battered passenger coaches and open freight ones. There was a scramble as the word went around that this would be the only way back to London until services resumed in the morning, if the lines hadn't been bombed by then. Billy launched himself into the crowds of passengers trying to find a spot. He managed to get on, keeping tight hold of his old grip, but there were no seats to be had. He was left with no choice except to stand in the corridor, but he didn't mind. It was better than freezing in a freight truck. He slipped his hand into his inside pocket and withdrew the last ham sandwich that the stranger on the down train had given him, which foresight had warned him to put away just in case. As he took the first bite, the train set off.

★   ★   ★

It was after dawn by the time the train limped into Waterloo station. All around him passengers were slumped, trying to catch what rest they could in their uncomfortable and cramped positions. Billy shook himself awake, having managed to doze off where he stood for an uneasy few hours. He glanced at his watch and assessed how many people there were on this

250

train, and how many other unscheduled trains were standing at the many platforms disgorging sleepy and rumpled passengers. He reached for his grip, placed firmly between his feet so there was no chance of losing it. He might as well walk. He could be at Jeeves Street in about an hour and would catch all of them having breakfast.

As he strode along, his intermittent night's sleep a thing of the past, he tried to plan how he would break the news. But his mind failed him. It was too much to contemplate, and for a moment he wondered if it had been a figment of his imagination, a strange dream born of the overlong journey. Then he would remember the sight of his friend's face, terribly injured on one side but without a doubt that of Harry Banham.

His body began to flag as he reached Dalston, but his brain was whirring, excited at the good news he was about to bring to the family who had already lived through so many terrible events. Finally he came to the front door. He could hear voices inside — Mattie calling to Gillian to stop doing something, Stan wading in with advice. Billy took a deep breath and knocked.

★ ★ ★

Alice arrived back at the nurses' home early after her morning rounds were finished. She didn't want to be overly optimistic but Dennis, the boy with the tubercular hip, seemed at last able to put a little weight on it. His spirits had picked up tremendously as a result. All the nurses who had worked with him admired his refusal to be downhearted, but now he was able to see genuine reasons for hope. She stowed her bike in the rack and went inside through the back door, wondering if she would have time to read the letter she had picked up that morning. Everyone else was still out and about and their meal would not be ready for some time yet. She recognised Dermot's handwriting and wondered what was happening in his hospital near Southampton.

Winston Churchill had made a stirring address on the wireless, telling the nation that 'never was so much owed by so many to so few', as the brave airmen fought their ongoing battle along the Channel and south coast and, more and more, over the airfields close to London. Dermot must be right underneath the action. While you could hear the guns and see distant planes over the East End, she knew it would be far worse where he was. For a fleeting moment she wondered what Mark was doing and if he was safe, then she dismissed the thought of him.

As she came up the back stairs to the main entrance hall, there was the sound of urgent knocking on the front door. Gwen beat her to it, appearing swiftly from the district room and opening the imposing door.

Billy stood outside. 'Is Edith here?' he said at once, all polite manners forgotten.

Gwen drew herself up to her full height and froze him with a glare. 'Is this a medical enquiry or is it of a personal nature?' she demanded. 'We simply cannot entertain young men coming here to importune our nurses. If you require a nurse, then one will be sent according to our procedure and you may not request a specific one . . . oh, good day to you, Mr Banham.'

The tall figure of Stan Banham came into view and Gwen immediately softened. She very much approved of him and his calm way of working and representing the ARP. 'What can we do to help?'

Stan ascended the steps so that he was on a level with the hall. 'Hello,' he said swiftly, catching sight of Alice. 'Excuse me, but Alice, is Edie here? We have something to tell her that can't wait.'

Gwen drew back in surprise to let the two men pass.

Alice ran forward. 'No, I'm back early, that's all. Whatever is it? Is it bad news?' Surely Edith had already had the worst news she could ever receive. For a moment she was gripped by fear. Was it Joe? But it couldn't be — they would not have asked for Edie if so. She breathed more easily.

'No, no,' Billy said, almost shaking with eagerness. 'Shall we tell Alice, Stan?'

'Yes, Edith will need a friend when she hears,' Stan said, instantly weighing up the situation.

Alice looked blankly at them both.

'The thing is, the thing is . . . ' Billy was still too agitated to form a sentence, despite having shared the news once already.

Stan took over. 'Prepare yourself for a shock, Alice,' he said gently but firmly. 'Harry's alive.'

Alice took a step backwards. She shook her

head, afraid that Stan had finally given in to sorrow and his mind had begun to wander. 'No,' she said, 'that's not right. I know it's dreadful but he died at Dun — '

'No he didn't,' Billy interrupted. 'We thought he did but he didn't. He's badly hurt and nobody knew who he was but I've seen him, Alice, seen him with my own eyes. You wouldn't believe it. He's in a hospital in Portsmouth. He's on lots of painkillers and hasn't been able to talk, but it's him. I wouldn't get that wrong.'

Alice tried to take it in but the change of fortune was too extreme. 'Harry? No, he can't be. After all this time? He's really been there since Dunkirk? Oh my goodness.'

'Alice, take it easy,' Gwen said hurriedly, afraid the young woman would faint at the shock. 'Deep breaths, now. That's it. Come, we'll get some tea from the service room. Follow me, Mr Banham and . . . ?'

'Billy. Billy Reilly.'

'Mr Reilly. This way, if you will.' Gwen swept ahead, clearly happiest at doing something while the shock-waves settled.

'Is it really true?' Alice asked as they went down the back stairs to the lower-ground floor and the big common room.

'I'm not going to make that up, am I?' Billy said. 'I know how you feel, I couldn't take it in when I first heard and I had days of getting used to it before I went and saw for myself. I thought it had to be a mistake but it isn't. When will Edie be back, Alice?'

Gwen led them to a table near the window, the

very one that Edith, Mary and Belinda had all at one time or another climbed through after breaking curfew.

'We can see the bike rack from here,' Alice explained. 'That's where she'll come in, as she's out on her rounds. We all sort out our bikes, then come in the back way for our lunch.'

'I'll fetch you some tea,' offered Gwen, going across to the service room and almost bumping into Gladys as she came through the little door. The young woman's eyes grew wide as Gwen quickly spoke to her, then she broke into a wide smile, nodded and went back into the small room. Gwen followed her, returning shortly with a tea tray. She poured for them all, while keeping an eagle eye out for the bird-like figure of Edith arriving at the bike rack. Outside it was overcast, gloomy for late August, and far from warm.

Alice had to stop herself from drumming her fingers on the table top as they waited, hardly speaking now the astonishing news was out. She tried to think what this might mean. Was Harry going to regain consciousness? How badly would his injuries affect him? Would he be the same devil-may-care young man they had known, or would his experiences have changed his character? She brought herself up short. None of that mattered right now. There would be nothing any of them could do to alter the future, at least not for a while. Then it would be a question of helping Edith and the Banhams as much as they needed, she supposed. Her mind raced, trying to work out what would be best to do, searching for answers when she didn't yet know the exact questions.

Finally Edith came into view, black curls peeping from under her nurse's cap, grabbing her Gladstone bag and heading through the back door.

'Alice! You would not believe the morning I've had,' she began, and then came to an abrupt halt as she noticed who was sitting at the table. 'Hello,' she said cautiously. 'Is everything all right? Have you got a day off, Billy, Mr Banham? It's not Mattie, is it?' she continued anxiously.

Stan came across to her and put his hands on her upper arms. 'Sit down, Edie. We've got news for you, and no, it's not Mattie, she's all right. No.' He waited until Edith sank down onto a chair beside Alice. 'Edith, you will find this hard to credit, but Harry's alive.' He waited until he was sure she had understood. 'It's a miracle, Edith. He's badly hurt but he's alive. He didn't die at Dunkirk after all. Edie, your Harry, our Harry, he's come back to us; he's in hospital but he's alive.'

Edith simply stared at him, her mouth open.

'Did you hear that, Edie?' Alice asked. 'Did you take that in?'

Slowly Edith turned her head to her friend. 'This is my dream again, isn't it? Only this time you're in it. I'll wake up in a minute and then I'll be back to normal.'

Alice smiled, shaking her head. 'No, it's not the dream, Edith. It's different. It's real this time. Harry isn't dead, he's in a Portsmouth hospital, and Billy's seen him.'

Edith frowned. 'What's he doing in Portsmouth?' she said, focusing on the least important detail as everything else was too impossible to comprehend. 'He doesn't know anybody there. He wouldn't go to Portsmouth.'

'I don't think he had much choice,' Billy said. 'Matron said he was one of a load of badly injured soldiers brought on board ship after Dunkirk. He's been there ever since.' He started to explain the circumstances but Edith waved him away.

'No, stop, Billy, I can't take it in. I'll wake up then it won't be true and then it's worse than ever.'

Alice put her hand over her friend's. 'It *is* true, Edith. You can believe it. You aren't going to wake up this time; this is really happening.'

Edith's wild-eyed stare began to relax and she blinked several times. 'No. Really? Al, really? You aren't having me on?'

Alice shook her head, never breaking gaze with Edith.

'I suggest you go somewhere quiet and try to come to terms with what you've just heard,' said Gwen, mindful of the impending lunchtime crowd. 'Go up to my room if you like and I'll have your food sent up. I'll arrange cover for your afternoon calls. Go on, before everyone else comes in and it's pandemonium in here.'

Edith, in a daze, allowed Alice to guide her out of the common room and up the stairs towards their deputy superintendent's big corner room. Alice paused at the bottom of the second set of stairs. 'I'll look after her,' she assured Stan and

Billy. 'When it's sunk in, maybe we will come over and work out what's best to do next. Thank you so much for coming. I . . . I can't believe it either.'

Stan's face creased into a smile. 'Come this evening. Flo has started baking as if he's arriving tomorrow, although she knows that's a long way off. You take your time, Edie. It's not every day you are blessed by a miracle. You take as much time as you need.'

Gwen went to show the men out, muttering her appreciation, all trace of her sternness towards Billy long gone. Alice and Edith slowly climbed the stairs to Gwen's room. At the door, Edith turned to her friend, a confused expression on her face. 'Did that just happen or am I going mad?' she asked. 'Billy and Stan were here, saying Harry's been found alive?'

Alice nodded. 'That's right.'

Edith drew in a long breath and then burst into tears. Alice stepped forward and gave her a big hug, as her friend repeated over and over, 'Harry's alive. Harry's alive.'

21

Edith was desperate to jump on the next train to Portsmouth, but Alice persuaded her otherwise. As they walked back from a very emotional evening at the Banhams', they talked it through.

'From what Billy says, it won't make any difference if you go tomorrow or at the weekend,' Alice pointed out. 'As neither of us is on duty on Saturday that means I can go with you. Wouldn't that be better? And with the trains being so crowded, we'd be safer together.'

'Are you sure, Al?' Edith asked. 'Giving up your day off like that? Won't you mind?'

'Of course not!' Alice insisted. 'Not when it's you seeing Harry again! What could be more important?'

Edith nodded. 'Then thank you. I'd rather you were there. What if I faint or something? That would be awful.'

'You won't,' Alice predicted. 'You're made of tougher stuff than that, Edith Gillespie. Tough as old boots, you are.' She paused at the postbox on the edge of Hackney Downs. In her hand she held a letter to Joe that Stan had written that evening, telling him about Harry.

'Why are you hesitating?' Edith asked, drawing her jacket tight across her chest against the cool breeze.

'I'm not. Well, not really.' Alice shuffled her

feet. 'I just wondered if — given the circumstances — we could ring him first.'

'How?' Edith was baffled. 'He could be anywhere by now, couldn't he?'

Alice nodded in acknowledgement. 'He could. But if he's still at his base we could get a message through. He gave me a number, for emergencies.'

Edith's eyebrows shot up. 'He did?' She knew this was highly irregular. 'You didn't say anything about it before, not even to Stan and Flo.'

Alice looked a little embarrassed. 'I know. I don't know if he was meant to. He was worried about Mattie — she told him she'd had that scare. He wanted to know as soon as anything happened, good news or bad. So he let me have the number in case I could call from the home. I promised not to use it except for real emergencies, but don't you think this is one?'

Edith couldn't hide her surprise. 'Blimey. He . . . he must think a lot of you, Al, to trust you with something like that.'

'It made sense, that's all, because we have access to that telephone. He knew I wouldn't misuse it or anything.' As ever she tried to play down the close connection she and Joe shared. It was hard to explain to anyone, even Edith. It was nothing like the intense passion she had had with Mark, and nothing like Edith and Harry's blazing love affair, but it was something deep and real. Him giving her the number proved it. 'So I thought, he'll want to know, won't he? And the letter might take ages to reach him. I could telephone tomorrow morning and ask to get a message for him to call the home either at lunchtime or when we're back in the evening. Do you think it's a good idea? I hope Gwen and Fiona won't be cross.'

Edith thought back to Gwen's reaction earlier that day. 'They won't be.'

Alice made up her mind and posted the letter with a flourish. 'There, that will reach him at some point. But tomorrow morning, I'll ring his base.'

★ ★ ★

It was a good job Billy had warned them about what the train was going to be like, Alice reflected, as they descended onto the platform of Portsmouth Harbour station. Being forewarned, they had packed plenty of fish-paste sandwiches, which Gladys had helped them to make because she was so excited about them going to visit Harry. They had also borrowed thermos flasks from the kitchen and filled them with tea, to keep their spirits up. Just before they had set off, Bridget and Ellen had found them and presented them with a small box. 'We had some ingredients left over from Joe's 'welcome home' cake,' Bridget explained, 'so this is a very small version.'

'We'll take it to the hospital,' Edith decided at once. 'Even if Harry can't eat it, his nurses can. That's perfect.'

Somehow they had managed to keep the box from getting squashed, and Edith now carried it gingerly along the heaving platform. Alice stuck close to her side, afraid that the crowds would separate them and then she would have no idea of where to go. Edith had the map that Billy had given them, carefully redrawn from Ron's attempt, this time with the correct street names.

They were swept along to the station's exit and disgorged onto the street beyond, at which point they could gather themselves and work out in which direction to head for. 'Are you sure you want to walk?' Alice asked.

Edith gave a little laugh. 'You don't have to treat me as if I'm sick, Al,' she chided. 'I'm nervous, of course, who wouldn't be, but I am all right. I'd rather walk. It was kind of those sailors to give us their seats, but we've been sitting down for hours. I need to stretch my legs.'

'Then by the looks of it, it's this way.' Alice pointed at the map and then at the road across from them. 'Over there.'

As they strode along, pausing only to consult Billy's drawing, Alice remembered the disbelief in Joe's voice as she had told him the news. With Fiona's permission she had rung his base immediately after breakfast on Thursday, and persuaded the clerk at the other end that this was no sentimental telephone call but a serious matter. Joe had called back while she was on her lunch break, just as she had hoped he would.

'Whatever's the matter? Are you all right, Alice? Is it Mattie?'

'I'm fine. Look, I can't stay on the line for long, but it's not Mattie, Joe. Prepare yourself for the most astonishing news. It's Harry. He's not dead after all.' And once Joe had protested his disbelief and then calmed down, she filled him in on the basic details. 'A letter from your father is on its way, but we're going down to Portsmouth on Saturday, Edie and me. How about that?'

There had been a pause as Joe drew a breath. 'I wish I was going too,' he sighed, his voice full of emotion. 'Give him my regards, won't you. Thank you for telling me, Alice. I'm so glad you thought to ring. I don't know if I would have believed it in a letter, it's too unlikely. Hearing your voice makes it real.'

Alice had silently thanked heaven that she had done the right thing.

'You go on, now. I know you've got to keep that line clear. But thanks again. I hope we see each other again soon.'

'So do I, Joe. Bye.'

For a fleeting moment she wondered if he would be granted extra leave to come down to see his brother, but then recognised that it would be very unlikely. How she would have loved to see him again. Those four days of his last leave were fading fast. There was no question about it; everything felt better when he was there. She felt alive in a way she never did otherwise. But at least she had managed to speak to him.

Now she wondered what lay in store for them at the hospital. She had tried not to dwell on it, as the very fact that Harry was there at all was cause for celebration. Yet she knew they must not get their hopes up. He would be unable to react to them; he might well not know they were even there. How would Edith cope with the stark reality of that? All Alice could do would be to comfort her if needed.

As they drew closer to the hospital, Edith's excited chatter faded and she sank into silence. Alice glanced at her friend's face. Edith was chewing her lip.

'What's the matter?' Alice asked gently.

Edith shook her head. 'I'm just a bit nervous, that's all. Not knowing how he'll be. I'm expecting the worst, you know. I don't expect him to hear my voice and suddenly sit up or anything like that. But I'm dreading it as well as longing to see him, so I feel a bit strange.'

Alice slipped her arm through Edith's. 'That's why I'm here. It's going to be a real mixture of joy and sadness, isn't it? You'll cope, Edie, that's what you do best.' She tried to keep any of her own trepidation out of her voice. That would not help at all. 'This must be it, behind those big gates. Yes, there's the sign. We go in and follow the main corridor.'

Edith swallowed hard. 'Right you are, then.' She broke into a swift, determined walk that left Alice struggling to keep up.

★ ★ ★

Edith's nerve almost failed her as she reached the double doors to the ward. Part of her was terrified at what she was about to see. Now that the shock of the news had faded, the grim prospect of what lay ahead taunted her imagination. Harry, terribly maimed, unable to speak, hear or see, a living corpse. She gave herself a mental shake. Nothing good ever came of letting your imagination run riot. She had to face the truth, whatever that turned out to be. Pushing open the big doors, she went in.

Quickly she found a nurse to direct her to the right bed. She passed by several injured men, bandaged or in traction, before drawing up to the corner bed. She could sense Alice right behind her, ready for whatever came next. There he was; this must be him. He was lying on his back, with one heavily bandaged arm raised, a sheet almost covering his head. Cautiously, she lifted the sheet a little away from the face, and took a short gasp of breath.

Half of his face was blistered and scarred, and she could not begin to think how that had happened nor how painful it must be now. Yet the other side of his face was her Harry, the handsome features still there, the hair on that side the gorgeous wavy chestnut brown, envied by every woman they knew. His eyes were closed, but the professional side of her noted that his breathing was regular and easy. Even though he was so heavily sedated, she took that as a good sign.

The nurse who had directed her came across, temperature chart in hand. 'Were you warned what to expect?' she asked quietly.

Alice answered for them both. 'Yes, we know he's not responding.'

'Yes, nothing has changed in that regard, although we have begun to reduce his pain medication now that we can address him using his name. We hope for a reaction soon,' the nurse said, deliberately cheerful.

Neither Alice nor Edith was fooled. They used that tone themselves.

Edith pulled up the hard wooden bedside chair and sat down. She reached across to take Harry's unbandaged hand. 'Hello, Harry,' she said, just as she would have done if she'd arranged to meet him at the local café. 'It's Edie. Alice and me have come to see you, to see how you are. Isn't that right, Al?'

If Edith could speak normally, then so could Alice. 'Yes, we came on the train.'

'Took us ages, it did,' Edith chipped in.

'Joe sends his regards. I spoke to him a couple of days ago,' Alice added.

'And your parents, of course. Mattie as well. You should see her; she's big as a barrage balloon. Only a few weeks to go now. You'll have a new nephew or niece very soon.'

Alice stepped back. Now she had said a few words, she wanted to give Edith some privacy. 'I'll just see if there's somewhere to buy a cup of tea,' she whispered to her friend. 'I'll bring one to you if I can.' Discreetly she slipped out.

Edith nodded, but her eyes never left Harry's face. Now that she could see the damage she was no longer afraid. This was still the Harry she loved with her whole heart, and if one side of his head was hurt, underneath it all he was the same man. He was more to her than just a handsome face — although that had been a big part of the initial attraction. Besides, he would always be handsome to her. She squeezed his hand.

'Harry, I'm so sorry you're lying here like this,'

she said softly, with a slight tremor in her voice. 'I don't know if you can hear me, but it doesn't matter. I'll keep coming back and telling you until you can. It won't make any difference to me, you know. I'll love you just as much. Even more, in fact, because you were so brave.' She fought down a sob at the thought of what he must have gone through but regained control and spoke again. 'You make sure you hurry up and get better for me, Harry. I can't wait. You and me, we're going to do everything we said we'd do, and more besides. We've got our lives ahead of us, Harry Banham, and one accident off Dunkirk isn't going to stop us.' She scanned his face for any trace of recognition but there was none. 'You've got to recover as the family need you. We all do. Billy says hello — did you know he'd been to see you? We brought you a cake. I'll tell the nurse who brought us here where to find it.' She paused to put the box in the bedside cabinet.

Taking his hand again, she resumed. 'I thought I'd die as well when I first heard you were missing. We all thought you were dead. These have been the worst few months of my life, knowing I'd met you and then lost you. Now you're here, I feel the same about you as I always did and I love you with all my heart, Harry. You hang on to that and get better for me.' She squeezed his hand again and leant forward, planting a tender kiss on his temple.

His face remained impassive, although she willed with all her might for it to show some kind of recognition. Then, so slight that she could almost have imagined it, she felt a pressure in her fingers.

Harry was squeezing her hand. He had heard her. He knew who she was.

★   ★   ★

Flo paced anxiously around the kitchen, unable to settle. First she rolled up her sleeves, then she rolled them down again. While Mattie had been downstairs she had done her very best to hide her nervous energy, but now Mattie had gone up for an early night, she could not sit still. She turned on the wireless, and the sound of Arthur Askey rasping out 'Bless 'Em All' filled the room. Usually she loved him, but tonight she switched him straight off again.

Finally she gave in and turned to Stan, who was for once not on shift.

'Do you think they're back yet?' she asked. 'Wouldn't their train have come in to Waterloo by now?'

Stan shook his head. He was every bit as keen as his wife for news of their son, but understood the difficulties. 'You know what Billy said about that train line,' he pointed out. 'We can't pretend it will keep to a normal timetable. They could be anywhere. If they get back late they won't come here, they'll need their sleep. The soonest we can reasonably expect to see them is tomorrow.'

Flo shut her eyes for a moment. 'Yes, he said it took ages, but what if they are back? Maybe they are already in Victory Walk but too tired to come over. Why don't you go over and see, Stan? You could ask that nice superintendent. You wouldn't need to disturb them if they've already gone to bed, but at least we'd know.'

Stan sighed. He was torn between the urge to hear the latest as soon as possible and the temptation of sitting in a comfortable chair in his own home for an evening. However, he could see that his wife would not settle while this was on her mind. Wearily he got up.

'There's no guarantee I'll find out anything,' he warned her, reaching for his light jacket. 'They're probably stuck in a siding somewhere.'

'I do hope they thought to take enough food and drink,' Flo fretted.

Stan could see she was getting herself into a state, which didn't happen often, but he recognised the rare signs. 'Bit late now,' he replied. 'But this is Edie and Alice we're talking about. They're sensible, they'll have packed enough to see them through any delays. Don't you go worrying about that.'

'You'll hurry back to tell me, won't you?' Flo asked.

'Of course.' Stan planted a kiss on the top of his wife's head. 'Now you stay here and I'll be back as soon as I can, then we can have a drop of tea and go up together for once.'

Flo saw him to the door and watched as he walked quickly down to the end of Jeeves Street to the main road.

Stan's long legs took him swiftly towards Victory Walk, although he doubted very much that the two nurses would be there when he arrived. The night air was marked by the anti-aircraft defence lights, piercing the black of the sky. Billy's account had made it clear that they would be very lucky to be home in anything like normal time. He was far from happy at the idea of the pair of them wandering around the centre of London in the dark, unable to find transport if they were very late, but there was little he could do about it. They were used to tackling difficult situations and looking after themselves. He just hoped there would be no enemy attacks. Earlier in the day they had heard gunfire from further east and towards the dockyards, and he was mindful that a bomb had been dropped on Harrow just a few days before. There had also been attacks on production factories in Portsmouth. Still, he reminded himself, the odds were that nothing out of the ordinary would happen this evening. There was no reason to believe that 24 August would be any different to any other night.

Before he rounded the last corner, someone called out to him. 'Stan! That you?'

Stan turned in the direction the voice had come from and saw a figure in ARP uniform, holding a shielded torch. It was Brendan Richards, the recent recruit from the market. 'Good evening! How's it been so far?' he asked affably.

'Not so bad around here, all things considered.' The man paused, as if debating whether to go on or not. 'However, we've been getting reports of heavy bombing on the south coast. Didn't you say your son had been found alive in a hospital down there somewhere?'

Stan swallowed hard. 'That's right. In Portsmouth.'

Brendan's face fell. 'Ah, well, that's where they say the worst of the bombs fell. Hope they haven't gone near the hospital.' He realised too late what he was saying. 'Well, they're bound to go for the docks or more factories, aren't they. That would make sense. Or the train station, somewhere like that.'

Stan nodded briefly. 'Thanks for telling me. I must get on.'

'Of course.' Brendan deferred to his more senior colleague. 'I'll carry on with my rounds, then. Good night.'

'Good night,' Stan said, now consumed with worry. It made no sense to bomb a hospital, but how accurate were the raiders? What sort of light conditions had prevailed over the south coast and what time had it happened? His colleague would have had no idea of Edie and Alice's trip, and so he had meant nothing by mentioning the station, but Stan's heart turned to ice. He ran up the stone steps to the nurses' home front door and knocked firmly.

Even at this hour there was an almost immediate response, as the nurses never knew when their services would be needed. A young woman he didn't recognise admitted him and promised to find Fiona. The only thing he registered about her was that she had lots of freckles and an Irish accent.

Fiona ushered him into her office with her usual brisk efficiency. 'You'll have a cup of tea, Mr Banham? Or something stronger?' she offered, her eyes bright.

'No, not this evening, thank you.' He ran his

hand through his greying hair as he took the seat she indicated. 'You'll know why I'm here, I'm sure. Are they back yet, Edith and Alice?' He was hoping against hope they had beaten the odds and found the one train running on time.

Fiona gave a small frown. 'Why, no. But I wasn't expecting them yet, to be honest. You know as well as I do what the transport situation is like.'

Stan nodded ruefully. 'I do indeed. I thought it was worth checking though. As it happens I've just heard some rather disturbing news.' He repeated what his colleague had told him, trying to play down his fears, but Fiona knew him too well to miss the slight tremble in his voice.

She set down the glass of water she had been holding. 'Well, that is a cause for anxiety, I agree. That was all he said? Nothing more precise?'

Stan shook his head and Fiona tutted. 'Very frustrating, not to have more definite news. Well, there is no point in worrying when we don't know the full facts,' she declared resolutely. 'We have no actual reason to suspect Alice, Edith or your son have come to harm. So we must remain optimistic.'

Stan nodded, but knew full well they were both thinking the same thing. How cruel it would be to have Harry returned to them after months of believing him dead, only for him to be killed by a bomb in what should have been a safe place. And then there was the pressing question: if Alice and Edith had not yet returned to the nurses' home, where were they?

22

They had never seen, heard or smelled anything like it. The smoke was so acrid they could almost taste it. The skies towards the south of the city of Portsmouth were orange with the flames, and the noise of crashing and crackling as buildings caught fire or collapsed was overwhelming. For a short while Edith and Alice simply stood and stared at the conflagration before them, unsure what to do. Then good sense and survival instinct kicked in.

'We can't stay here in the open,' Edith gasped. 'Come on, there must be public shelters somewhere.'

'I wish we'd checked,' fretted Alice, who liked to be well prepared. 'There must be ARP wardens here too, mustn't there? We need someone like Stan or Billy.' As they made their way back along the main road which led from the hospital in the direction of the station, they scanned the crowds, who all seemed to be rushing to every point of the compass. It was still only early evening and daylight, and yet the air was thick and murky, making visibility poor. Alice's eyes itched from the smoke but she knew rubbing them would make it worse.

'There. Look, over there.' Edith had spotted the distinctive uniform and hurried across to the ARP warden, catching Alice by the elbow and bringing her along too. 'Excuse me! Excuse me!'

The warden turned and to their surprise it was a woman, taller than them but not dissimilar in age. 'How can I help?' she asked, friendly but to the point.

'We're trying to reach the station to get back to London,' Edith explained.

The woman grimaced. 'Don't get your hopes up. It's been bombed and you won't find anything running from there for some time. Do you have somewhere you can go?'

Alice thought for a moment, then shrugged at Edith. 'We might as well help out, then. Are there heavy casualties?'

'We don't know yet but bound to be,' the warden said starkly. 'How can you help?'

'We're nurses,' Edith explained. 'District nurses. In the East End of London, usually.'

The warden nodded. 'Then I dare say your skills will be useful. Do you know where the hospital is?'

They both nodded. 'We've just come from there. We were visiting — '

The warden cut Edith off. 'Then your best course of action is to go back there and see where you can be placed. It's away from the path of the raid and so far safer than trying to head into the centre. I'm sorry but I must be off. Good luck.' She strode off to where another warden was calling her, beckoning urgently. The pair of them disappeared into the murk.

Edith looked at Alice. 'Will that be all right? Will they even believe us?'

Alice sighed. 'I don't know but they could always telephone Victory Walk, I suppose. I didn't bring my badge but I talked to the matron when I went to get the tea earlier and we discussed how different her cases are to what we've been seeing — I'm sure she believed me; it's not exactly the sort of thing you'd make up.'

Edith gave a short laugh. 'That tea probably saved our lives. If we'd gone straight back to the station after seeing Harry, then we might well be goners.' She sent up a silent prayer. After Alice had left her alone at Harry's side, she had held his hand for what felt like ages, telling him over and over again how she loved him and would be waiting for him when he got better, and her reward had been another gentle but unmistakable squeeze from his hand. Finally, a young, dark-haired nurse had come over and gently pointed out how long she'd been there and that Harry needed to rest. 'You can come back another time,' she suggested.

Edith had felt like crying but had not given in to the wave of emotion. Instead she explained that she had to return to London and her job, and that the next visitors would most likely be his parents. 'But I'll write,' she vowed. 'Would you be able to read the letters to him, Nurse?'

The young woman had beamed. 'It would be a privilege. I'm sure it's done him good, to hear your voice. Say your goodbyes now, but I'll make sure he gets your letters. Don't worry about that.'

Edith had held herself together as she left the ward, feeling a little guilty at not speaking to Alfie, but too wrung out by the events of the day to attempt a new conversation. She had met

Alice coming the other way along the corridor, bearing cups of tea, and they had sat on a bench near the ward doors, sipping in silence. It was only when she felt ready to face the world that Edith had stood once more. Those precious minutes had quite possibly saved their lives.

★　★　★

Back at the hospital, everything had changed. Ambulances were arriving, stretchers being lifted from them before the drivers set off back into the centre of the action for their next patients. Edith and Alice cautiously approached the main entrance, looking for anybody senior. By chance the matron Alice had spoken to earlier spotted them and came hurrying over.

'So you didn't get very far?'

'We've been told the station has been bombed and there won't be any trains, so we thought we could make ourselves useful here. If you'll have us, that is.' Alice was suddenly aware that they didn't look much like nurses, as they were in their cotton summer dresses and light cardigans, all of which were smudged with soot.

'The poor souls.' Matron took a moment to absorb the bad news. Then she was all determined energy. 'Right, well, some of our evening shift have failed to turn up, and I'm not about to speculate what might have happened to them, but you can indeed be of use here. You'd better come with me and I'll find someone to fetch you spare uniforms and show you where to get cleaned up — you can't go near patients in your frocks; we must maintain a professional appearance.' Gwen would have loved this woman, thought Edith, as she followed her through the entrance hall and down a short corridor that smelt of disinfectant. 'District nurses, you said? So you'll have had experience of all sorts of patients? Good. You — Miss ... Lake, was it? — will be needed on the women's surgical ward; they're very short of staff. You, Miss Gillespie, come with me, you're going to the children's ward. I trust neither of you are squeamish. Get changed, and prepare for a long night.'

★ ★ ★

It had been a long time since she'd been on a ward and, as Alice put on her loaned uniform, she wondered how she would adapt. The uniform was slightly too short and loose around the waist, but she supposed nobody would be paying it much attention. It would be the least of their worries.

With one of the local nurses escorting her to the ward and then leaving her to the overworked staff nurse, she had little time to dwell on it. Within moments she was comforting a woman in her late twenties who was recovering from having her appendix removed and very worried about the young family she'd had to leave in the care of their aunt. 'What if they've been hit, I'll never forgive myself,' she moaned, as Alice firmly took her hand.

'Now, you had no choice in the matter,' she

said kindly but firmly. 'When an appendix needs to come out, it needs to come out. You would have been in far greater danger if you had not come in to hospital, and that would have been no good for your children at all. Try not to move around so much,' the woman was twisting under the bedclothes in her distress, 'you don't want to break your stitches. The very best thing you can do for your family is to get well again as quickly as you can.'

The woman responded to Alice's calm authority and sank back against her pillows. 'Yes, Nurse. I know that, but it's so hard.'

Alice nodded. 'I'm not saying it's easy. Everyone will be shaken up by today's events but we can't change them. You have to concentrate on getting back on your feet again, and the only way to do that is rest. Will you try to do that, difficult though it is?'

The woman nodded meekly. 'I will, Nurse.'

Alice quickly filled in the woman's latest details on the chart at the foot of her bed and then moved on to the next bed, where an older woman lay sleeping. She filled her water jug and set it down quietly so as not to wake her. She went from bed to bed down the side of the long ward, checking the current patients were as comfortable as possible before the inevitable happened and casualties from the bombing raids began to filter through from the operating theatre.

'Over here, Nurse.' Alice was summoned brusquely by a young doctor, evidently keen to get back to surgery and hand over his patient.

'Kindly see to it that this lady is kept as still as possible until the next ward rounds. Here are her notes.' Thrusting them into her hands he was off, and Alice was left to decipher the scrawled handwriting. The woman had been crushed by a falling brick wall and had had both legs operated on. They were safe under a raised cage but Alice could see the rest of her needed attention; there was still a strong smell of smoke about her and she had bruises all over. Gently Alice washed her down, using a cold flannel to help reduce the inflammation, but she had barely finished when she was needed to attend to the next arrival.

The hasty surgery had dealt with the worst of this woman's injuries but not the minor ones, and Alice did her best to stop the loss of blood from the many deep cuts. She squeezed her eyes shut in an effort not to imagine the flying glass that must have caused them, pushing away the terror of being caught in a blast so strong it would shatter all the windows around. She couldn't let herself become mired in such a nightmare. If she let herself think about the bombers returning, flying over the hospital, then she could do no useful work at all. So she steeled herself to continue, swabbing and bandaging, all the while murmuring words of comfort without knowing if the woman could hear her.

This was the pattern for the next few hours; she scarcely had time to think, let alone build up a calming rapport with each patient. She was thankful that her training kicked in and she rarely had to ask what the next step would be; the most difficult thing was to remember where everything was kept, and her temporary colleagues' names. The familiar routine of assessing each patient, deciding what best to do and then doing it was the greatest help in simply keeping going.

It was the same for Edith over in the children's ward, which had seemed fairly quiet to begin with, and several beds had stood empty. That was not the case for long. Edith flew from small patient to small patient, comforting where she could, reassuring them that they were in the best place. Some cried pitifully for their mothers and Edith could only hope that the families had not been destroyed. The job of reuniting the children with their parents would fall to someone else, and she could not let herself even think about that as she fastened bandages, fetched soft toys to distract the youngest ones, and made careful notes about everything she did. The effects of the bombing raid had been indiscriminate and the children were suffering injuries as horrific as those of the adults, and Edith knew that for many this would be the first of a long series of nights in a hospital.

In all of this she had absolutely no time to think about Harry and the whirlwind of emotions that had assailed her earlier in the day. In a funny way, this was the best remedy to stave off worry about his future — knowing she had to get on with the job in hand, that she must do everything correctly and accurately but at top speed. There was no let-up whatsoever. If she had stopped she would have dropped with exhaustion, and so she did not stop. She barely had time to meet her fellow nurses, pausing only to ask, 'where's the witch hazel?' or 'can we give this child water if he wakes?'

None of the regular nurses had time to express surprise at a stranger in their midst, as they were just glad of another and obviously highly competent pair of hands. Occasionally one would frown at Edith's questions and then apologise, forgetting in the heat of the moment that the newcomer would not know some of the details of the ward. There was simply no time for the usual getting to know each other and all of the minor disagreements that might crop up. The hospital was stretched to its limits and everything else could wait.

★   ★   ★

Dawn was breaking over the ravaged city and its dim light filtered through the makeshift blinds — spare sheets pinned over a draughty window at one end of the large store room. Alice and Edith, along with several other temporary nurses, had been given this space to bed down in for a few hours. Edith stretched and her hands collided with the edge of a cupboard. It took her some moments to remember where she was. She had fallen asleep in her borrowed uniform, her pillow the cardigan she had chosen with such care just in case Harry had been in any state to see what she looked like. Now it was rolled up any old how under her head. She was lying under a scratchy hospital blanket, and all her limbs ached. She didn't care. The previous day was coming back to her. She had seen Harry and he had recognised her voice. She and Alice had narrowly avoided becoming caught up in the raid that had devastated Portsmouth station and more besides, and then they had worked themselves beyond what she would have believed possible until directly ordered by the matron to stop and catch a few hours' sleep.

Carefully, so as not to wake the others, she crept to the door, clutching her frock and shoes. She tried to remember where the bathroom was, found it and hurriedly washed her face in cold water to try to fully wake up. Then she washed all over as best she could with the rough pink carbolic soap. She caught sight of herself in the mirror and sighed. While they had carefully packed their bags with extra food and drink, they had not thought to bring hairbrushes. She scraped her fingers through her dark curls to try to bring them into some semblance of order.

Back in the would-be dormitory, everyone else was awake and a new matron had arrived. 'We cannot thank you enough,' she was saying. 'Now you will want to return to your own hospitals or places of work. Miss Lake, Miss Gillespie, there's a van leaving the front gate at eight thirty which will be taking supplies up to central London. I suggest you avail yourselves of that, as from what I hear there will be little chance of trains. There is also the complication that the West End was bombed last night, and so you might find transport at that end a little tricky too. Still, you have shown yourselves to be enterprising young women so I'm sure you'll think of something.'

With that she swept out, leaving Alice and Edith open-mouthed.

'The West End,' Edith said with dread. 'I wonder what happened — how many were hurt. I hope they haven't damaged Lewis's. I was counting on them to have something wonderful for when Harry wakes up properly.'

'I suppose we'll find out soon enough,' said Alice soberly. 'Come on, we've got to return those uniforms to be cleaned.'

'There must be a caféteria somewhere; I'm starving.' It suddenly hit Edith that — apart from their extra sandwiches — she had eaten nothing since leaving the train, which seemed like another lifetime ago.

'There is, I got the tea from there yesterday. I'll show you,' Alice said. 'I could do with something myself.'

Edith grinned as an idea struck her. 'Do you think we could go past Harry's ward?'

Alice frowned. 'It isn't exactly visiting hours, you know.'

Edith shrugged. 'Yes, but I'm not a visitor now, am I? I'm staff. Anyway, I bet after last night they won't say no. It wouldn't have to be for long.'

Alice nodded. 'All right. Tell you what, we'll see if there's anything for breakfast then you persuade whoever's on shift to let you in to see Harry. Meanwhile, I'll try to find a telephone to call Victory Walk. I don't know if they'll have heard about what has happened here. If they haven't, they'll be worried about where we are, but if they have it'll be even worse.'

Edith's face fell. 'I hadn't thought of that. Yes, that's a good idea. Then we'll still be ready for this mysterious van at eight thirty. Good job it isn't a limo. I'm not sure either of us look the part.'

'Speak for yourself,' said Alice, and she turned to head for the canteen.

23

Gladys had come in to help with breakfast at the nurses' home even though Sunday was meant to be her day off. She could have stayed away but there would be no peace in her house and she wanted to catch up on reading the *Queen's Nurses' Magazine*. She still found it hard to make out the longer words and felt that she was far too slow, but she was determined to persevere. Once her sister reached her next birthday, Gladys had decided she should formally sign up for the civil Nursing Reserve and do more to help the war effort that way. Making porridge for the district nurses no longer felt like enough.

She heard the telephone ringing but, before she could run up the stairs to the hallway, somebody else answered it, so she returned to the article she was painstakingly making her way through. Now and again she became stuck but refused to give up, skipping a very difficult word if she had to. It was frustrating, but she had to try to get to the end. She had promised herself that she would. 'Otherwise I might as well have stayed in bed,' she muttered under her breath.

A noise from the service room startled her and she looked up. It was one of the Irish nurses. Although they had their own kitchen next door, they usually came over to the main building for breakfast, but sometimes they sorted themselves

285

out at the weekend.

'Hello — it's Gladys, isn't it?'

Gladys nodded. 'And you're Bridget, aren't you?'

Bridget smiled. 'You remembered. It must be hard, keeping up with all of us coming and going. I bet you've met lots of nurses as they pass through this place.'

Gladys shrugged. 'It's not that many. I've got a good memory, or so me ma says.' She had to, she thought privately. It was how she had coped until recently, memorising whatever anyone said to her, as she knew she wouldn't be able to write it down.

'What have you got there?' Bridget craned her neck to see. 'Oh, it's the magazine. Stuffy old things, aren't they? I know I'm meant to read it, but somehow I don't have the time.' She settled herself on a stool beside the younger woman.

Gladys disagreed. 'No, you probably don't need to read it much because you're out on the district and practise all the time. But I like to read up about everything and then when you all come in talking about what you were doing, I can understand a bit better.'

Bridget nodded, impressed. 'That's showing initiative, that is. So you want to be a nurse one day, then?'

Gladys blushed to the roots of her lank hair. She rarely admitted her ambition, and only then to people she knew very well. Now here was this new nurse just coming straight out with it. Gladys hung her head. 'I suppose so. Yes, maybe one day. When my sister's old enough to look after the younger ones. That won't be for a little while yet, so I got to keep studying when I have a moment to spare.'

'What's that article about, then?' Bridget was at the wrong angle to read the page.

Gladys blushed still more furiously. She was struggling with the name of the condition. The word made no sense to her. 'It's about this,' she said, turning the page around, well used to dodging such questions, after years of not wanting to admit she couldn't read.

'Oh.' Bridget's face fell. 'I see. Giving injections when a patient has diabetes.'

Gladys looked up, relieved to hear the word spoken aloud. Now it all made sense. 'Yes, that's it. Do you have to do that much?' She was surprised to see the nurse turn away a little, as if something was wrong. Maybe she had over-stepped the mark somehow. She hastened to put that right. 'I know it isn't something that I would be doing. I'm not qualified to do much more than roll up bandages. I go to the first-aid lectures and everything, but I wouldn't assume that meant I could give anyone an injection,' she assured the other woman hurriedly.

Bridget briefly squeezed her eyes shut and opened them again. 'No,' she said slowly, 'but we don't know what's around the corner, do we? I'm just after coming back from early mass, and they're saying that a bomb just got dropped near the Barbican — that's not too far from here, is it? So I believe it's coming closer.'

'Oh no.' Gladys's dismay was evident. 'And there was one down at Bethnal Green. I saw my neighbour first thing and he was coming in from fire-watching.' She shuddered. 'That's a bit too close for comfort, isn't it?'

'Then who knows what we'll all need to do?' Bridget said, not really sure how near those places were or what it might mean. She pushed her flicker of fear away and strove to be practical. 'It's good that you go to those lectures. You might wind up somewhere when you're the only person who knows how to step in and look after a casualty.'

'I hope not,' Gladys said vehemently. 'I don't mind helping out, but that's all I could manage, I'm not a proper nurse.'

Bridget drummed her fingers on the counter-top. 'Tell you what, Gladys. Would you like to help me with something? Just you and me?'

Gladys looked at her in confusion. 'What could I help you with? You're all trained up and everything, and I don't know much at all.'

Bridget took a deep breath. 'Well now, you see, when you asked if I had to inject patients with diabetes, you caught me out a bit. Sure I have to do it, we all do, and there's a lady patient I've had to look after recently. She's very kind and no trouble at all, it's not that. But, and promise me you'll tell nobody,' she dropped her voice and Gladys nodded, although now rather alarmed, 'it's the worst bit of the job for me. By a mile. By a thousand miles. I don't know why. I've done it scores of times and yet every time feels like the first.'

'Blimey, miss.' Gladys was dumbfounded. She had assumed that once you were trained, that was it, everything fell into place. Now Bridget was telling her it did not always turn out like that.

'I know. Silly, isn't it?' Bridget's voice shook with nervous laughter. 'There's no rhyme or reason to it. I couldn't tell any of the others, and certainly not Fiona or Gwen. They might think I wasn't up to the job.'

'Oh no, miss.' Gladys was certain of this. 'They wouldn't. They're ever so fair. They been ever so good to me, letting me finish early sometimes to go to the lectures. And besides, you done all the exams, like I don't think I'll ever be able to do.'

Bridget shrugged her shoulders. 'I did, and yet I still come over all peculiar when I have to use a syringe. So what I wondered is, if I practised with somebody, then it might help.'

Gladys drew away. 'What, give me injections? Sorry, miss, I don't like that idea — '

'No, no.' Bridget saw the girl had got the wrong end of the stick. 'I should have said, practised *along-side*. When we began as trainees, we'd use a piece of fruit, but I don't suppose there's much spare nowadays.'

'No there ain't,' said Gladys, who was daily faced with finding enough ingredients for the nurses' meals. 'Hard enough to keep you all fed, without keeping some of it back to pretend it's someone's arm or whatnot.'

'Hmmm. Well, there must be something we could use instead.' Bridget paused to consider, casting her eyes around the small service room, with its rows of cupboards, counter and kettle. 'It needs to be something quite soft, with a bit of give in it.'

'What about a kiddie's ball?' Gladys suggested. 'My little brothers and sisters have got several, they won't miss one. They're all spongey. I bet that would do.'

'That's a really good idea.' Bridget's eyes brightened, and then she stopped abruptly as someone could be heard approaching the door. 'Not a word now,' she hissed.

Gladys blinked in acknowledgement as Gwen came in, almost running, which would have been to break one of her strictest rules.

'Ah, Gladys. I'm so pleased I found you here. I wonder if you could run a rather unusual errand for me?'

'Of course.' Gladys never had to be asked twice.

'We've had a phone call. Nurses Gillespie and Lake are safe and on their way back to London via road. Could you cycle over to inform the Banham family? They will want to know.'

'Of course, miss.' Gladys was forever grateful to those nurses in particular, who had been the first to help with her reading. She could see how urgent it was from Gwen's face, which hardly ever revealed her feelings, but was very close to doing so now. She would ask why later. 'I'll go right away.'

As she turned, Bridget tapped her nose and gave a small smile. Gladys could tell that their short conversation had somehow meant a lot to this new nurse, and it had come as a complete surprise to her as well. She would think about the whys and wherefores of that later too. But for now she had an urgent message to deliver.

★ ★ ★

Flo and Stan sat either side of their unlit fire, the blackout blind drawn and the gas lamp lit. Now that she knew everyone was safe, Flo was back to her old self. Hearing about their adventure direct from Edith and Alice had put her mind at rest and warmed her spirits.

'Such lucky girls,' she breathed, remembering that if they hadn't had a cup of tea after seeing Harry, they might have been right in the path of the Luftwaffe raid on the station. 'And brave with it. It must have taken some gumption to turn around and work a shift after all that.'

Stan nodded in agreement. 'Yes, but it's what you expect of them.'

'And to think it meant Edie got more time to spend with Harry.' Flo's eyes misted over. 'We have to work out how to go and see him, Stan. If he's responding to familiar voices we could help him get better. He'll know it's us, of course he will. It will do him good to hear us.'

Stan ran a finger around his shirt collar, one button of which was undone because of the warmth of the evening. 'And it's got nothing to do with you wanting to see him for yourself, of course.'

'Well . . . ' Flo rubbed her hands, reddened by tonight's washing up. Alice and Edith had come over as soon as they had recovered from their return journey, which had involved them sitting on packing cases in the back of the van, and the driver having to take detours because of the overnight bombing of the capital. They had caught a few hours' sleep back at Victory Walk and then come straight over to Jeeves Street. Flo had been baking ever since Gladys's visit earlier in the day, bringing out her precious saved rations to produce a proper Sunday tea. Sausage sandwiches had been followed by scones and the luxury of a choice of jam, and a moist cake made with grated carrot. Flo had been doubtful about the recipe, recommended by *The Kitchen Front* on the wireless, but she had been pleasantly surprised.

Mattie had offered to wash the dishes but Flo had refused flat out. 'You can hardly reach the taps, you have to stand so far from the sink with that bump,' she pointed out. 'Go up and have a decent night's sleep. Time enough for all that once you've had the baby.'

Mattie had agreed, knowing her mother was right. Besides, her ankles were swollen worse than ever and her back ached. Truly, that baby could not arrive soon enough.

Flo considered how far along their daughter was with her pregnancy. 'We should try to go before the birth, you know, Stan,' she said. 'She'll want me here for that, and I'll want you close by in case we have to send for help. There isn't long to go now.'

Stan sighed. 'Yes, but we can't rely on getting a lift in the back of a delivery van. I can't see you enjoying that all the way down to Portsmouth, and I'd have a job fitting in, even if the chance was on offer.' He stood up, stretching his long legs. 'We might be best to wait until the trains are up and running again. Heaven knows they weren't keeping to the timetables before, so God alone knows what this will mean. Look what Billy went through, and that was before the bombs.'

'I know.' Flo frowned. 'It's so hard, though, knowing he's lying there, no family around him. I feel like Edie when she said she'd swim there if she could.'

Stan shook his head with a smile. 'Flo, you never learnt to swim. And you'd have to get to the sea somehow to even start. No, we're best to wait. I want to see him as much as you do, but the girls said he was in good hands. They'll know if it's a well-run hospital or not. I trust them when they say he couldn't be in a better place.'

Flo knew all this was true and yet it didn't stop her strong maternal urge to go to her child. If there hadn't been Mattie and Gillian to think about, she would have been tempted to risk the journey anyway; as things stood, she realised that would be a reckless and probably pointless endeavour. She could not be selfish; family need must come first. 'You're right, of course.' Stan was always the sensible one. 'But promise me that as soon as the track is open — or there's another way of getting there — that we can go. If we time it right we can be there and back before it's Mattie's time. I shan't rest easy until I've seen Harry for myself.'

Stan gazed lovingly at his wife. He recognised that dilemma; he felt it himself. 'All right,' he said. 'I'll put the word out. As soon as it's reasonably safe to go, we'll go. How about that?'

Flo rose and came to stand beside him, slipping her arms around his waist as she used to do many years ago when they were first courting. 'Thank you, Stan. Let's do that.'

★ ★ ★

Edith had to force herself to concentrate over the next few days, as her mind kept returning to the hospital ward and Harry squeezing her hand. Sometimes she would wonder if she had imagined it, that it was just a reflex, and she had made herself believe it because that was what she so desperately wanted. This woke her at night and she would sit upright in her narrow bed, sweating, her thoughts racing. What if she had mistakenly given false hope to Stan and Flo?

Then she would recall the scene, and how it had happened again the next morning, and be flooded with relief. She knew there was still a very long way to go, there would be no instant recovery, but he was not the living corpse she had feared from Billy's first description. Somewhere under all that sedation, Harry's spirit was still very much there, and she would do everything she could to set it free again.

She was pushing her bike back along the pavement near Ridley Road market when she caught sight of a familiar face. 'Peggy!' she called out.

Peggy turned, sweeping off the headscarf that

she always wore when at work. Edith realised she must have just finished her shift. Guiltily she knew that she had been avoiding the other woman ever since the news had come about Harry's survival, not wanting to rub it in that he was still alive while Pete was not. She wasn't sure what to say, but this state of affairs couldn't go on, and so she took it as a turn of fate.

'Hang on — I'll catch you up.' She pushed harder on the old handlebars, the wheels creaking around. She had neglected to oil them in all the upheaval and they protested loudly as she drew closer to her friend. 'How are you, Peggy? Haven't seen you for ages.'

Peggy smiled, so clearly she bore no grudges. 'Hello, stranger. No, not since they came and took away all the metal railings from this street. Looks odd, don't it? Suppose we'll have to get used to it — the council said they'll have them from our road too.' She paused. 'Have you time for a cuppa?'

'Not really,' Edith admitted. 'I'm due to take one of the first-aid classes this evening, so I need to get back to Victory Walk and grab something to eat first.'

'I'll walk along with you, then,' Peggy suggested. 'I'm in no hurry to get back to Pete's mum.'

Edith raised an eyebrow. 'Is she still driving you crazy?'

'Not half.' Peggy mock-shuddered. 'She's going on and on about me joining the WVS. It's all right for her, she's got nothing else to do with her time, and she enjoys knitting, which is what they seem to do a lot of. I can't think of anything worse.'

Edith laughed. 'She probably thinks it'll keep you out of mischief.'

'She probably does.' Peggy paused. 'So, I heard about Harry. It's a miracle, Edie, I'm so happy for you. Well, and for him and all the family too, of course. Have you seen him yet?'

'I have.' Edith described her visit. 'I know it's early days yet, but I really believe he'll get better. You have to look on the bright side, don't you? Thinking the worst won't help anybody.'

Peggy nodded, thrusting her hands into her jacket pockets as she walked along. The late afternoon light was changing; autumn was on its way. The bare stone tops of the walls looked bereft without their elegant railings. She gave a little shiver. 'That's the way to look at it. The more you tell him that's what you believe, the more it'll buoy him up. It's almost unbelievable, isn't it, that he's back from the dead like that? Don't get me wrong,' she added hastily. 'I mean, I wish for all the world that Pete would turn up in a hospital bed somewhere, but I know it's impossible. But if he did I'd want to think he'd make a full recovery too.'

Edith looked down at the creaking front wheel. 'Well, I know Harry might not. I'm not daft; I've got a good idea how badly he must have been injured to be sedated like that for so long. That's not just a few cuts and bruises. Also, I can't see how his arms will be like they were before. One especially is really badly injured. His days of being a boxing champion are over.'

'Oh, Edie.' Peggy stopped, stricken. 'He loved his boxing. He could have gone all the way to the top, he was so good.'

'Yes, his life revolved around it,' Edith said, 'but now it'll have to change. And we don't know what else will be affected. He's all scarred down one side of his face and they don't know if his hair will grow back on that side or not. He may have lost his looks for good.'

Peggy gave a rueful grin. 'Well, he certainly made the most of them while he had them. Sorry, Edie. I mean, before he met you, that is.'

'Don't worry, I know what sort of a reputation he had, and he probably deserved it and more,' Edith said. 'But I don't care what he looks like, Peggy, as long as he's still Harry underneath it all. I know I fell for his looks to begin with, but it was because he was him that I loved him. That doesn't change.'

Peggy began to walk along the pavement again. 'Yes, I know what you mean. I wouldn't have cared what sort of state Pete was in, if only he'd come back. Looks are all very well but you can't rely on them. Take that bastard Kath was married to. You never met him, did you, but he was all charm till you got to know him. She's better off now he's dead, scuse my saying so. I know it's awful, but still.'

'Poor Kathleen, but at least he's not going to return to beat her now.' Edith shook her head, aware of how very different their situations were. 'Part of me wants to steel myself against the news that Harry will be permanently disabled in some way, but really, I think I'll worry about that if and when it happens. When it comes down to it, to have him back in any kind of shape is beyond what I could have hoped for. So what if he can't box and he looks different. Doesn't really matter, he's alive.'

Peggy laughed again. 'So I suppose that means I can't persuade you to come out dancing then?'

'Are you planning to get back on the dance floor?' Edith had to admire her friend's refusal to be knocked down for long.

'Certainly am. We might go all the way over to the Hammersmith Palais if the buses haven't been put off by the West End bombs. Me and Clarrie, that is.'

'Sounds like fun.' Edith's eyes lit up, but she knew she wouldn't enjoy it. 'Have a lovely time, the pair of you. Don't do anything I wouldn't do.'

'Well, I know one thing you can do,' Peggy said as she prepared to take the side road back to Mrs Cannon's house.

'What's that?'

'Oil the wheels of that bloody bike!'

24

Mattie hugged Flo as the older woman drew on her coat. 'Now mind you don't overdo things,' Flo instructed her. 'I know what you're like: the minute my back is turned you'll be trying to move furniture or something silly.'

Mattie laughed. 'I shan't, I promise.' She knew her mother was secretly fretting about seeing Harry after all this time without wanting to admit it, so she was fussing over her daughter instead. 'Have a safe journey and don't worry about me and Gillian. We'll be safe here.'

'Now you know that if the siren goes you've got to get into the shelter at once.'

Mattie sighed loudly. 'Ma, we've been at war over a year and there haven't been any raids close by. We got all het up for nothing. It's hardly going to happen now, the very moment your back is turned.'

'All the same.' Flo held her daughter's gaze.

'Yes, yes, I promise that too. The first peep from the siren and Gillian and me'll be in the shelter quicker than you can say Jack Robinson. I shall pop her into that new siren suit Kath made for her after she did Brian's. They'll look like two peas in a pod in that green material she came up with. Now, off you go, Pa is waiting.'

Stan had managed to get them a lift with one of his ARP colleagues who had to go to the south coast for some reason to do with defence training, and so they would not have to worry about the damaged train tracks. It had taken until now, the end of the first week in September, to arrange transport to Portsmouth. They were setting out at first light so as to waste no time.

Mattie watched her parents turn the corner at the far end of Jeeves Street and then went back into the kitchen to put the kettle on for her second cup of tea of the morning. 'Do you want to go back to bed?' she asked Gillian, who was toddling to and fro in front of the table, very proud to manage the steps so well. 'It's still early. Mummy might want to have forty winks at any rate.'

Gillian plonked herself down and Mattie settled onto the sagging sofa, pulling the little girl up beside her. 'There we are,' she said, making sure her tea was within easy reach. 'A nice cuppa and then a little doze. Then we'll be fresh as daisies.'

'Daisies,' Gillian did her best to say, and burst into her carefree chuckle. Mattie smiled, and wondered if her next child would have such an infectious laugh. Whatever happened, she would move heaven and earth to ensure both her children were shielded from the grim realities of war.

*　*　*

Mattie wasn't sure what time it was when she woke up again. The light had changed and it was no longer early morning. She was not sure if it was even morning at all. Gillian had nodded off beside her and was snuffling gently, her arm curled protectively around her teddy bear. 'Dear me, this won't do,' Mattie muttered. 'Look what silly Mummy has done, gone and missed the best of the morning. Let's hope Aunty Kath hasn't come round, found the door shut and gone away again.' Moving as carefully as she could, she pushed herself out of the seat and walked, with her painfully waddling gait, to the front door. She made sure it was unlocked and that Kathleen could get in, as she had promised to drop by after going to the market. Despite what she'd said to her parents, Mattie didn't fancy being on her own all day with Gillian. Everyone said the bombs over London had been a mistake by one of Hitler's generals, but she felt nervous nonetheless.

In fact she felt on edge, caught between a desire to walk around restlessly, and to clear out the kitchen cupboards. She knew she should not as the pots and pans were heavy and she didn't want another scare. But she couldn't settle. 'Serves me right for dropping off like that. I never meant to sleep so long,' she told herself firmly. Her gaze was caught by a small pile of handwashing that needed doing. That could not possibly count as heavy work. Checking that Gillian was safely wedged in by a cushion and showing no sign of waking, Mattie went into the back kitchen and picked up a tin bucket. It was as she bent down to the lower shelf for the soap powder that the first pain hit her.

At first Mattie thought she could carry on. The weather was warm, there was a bright blue sky and she wanted to get her washing out. After such a dull end of summer she couldn't afford to waste a day. So Mattie gritted her teeth, clung to the edge of the countertop, and when the worst of it had gone she resumed her attempts at getting the food stains off Gillian's bibs.

The second pain caught her just as she turned to rinse the little pieces of flannel, making her gasp. Her hand flew to her mouth to stifle the groan. She didn't want to wake her daughter, no matter how much she wanted to cry out. A couple of the bibs fell to the floor but suddenly the idea of reaching down to retrieve them was too much. Grimly, Mattie steadied herself and went back to the sofa, lowering herself carefully, and braced herself for the next wave of pain. Her eyes went to the clock. Surely Kathleen must come soon.

It was almost an hour later when the front door opened and her friend called out. 'You there, Mattie? Sorry I've been so long, you'll never guess who I saw — '

Kathleen, with Brian following, came into the kitchen and abruptly stopped. 'Oh, Mattie. Are you all right? What's happened? Is it the baby coming already? Isn't it too soon?'

Mattie gasped, at the same time almost crying with relief. 'Kath. Thank God you're here. It's coming. It's a couple of weeks early but then so was Gillian. I thought it was just first babies that

302

were early but maybe not. Ma's gone to Portsmouth, so am I glad to see you.' She fell back against the faded cushions, sweating with the effort. Gillian had woken up by now and started to fret at the sight of her usually cheerful mother in distress.

Kathleen weighed up her options and then took charge. 'Right. I see. Well, then.' She went to the sink and swiftly grabbed a glass and filled it with cold water. 'You have this and I tell you what I'll do. The children can go to Mrs Bishop; she's in on her own today cos I saw her earlier. I'll take them over there now and be back in two ticks. Brian, you play nicely with Gillian while I go and find her a change of clothes and a cardy, then we'll go to Mrs Bishop's back yard — you'll like that.' She dashed upstairs, before returning with the small articles of clothing in a paper bag. 'Off we go, into the sunshine, won't that be nice?' She didn't stop to think; she knew she had to act. It was down to her now. After all the times the Banhams had come to her rescue, this was her turn to repay them.

★　★　★

By the time Kathleen returned, a matter of ten minutes or less, Mattie felt calmer. She wasn't going to be left on her own. This was a natural and normal turn of events. Even though she wished Flo was there, she knew what would happen; it was less than two years since the last time she had done this, after all. It would hurt but she'd have a beautiful baby at the end of it.

303

Better still, she trusted Kathleen, who had given birth around the same time as she had. They were old hands at this.

Kathleen went around the house, collecting items that would be useful for the birth: old sheets to put on the sofa, newspapers, towels. She set the copper to boil and then encouraged Mattie to eat a little, to keep her strength up. 'You don't know how long this will go on,' she pointed out. 'Better have a bit of something while you can.' She set about heating some soup and making a few pieces of toast, and then joined her friend in the hastily cobbled-together dinner.

Mattie felt better for a while, as the contractions had settled into a pattern, not too close together as yet. Kathleen felt confident enough to leave her to finish the handwashing, making the most of the sunshine. 'I don't know why you didn't leave it to me in the first place,' she scolded. 'You knew I was coming. You know I never mind doing it.'

Mattie flashed a grin. 'Yes, but it didn't seem like much. I thought it would be no trouble. Thanks, Kath. It's so hard to keep enough clean bibs.'

'I know exactly what you mean.' Kathleen rolled her eyes, as she dried her hands on an old tea towel. She felt in control. All was going well. Mattie's pains were steady but not urgent as yet, and so Flo would probably be back in time to take charge when the real pushing began. The children were safe with her old neighbour; even though she complained non-stop to Kathleen, she was in fact very good with the young ones. Kathleen began to think about preparing something for tea from the shopping she'd brought from the market. Maybe some corned beef and salad — that would be light enough in this warmth.

She was just getting to her feet when the air-raid siren sounded.

For a moment she thought it was a mistake, that she was imagining it. But when it showed no signs of stopping she realised that it was all too real. She knew she had to stay calm and help her friend who instantly sprang upright, cradling her swollen stomach. 'What . . . no, it can't be. Kath, why is this happening today?' Mattie's voice rose in panic.

Kathleen tried to remember how Alice and Edith acted when there was an emergency. She kept her voice very level as she replied, 'It's probably a mistake. You know, like that alarm last year when war was declared. All the same, we'd better get you into the shelter, and then I'll bring everything we might need across as well.' She gave Mattie her arm and together they hurried to the Anderson shelter, dug out by Harry and Joe before they had joined up, and carefully kitted out by Stan and Flo.

Kathleen remembered how Mattie had teased her parents, accusing them of doing it out like a holiday caravan, but now, as they crept inside, she was grateful for the small comforts: a table, torches, some old cushions from a long-discarded armchair, a rag rug on the hard earth floor. 'You stay here and I'll be back in no time,' she said, hastening to the kitchen. Good job she knew exactly where everything was, she thought, as she found two flasks, made tea from the recently boiled kettle, and then — as an afterthought — some meat-paste sandwiches, in case this lasted for a while. She tucked more cushions and towels under one arm and returned to the shelter, the siren wailing incessantly as she did so.

Mattie clutched her arm as she crouched beside her. 'We're going to be all right, aren't we?'

Kathleen nodded steadily. 'Course we are. Mrs Bishop will take care of Brian and Gillian so we don't have to worry about them. Anyway Gillian just popped out, didn't she? So there's no need for you to get het up.' She hoped that would prove to be true.

⋆ ⋆ ⋆

Mattie was sipping at her tea and Kathleen had poured one for herself when an explosion rent the air, making them both spill the hot liquid.

'Put it down, Mattie.' Kathleen's first reaction was automatic, snatching the cup away from her friend to stop her getting burnt, almost as if she was a toddler.

Mattie turned to her in the gloom of the shelter, her eyes wide. 'That was close, wasn't it?'

'I bet — ' Before Kathleen could finish her sentence, another explosion assailed them and then another. They were louder than she could ever have imagined. Her ears rang, her vision

306

blurred, and she could barely think straight, let alone form a sentence.

'Kath.' Mattie gripped her wrist. 'The contractions are getting stronger. I think they're closer together. Oh, God. They really hurt now.'

Kathleen took a deep breath and aimed to speak slowly, not to show her own fear. 'Try to hang on,' she said, as another explosion rocked the shelter. 'Just a bit longer then this will pass over.'

Mattie gasped and gripped even tighter. 'I'll try, Kath, but I don't know if I can.' She gave a sob. 'What if it goes wrong? After my scare, I mean? How do we get help in all this?'

'It won't,' Kathleen said staunchly. 'It's going to be all right. It was just a little scare. You won't need anyone.'

Mattie nodded and shut her eyes, as if willing the pain to fade along with the crashing and banging outside. In between those noises there was a faint rushing sound accompanied by a smell, barely noticeable at first, but which grew stronger with every passing moment. It was smoke. Something was burning.

Kathleen raised her head, as if that would help determine the direction of the fire. It was becoming more and more pungent. She gave a cough. As long as it didn't get any closer, they should be all right.

'Do you think I should go and look?' she asked, unsure what would be best. She hoped against hope Mrs Bishop had got the toddlers safe in her small shelter.

'No, stay with me,' Mattie said at once. 'What

difference will it make if you look or not? Stay here with me, we're safest under this roof.'

'Good job your brothers got it done in time.' Kathleen looked up at the curved corrugated metal, which was heaped with earth on the outside for insulation and protection. 'You could grow veg on top of this; I've heard people have started doing that.'

'Yes, we could get fresh salad for the kids.' Mattie's brief burst of enthusiasm was cut short by another contraction, and her face convulsed with the pain of it. 'Kath, I don't want to worry you but . . . I don't know. It doesn't feel like before.' She hesitated. 'I don't think it's right, somehow.'

Kathleen tried not to show her alarm. 'How do you mean? Isn't it because we're stuck in here and not in the house with everything around you?'

Mattie miserably shook her head. 'I don't think so. I tried telling myself that but it just doesn't feel like before. It's too sharp; it's like something's twisting inside. Kath, what shall we do? It's got to be all right. You know . . . for Lennie. It would kill him if — '

'Don't talk rot,' Kathleen interrupted. 'None of your 'ifs'. You got to believe it will all work out. You hold on to that. Then,' she swallowed hard, 'if, when all the explosions have stopped, you still feel bad, I'll go for help.'

'Promise?' Mattie's eyes were larger than ever.

'I promise,' said Kathleen, hoping it would not come to that. She had no desire to leave the safety of the shelter, but she knew she could not cope with a difficult birth on her own.

They waited.

★ ★ ★

It seemed like an eternity before the noise abated, leaving just the faint roar that they both knew must mean a fire somewhere, not too far away. Kathleen looked long and hard at Mattie. 'Do you still need me to go?'

Mattie paused and then nodded. 'I wouldn't ask if I didn't have to,' she said in a whisper, barely there. Her fear was all too obvious on her face in the dim light.

'I know.' Kathleen understood that this was a situation of the utmost gravity. Mattie was not given to flights of fancy. If she did not go, something terrible might happen to the baby, or her friend, or both. And yet if she did go, she herself might be in danger. It was an impossible dilemma. Yet she had promised.

'All right, I'll make a run for it,' she decided, unfolding herself from the wooden bench running down one side of the shelter. Mattie was on a similar one on the other side, propped up with the cushions. As Kathleen opened the shelter door she could see her friend more clearly, lit by the strange orange glow of the sky beyond. 'Stay here, whatever you do. I'll be as quick as I can.'

'Please.' It was the only word Mattie could manage as another contraction took hold.

Kathleen scrambled out of the metal door, propping it carefully shut after her. Then she ran

309

through the house, which was thankfully undamaged, and out of the front door, hurriedly pulling her handkerchief out of her patch pocket and holding it over her nose. She'd left her gas mask in the shelter, the one time she actually needed it. Then again, perhaps it was better that Mattie had it. In all the commotion of her going into labour, Mattie's mask was overlooked. It was probably still in her bedroom, Kathleen thought.

What had been a glorious early September afternoon just a few hours ago had changed to something unrecognisable, everything lit by a strange orange glow, though Kathleen could not see over the roofs of Jeeves Street to work out what was on fire. As she rounded the corner, it looked as if the main source of the light was to the south, where the docks were. But there were also fires closer to hand, in all directions. The stench was vile, catching in the back of her throat, as she ran, heedless for her own safety, desperately searching for anyone in authority.

'Miss! You shouldn't be here!' A cry came from a shop front further down the road. Kathleen ran towards the voice, making out the shape of a man with the distinctive ARP warden's hat. Not Billy, and not Stan, who she hoped had stayed put in Portsmouth, but their colleague, the market trader.

'I need help!' she cried as she came closer. He ducked into a doorway and she joined him.

He looked at her in recognition. 'I know you,' he said. 'You go down Ridley Road with your nipper, don't you? You're Billy Reilly's friend.

What are you doing running around in all this?'

'Is Billy here?' She cast around, desperately hoping to see his familiar face.

'No, miss, he's on duty a bit later on. What's the trouble?'

Kathleen took a moment to catch her breath. Smuts and soot drifted in the air, and stupidly she could only think that the washing would be ruined, that it would have to be done again. Then she gathered herself together and told him.

He pulled a face. 'Trouble is, with all this going on, the ambulances are busy,' he said. 'Do you think she's so bad as to need one? It's poor timing and that's a fact.'

Kathleen sighed in exasperation. 'Yes, but the baby doesn't know that. It's just decided to come a bit early. I don't know if she needs to go to hospital or what, but we can't get her there on foot. She's in ever so much pain.'

The man seemed lost for words. Trust it to be the one time that neither Stan nor Billy were on duty, she thought. Then the solution struck her.

'Can you get a message to the district nurses?'

The man gave her a sharp glance and then nodded in acknowledgement. 'That would be easier. They aren't far away, and I could use the ARP telephone to call them directly.'

Kathleen agreed. 'It's no distance. They all have bicycles. And to save even more time, could you ask for one who knows the house — several of them do. Then they could just come straight over. Ask for Edith, Alice or Mary. My friend would trust any of them.'

The man's expression grew stern. 'They're all

equally well trained, miss. They would all do as good a job as any of the others.'

Kathleen gritted her teeth in her effort to make him understand. 'Yes, I realise that. I didn't mean to cast aspersions. It's just, she's had one scare in this pregnancy already; she knows this isn't the simple birth she's had before, and to top it all her husband's a prisoner of war. If we didn't have to explain all of that all over again, it would save time. So please, would you ask for one of them?'

The man gave in to her insistent pressure. 'Well, it ain't regular,' he admitted. 'But seeing as it's you, and I don't want Billy to bite my head off or nothing. Edith, Alice or Mary, you said?'

Kathleen's shoulders began to sag with the stress of it all. 'Yes please. Any of them. If they aren't there, then any of their colleagues. Please, just call the nurses of Victory Walk.'

25

Bridget huddled against the wall in the service room, Gladys close beside her. They were meant to be in the refuge room, the space in the nurses' home that had been deliberately set aside for raids as there was no possibility of a shelter in the paved back yard. However, they had decided to risk it and take the time to practise injections on the sponge ball. Gladys reckoned the service room was as safe as anywhere, being on the lower-ground floor, surrounded by stout walls and with only one small window.

All the same, once the bombing started, her confidence dwindled.

'I'm not so sure about this now,' she confessed, staring out of the glass panes that had been crisscrossed with tape to prevent them shattering. 'My mind's not on it, miss.'

Bridget sighed with relief, as her hands had begun to shake, and not from fear of syringes for once. 'No, I feel the same,' she admitted. 'We can maybe try again another time. This won't do us any good.' With that, the sky above them lit up in a burst of orange. 'Shall we go to the refuge room?'

Gladys shook her head. 'You go ahead, miss. I would rather stay here where it ain't so crowded, then I can hear if anyone comes to the door or whatnot. Heaven knows what's happening out there. You nurses might be needed.'

Bridget gulped at the idea of venturing out into the heart of an air raid. The reality began to hit home that this was what she had signed up for. What had started as an adventure, leaving Dublin for a new country, was suddenly no longer fun but a very real danger. 'Do you think we will?'

'Bound to be,' predicted Gladys, and then an even louder bang prevented her from saying any more. They pressed themselves against the thickest wall and stared out of the window, watching as the flame-coloured sky grew brighter still.

Eventually the noise died down and they stood upright again, neither one wanting to admit to how terrified they had been. Then came the sound of the telephone.

'I better go. I don't know if they'll hear it in the refuge room,' Gladys said.

'Be careful. We don't know if the upper floors are damaged,' Bridget warned her.

Gladys wiped her hands on her apron. 'I'll find out soon, won't I.' She slipped out of the door, through the canteen lit by the weird orange light and up to the hallway. The building around her was still sound.

'Victory Walk Nurses' Home,' she said, as she had heard Gwen do many times. 'Er, right, I see . . . yes, I will enquire for you. Please hold the line.' Then she rushed to the refuge room with her message, full of dread for what was taking place a few streets away.

★ ★ ★

'Are you certain that you both want to go?' Gwen regarded Alice and Edith, ready in no time at all with their refilled Gladstone bags at their feet.

'Yes, it's best if there are two of us.' Alice didn't need to add that it was because if one of them was injured on the way, at least the other one would make it through to the emergency. Gwen would know that as well as they did.

'Very well.' Gwen waved them off, trying to keep her anxiety for their safety from showing. It would do them no good to realise that she, with all her years of experience from the Great War, was thoroughly alarmed atthe conflagration all around them. Coughing, she retreated back into the relative safety of the nurses' home and headed back to the refuge room. There was no point in putting herself in danger as well.

★ ★ ★

'You all right there, Al?' Edith was pedalling ahead, squinting through the unfamiliar light so that she did not take a wrong turning on this, the most familiar of routes in her adopted home borough. 'Not fallen off, have you?' The noises all around drowned out the gentler sound of her friend's bicycle.

'I'm right behind you,' called Alice, her eyes smarting. She kept her gaze firmly on Edith's back, refusing to be distracted by the evidence of bomb damage in the area. Victory Walk was unscathed, and the road that linked it to the high road, but just further south towards Dalston

Lane there appeared to be major problems. She couldn't do anything about that now; other medical staff would have been called there. She had one job to do, and that was to deliver Mattie and Lennie's baby on this unluckiest of days to choose to be born.

'Nearly there,' Edith replied, as they crossed the main road and hurried towards the Jeeves Street turning. None of the houses here had been hit but everything was speckled with soot, and loose bricks and window panes had been dislodged, littering the road and pavement. 'Mind that pile of glass, Al, we don't want any more punctures.'

Alice could hardly reply as the smell was catching at her throat, making it hard to speak. She swallowed hard. 'Look, there's Kathleen at the door. Quick.'

They swung themselves off their bikes. 'Bring them into the hallway, I'm sure Stan and Flo won't mind,' Edith suggested. 'We don't want those loose bricks landing on them. God knows they're rickety enough already.'

Kathleen helped them and then gave Edith a big hug. 'I'm so glad to see you. I didn't know if you'd come. Mattie's so worried, and I don't know what to do.' She began to move swiftly through to the kitchen and out to the back door. 'We're in the shelter.'

'Will there be room for all of us?' Alice wondered, manoeuvring her bag past the familiar furniture made strange by the weird light.

'Have to be,' replied Edith bluntly, feeling in her pocket to check for spare torch batteries.

Allowing Kathleen to forge slightly ahead, she took Alice by the arm. 'Al, have you ever delivered a baby?'

'Of course. When we did our training.'

'Yes, but on your own, on the district?'

'No,' Alice admitted. 'Only when someone else was in charge.'

'Me too.' Edith looked up at her friend. 'Oh well. Here we go.'

★　★　★

Mattie was panting for breath as they squeezed into the shelter. At first she was too overcome by the latest contraction to acknowledge them but then, once it had passed, she looked up, her face pale and slick with sweat. 'Oh thank God. I thought I'd have to do it on my own. I was afraid Kath had got killed. And now you're here, I'm so glad it's you. Aaaah . . . ' And another contraction overwhelmed her.

Edith glanced at Alice. Two so close together could only mean the birth was imminent. 'Right, I'm going back into the kitchen to get some hot water and then we'll get cleaned up and see how you're coming along,' she said, switching into professional mode, trying not to think of Mattie as her close friend.

Alice took over the role of making Mattie comfortable, rearranging cushions and Kathleen's makeshift equipment. 'Kathleen, if you could sit by the door please. We'll need a bit of room to work,' she explained. Kathleen was only too happy to do so, now that proper help was at hand. She knew she had done what she could and now the experts were taking over. 'I'll go with Edie and make some tea,' she offered.

Alice knew that was a risk, as the shelter would still be the safest place, but tea would be a comfort to everybody, and making it would give Kathleen something to do. Now they had to concentrate on the reason they were there: delivering the baby. Once Edith returned with hot water, they carefully set aside their cloaks, cleaned their hands and began to assess their distressed patient.

In the shadowy darkness lit by their torches and the slightly open door, they worked together, scarcely having to say anything other than murmur vital notes: temperature, respiration, pulse, frequency of contractions. Edith thought there was much to be said for training together month after month. They didn't need to ask each other anything unnecessary, but worked as one. She wondered if Alice had had the same concern that was at the forefront of her mind: that this could indeed be related to the scare, and possibly a problem with the placenta.

'I want to push!' Mattie suddenly screamed, half sitting up on the rudimentary bed. 'I have to!'

'Right, I'll stay here at your head and Edith will be at your feet,' said Alice as calmly as she could, hoping the twisting pain Kathleen had told them about was nothing too out of the ordinary. Edith moved into position, helped Alice to pull back the sheet that Mattie had been huddled under, and prepared for what was to come next.

Mattie squeezed her face as tightly as she could and pushed with all her might but nothing happened. She lay back on the cushions, exhausted. 'I can't do it. It's no good.'

Alice rubbed her hand. 'You're doing really well. You just have to give it another go. Wait for the contraction then push into it. Big breath, now.'

Mattie screamed as she gave it all she was worth, but still there was no progress.

Edith grabbed her torch and shone it on Mattie. 'Come on, even in this light I can see something's happening. It's nearly here, Mattie, honestly. Give it one big effort. All right, one, two, three . . . '

Mattie screamed even louder and Kathleen turned her face away, not wanting her best friend to see the tears of anxiety coursing down her face. She couldn't help it. She had been holding herself in check all afternoon, and now that she was relieved of responsibility, she recognised that she was wrung out. But Mattie didn't need to know that.

Edith pursed her lips. 'Kath,' she said quietly, 'go back into the kitchen and get Flo's biggest cooking pot and fill it with cold water. Quickly now.'

Startled, Kathleen did as she was asked.

Alice flashed a glance at Edith but then composed her face and encouraged her patient to try again. 'Next one's coming — here we go, big push. Hold my arm tight.' Mattie gripped her like a vice and again gave it all she was worth, but still there was no baby.

Then as Kathleen came back, balancing the biggest stewpot in front of her, by the light of the fully open door Edith could see a glimpse of what she was looking for. 'Here we go, Mattie. That's the top of baby's head showing. Almost there! Big push!'

Mattie, at the end of her endurance, lay back against the cushions, gathered her energy and gave one last almighty push, yelling at the top of her voice as she did so.

'Yes! The head's coming through!' Edith got into position and neatly prepared to give the baby a helping hand. Gently she pulled as the shoulders emerged, pausing discreetly to loop the umbilical cord from where it had wound itself around the child's neck. She registered that Alice was giving her anxious glances but said nothing, giving all her concentration to the baby, to see if it would cry or not. Finally, the body and legs slithered out and she could lift it. It was small, but perfect, its hair dark, and . . .

'It's a boy,' she proclaimed, all the joy flooding back now he was here. 'A beautiful baby boy. I'll just clear his mouth . . . ' She surreptitiously moved to one side where the light was better, cleared his airwaves and patted him on the back. After a few moments a small noise, almost like a mew, came out. Then, progressively louder, until he sent up a wail. Edith had never been so glad to hear a baby's cry.

'A boy!' echoed Alice, delighted, setting aside her fears. She had known what was on Edith's mind. She had planned to do her best if the baby needed reviving by alternating hot and cold baths — except they would have had to make do with Flo's big metal pot.

'Let me see him!' Mattie pushed herself up onto her elbows with an energy she didn't know she still had. Edith leant forward, presenting the child to his mother. Mattie gasped at the perfection of him.

'A son for Lennie,' she breathed. 'He'll be so proud. He'd have loved another girl, but to have a boy is extra special . . . he is all right, isn't he? After all our worry?'

'He is,' Edith confirmed. 'A little small but that's only natural as he was a bit early. We can weigh him later, but he's got everything in working order as far as I can see.'

'Let me hold him,' Mattie said, wriggling into a seated position. 'I have to see his face again. To tell what sort of name he should have.'

Kathleen leaned forward to see the newborn. 'Will you call him Lennie as well?'

'He can have that as a middle name,' Mattie decided. 'I'm going to think about a name he can have all of his own. But first I think I'll sleep.'

Edith stepped forward to relieve her of the baby. 'You do that,' she said. 'We'll make a little cot for him from this box. There, you tuck in that towel, Kath, and he'll be snug as a bug in a rug.'

Once the baby settled, Kathleen brought out the new flask of tea she'd made while hunting for the big pot, and the last of the paste sandwiches. Then, as the three of them huddled on the wooden bench opposite the now-sleeping Mattie, they caught the sound of planes overhead once more — and the start of the next round of bombs.

★ ★ ★

On and on went the bombing, and yet the baby and an exhausted Mattie slept through it. Kathleen grew more anxious as the raid continued, stirring on her one hard cushion. 'It's no good,' she whispered in a brief break in the cacophony. 'I should try to fetch Brian. My neighbour doesn't mind having him in the daytime, but she won't want him overnight. I didn't bring enough clothes or rusks either.'

'Does she have a shelter?' Alice asked quietly.

Kathleen nodded. 'Yes, a really small one, or I'd have been round to get him and Gillian before now. But if this is set to go on . . . I don't know what to do for the best.'

Edith pulled a face. 'Now that Mattie is safely delivered we ought to try to go back anyway. We might be needed elsewhere. Can't say as I'm looking forward to it, but I reckon we should.'

'If we aren't in here, then there would be room for Brian and Gillian,' Alice pointed out. 'You've got all these cushions and towels — you could make up little beds for them. If only we could get them back safely.'

'It's only five minutes away, if that,' Kathleen said. 'If there's a proper break in the bombing I'm going to risk it. I can't stand the thought of being apart from them a moment longer. Especially when I saw that look on Mattie's face when she held her son. I can't have Brian away from me for all this time. He'll be scared and Mrs Bishop won't be enough for him.'

Alice sat up straighter. 'Then what we'll do is all three of us go into the house. Edie or I will wait inside and then two of us can run to Jeeves Place and fetch the children back. How's that? The raid can't go on at this intensity much longer. We'll make a run for it.' She had no idea if this was the right thing to do, but they could not let Mattie sleep alone with the new baby and wake up to nobody. At least this way, if the worst happened, one of them would still be here to help her.

Edith stood up. 'Come on. It seems to have gone quieter. Let's do it while the going is good.'

Swiftly the three of them ran into the house, hands over their mouths against the all-pervasive smell of burning. Edith swung her torch as they reached the hall, so that they didn't crash into the bikes and knock them over. 'Shall I go?' she asked Alice. 'The children know me a bit better than you.'

'Yes, but I'm taller and I can carry more of their things,' Alice pointed out, as Kathleen cast them a look of frustrated despair. Their discussion was cut short by a knocking at the door. 'Who's that?' Alice breathed, gripped with a fear there was bad news about Flo and Stan on their journey back from the south coast — or, by some dreadful twist of fate, Joe.

Kathleen went to open up. 'Billy!' she cried, and it was all she could do not to fall upon him in delighted relief. If ever there was a time when she could have wished for his reliable, dependable face, this was it.

Billy stepped inside. 'I shouldn't really be here but I thought I'd check everything was all right. Brendan filled me in on what was happening. How's Mattie?'

Edith hurriedly told him, as Kathleen twisted with anxiety beside her. 'And so now we need to get the other children back,' she finished.

Billy nodded. 'It's no picnic out there, you know. I'll be all right, I've got my tin hat.' He tapped it and smiled. 'I'll come with you, Kath, then you two can stay here till we get back. That way we're as covered as we can be. How does that sound?'

'Really, Billy? Would you?' Kathleen could hardly believe her ears. She would trust him above anyone to keep her boy safe.

'Of course,' he said seriously. 'Come on, let's go while we have a chance. See you girls later.' Taking Kathleen's arm he hurried her out of the front door, leaving Edith and Alice to keep their fingers crossed.

★   ★   ★

It felt like hours but it was actually only a matter of minutes before they returned with the two toddlers safely in their arms, Billy with Gillian and Kathleen with Brian, whatever bits and pieces they could bring with them stowed in a shopping bag slung across Billy's broad back. Mrs Bishop had been evidently relieved to hand over the children after having had the responsibility of minding them through the lengthy raid.

Kathleen had been glad to take them away and to say goodnight to her useful but frequently miserable neighbour. The toddlers were all but oblivious, having nodded off, still blessed with the ability to sleep through anything.

Now Kathleen stood in the Banhams' front doorway, having settled the little ones and then having waved goodbye to the nurses, who had pedalled off back to Victory Walk, where they fully expected to be called out to tend to injuries resulting from the raids. 'I'd better send you on your way then, Billy,' she breathed, filled with gratitude and admiration for what he had done. 'You better get back on patrol, you'll be needed tonight.'

'Reckon I will be, an' all,' he replied. 'You know what they're saying? The first raid this afternoon dropped so many bombs on the docks and around that the fires guided the second lot over. Bloody marvellous, we get it in the neck twice in one day.'

Kathleen shook her head sadly. 'We'll find out the damage tomorrow, won't we.'

'We will. Kath, I'd better go,' Billy said, his voice heavy with reluctance. His eyes shone as he looked at her.

'Thanks again, Billy.' She almost leaned in to his face, but common sense pulled her back. Despite what he had done for her and the children this evening, he wasn't hers and it wouldn't be right, never mind what she truly wanted in her heart. She put her hand on his arm and gave it a little squeeze. 'I won't forget tonight, ever.' Her eyes stayed locked on his for a precious moment longer and then she dropped her hand. 'I'll get back to the shelter. Goodnight, Billy.'

He waited until she had gone inside and shut the door, and then he turned to resume his duty. His shoulders slumped at being parted from her when every inch of him longed to stay, but then he stood straight again with pride. He had helped reunite the little family and they at least were safe for the rest of the evening.

Whether that would be the case for the other families around Dalston, he could not say. But he doubted it.

26

The next day was Sunday and, despite the bombing having gone on for most of the night, many of the nurses went to church as usual. 'I shan't let the Luftwaffe stop me going about my usual business,' Mary declared, dressed in a new coat with a stylish patent belt to show off her trim waist. 'That would be to admit defeat. Are you coming, Alice?'

Alice nodded, and the two of them set off down the narrow corridor that led between the attic bedrooms. Edith, though, had decided to miss Mass; she felt she needed to catch up on her rest after the events of the previous day.

Plenty of the nurses reported back that there had been damage all over the area, and that the church hall was being used to accommodate anyone unlucky enough to have been made homeless in the raids. The vicar's wife was organising a canteen to feed not only the homeless but any of the volunteer firefighters or other local service members who needed a hot drink or sandwich to tide them over until they could return home. Mary had offered to help but was gently turned down. The vicar's wife was sure she would be needed in her professional capacity only too often.

'Well, I tried,' Mary said as she settled into an easy chair in the common room. 'I don't mind serving cups of tea to firemen, but I suppose I'm of more use as a nurse. They've got it all set up, Edith, you should go and see it. They've thought of everything — even little toys to keep the children amused.'

'We must tell Billy, then he can direct people to go there, if he doesn't know already,' Edith replied. 'He didn't mention it yesterday — mind you, we had other things on our minds.'

Alice pulled up a chair beside them. 'I wonder if I should write to Joe and tell him he's got a new nephew. Mattie will be too busy with the baby, and who knows when Flo and Stan will be back? At least they aren't relying on the trains.'

'We heard that London Fields station's been damaged — a high explosive hit the tracks,' Mary reported. 'Heaven knows what the big stations are like.'

Alice's face creased with worry, but she knew there was nothing she could do. She just had to trust that they would return as soon as they could. 'I might wait until they've chosen a name,' she decided. 'That would make sense.' She looked up as Fiona swept across the room, clutching a pile of folders.

'Everybody all right?' the diminutive superintendent asked them. 'My, we all took a bit of a pasting last night, didn't we? Did you manage to catch some sleep? Can't have my girls too tired and weary.'

They all nodded, and Fiona smiled. 'That's the spirit.' Then, too busy to talk further, she was off again.

Fiona hurried up the stairs to her office, weary herself, but with no time to give in to the urge to sleep. There was simply too much to do. She was proud of the way her nurses had coped so far, but had a gut feeling that this was the beginning of the onslaught. Somehow she had to keep them up to scratch and fully ready for whatever the air raids might fling at them. Yesterday's emergency had sparked an idea that she had long been harbouring but had not yet acted upon.

'Send more nurses on specialist midwife training,' she wrote in the notebook she always kept on one side of her desk. She paused. Somewhere she had read that there were bursaries for this. 'Find details of funding,' she scribbled, knowing that the more of her charges who could confidently deliver babies, the better. Not everyone would have been able to cope in the way that Alice and Edith had, in the restrictions of an Anderson shelter.

★ ★ ★

Edith couldn't rest no matter what she did. She had tried staying in her room and lying down, but she just could not settle. She'd come down to the common room and picked up a book but couldn't focus on the words. Her mind was in a whirl. She had been hoping to see Flo and Stan, to hear how Harry was. Had he recognised their voices and responded? Had there been more improvement? In her deepest heart she had longed for them to say he had spoken and asked for her, and they would be able to bring him home soon. Yet she knew that was about as likely as flying to the moon. Any improvements would be slow and she must not get her hopes up. All the same . . .

She put the book down and got to her feet. The only way to still her anxious thoughts would be physical activity of some kind. 'Fancy a walk?' she called over to Alice. 'We could wander over to the Downs before dinner.'

'Good idea.' Alice swung her legs down from the stool she'd been resting them on, and stood up, shaking the creases out of her cotton skirt. She'd been so exhausted this morning that she hadn't ironed it, but supposed nobody would notice, or mind if they did.

As they made their way along Victory Walk, they could still smell burning, as some of the fires had raged all night. Debris littered the road and pavement: glass, tiles, bricks, and an assortment of burnt shapes that could have been anything. 'Glad I didn't wear my sandals,' Edith muttered, swerving to avoid a sharp shard which must have once been a window. 'My toes would have been cut to ribbons.'

Other people had had the same idea and they noticed couples, family groups and solitary walkers all out to assess the damage that had been done. Some of the smaller children were running around, not caring that they'd had to sleep in shelters. The change in routine was a cause of excitement rather than fear. Their parents' faces told a different story, many visibly exhausted. Others showed a quiet determination to have their Sunday walk as usual, raids or no raids.

Alice linked her arm through Edith's and they

wandered along the outer path of the Downs, the first of the fallen leaves crunching beneath their feet. The trenches that had been dug before the beginning of the war would have provided little shelter from the severity of the raids the previous night. 'I wonder how Mattie is feeling this morning,' she said. 'I hope she got more sleep than we did.'

Edith gave a brief laugh. 'I didn't really sleep at all until about four,' she said. 'What with the bombing, and the anti-aircraft guns. I thought I'd catch forty winks this morning but I couldn't. I'm too wound up, wanting to hear how Harry is. I do hope his hospital hasn't been hit.'

'There wasn't anything on the news about south coast cities,' Alice said comfortingly. 'We'll know when Stan and Flo get back. I'm sure they'll send word. Won't they be thrilled to find Mattie's had her baby safely?'

'Flo will be sad to have missed it,' Edith predicted.

'I wonder what he'll be called?'

'Maybe Mattie has already decided,' Edith guessed. 'Something that goes with Lennie as a middle name. Or Leonard. I suppose that's the full thing, isn't it?'

'I can't imagine Lennie being called Leonard — it sounds far too stuffy,' Alice smiled. 'Not like Lennie at all.' She fell silent, wondering how he was faring in his prison camp so far away, with no prospect of meeting his newborn son.

Edith nodded, knowing what her friend was thinking. The baby would start his life with no father, and most likely neither of his uncles either; but he would have a doting mother and grandparents, who would make sure he wanted for nothing. This was a child who would be showered with love. She thought of her own family for a brief moment and wondered what her brothers were doing. What a contrast to the Banhams.

'Look over there.' Alice pointed to a clump of trees some way away, beyond the closest line of trenches, where some people were walking. One of them had distinctive red hair. 'Is that Clarrie? Or her sister?'

Edith squinted. 'You're right, it does look like Clarrie. Let's go over and see if it is her.' She sped up and Alice hurried after her.

The young woman across the park looked up and nudged her companion, who immediately pointed and waved. Alice shielded her eyes to see them better. 'It is Clarrie. And that's Peggy, if I'm not mistaken.'

The four of them met halfway, out in the open space where often children would play football but which today was empty.

'Fancy seeing you here,' Edith smiled. 'We fancied a quick stroll before dinner to wake us up a bit. How did you get on last night?'

Clarrie and Peggy looked at one another and then broke into peals of laughter. Edith and Alice glanced at each other, bemused. 'Come on, share the joke,' Edith urged.

Peggy recovered first. 'Don't mind us, we're so tired we don't know if we're coming or going,' she admitted. 'But look at us — doesn't anything strike you as odd?'

'Odd?' Edith could not at first work out what her friend meant. Then she noticed the two young women were wearing high-heeled shoes, and their dresses were not what she might have chosen herself for a casual Sunday stroll. 'Well . . . I'm not sure about your clothes . . . '

Peggy broke into another whoop of laughter and shimmied her shoulders, making her shiny rayon frock swing about. 'We haven't been home! We've been up all night! It was such a hoot!'

Edith's eyebrows shot up.

Clarrie cleared her throat and began to explain. 'We decided to go to the Hammersmith Palais for a change, like we've been talking about for ages. It's really good there, the dancing is second to none. You'd love it, Edith.' Edith tried to smile but knew that, with Harry unable to move — let alone dance — for the foreseeable future, a night at the Palais was very low on her list.

'There was a band playing, with singers and everything,' Peggy chipped in. 'They were as good as the Ink Spots, honest.'

'Anyway, we'd already set off before the first sirens so we thought we might as well keep going as turn around and come back. So we did, and for a while there was lots of dancing, but then we all got evacuated and we had to go to one of their big shelters,' Clarrie went on.

Edith's eyes widened. 'Was it very crowded?'

'Oh, ever so,' said Clarrie. 'But I'd met these nice off-duty firemen and they looked after us. They were terribly kind. Shared their flasks of tea and everything. Proper gentlemen, they were.'

Edith nodded. She could imagine that Clarrie had given as good as she got, laughing and flirting with the firemen. When she had first met the redhead, she had feared that she had Harry in her sights. Then she realised that Clarrie just liked to flirt, and that she and Harry were nothing more than old school friends.

'Then two of them had to go as they were working a late shift,' Peggy added. 'There weren't any bombs near us but they were due to go into the centre of town and so I suppose they would have been in the thick of it. We sat up with the other two and played cards until the all clear. Then they had to go to catch a few hours' sleep before they were back on duty and so we started walking and managed to get a bus before too long.'

Clarrie grew more sober. 'The closer we got to home, the worse it got. The buses were diverted; I think a lot of gas pipes were hit, or that's what people were saying. And there were craters in some roads. Down by the docks is a mess. There were fires everywhere.'

'Blimey, I'm surprised you didn't both go straight home,' Edith said.

Peggy shook her head. 'We fancied a quick stroll to get some fresh air, only it's not very fresh, is it? We'd better get back now, though. Pete's mum will be worried. She was going round to her friends' last night, but they have a shelter so she should be all right.'

'We could walk back some of the way with you; that'd make it a round trip for us,' Alice suggested, and the four of them fell into step, finally parting near Dalston Lane.

Edith shoved her hands into the pockets of her light jacket. 'Let's go along here a bit,' she said. 'I don't want to get back too soon before dinner. I'd rather be outside.' They strolled along the road and then turned into one of the side streets, Edith following a path from earlier in the summer almost without realising it, and Alice happy to stroll along aimlessly. Broken roof tiles littered the pavement and clouds of dust puffed up into the air.

'How silly of me, I've only just realised where I am,' Edith exclaimed. 'This is the street that Vinny lived on. Do you remember, that little boy I used to come to treat, when there were all the precautions against spreading infection? I don't know how his poor mother managed. She had five of them, and she had to keep all his food separate . . . oh no.' She came to a halt in front of the house — or rather, where the house had been.

Now there was just a crumbling mass of walls, lopsided window frames hanging in mid-air and lone pieces of furniture marooned on what had been solid floors. A curtain flapped in the light breeze, but everything behind it was burnt and ruined. Edith gasped as she remembered how this had been one of the best-kept houses in the little street, the way Mrs Bell had made the effort to make it clean and tidy, even while looking after five children.

'This was their home?' Alice stared at the wreckage, aghast.

An elderly man came across from the opposite

pavement. 'Did you know them?' he asked, his voice croaky and wheezing. Alice wanted to tell him to save his breath, but shook her head.

'I did,' said Edith sadly. 'Well, Mrs Bell and the two youngest anyway. They were going to move to Northampton, weren't they?'

The old man nodded. 'Good job they did. She took the younger kiddies with her but Terry and their eldest stayed behind. Awful business, it is. Terry's the hardest worker you ever knew and then on top of that he went fire-watching. He was on duty last night, God bless him, then he come home this morning to find his house was gone. His oldest boy was inside, didn't stand a chance.'

Edith shut her eyes for a moment. 'Vinny's big brother was in there, you mean?'

The old man coughed again. 'Wouldn't have known anything about it — that's the only comfort,' he said. 'It was a direct hit. Went up in flames at once, it did. He couldn't have got out of there. Nice lad he was, too. His poor father, he's almost lost his mind. The warden took him away, I don't know where he's gone. There ain't nothing left for him here, that's for certain.'

Edith turned to Alice. 'I can't take it in. That little boy was so brave and he nearly died of pneumonia — it doesn't seem fair that they got through that, only to lose their oldest son. It seems so senseless. It could have hit anywhere, but for some reason it landed here . . . Vinny might be too young to remember his big brother, but his sister will. She always had plenty to say about everything.'

The old man wheezed as he tried to reply. 'Ain't the only house that got hit round here but I don't know the folks in the others. Yes, it's a crying shame; a fine young lad like that, cut down in his prime. Well, he wasn't the first and he won't be the last. Good day to yer, miss.' He shambled his way back across the road and went into a house very like that of the Bells' but shabbier.

'Come on, Edie, we can't do anything here.' Alice tucked her arm into her friend's once more. 'It'll be time for dinner soon. You've got to keep your strength up. We don't know what we'll be called on to do later.'

Edith squared her shoulders. 'You're right, of course. Still . . . no, it's no good, there's no sense to it, is there? I'm just grateful that Vinny wasn't there too. I know it isn't a matter of things being fair or unfair — but all the same, how unfair it would have been to have survived what he had and then get bombed. At least he's been spared that.'

★　★　★

Flo leaned on Stan's broad arm as they walked slowly along Jeeves Street. She was gladder than she ever could have imagined to see her home again. She didn't like leaving it at the best of times, and only the prospect of visiting Harry had enticed her to go. Now she felt like touching the brickwork to check it was actually still there and all in one piece. The sights they had seen on their much-delayed journey back

337

from Portsmouth had made her fear the worst. As they had approached the East End, the smoke was still rising over it and down towards the docks. Stan's colleague had laughed and joked for most of the way, making light about having to change his route again and again because of the bomb damage, but even he had fallen silent as the realisation of what had happened to the area hit them all.

Yet their worry had been for nothing. Flo pushed open her front door and called out, 'Mattie! We're home!' She had expected her daughter to be anxiously awaiting their return and was a little surprised that she didn't come running at once. 'Mattie!' she called again. The girl might be outside, she reasoned. 'Sorry we had to stay away overnight!' she shouted.

There were footsteps on the stairs and then Kathleen appeared, beaming widely. 'Oh, you're back! What a relief. We were wondering. How was Harry?'

Flo smiled back. 'Oh, I'm glad to see you too, Kathleen. It's good that Mattie hasn't been here on her own. If you just fetch her I can tell you both all the news. Why don't I get the kettle on — I'm parched, and how about you, Stan?'

'A cuppa would be lovely,' he said. 'What's wrong, Kathleen? Is there some kind of trouble with Mattie?'

Flo stopped dead in her tracks. 'Is she all right?'

Kathleen chuckled. 'Well, I won't fetch her just now if you don't mind. She's fast asleep upstairs. You might want to come up though.

There's someone there you'll want to meet.'

Flo stared at her and then her jaw dropped as she cottoned on to what the young woman meant.

'She's . . . she's . . . ' Flo turned to her husband, who still had one hand on the front door handle. 'Stan, I do believe . . . we've missed it, haven't we? Mattie's gone and had the baby while we were away.'

'That's right.' Kathleen could not keep the delight form her voice. 'He's ever so small but he's perfect. Come upstairs and meet your new grandson.'

'A boy!' Flo breathed, and then she dropped her carpetbag on the worn hallway runner and quickly followed Kathleen up the stairs as if she was young again herself.

★   ★   ★

Kathleen loaded the old wooden tray with teapot, cups, milk and a small bowl of precious sugar, then carefully carried it up to the family gathered in Mattie's bedroom. She was glad to be able to help, so that Flo could spend even more time with her new grandchild. Stan's eyes had lit up when he realised he had a grandson, and Kathleen could see he was bursting with pride as he looked at the swaddled bundle for the first time.

'Here we are.' She set the tray down on the dresser, well out of the way of an over-excited Gillian. Mattie was sitting up against her pillows, a crocheted bed jacket thrown around her

339

shoulders, and her son was snuggled against her.

'Isn't he good?' Flo breathed. 'He barely makes a sound.'

'Oh, don't worry, he can when he wants to,' Mattie assured her mother, eyes dancing brightly. 'Can't he, Kath? He knows how to make himself heard.'

'Can't think who he takes after,' Stan said. 'But I reckon he looks like his dad — he's got the same round face. Hard to tell about the rest of him yet.'

The proud grandparents leant forward to see the child better, and Gillian scrambled up on the foot of the bed to join in.

Mattie turned the baby a little to make it easier.

'So, don't keep us in suspense,' Flo said. 'Have you chosen a name for him yet? Did you decide on one ages ago and not tell anybody?'

Mattie glanced up at Kathleen and then at her parents. 'No, I wanted to wait until I saw him or her and then make up my mind. Lennie always said I could choose; he'd be happy with whatever I liked. I didn't want a family name as people always feel left out if their names aren't picked.' She paused, to draw out the moment. 'Well, I like Alan. We haven't got any others in the family; it'll be a name just for him. Alan Leonard Askew. How about that?'

Flo found her eyes were misting with tears as she reached out and stroked the tiny face, very gently so as not to wake him. 'Hello, Alan,' she said. 'Welcome to the world. We're going to take the very best care of you so that your daddy will

340

be proud of you when he comes home.'

Stan reached across and squeezed her shoulder, to show that he was feeling the same.

Flo sat back on the bed and gave Gillian a hug so that she wasn't left out. Despite the horrors of the journey back from the hospital, she was content. It had been hard to see Harry in such a terrible condition, but the doctors had assured them that he was responding to treatment now. When she spoke to him he had reacted, and especially when she had mentioned Edith's name. She was convinced that not only did he know her voice, and Stan's, but also that he understood what they were talking about. Somewhere under the bandages, and within the fog of painkillers, the Harry they knew was still very much alive.

Tomorrow she would send a message to Edith to let her know how the visit had gone. Perhaps she would invite Edith and Alice round to thank them for taking such good care of Mattie in her hour of need, when she could have done with a mother's experience to guide her through. Yet what more could she have asked for than two excellent nurses who were also the best of friends?

Flo took a sip of her tea and looked around at this small group of people crowded into the bedroom. These people were her world. Now that she knew Harry was on the mend she could enjoy every minute of looking after the latest addition to the family, the precious creature who was beginning to stir. Stan had warned her that last night's raids might be the first of many, but no amount of Luftwaffe bombing would spoil her pleasure at having a grandson. They had a shelter, now tried and tested; they had each other. Whatever the onslaught, they were ready.

27

Fresh from a last-minute trip to the market, Kathleen laid out her ingredients for a stew. She'd been lucky and caught the butcher just before he shut his stall, and he'd been happy to let her have some offcuts as a bargain. As meat was rationed by price and not weight, that meant she still had enough coupons for later in the week. She would put it in the pot with vegetables and pearl barley and then that would last for two days. Not bad for half an hour's work, she thought.

She hadn't been able to go to Ridley Road first thing in the morning because she'd slept in. For the last few nights there had been more bombing raids; the East End was bearing the brunt of the attacks, with many buildings destroyed and much loss of life. It was changing everyone's daily routine, turning everything they were accustomed to do upside down. Kathleen had been at a loss to know what to do for the best, as there was no room for a shelter in her shared back yard. She couldn't run around to the Banhams': they were full to bursting. She supposed she could have asked Mrs Bishop to share her small shelter, but the idea of putting up with the woman's moaning while trying to quell Brian's fear was unbearable. Some people declared you were safe on the ground floor of a building, and Kathleen was tempted to believe it;

that the Coynes upstairs would cushion the blow if it came. However, she knew that was far from always the case and Billy had often told her not to listen to gossip but to follow the official guidelines. Although she would far rather have stayed in her own home, she could not take the risk with Brian's safety.

So they had bundled their essentials together in a big bag, Brian wrapped in his new siren suit, and set off for the church one road over, which had a basement and was opening its doors to people with no shelter of their own. In some ways it was comforting to be with others in the same situation. It was noisy and there wasn't much privacy, but they had gas and running water so the conditions weren't as bad as in some places. It was easier to hide her fear with other people around, and to persuade Brian that it was a big adventure. She didn't want him to pick up on her constant alarm until the all clear sounded.

Brian was singing to himself as he tried to build a wall with his wooden bricks, and Kathleen began methodically to slice potatoes. She wished she had an onion to add but they were scarce these days. She lined up her peeler ready to prepare the carrots next, and reached for her heaviest saucepan to brown the meat.

She loved the feeling of being ready to cook her son a good meal. Now that he could eat most things if she cut them up and mashed them, there was great satisfaction in knowing he was well fed. What a change from last year, when it had been an almost impossible job to feed herself, and she had such poor milk for him. He'd been malnourished for his first few months of life and she could never quite forgive herself for that, even if it had not been her fault.

'You all right over there, Brian?' she called out, but he simply carried on with his song and collapsing his bricks. Maybe he was not cut out to be a builder, she thought, as she chopped the end off the first carrot. She wondered what he would become. Perhaps an engineer like Joe. It didn't hurt to dream.

She was lost in her thoughts when the front door handle turned. At first she did not react. Perhaps it was one of the Banhams, or even Billy. Her heart beat a little faster at that. Then a voice that she thought she would never hear again spoke to her.

'Hello, Kath. Bet you didn't expect to see me.'

Silhouetted in the light from the open door was the frame of a man: tall, broad, menacing. Kathleen thought she was imagining things. This could not be.

'I just come to see how you're doing without me.'

She stared in disbelief. This was all wrong. The man was meant to be dead. She had the telegram, the official letter, the pension. Yet it looked and sounded like him.

'Ray?'

The man stepped forward. 'That's right, Kath. Back from the dead. What's the matter? You don't look very pleased to see me.'

'I don't . . . I don't understand.'

Ray advanced into the little room, needing

345

only a few steps to reach Kathleen at her kitchen counter. 'No, I don't suppose you do.' He laughed but there was no warmth in it. She drew back, confused and also repulsed. He smelt as if he hadn't washed in a long while. She could see he was dirty, his clothes grimy, dust on his hands and face. This was not the dandy who had used his shallow charms to seduce her years ago. His eyes glittered and she sensed the danger radiating from him. Was he on the run? How could this happen? Then she noticed a detail of his shabby shirt. It was fastened with dark brown buttons, and one was missing. That one she'd found on the floor . . . he'd been here. She hadn't imagined being watched. He could have walked in on her at any time. She thought she might be sick.

'Why don't you offer me a cup of tea, Kath? Or something stronger?'

Once she would have dropped everything to do his bidding but now she hesitated, numb with shock. 'What are you doing here, Ray? Why are you here at all?'

He folded his arms and scoffed. 'Oh that's charming, that is. Not a word of welcome for your old man. All these months and that's what I get.'

Kathleen slowly shook her head. 'You're dead, Ray. I saw it in black and white.'

He laughed again, louder this time. 'That's what you were all meant to think. Why would I want to hang about when everyone was trying to kill me? You can't imagine what it was like, men getting shot all around, kids dying like flies. I

346

wasn't sticking around for it to be me next. It was easy enough to disappear in all the confusion, and then of course they thought I was dead.'

Kathleen thought of Billy's bravery, heading over to Dunkirk when he had hardly ever been on a boat before, sailing right into the centre of hell to rescue the survivors. What a contrast to this coward who stood before her, mocking the sacrifice of so many. Her pulse beat hard with disbelief as she tried to absorb the sight of the man whose good looks used to make her knees melt. How could she have been so blind to what he really was?

'So what did you do?' she asked, playing for time. She had to work out a way of getting him out of the flat. Her eyes flew to Brian but the toddler was still absorbed in his game. She prayed he would stay that way; that he wouldn't demand attention and set his father off into the all too familiar rage. Something she had believed she would never have to endure again.

'Oh, I swapped my merchant-navy gear for some civilian's clothes; he was dead and wasn't going to miss them,' Ray said easily. 'One of those little boats was happy to take me back, didn't ask no questions. Then I got a lift and ended up back in Liverpool. Elsie took me in. I believe you've met.' His face darkened.

'Not for long.' Kathleen had no wish to talk about that woman.

Ray settled back to lean against the wall opposite her. 'She had her uses, I must say. She was ever so obliging at first. Knew how to keep her man happy.' He sighed. 'It all changed when I brought her down here, I don't mind telling you now. Got a bit above herself, she did. I had to teach her a lesson or two. I'm sure you remember what that was like.'

Kathleen forced her face to remain neutral, although she remembered all too painfully.

'She didn't do a great job persuading you to cough up half the pension, did she? I told her she was wasting her time. Still, it was worth a go.' He rubbed the knuckles of one hand with the other, and Kathleen felt the blood pounding in her ears.

'Anyway, she was soon up to her old tricks so I kicked her out. Told her to take that snivelling kid with her. He ain't none of mine, despite what she'd like me to believe. Led me a right song and dance about that.'

Kathleen felt a surge of relief. Brian didn't have a little bastard brother somewhere out there; it had all been a tissue of lies and Billy had been right.

'I'll get to the point, Kath.' Ray looked directly at her. 'We could do a bit of mutual business, you and me. You see, that little place I had with her got bombed. Nothing left of it but a shell, and I can't live in that.'

Kathleen recalled Billy saying something about Elsie coming out of a shop in Poplar. Perhaps they had lived near it. Poplar had suffered badly in the raids of the last week.

'So I thought I'd come back and live here.'

'Here?' The word burst from her before she could stop it.

348

'Yes, here. With my very own wife and child. I been back a couple of times to check you was still at the same address, and I have to say you been very careless. That spare key to the back door is where you always left it, tucked under the pot by the drainpipe. Anyone could get in.' Ray had made no effort to look around for Brian. He obviously still didn't care one iota about the boy. 'See, Kath, it makes sense. You got my pension. You can afford to keep me. You can't report me for going AWOL because, if you do, you lose the money. But if you fail to report me you're committing an offence. You got no choice. I'll see to it that someone shops you if you even try. Neat, ain't it? Your own beloved husband back from the dead after all this time. Now we can play happy families all over again.' He leered in the gathering gloom.

Kathleen gasped. He was crazy. Even if she wanted him to, he couldn't stay here for long. Everyone knew everyone else's business in Jeeves Place. It would be madness. They'd be discovered, he would be under arrest and she would be prosecuted for aiding and abetting. What a nightmare. She cursed herself for not checking on that key.

There was a bit of her that automatically wanted to agree, just as she had always done for years. It was so much easier. Crossing Ray never worked; he would be free with his fists and twist whatever she'd say, mocking her, belittling her. For a moment she could imagine how it would be: her doing everything he asked; cooking, cleaning, suffering his pawing hands, putting up with whatever he wanted. Him spending all the money on drink, her being hungry all the time.

Things were different now. She had Brian to protect. She would not allow this lying excuse for a man to hurt her boy, or to ruin her life all over again. Her hands were shaking in fear but also in rage. 'No,' she said.

Ray looked at her in surprised amusement. 'No? What do you mean, no?'

She met his gaze and held it. 'No, Ray. You can't just turn up here after all those months and expect to be welcomed with open arms. Not after you been off with your fancy woman.'

Ray's face burst into a smile. 'Ah, you're jealous. I might have known it. Still holding a candle for me, are you? Course you are. Let me tell you, she was only ever a bit of fun on the side. Not like you. You're my wife, Kath.' He stood away from the wall.

'No, Ray. Don't come any closer.'

He frowned in incomprehension. 'You don't mean that, Kath.'

Kathleen pushed herself up to her full height. 'I do, Ray. Don't you try and lay your hands on me. You stay back, now.'

Ray's eyes flashed at the challenge. 'That's not like you, Kath. I don't believe you.' He took a step closer.

'Get out, Ray!' She raised her voice a little, desperate not to scare Brian, but refusing to give in.

He advanced still further. 'Get out? Why should I? It's my house as much as yours. More, as I'm the man. I'm not getting out. Are you going to make me?' He smiled at the ridiculous idea.

Suddenly fury flooded through her. Without thinking what she was doing, Kathleen reached behind in one swift movement and picked up the heavy pan she'd had ready to brown her meat in. In one smooth swipe she aimed it at her husband and connected with the side of his head.

He cried out in agony but the look on his face was more one of disbelief: that his obedient wife should suddenly turn against him.

'Get out,' she repeated, realising he was on the back foot now. She made to swing the pan again and he retreated to the door, flinging it open.

'You haven't heard the last of this,' he threatened. 'You remember what I said. You don't have a leg to stand on, not if you want to keep getting the money.' Then he turned and was gone.

★   ★   ★

Kathleen sank down at her small wooden table, clutching the sides of it. Brian, sensing that she was upset, came over and hugged her around her knees and she bent to pick him up and set him on her lap. She was still trembling from shock, fear and overwhelming anger.

If it weren't for the pan on the floor she would not have believed what just happened. It was so far beyond credibility. She had thought she was safe from Ray, from his violence and selfishness, and did not want to recognise that he was all too real. She had loved him once, but his behaviour during their marriage had killed off any affection, leaving only terror and then intense dislike. She had borne the burden of guilt all summer, ashamed that his death had brought her such relief. She sniffed. She had been wasting her time. She had thought she was a widow, but had felt too weighed down to take advantage of her new freedom. Now it seemed as if she was back in the old prison, being shackled to someone she no longer loved, but hated from the depths of her being.

She stroked her son's hair, so silky and smooth. 'Don't worry, I'm going to keep you safe,' she murmured, loathing that Ray still had the power to shake her to her core. Now the shock was wearing off she knew she had to face the dilemma that he had described so brutally. If she reported him to the authorities, she would lose his pension. If she didn't, she was conniving in his deception. Neither route offered her any comfort. She was certain only that she would not take him back to live under the same roof. The very thought made her feel sick.

Kathleen gritted her teeth and realised she had to ask for help. She could not think this through on her own, she was too agitated. The Banhams had enough on their plate, what with the new baby and the news about Harry. A sob caught in her throat as she pictured how thrilled they had all been at his return from the dead. Everyone had been delighted. It was the complete opposite of learning about Ray. How thrilled Peggy would have been if it had been Pete — but he had been killed, without a shadow of a doubt, in the waters off Dunkirk. It was sod's law that Ray had survived, intact, when those other good men would have deserved it so much more.

As ever, she would have to speak to Billy. He knew Ray as well as anyone. How she longed for him to make this problem go away, but for the life of her she couldn't see how. Perhaps it was a good thing after all that she hadn't responded to that look in his eyes; if she had given in to that powerful temptation she would have committed adultery, albeit unwittingly. What a mess. Perhaps he should get on with his life and forget her completely, now that he'd met Belinda . . . and yet, from the way he had gazed at her that first night of the blitz, she knew what he still felt for her. It had not gone away. But now she could do nothing about it, in all conscience. It was too late.

The clock showed it was six o'clock. Wearily she lifted Brian back onto the worn rug. 'Time to make your tea,' she said, retrieving the heavy pot and wiping it clean. If she hurried there would still be time to make their stew before the raids began after dark. Then they would wait for the call of the siren before struggling over to the church basement. Yet if there was a raid, that meant Billy would be out on duty. She would intercept him somehow and arrange to see him to share her bad news. She absolutely had to tell him.

28

Alice had wondered if she would one day be called out to this particular household. Ever since Pauline had mentioned that her gran had leg ulcers, she suspected that time was growing closer. Now the message had come through and Alice happened to be the nurse with space on her morning round. She steeled herself. Her previous encounters with the elderly woman had not gone well.

At least the house was not far from the nurses' home. However, even on this narrow street of rundown two-up, two-downs, the place stood out in its dire state. Alice wondered if any of it was due to the air raids, which were happening virtually every evening now. Many of the roads around Dalston had suffered direct hits, and gaps were appearing along many of the terraces. Other houses showed signs of bomb damage — broken windows, missing roof tiles. Still, as she drew closer, she decided this place was suffering from years of neglect, with its peeling paintwork, rotten woodwork and sagging roof.

Alice sighed. She was bone tired, as the raids cut into their sleep. She didn't want to risk leaving the home's refuge room to go up to her own cosy bed until the all clear sounded, but she found it hard to sleep on the floor, or in a chair, with so many others packed into the same space. Some of them found it easier than others.

Edith could drop off with no problem, claiming the crowded conditions reminded her of when she was younger, and didn't mind at all. Mary had an eye mask to shut out any light and was determined that nothing would get in the way of her beauty sleep. Alice admired her single-minded resolution, but it didn't work for her.

Nevertheless, she had to do her best for this difficult old woman. Blinking quickly to try to wake up a little more, she knocked on the door. Flakes of faded green paint fell off.

'It's open,' came a shout from inside.

Alice pushed the door, which led directly into a small room. It was no bigger than the main room of Kathleen's small flat, but it was completely different in every other way. The filthy net curtain blocked out much of the light. There was an unpleasant smell, a combination of damp, stale food and unwashed human bodies. Everything was covered in a layer of dust, the fire had not been swept, dirty dishes were piled on the wonky table and used cups littered the floor. It took Alice a few moments to make out the old woman, who was sitting in a chair in the far corner, near the uncarpeted stairs.

'Oh, it's you,' were her first words of welcome.

'Hello,' said Alice, as brightly as she could. 'Yes, we've met before. I know Pauline from St Benedict's school. Her favourite teacher is a friend of mine.'

The woman snorted. 'You can save your breath if you've come to try to get her evacuated. She ain't leaving and that's that. I ain't having her go off to total strangers. She's stopping here with me.'

Alice set down her bag. 'No, I haven't come about that. I'm here to check on your legs. Pauline said you'd had trouble with your ulcers and now Dr Patcham has decided we're to come regularly to make sure they're properly cleaned and dressed, so they'll heal faster.' She couldn't imagine how anything could be clean in this place. No wonder the ulcers were failing to improve.

'Is that a fact?' the woman said grimly. 'Suppose you'd better have a look, then. Hope you got a strong stomach, they fair turn mine.' She shifted her weight in the chair and stuck her legs out straight in front of her so that they were nearly in the ash-filled hearth.

Alice cast around and noticed a small footstool. 'Is it all right if I move this across, and then you can rest each leg on this while I take a closer look?'

'Suit yerself.' The patient clearly wasn't going to make it easy. Alice wondered if it was because the woman already distrusted her, or if she was like this with everybody. She pulled the stool across, setting down all the unwashed clothes that had been piled on it, and then drew up her bag.

'Do you have a waste bin in here?'

'Are you bleedin joking? Where would I put it? We chuck most things straight out in the back yard.'

'I don't think it would be a good idea to do that with used dressings,' Alice said firmly. 'You have young children around — we can't have them picking them up.'

The woman snorted again. 'What, Hitler's blowing half our houses to smithereens and you're worried about a few old bandages? I should have thought you had more important things to worry about. Don't you get in a flap and blame me for not having a la-di-da bin.'

Alice counted to ten. 'I'll remove them and then dispose of them safely, then. We've got to try to maintain standards of hygiene, raids or no raids.'

The woman looked at her as if she was mad, but made no further comment as Alice swiftly removed the old dressings and got her first look at the ulcerated legs. Now she could see why the old lady was bad-tempered. They were among the worst ulcers she had encountered, and despite her strong stomach she came close to backing away.

'Bet you never seen anything like these,' the woman cackled.

Alice took a swift breath through her mouth and controlled her voice carefully. 'They aren't very nice to look at, are they? They must be causing you great discomfort.'

'Hurt like hell, they do,' the woman confirmed.

'Well, let's get them cleaned up.' Alice got to work, gently swabbing the affected parts of the leg, cleaning and then disinfecting them before rebandaging the limb. 'Right, now the next one.'

The woman leant back as Alice did what she had been sent there to do, gritting her teeth but not crying out. Alice admired her stoicism. 'You're taking this very well,' she said.

The woman replied only when both legs were finished. 'Used to it, ain't I? I usually does it for myself. Lap of luxury having someone else to see to it. Will you do this all the time now?'

Alice checked the doctor's notes in her mind's eye. 'Me or one of the other nurses, depending on who is available. We have to share patients now, as we're being called out to tend to injuries after every raid.'

The woman became more animated. 'Bleedin' nuisance, they are. I can't get me gin. One of the pubs got bombed and the other one won't serve Pauline. I had to go over there myself — in my condition, I ask you. I said to them, we ain't ever had no trouble before. You'll get paid if that's what yer worried about. The nipper don't drink it, she knows she got to bring it straight back to me, but he wasn't having any of it. Bleedin' busybody.'

Alice nodded. She knew Pauline went on errands for her grandmother, including buying her gin, which the old woman was never without. 'Maybe it's just as well not to send her out in the evenings, in case she gets caught when the siren goes,' she suggested.

'She knows how to look after herself,' the old woman claimed. 'It's all I can do to mind her little brother. We stay here, we're as safe as anywhere.'

Alice thought about advising her patient to make for the nearest shelter, but could see that walking anywhere would be difficult for her. She would speak to Pauline's teacher, and make sure the little girl knew she could take her brother to a nearby church hall, which Alice remembered had a big shelter. That might be the most diplomatic course of action.

'Right, I must be on my way,' she said, wondering if she would be allocated to this patient again.

The woman nodded in the gloom. 'Go on then, bugger off. See yerself out.'

Alice turned, having expected nothing other. As she opened the door, the woman called out again.

'Meant to say. Thank you, Nurse. I know it's not a pretty sight. So thank you.'

Alice bit back her gasp of surprise. 'Not at all,' she said. 'Don't you worry, we'll get you on the mend in no time.'

Cycling off to her next patient, she reflected that those few unexpected words of thanks had meant more to her than many of the loud outpourings of gratitude from easier patients. Perhaps Pauline's gran wasn't so bad after all. She would hang on to that moment to lift her spirits in the dark days to come.

★　★　★

'You look as if you got something on your mind, Bill.' Ron came out of the warehouse and pulled a face at his colleague. 'What's up?'

Billy raised his eyebrows. 'What, as well as night after night of being kept up by the raids, idiots who won't go into their shelters and think they know best, and half our goods here being set on fire and no use to anybody? Leaving us to try to sort out the mess?'

'Just thought you looked a bit down in the dumps,' Ron said. 'Want a cuppa?'

'Yeah, all right.' Billy knew it wasn't Ron's fault, but he was short-tempered that morning. Yes, it was down to lack of sleep and all the reasons he'd given his mate, but on top of that was the astonishing news that Kathleen had told him yesterday when she had waylaid him outside the big church around the corner from Jeeves Street. At first he hadn't believed her, but her evident distress had convinced him before long.

He had tried to allay her fears, pointing out that Ray was a man on the run. 'Why does he think he's safe staying with you?' he had asked. 'Why not go to his mother's? At least she loves him.'

'I know, I wondered that,' she'd said, twisting her hands together. 'You'd think he'd be noticed at once on my street, but he seems prepared to risk it. It's because of the money. He's got one over on me, whereas if his ma decided to hand him in, there'd be no comeback on her. Or any of her neighbours could shop him but she'd be no worse off. It's me who stands to lose the most. So I'm the easy target.'

Billy had gazed at her sorrowful face and felt his heart melting all over again. 'You leave it with me,' he said. 'He won't hurt you any more, Kath. I'll make sure of it.' He had all but taken her in his arms there and then, but the sirens had wailed and there had been no chance to. Every time he drew close to her, he was foiled. So he had to help her in whatever way he could. She had nobody else to turn to and he could not let her suffer. The very thought of it tore him in two.

'How's your Alfie coming along? Have you heard any more?' he asked now, accepting a steaming mug of tea.

Ron launched into an account of Alfie's latest news, as dictated in a letter written by the pretty nurse with the dark hair.

It was towards the end of their lunch hour that Billy spotted his most unreliable colleague, Bertie. He was striding along the wharf with a face like thunder. Normally Billy would have given him a wide berth in that mood, but today that wasn't a choice. He matched the other man's pace and Bertie rounded on him.

'What d'you want, Billy? I'm busy, so get out of my way.'

Billy did not back down. 'I need a word with you,' he said steadily.

'Then you'll have to walk along with me, I got somewhere to get to in a hurry.' Bertie started off again and Billy kept up, the wind off the water ruffling his hair. Dust whipped around their feet.

'Ray's back, isn't he?' Billy said.

Bertie stopped and turned to him. 'What do you mean? Ray died at Dunkirk.'

Billy supposed he should have expected Bertie to deny it, but he didn't have time to waste. 'No he didn't, and you know it. He's been living in Poplar, but now he's been bombed out and is back causing trouble. Where is he? Are you hiding him?'

'Me!' Bertie abruptly dropped his pretence of not knowing. 'You got to be joking. Ma would kill me.'

Typical, thought Billy. Bertie was happy to lie about Ray but he was still afraid of his mother. 'So he hasn't been cutting you in on his latest deals, then,' he said, taking a guess at how Ray had been making his living since reappearing in the docklands.

'His deals!' Bertie was incensed, responding to the provocation better than Billy could have hoped. 'He's in no position to do his own deals, is he? He has to rely on mine. He does what I tell him to, not the other way around.'

'I see,' said Billy.

'Don't you be getting the idea that he's in charge,' snarled Bertie, his pride deeply hurt at the suggestion. 'I'm the brains around here. All he gets are the crumbs from my table.'

'And what are they?' Billy asked curiously.

Bertie rounded on him again. 'Well, I can tell you what they *aren't*, for a start. They aren't acids what certain people near here would pay good money for. You had to go sticking your nose in there, didn't you? Playing the hero, rescuing that kiddie and that tall nurse. Yes, I heard all about it. I was all for making the pair of you pay for that, but it was too risky, might have blown my cover. All the same, you can consider yourselves lucky. Next time I might not be so generous.'

'Don't you dare hurt Belinda.' Billy was horrified. He knew she had been moments away from being burnt by that spilt acid in the yard.

She'd only been doing her job. That would mean nothing to someone like Bertie. He put his black-market profits above everything.

'Oh, Belinda, is it? Touched a nerve, have I?' Bertie crowed. 'You're more of a ladies' man than I thought, Billy. Course we all know you been sniffing around Ray's woman for ages, but nice to hear you got a backup plan now she's got her old man back.'

Billy bit his lip hard so he would not react. He counted to ten. 'So where is Ray?'

Bertie had had enough. 'Nowhere that concerns you. Why would I tell you, when I need him to button his mouth? Can't have him blabbing all my business to the likes of you. Now get out of my way, I got enough on my plate without you bothering me.' He wheeled around and strode off.

Billy watched him go. While he hadn't managed to learn Ray's exact whereabouts, Bertie had given away more than he realised. Ray and Bertie were working together; that was no surprise, but it was useful to have it confirmed. Ray was not living with Bertie, though, and from Kathleen's description it sounded as if he was roughing it somewhere. There were plenty of places to hide around the docks, but as he had complained to Ron earlier, the docks were prime targets for the enemy's bombs. Plenty had already been damaged. No wonder Ray wanted to move into the comparative safety of his wife's flat.

If Bertie was planning on siphoning off some of the incoming goods, as was his habit, or even storing his own around the dockside warehouses, no wonder he was in a bad temper. He had already lost one of his safe houses when the acid was discovered. He must be under pressure from all sides. Billy decided to watch the man more closely. If he was this much on edge, it might not be long before he cracked.

29

Bridget was gradually mastering the strange habits of her bicycle. She had been well warned by everybody in the home about it, how all the bikes were unlike any she might have learnt on back in Ireland. 'They have minds of their own and there's not a thing you can do about it,' Edith had cautioned her. 'You have to make the most of it and then it won't be so bad.'

Bridget had laughed at the tradition of every nurse putting something personal on her own handlebars, the quicker to identify her bike in the communal rack. You didn't want to get stuck riding someone else's, which would have its own tricky habits. Bad enough coping with yours. Mary showed her the scrap of blue ribbon she had tied on hers, and Bridget had immediately gone for a piece of green lace. 'Green for Ireland — then you'll know whose it is,' she pointed out. 'Sorry, Ellen — you'll have to find something else.'

Now the little fragment of lace blew in the early evening breeze as she came closer to Victory Walk. It had been a long day and the final visit had gone on for what felt like hours. An old man had been hurt in one of the raids and needed his wound seen to, but he was reluctant to let her leave. She had realised he was simply lonely. His sons had been called up and his daughters-in-law and their children evacuated. He told her she was the only person he had seen to talk to all day, and she didn't have the heart to leave him immediately after that.

So now she was late. 'Ellen had better have saved me something to eat,' she muttered under her breath. The streets were quiet now that most sensible folk were in having their tea. She had passed a couple of WVS vans, the women preparing to hand hot drinks to the ARP wardens and whoever else might be called out this evening: fire-watchers and the like. Otherwise the day was winding down. She was just wondering what tonight's meal was likely to be when the dreaded sound of the siren began.

Bridget was tempted to risk it and try and make it back to the nurses' home, but common sense told her she was too far away. She cast around for the best place to go. Then she recognised a side road; she knew it was where Dr Patcham lived, as she had had to visit the surgery in his house on a few occasions. He had a shelter in a secure basement — she could go there. She liked the kindly old doctor, whom everyone had welcomed back with relief once his unpopular latest locum had left.

Someone was putting up the blackout blinds as she approached and, moments later, the door opened. It was his housekeeper, who immediately remembered the freckle-faced nurse before her. 'Ah, Miss O'Doyle, isn't it? Come in at once. You don't want to be out on the streets in these raids. We can't lose any of our highly trained nurses, can we?' She ushered Bridget inside.

Bridget was astonished to see the surgery was full, and recognised one of the patients, Millicent from near Cricketfield Road. Dr Patcham rose from his desk. 'Excellent! Help is at hand!' he exclaimed, moving across the room to greet her at a speed that belied his years. In other circumstances he would have been thinking of his retirement but, with so many younger doctors going into the armed services, that was out of the question.

In the distance, there was a distinctive bang. The bombing had started.

'You are just in time,' he went on, his white eyebrows twitching. 'Out of the bombs and into our clinic.'

Bridget suppressed a shiver as another, louder explosion went off. 'What clinic is this?' she asked, struggling to maintain her calm, but knowing she had to. Nurses could not be seen to panic.

'Ah, of course, you won't have been back to Victory Walk to see my memo.' He turned and waved expansively at the patients sitting waiting on a variety of chairs around the room. 'What with all the raids, many people aren't in their homes for their regular morning appointments, and their daily schedules are disrupted. So I've opened an evening clinic to ensure they can have their injections. Not ideal, but better than missing a day, wouldn't you say?'

Bridget had a horrible realisation what she had just walked into. 'Wh . . . what injections?'

'Why, insulin of course. This is the diabetic clinic. These poor people have to adjust their eating patterns on top of everything else, and yet without the injections . . . well, I don't have to tell you. I can see at least one of the people here knows you.'

'Oh yes, Doctor, Nurse O'Doyle is very good, very reassuring.' Millicent spoke up from the corner.

Bridget wanted nothing more than to run out of the door. She would take her chance with the bombs, make it back to the haven of the refuge room, settle in with Ellen and Alice and Edith. But she could see that Dr Patcham would not be best pleased. Moreover, with the number of patients waiting, she could tell that in fact her arrival was a godsend. The old man would be working until heaven knew what time if he had to do this on his own. 'R . . . right,' she said. 'I'd better wash my hands.' There, she'd said it. She had committed to helping, despite her fear of the syringes.

As she emerged from the little cloakroom, more loud bangs reverberated through the elegant old house, shaking the Victorian mirrors and finely polished dark furniture. The house-keeper apologised, but had to turn off the electricity and gas. 'I'll bring the Tilley lamps,' she promised.

So, by the flickering flames of the improvised lighting, Bridget worked her way through the patients, administering insulin as more and more bombs fell. Flashes of orange from outside lit the room from where a square of blackout material had been dislodged. The housekeeper tried in vain to pin it back but found the window frame was too damaged. 'Keep away from there,' Bridget called in alarm. 'You don't want to be caught by breaking glass. Better that a little light escapes — in all that fire outside, it's the least of anyone's worries.' The housekeeper nodded and hastily moved to an inside wall.

'Why don't you take all the patients who have had their insulin down to the basement?' the doctor suggested to the shaking woman, who, evidently glad of something to do, led a row of people out of the room and down the corridor.

'Not long now,' Dr Patcham said cheerily, and Bridget wondered where he got his energy from. He was bustling around like a man half his age, indefatigably cheerful, calming the frightened patients who were shivering too much to inject. Her admiration for him doubled. Straightening her shoulders, she knew she had to emulate him. There simply was no space for her previous nervousness; there was too much to do.

As swiftly as possible, she worked her way to the last patient, Millicent.

'I'm so glad it is you, Nurse O'Doyle!' the woman said, grasping her arm. 'I know you are all specially qualified, but you are my favourite, though I shouldn't say.'

'Now, really!' Bridget laughed it off in embarrassment. 'Tell me, how is your nephew?' As she talked, she swiftly administered the insulin.

Millicent beamed in delight, her face visible in the light from the Tilley lamp. 'Oh, very well indeed. How good of you to remember. See, that is typical of you. Thank you so much.' She rolled her sleeve back down and rose.

'Come, Nurse, we'll all go down to the basement now,' the doctor said, having treated his last patient as well. 'Much the safest place. None of us is to leave until the all clear. My housekeeper has extra stores of tea for emergencies just such as this.' He escorted them down to the basement door, and both patients went in.

'Just one moment, Nurse.' He stepped a little away from the opening and turned to Bridget. 'I wanted to take the chance in this lull between bombs to thank you. We've never had so many patients in the surgery. I don't know what I would have done if you hadn't turned up when you did.'

Before Bridget could reply, the loudest explosion of the evening rocked the building, the very walls seeming to shake. Dr Patcham stumbled, and his glasses fell and broke. Bridget bent to pick them up.

'Dash it.' For a moment he looked his age, in the shadowy light. Then his customary cheerfulness returned. 'No matter, I have others. In my mahogany desk upstairs. That was my grandfather's — it will take more than a bomb to wreck that.' He exhaled heavily. 'As I was saying, Nurse — no, hear me out, indulge an old man if you will. I confess, it's hard to remain calm under such circumstances. Your steady demeanour was an inspiration this evening. The way you conducted yourself made me believe that I too could maintain an encouraging manner, reassure the patients.'

Bridget gasped aloud and brought her hand to her mouth. 'But . . . but . . . that's how I felt. I'm a mass of nerves underneath, but I saw how you were with the patients and made my mind up to be like that too.'

Dr Patcham let out a guffaw of laughter, and his tweed jacket shook. 'See what a good team we make, Nurse! Of course you're afraid. I'm afraid, and I've been through a war already. Doesn't matter. As long as you can keep your head and treat your patients, you can be as afraid as you like. That shows you are human. But make no mistake, Nurse, you did sterling work tonight, in conditions that would have floored many a man. Now come and have a well-deserved cup of tea.'

Bewildered but buoyed up by his words, Bridget followed him into the big basement, suddenly aware that in all the terror of the falling bombs, her fear of syringes had faded.

★   ★   ★

Flo stood in her doorway, waving at Gillian, who was facing backwards in the big pram. Little Alan was out of sight, closely swaddled for his first ever trip outside. Mattie was pushing the pram like the expert she was, fully recovered from the rigours of his birth, and Kathleen was alongside with a toddling Brian on his new woollen reins. 'Look after them!' Flo called cheerily as Kathleen turned.

'I will!' Kathleen shouted back. They were only going as far as the small local park but it was a big step for Mattie and Alan.

Flo went back inside and reached for the key she had seen Kathleen leave on the ledge by the coat hooks. She knew it was sneaky but she wanted to give the young woman a surprise. After all, she was almost like another daughter to Flo, and her own mother never gave her treats of any kind. Flo had baked an extra little carrot cake, and wanted to decorate it in Kathleen's kitchen. She was going to arrange pieces of dried fruit on top to spell 'Thank You', inspired by the lemon-peel arrangement those nice nurses had produced for Joe's homecoming. Swiftly she gathered her things in a wicker basket and hurried around the corner to Jeeves Place. It shouldn't take long.

Somehow both Jeeves Street and Jeeves Place were still unscathed by the raids, unlike plenty of places nearby. The roads were quiet. Many people would be snatching forty winks to compensate for all the disturbed nights of sleep. Flo wondered if she could do the same once she got back, before the children returned and the house became noisy again.

Even though Kathleen's house had not been damaged, the front doorstep was still filmed by a layer of light ash, which must have drifted down from fires close by. Flo tutted as she opened the door. She would brush it clean so the girl wouldn't need to bother. She knew how Kathleen would hate to see such dirt.

She set down her basket and took the brush from where she knew it was kept in the back kitchen, and went out again. Inspecting the step

372

more closely she could see there was a footprint. That was strange. The shape looked as if it had been made by a high-heeled shoe — the kind Mattie had tried to wear before she settled down and married Lennie. That phase hadn't lasted long as she could never balance properly. Flo smiled at the memory. Mattie had been such a handful back then. Then she wondered who Kathleen might know who wore such shoes.

It was as she eased herself back up to a standing position, the step now pristine, that Flo saw who the shoe belonged to. A young woman was striding down the street, the high heels presenting her with no problems. She was pushing a pram, under which was a bulging duffel bag. Flo folded her arms over her dog's-tooth print frock, every instinct telling her this young woman, with her brightly bleached hair and scarlet lipstick, meant trouble.

The woman stopped before her and glared. 'Where's Kathleen?' Her voice revealed she was not from London.

The cogs turned in Flo's brain. Mattie had told her a potted version of Kathleen's unwelcome visitor and her extraordinary claims. Those two words clinched it: a Liverpool accent. She knew exactly who this was but that didn't mean she had to show it.

Instead she smiled blandly. 'And who might you be?'

The young woman squared up to her as if for a fight. 'I might ask the same of you.'

Flo nodded. 'Indeed you might.' She waited, her face a mask of patience.

The young woman glared some more but then her bad temper got the better of her. 'Is she in there?' She stepped forward. 'Get out of the bloody way. Let me see. I've got a bone to pick with her.'

Flo stood her ground. She might be shorter than this woman in her tall spindly heels, and twice her age, and her hands might be stiff with arthritis, but she had no intention of being a pushover. 'Now then, young lady, I don't think I can let you into this house unless you tell me who you are.'

The woman's face was reddening with fury. 'That should be my house by rights. She gets everything while I get nothing. Well, she won't get away with it.'

Flo did not move. 'You'd better tell me what you mean by that.'

'Oh, I'll tell you all right. I'll scream it loud enough so everyone can hear.'

Flo glanced along the street. The weather had turned and people had kept their windows closed, against the increasing chill as well as the drifting remnants of ash from all the fires. If this visitor chose to shout her business from the pavement, then no one would hear.

'She might be Ray's official widow, but I'm his most recent woman, so that should count for something. She gets all his pension, when it should come to me. Well, I'm here to ruin her plans. Just you tell her Elsie came by. I know how to stop that money coming in, and she can see how she likes it, to be left penniless by Ray Berry.'

Flo was tempted to say 'I think she knows', but bit it back. 'I'll tell her no such thing,' she said calmly. 'I think you should take your nasty accusations and leave right now.'

Elsie flew at her. 'I'm not going nowhere. You listen to me if you're so keen to stick up for her. Let's see how much you really know about your precious friend. Or are you her mother? You look old enough all right.' Flo didn't react, which goaded Elsie still further. 'She's been living a lie. She's been taking that money even though she knows full well that Ray Berry's still alive. There! Bet that shocked you, didn't it? What do you have to say about that?'

Flo kept her face impassive. True, when Mattie had told her and Stan that the despicable coward hadn't died at Dunkirk after all, she had been shaken to her core. Mattie had sworn them to secrecy, asking them not even to let Kathleen know that they had been told, as Kathleen was desperate to keep it quiet — not because she wanted to fraudulently keep the pension but because she wished to protect Brian.

'I think you are talking stuff and nonsense,' she said.

'It's true all right. And now the bastard's kicked me out, and his little boy too! How about that! So I've got nothing to lose.' Elsie's eyes grew crafty. 'You can tell your precious Kathleen that I'm going to shop him to the police. Then he'll be for it, and she'll be arrested for protecting him. I know he's been round here. She'll be in water so hot she'll squeal.' She pushed angrily on the pram and it swung around so that Flo could see the small child's face.

She considered her next move. While she didn't usually approve of breaking the law, she had no wish to bring the police to Kathleen's door. And what if Ray got wind of this, and thought it was Kathleen who had reported him? What might he do to her or Brian in retaliation? Flo had seen the results of the last beating he had inflicted on his wife, and had no intention of letting that happen again. She had to take a gamble.

'You got no proof,' she said.

'What? You can stand there and say that?' Elsie shouted. 'What proof do I need? I'll tell them my story and they'll see how wronged I am. Besides, look in front of you! Here's my proof — my son! Ray's son!'

Flo slowly shook her head. 'You're wrong. They won't have no reason to believe you. They'll think it's a case of sour grapes. Or, if they do believe you, they'll want to know why you've waited all these months to tell them. They might well think that you're not doing it out of public spirit, or the goodness of your heart, and have you in for questioning instead, for harbouring a fugitive. And as for your boy,' she paused and refolded her arms, 'he's no more Ray Berry's son than I am. Is he?' She stared at Elsie until the young woman could no longer hold her gaze.

'You'll be sorry for this,' she hissed.

'No, Elsie, I don't think so. And don't you presume to threaten me.' Flo drew herself up to her full height. She hadn't raised three children in the East End for nothing. She'd had to battle to keep them on the right track often enough, and she was never one to back down from an argument. This young woman's threats were empty ones. 'You take your boy and get out of here. Don't you dare to come back and try anything to hurt Kathleen. You take your tricks elsewhere. There's nothing for you here.' She kept her voice level and her gaze steady until Elsie turned the pram around with a howl of frustration and set off back down the short street, her high heels clacking on the road's surface.

Flo brushed her hands down the sides of her frock. 'Good riddance,' she breathed. She doubted the woman would be back, now her bluff had been called. Flo debated telling Kathleen about it but decided it would only worry her, and she was pretty sure there was nothing to worry about any more. 'Right,' she said to herself. 'I'll give my hands a good wash as I feel dirty just for talking to that creature. Then I'll get on with that cake.'

★ ★ ★

'You're so lucky to have this kitchen to yourselves.' Edith gazed around the small, neat room that the two Irish nurses shared. 'I know we've got the service room, but sometimes it's so busy that I don't bother making myself a drink even if I want one.'

'Well, you're always welcome to come over here,' Bridget offered, setting the kettle to boil. 'We can do with the company. Otherwise we'll be bored of the sight of one another.' She smiled at Ellen to show she didn't mean it. 'Will you have a cup of cocoa now?'

'Yes please.' Edith perched on one of the stools that just fitted under the narrow table pushed beneath the window. The kitchen was not really big enough to sit in, but as the living room had been turned into a bedroom for Ellen, this was the only common space. She didn't feel she knew either of the two nurses well enough to sit in their rooms yet.

'And we have biscuits!' Bridget produced a packet from the freshly painted cupboard. She noticed Edith peering at the unfamiliar packaging. 'Mammy sent them from home. Don't worry, they taste just as good as your English ones.' She slid some onto a china plate.

'I'm sure they do.' Edith wasn't about to complain.

'Now tell us,' Ellen began, 'what is the latest news about your boyfriend? His parents went to see him, didn't they?'

Edith nodded, licking crumbs from her upper lip. 'They did. Right at the start of the bombing raids. They were ever so relieved to find him in one piece, you can imagine.' She popped the rest of the biscuit into her mouth. 'Delicious. Thank you.'

'I'll ask Mammy to send more,' promised Bridget, putting three cups of cocoa on the little table top. 'That was several weeks ago now, wasn't it?'

Edith smiled broadly. 'He's come on a lot since then. One of the nurses writes to me on his behalf now, and reads him my letters. As soon as they knew who he was, they started using his name and talking about Dalston to him and he began to respond. There's someone else on the ward from around here and he goes and chats to him about people they know in common and it really helps. Harry's now just able to chat back a little. The nurse says it's wonderful to watch, as this other man almost lost his eyesight but now he's got some of it back. She says they're her favourite patients.' Edith beamed. 'I wish I could swap places, but I don't suppose I'd get much work done if I did.'

Ellen helped herself to a biscuit. 'No, you're needed around here. Will you go to visit him again?'

Edith pulled a face. 'I would love to, but it's so hard getting there and back, and really I can't take up a space on the train when other people need it more. I'll have to wait a while. Still, I get the letters. Just knowing he's alive is like a wonder — that will have to do for now.'

Bridget stirred her cocoa, made mostly with water and just a tiny pinch of sugar. She dunked a biscuit in it. 'Excuse my manners but it makes it sweeter. You should give it a go. Edith, did I tell you that Fiona asked us about midwifery training?'

'No.' Edith looked up encouragingly.

'Well, she did. It's all your doing — you and Alice, having to deliver that baby in the air-raid shelter. She wants several of us to go on a course so that we're all set to handle difficult births in all manner of circumstances.'

'Not that they'll train us in a blackout with just a few candles for light, I dare say,' Ellen added. 'Wasn't that how it was?'

'Just about,' Edith admitted but, before she could say more, the all too familiar wail of the warning siren started up, ruling out any further conversation. 'Not again. Good job we'd just about finished our cocoa.' She drained her cup and stood. 'I'd better get over to the refuge room. You coming?'

'Take the rest of the packet.' Bridget passed her the remaining biscuits. 'We'll be over in a mo. I just want to get my knitting — no sense in wasting time if we don't have to.'

Edith left swiftly and Ellen stacked the used cups and plates beside the sink. 'These can wait until the all clear.' She looked at her friend. 'Are you still glad we came? Sometimes when that siren goes, my stomach turns over, I don't mind telling you.'

Bridget halted in her tracks, amazed. She always thought of Ellen as fearless; in all the years she'd known her, the other woman had never admitted to being afraid of anything, apart from wasps. She had considered herself the fearful one. She turned to her friend, her face thoughtful. 'Well . . . yes, I'm still glad.' She took a moment to consider her reply. 'I know it's dangerous, and it was one thing sitting in the staff room in Dublin wanting a bit of an adventure — another kettle of fish altogether now we're here and in the midst of it. But yes, I don't regret coming for one moment. Not even that evening in Dr Patcham's clinic, which was pretty bad now I look back on it. It's not only getting the chance to do extra training, although I can't wait to do the midwifery course — I love babies. It's more than that.' She hesitated, cleared her throat and then took the plunge. 'You'll think I'm crazy . . . '

'Well, that's nothing new.' Ellen smiled warmly but her eyes were quizzical.

'The thing is, I'm less afraid now. Not more. That sounds daft, doesn't it? But I used to be afraid all the time, of silly little things, and felt I wasn't good enough.'

'You never said!' Ellen cried. 'You should have told me, I could have helped.'

Bridget shook her head. 'I felt too stupid. Here I was, trained for years to do my job, and yet every time I went to inject somebody I thought I'd do it wrong. That made me doubt I could do all the rest of it too. And yet somehow, now we're actually being bombed, it's getting better. When there were all those people looking at me in the clinic, there just wasn't a choice. There's no time to think, we have to get on with it. I don't know why, it's completely the wrong way round, but I'd rather be here, in the heart of it all, than watching from the sidelines.'

Ellen's expression was full of sympathy. 'I never knew you thought like that. You've kept that quiet for so long, I don't know how you've managed. I'm scared out of my wits every time that blessed siren goes, but I'm not planning to run away. I just hope it's over soon.' She squared her shoulders. 'Better grab your knitting, we've to get over to that refuge room before we're blown to bits. We'd be no use to man nor beast if that happened.'

Bridget nodded. 'And we wouldn't be midwives either.'

'Wouldn't want to miss that,' Ellen agreed. 'Come on, quick, let's get to safety as fast as we can.'

30

Billy had kept his eyes peeled following Kathleen's news about Ray's reappearance, all the while wondering if the man he hated more than any other would return to his old home. Sometimes his mind flickered to the thought that Ray might go round and hurt her badly if he was desperate; or, even worse, do away with her. Yet what would be the point of that? If he really intended to live off his wife's pension then she would have to be able to draw it. Even that was ridiculous, he reminded himself. Ray must know deep down that there would be no hiding for long in Jeeves Place. The gossip-hungry neighbours would be on to him like a shot.

He had to hope that Bertie would let something else slip during the course of the day, as he was the only source of information. Bertie, however, appeared to regret having been so outspoken and spoke very little. Billy was sure the man was becoming more and more stressed, snapping at the least thing, frowning all the time, his nails bitten to the quick. He just needed to be patient. As long as Kathleen was safe, he could wait.

Meanwhile the Luftwaffe continued to drop their nightly bombs on the docks and the East End, meaning that everyone was bone tired, and the strenuous work on the wharfs and in the warehouses took longer as everyone dragged their exhausted bodies through the shifts. Fires raged through the night and lasted throughout the days, each one with its own strange characteristic. Pepper fires filled the air with tiny particles, which stung anyone who breathed them in. Rum fires resulted in torrents of blazing liquid pouring from the sheds, and the barrels themselves would explode. Rubber fires produced a vile stench and nobody could approach too closely, meaning they lasted for even longer. None of them knew what they would encounter when they turned up for work. Billy reflected that anyone who thought the dockers had a cushy job which meant they could avoid being called up was totally wrong. This was like being on the front line.

Today had started with fresh revelations of destruction, this time a large storage shed which had taken a direct hit. It had been made partly of timber and so had instantly gone up in flames, leaving little but charred beams and twisted steel in smoking heaps. Whatever had been stored there had mostly perished, but Billy, Bertie and the rest of the team had been ordered to recover what they could and move it to the other end of the wharf.

When Bertie saw where they were to work, he went white as a sheet.

Billy flicked him a glance but Bertie looked away, chewing his lip. Billy watched him closely, waiting for him to try to give the rest of them the slip. The others would be pleased if he did; they often complained at having Bertie in their group as he was nowhere near as fit as most dock workers, and was unable to pull his weight. They were better off without him. But Bertie hung around for most of the morning, pretending to help lift crates, shuffling around in the background.

It was only as lunch time drew near that he made a sly break for it, but Billy was ready for it. He followed his colleague as he made his way to the back of the ravaged shed to an area none of the work party had yet reached. Some crates there remained intact, but others lay partly burnt on the ground, their contents ruined. Behind them there appeared to be a row of smaller crates, which looked to have contained cardboard boxes, but little remained of them other than singed scraps, which smelt strongly of burnt paper. This was overlaid by a meaty stench, pungent and choking.

Bertie was coughing so much that he didn't hear Billy approach. Then he came to an abrupt halt. His hand flew to cover his mouth, then he started to gag. Wildly he turned around; only at that point did he realise he had been followed. He froze, his eyes watering from the appalling stink.

Finally he gave Billy a short nod. 'Might have known it would be you,' he croaked. All his previous belligerence had gone. 'Well, you'll be happy now. Got what you wanted at last.'

Billy shook his head, unable to work out what the man was talking about. 'What do you mean — was this where you kept your stuff? Those boxes over there, were they yours?'

Bertie turned regretfully to gaze at the smaller

crates. 'That would have made me a fortune,' he said, his voice so low that Billy could hardly hear him.

'What was in them?'

Bertie shook his head, as if he could scarcely take in the fact that his stolen goods were gone. 'Medicine,' he said shortly. 'Boxes and boxes of it. Everyone would have paid through the nose for it, there'd have been such a shortage. All these people getting hurt in the raids, the demand for this stuff has gone through the roof.'

Billy couldn't believe it. Surely not even Bertie would sink this low? 'This was meant for hospitals,' he gasped in horror. 'You've been stealing stuff intended to help the sick?'

Bertie shrugged. 'They'd still have got it in the end. Just had to pay more for it. Now they won't get it at all.'

Billy gazed at his colleague in complete incomprehension. Didn't he realise what he was doing? Had he no conscience at all?

'Don't be soft, Billy.' Bertie's voice was regaining some of its strength. 'It goes on all the time. I'm not the only one at it. Still, you'll be pleased. There's one less person to worry about. Haven't you noticed what's over there? What do you think's making that smell — how many medicines smell like a Sunday roast?'

Billy followed his gaze and his eyes blinked in shock. From behind one of the half-destroyed crates a pair of boots was visible. He had come across several dead bodies now during the course of his ARP duties; the first one had been the worst, but he still recoiled in horror each time, although he took care to hide this from any relatives of the unfortunate victim, or if there were people nearby waiting for his advice. He also knew that many dock workers had lost their lives in the weeks of the Blitz, and this was just one more of a sad and ever-growing list. However, Bertie's reactions told him this was of some significance.

'Come and see for yourself. I warn you, it ain't a pretty sight.' Bertie moved so that Billy could get a better look. He shifted a few burnt boxes out of the way and glanced down.

It was a man in his twenties, dark-haired, tall and broad of build, his face obscured by a fallen cardboard box. Billy reached in to lift it and gasped in recognition.

'Happy now?' Bertie taunted him. 'He's not escaping this time. No third time lucky. Knew it was him by his boots — I lent them to him myself. I don't think I want them back now.'

Billy stared at him, amazed by his callousness. 'He was working for you,' he breathed. 'If you hadn't cut him in on your deal, he'd still be alive.'

Bertie shrugged. 'Nah, he was hiding out down here anyhow, so he'd have copped it soon enough one way or another. Now pardon me, Billy, it was nice passing the time of day with you, but I must be off. I don't intend to end up like him, and if the people who were expecting this stuff delivered learn they aren't going to get it, then I don't fancy me chances. So toodle-oo.'

Before Billy could stop him Bertie, having recovered his breath and apparently over the shock, made a dash for it, running out of the remains of the shed and off down the wharf. Billy made no attempt to follow him. Best to let him go.

He returned his gaze to the corpse in front of him, noticing the burned flesh, the grisly black blisters. Perhaps he had passed out through smoke inhalation. It was only human to hope it had been as fast and as painless as possible, even if it must have been a terrible way to die. Yet Billy was aware that his main feeling was relief — because Ray Berry could never hurt Kathleen ever again.

★   ★   ★

Mattie bounced her growing baby in her arms, gazing into his round little face. His mouth puckered but he didn't cry. She reached in and touched the tip of his snub nose. 'Just like your daddy's,' she told him.

Flo came out into the back garden to see what they were doing. 'Don't let him get cold,' she warned. 'There's a real nip in the air now.'

Mattie tutted. 'See how well he's wrapped up. He couldn't get cold if he tried.' She shifted so that he was resting more comfortably on her shoulder. 'I was thinking about all that grass laid over the top of our shelter.'

Flo turned to look at it. They had piled slabs of turf over the metal for better insulation and because it looked nicer, although it had taken a battering from all the falling tiles and flying pieces of burnt debris. 'What about it?' she asked.

'We could grow something more useful there come the spring,' Mattie suggested. 'We could have big flowerpots as well, grow our own fruit and veg. You're always saying that onions are rarer than hen's teeth now, so we could try to grow our own. Or it wouldn't have to be flowerpots, we could use anything that was the right size.'

Flo nodded. 'That's not a bad idea. Where did you get that from?'

'Kath said something about it but I was too busy at the time to take much notice,' Mattie admitted. 'It's getting too late now, I suppose, but when the weather warms up again, we ought to try. I don't want the kids to get rickets.' Alan wriggled against her and she held him tighter, not wanting to think about him going short of good food. It was up to her to do the best for him, with no Lennie around to sort out the garden.

'All right then. I'll ask around to see if anybody has spare seeds we could have,' Flo replied, taken with the idea. 'Mind you, we got a winter to get through yet. Once we've had a rest from those blessed raids we'll all feel better. What we need is something to cheer us up.'

Mattie nodded. 'I been thinking about that too. I want to get Alan christened and do it proper. I know I'm not much of a one for going to church but I think Lennie would like it. There's no point in waiting for him to come home. We'll just do it with those who are here, but we could invite everyone back for a special dinner or something like that.'

Flo beamed in delight. 'That's exactly what we need. Something to celebrate. If I speak to the vicar this week, then we could get it booked in before Christmas. I can start saving my coupons right away. We'll have a cold buffet, then everyone can help themselves, and we wouldn't have to cook as soon as we got back from church . . . '

'Hang on, hold your horses,' Mattie laughed. 'We don't have to plan everything right away.'

'Oh yes we do.' Flo was in her element now. 'Come back inside and we can start on a list. If we want to do this thing properly there isn't a moment to lose. Alan is going to have the best christening party we can manage and that's all there is to it.'

★　★　★

Billy didn't bother getting changed after his shift ended. He could hardly bear to wait at the bus stop; if a bus hadn't come along smartish he would have run all the way to Jeeves Place on nervous energy alone. His desperation to tell Kathleen the news overrode everything.

As he took his seat, he noticed that the older woman next to him looked at his clothing slightly askance, and he realised he had soot on his overalls, as well as the usual dust and sawdust. Then again, plenty of the people on the crowded bus showed signs of having to cope with the bomb-damaged buildings. Perhaps he should have made the effort to smarten up — but that was of secondary importance. Kathleen had to be put out of her fear-filled misery as soon as possible.

A younger woman got on and Billy noticed she was carrying heavy shopping, and so he gave her his seat. He went to stand by the opening at the back of the bus, feeling the cool air on his face, trying to rid his mind of the image of Ray, lying there among the ruined crates. He had had to report the discovery of the body, but it was far from the only one on the docks that day in all the confusion of the clear-up. Nobody had questioned him about the corpse's identity. There had been nothing on him to pinpoint who he was, and there were so many people coming and going every day in the area that it was no surprise that this one remained unnamed.

As they drew closer to the stop, his heart began to beat faster. He wasn't sure how Kathleen would react. His palms were sweating as he pressed the buzzer. All he could do was to tell her the truth and reassure her that she would truly never have to endure her husband's spiteful torment ever again.

Pulling himself together, he walked quickly from the stop to her front door. He could hear the Coynes arguing from halfway down the pavement; Mrs Bishop's curtain twitched as he passed by. A normal day on Jeeves Place.

'Billy.' There she was, dressed in a faded blue blouse that set off the warmth of her colouring, her well-worn dark skirt covered with a print apron around her waist. Her eyes lit up at once at the sight of him, but then immediately clouded with anxiety. 'You've got news?' Her voice was full of dread.

He wanted to sweep her into his arms at once but instead he said, 'Yes, it's important. Can I come in?'

She stood back to let him pass and then closed the door against the gossips' hungry ears.

'Where's the boy?' Billy asked, glancing around for signs of Brian.

'He's round at Mattie's. I took the chance to have a good clean and just finished. Do you want a cup of tea? I was going to have one.' Kathleen was talking very quickly.

'Sit down, Kath.' For once Billy didn't care about tea or anything else. It was lucky that Brian wasn't there; they could get all the details out of the way without scaring him. Billy waited until she took a seat at the little table, watching him closely, uncertainty written all over her face.

'What's — ' she began.

'Ray's dead.' He didn't give her a chance to say any more. 'He really is. There's no coming back this time. He got caught in a warehouse fire and collapsed. I saw his body with my own eyes. There's no mistaking him, so you can be completely sure. He's gone, Kath. He won't ever trouble you again.'

For a moment she didn't speak or move, but simply stared at him.

'It's true, Kath. I swear it on my own life.'

Slowly she brought her hands up and covered her face. 'Oh, Billy. Oh my God.' Then she looked up at him, her shoulders shaking, her eyes wet. 'I almost don't dare believe it. I thought I was safe before and then he came back and I was so terrified . . . I thought that might be him at the door when you knocked. I hid the spare key but he might have tried to get in somehow anyway. I've been jumping at every noise. That's why Brian's not here, I keep him away when I can.'

'Now you don't have to.' He gazed at her, at the lines of worry slowly leaving her face.

'No.' She shook her head slowly, as if taking it in. 'He's really dead. It's wrong to say it, but thank God, thank God.'

'You're safe, Kath. You and Brian.' Billy took a step closer. He hesitated. 'You're a free woman now. You really are.'

Kathleen met his gaze and her mouth slowly broke into a smile. 'I am. I really am.' She ran one hand through her hair, as if adjusting to the new idea. 'Even when I thought I was before, you know, when that telegram came, I didn't feel it. I was so guilty at being glad he'd gone. I wasn't free at all, really.'

'I know, Kath.' He pulled the other wooden chair across so he could sit beside her. Tentatively he reached for her hand, and it trembled beneath his fingers.

'Thank you, Billy. I don't know what I'd have done without you.' Her expression was serious now as she stared into his grey-blue eyes. 'If it hadn't been for you I'd have gone crazy. You've never turned me away, even when you were working so hard. I don't blame you if you and Belinda . . . '

He sat back, puzzled. 'Hang on, if me and Belinda what?'

393

She looked away. 'You know. I heard . . . you'd been seen together. So if you and her — '

'No, no, stop right there.' He hurried to put her right. 'I've walked her home a couple of times and that's all. She's a lovely girl but honestly, Kath, how could you even think such a thing? There's only one woman for me.' He paused. 'Kath, you must know that. There's only ever been one.'

She turned back and met his gaze once more, her eyes now alive with hope.

'Really, Billy?'

He swallowed hard and gathered his courage. 'Of course. It's you, Kath, it's always been you.' He waited, on tenterhooks, unsure if he'd said too much, if it was too soon, or if he'd misread her. Perhaps she had only wanted friendship all this time and he had let his longing for her cloud his judgement.

Then she reached around and hugged him, half laughing, half crying, her tears falling on his neck. 'Billy, I was so afraid you'd chosen her, that it was too late for us.'

He leant back to study her face. 'No, Kath, never. I just wanted to give you time, to adjust to being a widow and all that . . . it can't be too late for us. Not if you want us to be together as much as I do.'

'I want it more than anything.' She dashed the tears away with her free hand. 'I don't know why I'm crying. It's what I've wanted for ages, only I never dared to say.'

He took her other hand in his and squeezed her fingers very gently. 'I love you, Kathleen Berry.'

She gave a gasp and then smiled the broadest smile he had ever seen. 'And I love you, Billy Reilly. There, I've said it out loud. I've felt like telling you for years but I couldn't.'

'Now you can.' He pulled her to her feet.

'Now I can.' She leaned forward and he held her as he had longed to do for so long, kissing her gently and then more passionately until she gasped and pushed him a little away, her face flushed. 'Oh Billy. If I didn't have to go to fetch Brian . . . '

'Doesn't matter,' he said, pushing his hair back off his face and only then remembering how dusty he was. 'We've all the time in the world now, Kath.'

She hugged him again, planting a kiss against his chest. 'We have, haven't we. The rest of our lives — and we can be together at last.'

31

'Lots of post this morning!' Alice waved a collection of envelopes at Edith and Mary, who were finishing their toast and porridge. For once they'd had an unbroken night, even though Mary had had to attend an accident in the middle of the evening. Compared to the non-stop sirens and anti-aircraft guns, though, it counted as restful. Someone had turned up the wireless to celebrate, and Glenn Miller's 'In the Mood' filled the room, accompanied by the scraping of cutlery as the young women ate their breakfasts.

Mary accepted hers with a happy nod. 'From my godmother,' she said, ripping the letter open with her thumbnail and scanning it. 'She wants to take me for tea at Claridge's. It would be rude to say no, wouldn't it?'

Edith grinned. 'It certainly would. You have a very kind godmother. That's something to aspire to.'

Mary frowned, confused. 'What do you mean? Have you been asked to be a . . . Oh, I see. Congratulations.'

Edith blushed a little. 'I'm tickled to bits, to be honest, and I never thought Mattie would ask, specially as I'm Catholic and strictly speaking shouldn't even go to the church. But it's all different in war, isn't it? So I said yes.'

Mary looked stern. 'So what will you wear to

the christening? You can't wear your old coat, pardon me for saying so, but it's showing its age.'

Edith pulled a face.

'Well, it is. It's only fair that someone tells you, and you know I have your best interests at heart,' Mary pointed out. 'I'd lend you something only I'm bigger than you. My clothes would swamp you. We'll have to think of something.' She rose to leave, picking up her plate and bowl.

'How about you, Al?' asked Edith. 'You're coming too, aren't you?'

'I wouldn't miss it for the world,' said Alice. 'Mary, would you lend me your dark green handbag? It would go with my scarf with the leafy patterns on it and then it wouldn't matter if everything else was plain.'

'Of course.' Mary was only too happy to oblige. 'After all, you lent me that scarf when I fancied a change, the last time Charles took me to the cinema. It's only fair.'

'You could wear it to Claridge's as well,' Edith suggested.

'That's a good idea.' Mary was pleased. 'I must be off, see you later.'

Alice watched her go and then said, 'So what are your letters, Edie?'

Edith flicked through them. 'I don't believe it,' she said when she saw the scrawled writing on the final one. 'Unless I'm mistaken . . . ' She ripped it open. 'No. There's only one person with terrible writing like this. It's my young brother Frankie.'

Alice's eyes widened.

'Yes, you might well stare,' said Edith. 'Who'd

have thought it?' She skimmed the single page of cheap notepaper. 'Well. That's a turn-up for the books.'

Alice raised her eyebrows. 'What does it say?'

'I suppose it was asking too much for it to be a thank-you letter,' Edith said, but she didn't sound bitter. 'It's a bit late in the day, but he's letting me know the money arrived. No thanks or anything like that, but the very fact he's written — it's a big step for him. At least I don't have to worry about him, or not as much as I did when Mick had a go at me.'

'Edie, I'm really pleased for you.' Alice knew her friend would never have admitted to wondering what had happened to the money and her wayward brother. 'Perhaps he'll come round in time.'

'Perhaps.' Edith was keen to change the subject. 'And what have you got there?'

Alice opened her letter. 'It's from Joe.'

'Can he come to the christening?'

'No.' Alice sighed. 'Well, we didn't think he would. They won't let him go all that way for his nephew. It's why Mattie has asked Billy to be godfather, isn't it? He'll be able to be there in person.'

'That and he'll be a lovely godfather,' Edith predicted. 'You know what he's like with Brian and Gillian. Alan will be a lucky little boy to have Billy watching over him. I'm sorry Joe won't be there too, though.'

'Can't be helped,' said Alice, trying not to let her disappointment show. She knew it would have been a very long shot, but part of her had hoped that he would have managed to persuade the powers that be to give him leave. She would have to wait for that very special friend to return. 'I'd better get ready. I'm due to see Dennis first thing. Check how he's coming on now he's walking more regularly.'

'Do give him and his mother my best,' Edith said, full of admiration for the teenager recovering from the tubercular hip and his long-suffering mother. Alice nodded and took her breakfast things away to be washed. Once she had gone, Edith turned to her final letter, with its Portsmouth postmark. Gently she eased it open and then, as she read the precious words, her face broke into a smile of excited delight.

Closing her eyes, she briefly recalled the all-too-short visit that she had managed to the coastal city. Ronald had suggested, via Billy, a most unexpected way of him going to see his brother and her seeing Harry. He'd borrowed a motorbike and learnt to ride it, not telling anyone what he had done until he was good enough to go public. He would pull some strings around the docks to get enough petrol for the trip, and Edith could ride on the back. At first she had thought it a hare-brained idea, and then when it became apparent that he was serious, she was terrified — but not so terrified as to refuse. Blocking her ears to everyone's entreaties not to go because it wasn't safe, she risked life and limb and accepted.

It had all been worth it for a few hours at Harry's side. His damaged arm had been released from its hoist, and he was slowly learning how to use his hand again. She held it while he practised clenching and unclenching his fingers, awakening all those muscles he had once honed to perfection. Better still, he could speak. It wasn't the deep, confident voice she was used to, but it was still full of the essence of Harry, and when he managed to say her name she almost cried.

She would not cry in front of him though. He had been through enough, and she would not cause him any further pain. Instead she told him all about his new nephew, glossing over the worst parts of his arrival into the world, and how the rest of the family were adapting to the newest member. He had mostly listened, as every word he spoke clearly cost him a major effort. His eyes were sharp with interest, however, and Edith was sure that he was absorbing all she said. She was full of relief that her worst fear had been unfounded: that the brain injury would affect his understanding and change him irrevocably. He was still her Harry.

Finally she could tell he was tiring, and gently released his hand. 'I'd better go,' she had whispered. 'You're falling asleep.'

'Never.' His eyes had widened. 'Edie. Never tired of you.'

She had laughed and bent forward, giving his scarred mouth a soft kiss. 'This is just to be going on with,' she promised. 'I can't wait for you to be well enough to kiss properly. That won't be long, will it?'

His eyes brightened despite their evident

tiredness. 'For you, Edie,' he managed to say, 'for you, anything.'

⋆ ⋆ ⋆

Flo had risen before dawn to ensure that everything was ready, spreading butter very thinly on bread for sandwiches, baking savoury tarts using the margarine where its taste wouldn't be noticed as much, putting out as many plates and cups as she could find. She covered the food with damp tea towels to keep it fresh as the rest of the family emerged. 'Right, you can help yourselves to breakfast and then clear up,' she announced. 'I'm going upstairs to put on my Sunday best.'

Stan carried his grandson around the kitchen to keep him quiet while Mattie tackled the problem of feeding Gillian without the little girl covering herself in marmalade or ruining her new dress. Flo had made it from a bolt-end of material from Ridley Road, cleverly cutting it out in panels so it didn't look mismatched, and decorating the bodice with smocking. Mattie was determined her eldest child would look smart for the christening service but Gillian had other ideas.

'He might sleep all the way through if we're lucky,' Stan said, rocking the baby gently.

'I bet he wakes up when he feels that cold water on his head,' Mattie said. 'No, Gillian, wipe your hands on your bib. Don't make Granny's table all sticky.' She was nervous about the forthcoming day but didn't want to say so.

What she wanted more than anything was Lennie here beside her to share it, the first public outing of their beloved little boy. She missed her husband all the time, but on occasions such as these it was particularly painful. He was always so calm and cheerful. Maybe their son would take after him in temperament as well as looks. Gillian certainly didn't. 'Right, over to the sink, now!' Mattie ordered as her daughter gleefully rubbed her hands together, successfully covering them in marmalade.

Stan sat down with the sleeping Alan, watching the scene play out. He could tell what was on his daughter's mind. It was hard to hold a family gathering with no Lennie, no Harry and no Joe. He was proud of each of the young men, and of his daughter too for being so stoic. She got that from her mother, he thought.

Flo reappeared, in a neat cream twinset with a silver chain around her neck.

'Haven't seen that in a while,' he said.

Flo smiled, pleased that he had noticed. 'I haven't worn it since Gillian's christening,' she said, touching the slender chain from which hung a small diamond shape decorated with four tiny pearls. 'You gave it to me for Christmas just before she was born. Then she almost broke it by pulling on it, so I'll be careful with it today.' She regarded her husband in his brick-coloured dressing gown. 'You aren't going to church in that, are you? Do you want to get changed now? And you, Mattie?'

Mattie nodded but looked dubious. 'That means you'll have to take charge of these two, and you're already dressed up,' she pointed out.

Flo reached for her old housecoat which hung on the back of the kitchen door. 'You leave them to me,' she said cheerfully. 'I'd rather take care of these two than anything else in the world.'

⋆   ⋆   ⋆

As she stood at the front of the church in a berry-coloured jacket that Bridget had spotted on one of her rounds and tipped her off about, Edith stated her vows to take care of Alan Leonard Askew. She reflected this would have been the one way to provoke a reaction from her mother, who would have been horrified at any of her children setting foot in a Protestant place of worship. Edith didn't mind in the least; she would be a better mother to Alan, heaven forbid the need should ever arise, than her own mother had been to her. That was more important than a difference of denomination.

She glanced sideways at Billy, standing stiffly in his rarely worn good suit. Edith was sure he had been looking extra warmly at Kathleen, who sat behind them in a pew with Flo and Stan, and wondered what that was about. Then she realised the vicar was speaking again and hurriedly brought her attention back to the service.

Alan scarcely cried when he was anointed with water from the font, proving yet again he had inherited his father's calm nature, not his mother's and sister's. Members of the congregation nodded to one another in approval. Here was another generation of fine Banham men to serve their community. Alan simply snuffled once more and fell back to sleep in his mother's arms. He was wrapped in a fine white wool shawl that Flo had carefully unpacked from the attic, shaking off the lavender flowers which had deterred the moths since its last airing.

The service finished with a final hymn and the Banhams prepared to walk back the short distance to Jeeves Street. 'Were you nervous?' Alice asked Edith as they stepped through the church door. She had noticed that her friend seemed a little on edge. 'You're used to speaking in front of a crowd at the first-aid lessons, after all.'

Edith shook her head. 'No, not nervous. A bit excited, maybe. I've never been asked to be a godmother before.' She fiddled with her jacket collar to make it lie flatter. 'Shall we catch up with Mattie?' She strode forward, and Alice frowned. She wasn't completely convinced.

As they rounded the corner to Jeeves Street, Flo gave a gasp. 'What's that ambulance doing outside our house?'

Stan put his hand on her arm. 'Don't worry, it can't be for us. There's nobody inside, we're all here. It must be a mistake.'

'I hope none of our neighbours have been taken bad.' Flo didn't want anything to happen to spoil her grandson's special day. 'Stan, you go and speak to them, direct them to the right house.'

Stan stepped forward, but could see nobody inside the vehicle. 'They must have gone into one of the other houses,' he told his wife. 'We'll find out later, I'm sure.'

Flo was not satisfied but put the concern from her mind. 'Yes, you're right. Now let me go inside first and put the kettle on. Stan, you take everyone's coats and make sure people know where to go.' In addition to the immediate family, various friends and colleagues had been invited to the buffet, and not all were familiar with the house. Stan nodded to Lennie's uncle, who was the only one from the Askew side of the family living near enough to come. They didn't know him well but both Stan and Flo thought it important to have somebody representing Alan's father. Then he started at a cry from the kitchen. 'Flo, what . . . '

Flo burst out of the kitchen and back to the front door. 'It's Harry! Harry's sitting in the kitchen waiting for us! They let him come home in an ambulance especially!'

As a chatter went up among the guests, Alice turned to Edith. 'You knew, didn't you. That's what you were so keyed up about.'

Edith considered denying it but realised there was no point. Alice could read her like a book. She shuffled her feet a little then met her friend's gaze.

'All right, yes, I did know. I wrote to that nice nurse we met and told her about the christening, asking if there was any way for Harry to come to it. I understood it would be impossible for him to go to the church as he can't stand, but if he only had to lie in the ambulance and then sit still in a comfortable chair, I thought there was a chance. Fortunately his doctors agreed with me.

They think he's ready for a taste of the outside world. I know he'll have to go back for more treatment afterwards, but with no Joe and no Lennie . . . well, it seemed right that he should be here.'

Alice was dumbstruck for a moment. 'You kept all that to yourself?' she gasped. 'You sly thing, Edie. There was I thinking you'd come over all shy at standing in front of everybody, for the first time in your life.'

'No,' said Edith happily. 'Never been shy and never will be. Wouldn't have done me any good when I was younger, that's for sure. Let's go on in. I'm dying to see him again but I dare say there'll be a bit of a queue.'

Edging through to the main kitchen, Alice could see Edith was right. There were Peggy and Clarrie, dressed up to the nines, fussing over their old school friend, not at all put off by his scarred face and head shaved down one side. He was propped on the sofa with plenty of cushions, and one arm was still heavily bandaged, but the nurse had managed to find him a smart jacket and drape it around his shoulders. As he caught sight of Edie, his face transformed. If she had ever had any fears that he had been so badly injured he might forget who she was or what they had shared, that look told her all she needed to know. 'Edie,' he croaked. 'Come here.'

She flew across the room to him, thrilled to hear him speak, even if his voice was still far weaker than it used to be. Her eyes welled up as she reached him and took his uninjured hand. 'Harry.' Then she was half laughing, half crying with joy, as he used all his strength to pull her down with his one good arm to sit beside him.

'Are you sure this won't hurt?' she checked anxiously, not knowing how sensitive his skin was or how many wounds remained, now hidden under his baggy street clothes.

'It would hurt more if you didn't sit beside me,' he said, his eyes bright, and she snuggled against him, buoyed up by his old humour and feeling safer than she had done for many months.

Flo was handing round cups of tea but Stan had brought out the Scotch, which he reserved for the most special of occasions. He poured out several tots and passed them around. Billy took one eagerly. Harry demurred. 'Better not, Pa,' he said. 'Too many pills inside me already. Isn't that right, Edie?'

Edith nodded. 'Yes, best not to mix them. I'll have yours,' she said daringly, and Stan laughed as she took a sip and pulled a face. 'Delicious!' she said with determination.

Kathleen was smiling at Billy. 'Scotch at this time of the day, and on a Sunday too!' she remonstrated gently. She dug him in the ribs.

He glanced sideways at her. 'Dutch courage,' he muttered.

She raised her head to his. 'Really? Are we going to tell them?'

Billy hesitated and then nodded. 'I reckon we should. I don't want to steal young Alan's limelight, but what with Harry being here an' all, it seems right. We'll pick our moment.'

They allowed the other guests to eddy around

them, loading plates with food, setting down their drinks, chatting to one another, sitting down to rest their feet. Billy answered everybody who came over to ask if he was a proud godfather and how he was going to help look after the boy, but half his mind was on Kathleen. In fact, his mind had been on Kathleen every waking minute from that day when he had finally told her that he loved her and she had made his life complete by admitting she loved him too. Through all the difficult days of trying to keep the docks operating despite the damage, the nightly ARP shifts, the everyday ups and downs, his heart was singing. Nothing could touch him; her love had made him invincible. He sailed through his work, despite the perpetual threat of danger from the skies, happier than he had ever been, knowing she was his at last.

Stan stood up and called for everyone's attention. 'I'd like us all to raise a toast to the newest member of the family,' he said. 'We all wish his father was here with us, and his uncle Joe who's dying to meet him, but I'm more pleased than I can say to have our Harry here, when we never thought we'd see him here again.' He paused so that his voice did not betray his strong emotion at having his own son there with them, where he belonged. Then he steadied himself and continued. 'To his lovely mother, and to the two marvellous nurses who helped with the birth, and to our very good friend Kathleen, who raised the alarm, with the help of the new godfather, Billy. But most of all, to Alan.' He lifted his drink and everyone followed suit, whether it was a teacup, bottle of beer, glass of whisky or simply water.

'To Alan.'

Then, as the noise died down, Billy stepped forward.

'I'd like to add something, if that's all right with you, Stan.'

Stan nodded immediately.

'I'm very proud to be this baby's godfather,' Billy began, running his hand through his dark curls, trying not to feel too awkward in his formal suit and tie. 'None of us who were there that night will forget his birth in a hurry.' A ripple of laughter went around the room, as everybody had heard the story by now. 'But, and don't take this the wrong way, Alan, I'm even prouder . . . even prouder . . . ' For a moment he could not continue. 'Prouder to announce that Kathleen here has agreed to be my wife.' A gasp went up and then murmurs of congratulation. 'Now that Ray's been dead for some time' — he quickly glanced at Kathleen and then away again — 'we thought it would be all right to go ahead. So perhaps the next party invitation will be to our wedding.'

'Hear, hear!' shouted Peggy, as she knocked back the rest of her whisky and accepted another from Stan, who was doing the rounds.

Mattie hurried over to congratulate her friends and hug Kathleen, followed by Alice and Flo.

Edith looked up at Harry and squeezed his hand very carefully. He gazed back at her, amusement in his eyes, a smile on his face despite his scars. 'Well, Miss Gillespie?' he murmured. 'What do you say?'

She tutted. 'What do you think? I say yes, just like I did the first time you asked.'

'Even though I'm an old crock now? I'm not the man you first knew, so you got to be sure.'

Edith glared at him in a mixture of exasperation and love. 'Harry Banham, you are exactly the man I knew before, the man I fell in love with. You'll have to do better than that to shake me off, I warn you now. I'm not going anywhere but by your side. I've never been more sure of anything in my life.'

Harry nodded. 'Good. Just checking.' Then he slowly leant forward and, ignoring all the people around them, kissed her softly on the mouth, as if she was the most precious thing in the world.

Other titles published by Ulverscroft:

THE DISTRICT NURSES OF VICTORY WALK

Annie Groves

Alice Lake has arrived in London from Liverpool to start her training as a district nurse, but her journey has been far from easy. Her parents think that she should settle down and get married, but she has already had her heart broken once and isn't about to make the same mistake again. Alice and her best friend Edith are based in the East End, but before they've even got their smart new uniforms on, war breaks out and Hitler's bombs are raining down on London. Alice must learn to keep calm and carry on as she tends to London's sick and injured, all the time facing her own heartache and misfortune while keeping up the spirit of the blitz . . .